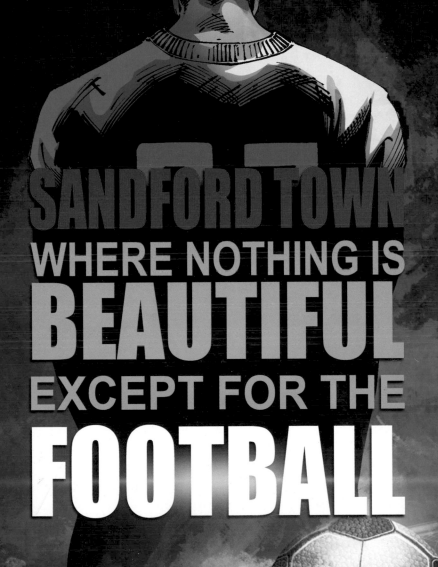

SANDFORD TOWN
WHERE NOTHING IS
BEAUTIFUL
EXCEPT FOR THE
FOOTBALL

THE BEAUTIFUL GAME

Author	:	Jason Quinn
Illustrator	:	Lalit Kumar Sharma
Inker	:	Jagdish Kumar
Colorists	:	Vijay Sharma & Ashwani Kashyap
Editors	:	Shabari Choudhury & Sourav Dutta
Letterer	:	Bhavnath Chaudhary
Designer	:	Mukesh Rawat

CAMPFIRE®

Published by Kalyani Navyug Media Pvt Ltd
101 C, Shiv House, Hari Nagar Ashram, New Delhi 110014, India
ISBN: 978-93-81182-11-6
Copyright © 2016 Kalyani Navyug Media Pvt Ltd

Printed in India

Chapter 1 WELCOME TO SANDFORD TOWN

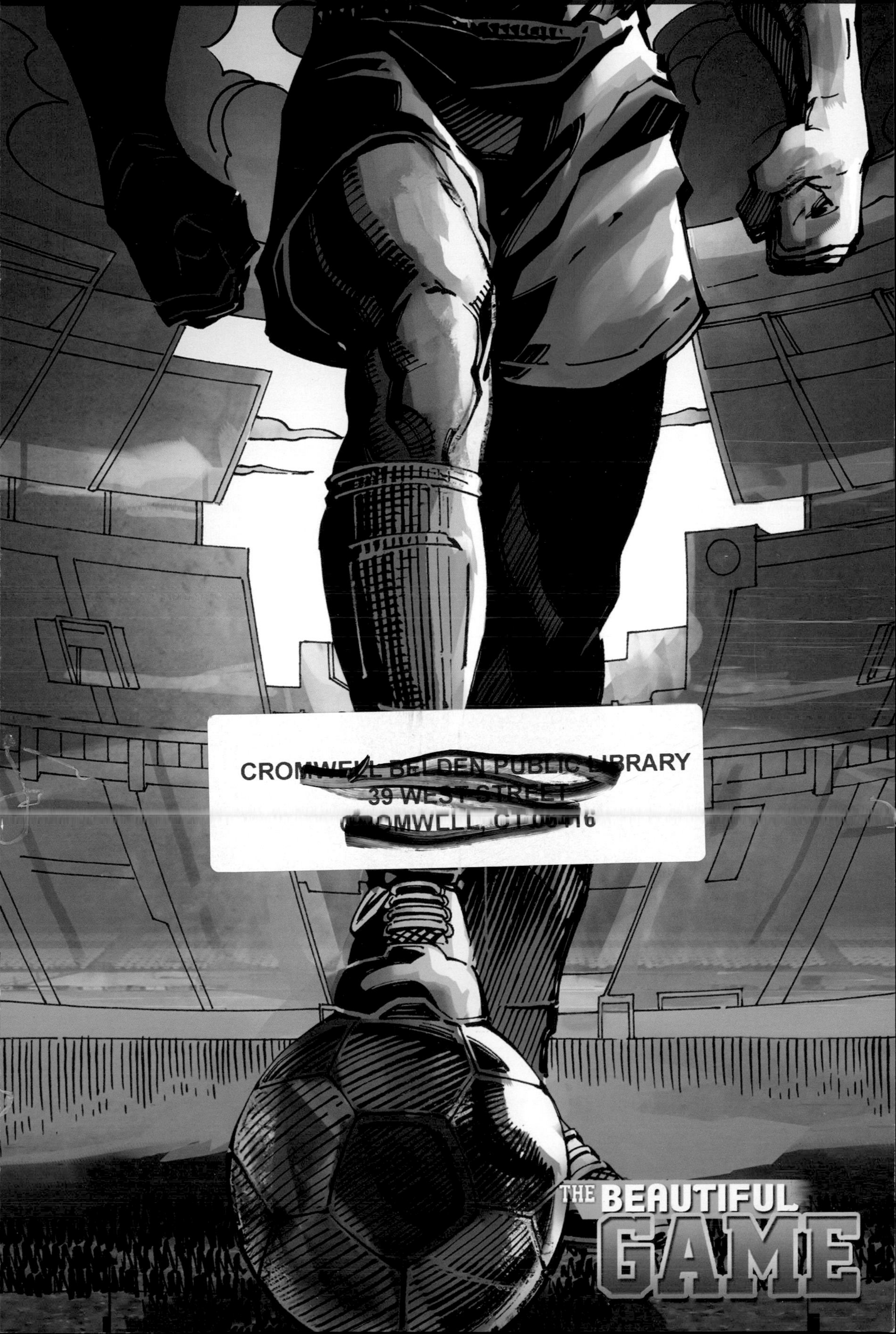
THE BEAUTIFUL
GAME

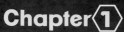

WHO'S WHO

BARRY BENNETT

Age: 18
Football player

Born and brought up in Sandford along with his twin brother Billy, Barry is the calmer of the two brothers and fiercely protective of his older sister, Claire. He hates bullies and has a long-standing rivalry with Russell 'Crab' Craven. Their rivalry goes back to primary school when Crab broke Barry's nose in a fight.

BILLY BENNETT

Age: 18
Football player

Billy Bennett is the more volatile of the Bennett twins. Exceedingly talented on the pitch, his spontaneous nature often gets him into trouble. He has been playing for the Sandford Town youth team for three seasons now and, along with his brother, seems certain to make it as a professional footballer.

CLAIRE BENNETT

Age: 20
Hairdresser

Claire Bennett is big sister to Billy and Barry. She has been working at Scissorz Booty Bootique as a hairdresser, ever since leaving school at eighteen. Claire has a mind of her own, and a quick temper like her brother Billy.

HARRY BENNETT

Age: 55

He is the father of Billy, Barry and Claire. Harry Bennett has worked hard to make sure that his kids have a good life. He was an amateur footballer during his schooldays, and along with his best mate Andy Shelldrake, he was a force to reckon with on the field.

BOB EVANS

Age: 65
Retired football player

A Sandford Town prodigy, Bob Evans started playing at the age of seventeen. He went on to make several appearances for Town before his playing career was cut short in 1983 by the Swiss coach disaster. A believer in team spirit, Bob has no time for people who give anything less than a 110 percent.

IN THE BEAUTIFUL GAME

STEVEN HUNTER

Age: 33
Football
player

Captain of Sandford Town, Steve Hunter has been their star player, up until now. He is no longer as fast as he used to be, but is still passionate about the game. He loves the club, but his wife Sharon wants him to leave Sandford for a bigger setup. Arrogant and hot-headed, Steve's discipline issues have made him a target for referees.

CRAB CRAVEN

Age: 20
Unemployed

Happiest when fighting, Crab loves to lead his gang—the Sandford Soldiers, a local crew of football hooligans—into battles against fans of rival teams. Crab is passionate about Sandford Town and Claire Bennett, on whom he has had a crush all his life. The two of them have been an item, on and off, for some years now.

STAN LYDON

Age: 60
Chairman,
Sandford
Town FC

A thorough professional with good business acumen, Stan Lydon is always thinking of the bigger picture. He doesn't hesitate to take tough decisions, as long as it benefits the club's future.

GUY TALK

Music group

A London based boy band that has become a worldwide sensation. With five hit numbers, members Larry Holmes, Vijay Nagar, Kieron O'Hagan and Ken Lee are ruling the charts at the moment. Vijay and Larry love football as much as they love driving their manager, Justin Taylor, up the wall.

HALTON MOOR

HALTON MOOR

Football club

A football club as old as Sandford Town and one of the founding members of the Football League formed in 1888. Moor's defenders are top-notch; especially Juan Perez who can slither his way in and out of the tightest corner. An old rival of Town, there is bad blood between the two clubs and things often tend to go out of hand during a match between the two.

SANDFORD EVENING POST

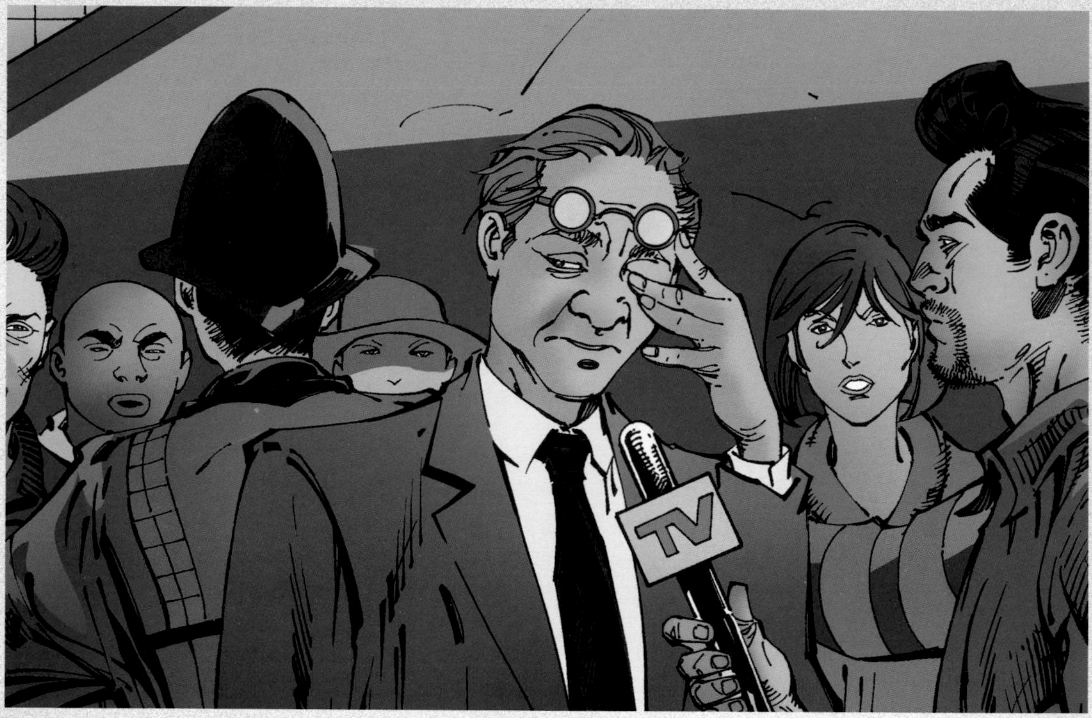
TV

For the chop? *Kurt Olaffsen feeling the pressure.*

ARE SANDFORD TOWN GOING DOWN?

These are dark days for Sandford Town FC as they are anchored to the foot of the table and look set for relegation come the end of the season.

Brought in just nine months ago, Kurt Olaffsen, the Sandford coach, has been unable to repeat the success he had at Cartagonova in Spain, when he led them to the Champions League semi-finals just two seasons ago, and reports of dressing room unrest are only adding to his problems.

Taking the manager's position at Sandford Town is sure to be seen by many as a poisoned chalice rather than a challenge, and we have to ask—who are the main contenders for the job? Martin O'Neill has already expressed a distinct lack of interest in the position, which leaves two main candidates—former Sandford Town hero Bob Evans or his ex-teammate, T.V. pundit Kenny Gilchrist. Evans has supposedly retired from the game, but it is well known that he has always held Sandford Town close to his heart. He would certainly be a firm fan favorite. We ask the question, is it time for the board to cut their losses and let Olaffsen go before it is too late? Saving the club from relegation will certainly be a Herculean task, but if something is not done soon then a difficult situation is sure to become impossible. Booed by his own supporters at every match, Olaffsen is proving an unpopular figure in Sandford. Although, we are sure that rival team Sandford Rovers hope he will remain in charge of the club and complete the dismantling of this once great team.

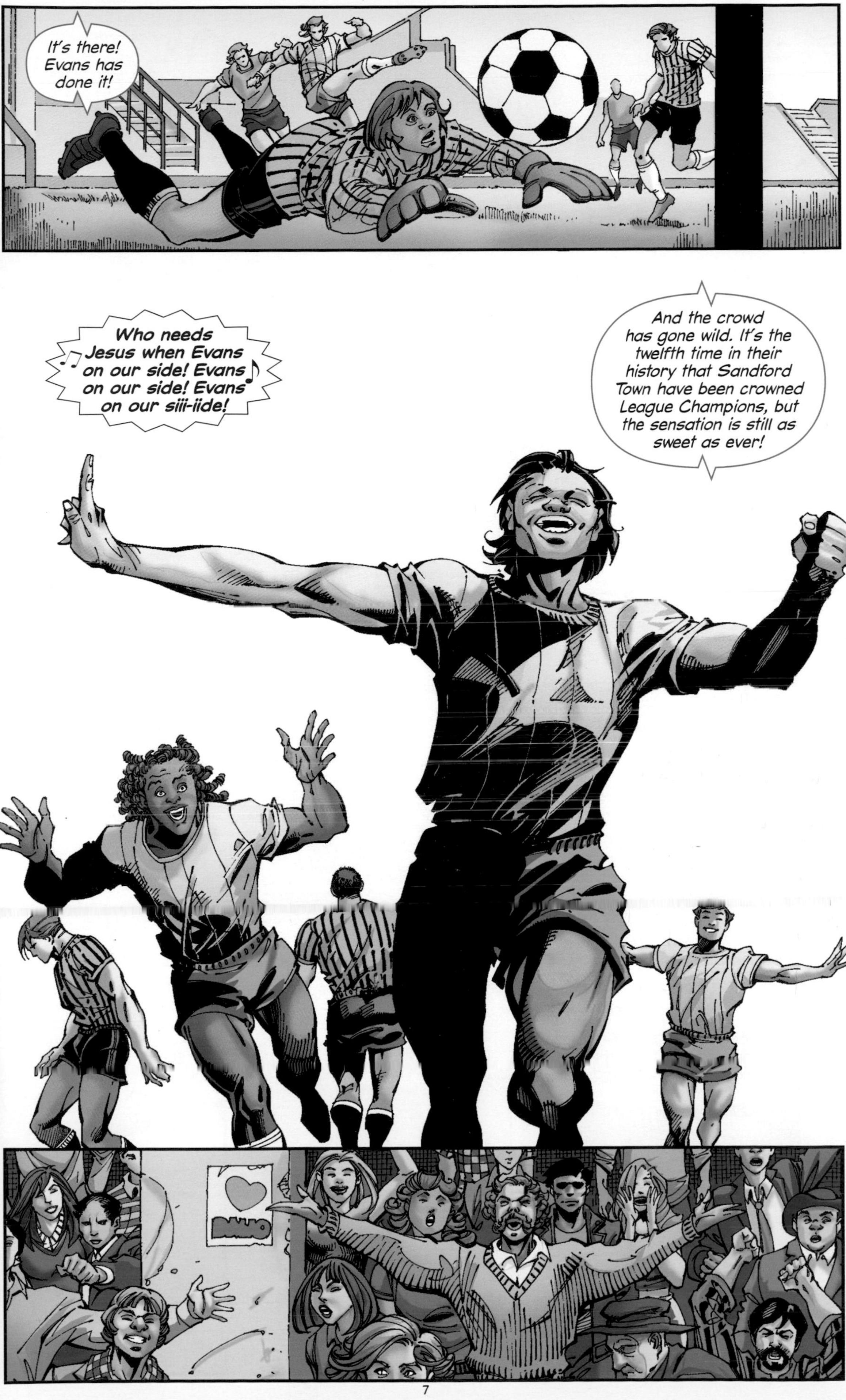
It's there! Evans has done it!
Who needs Jesus when Evans on our side! Evans on our side! Evans on our siii-iide!
And the crowd has gone wild. It's the twelfth time in their history that Sandford Town have been crowned League Champions, but the sensation is still as sweet as ever!

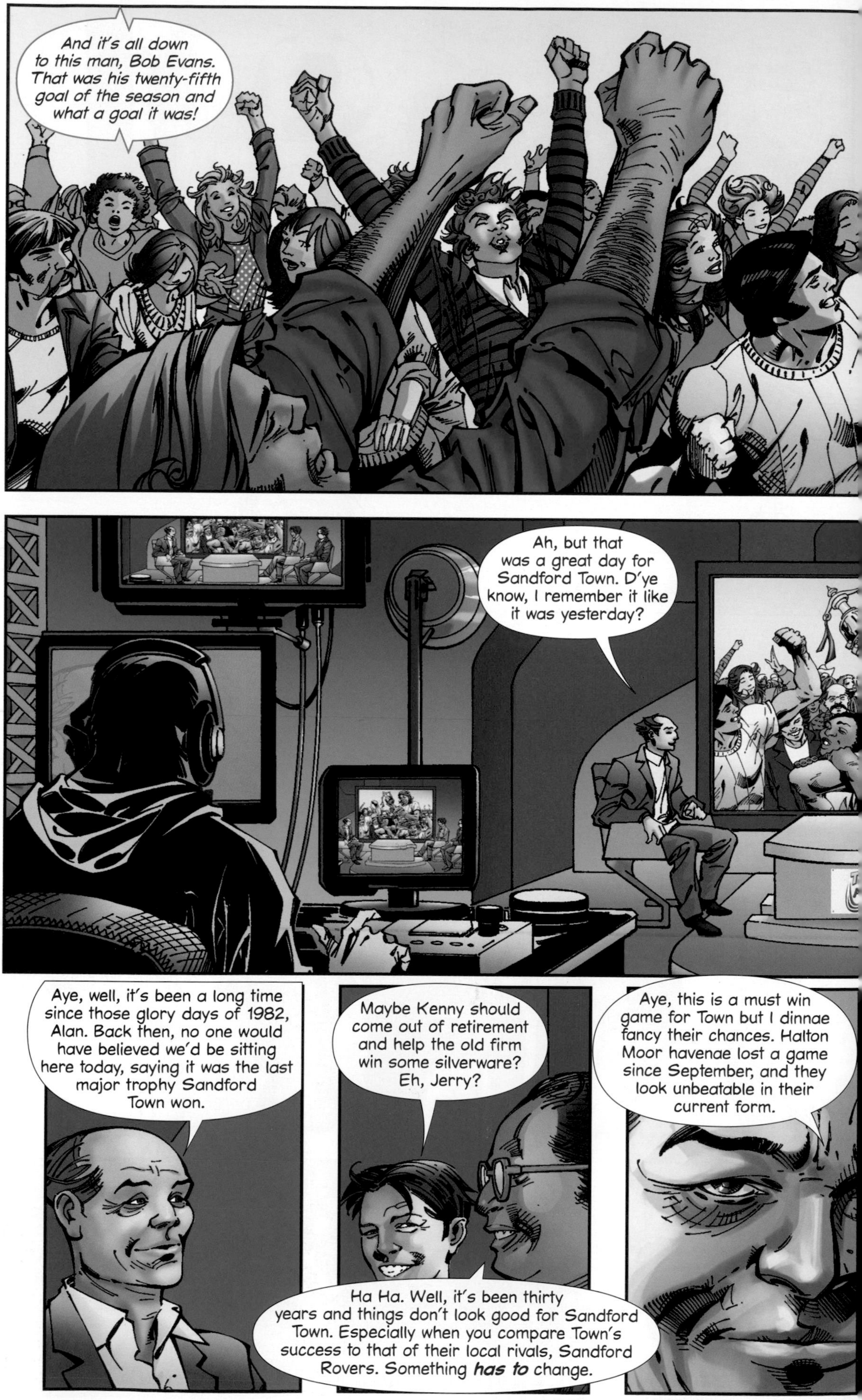

And it's all down to this man, Bob Evans. That was his twenty-fifth goal of the season and what a goal it was!
Ah, but that was a great day for Sandford Town. D'ye know, I remember it like it was yesterday?
Aye, well, it's been a long time since those glory days of 1982, Alan. Back then, no one would have believed we'd be sitting here today, saying it was the last major trophy Sandford Town won.
Maybe Kenny should come out of retirement and help the old firm win some silverware? Eh, Jerry?
Ha Ha. Well, it's been thirty years and things don't look good for Sandford Town. Especially when you compare Town's success to that of their local rivals, Sandford Rovers. Something has to change.
Aye, this is a must win game for Town but I dinnae fancy their chances. Halton Moor havenae lost a game since September, and they look unbeatable in their current form.

But it wasn't yesterday, was it, Kenny?

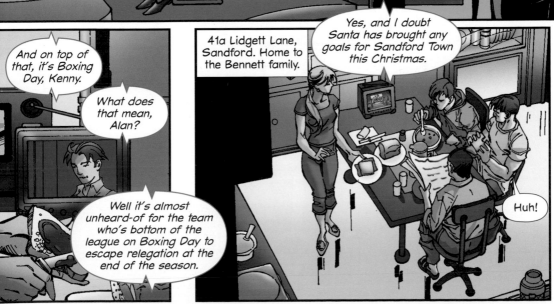

And on top of that, it's Boxing Day, Kenny.

What does that mean, Alan?

Well it's almost unheard-of for the team who's bottom of the league on Boxing Day to escape relegation at the end of the season.

41a Lidgett Lane, Sandford. Home to the Bennett family.

Yes, and I doubt Santa has brought any goals for Sandford Town this Christmas.

Huh!

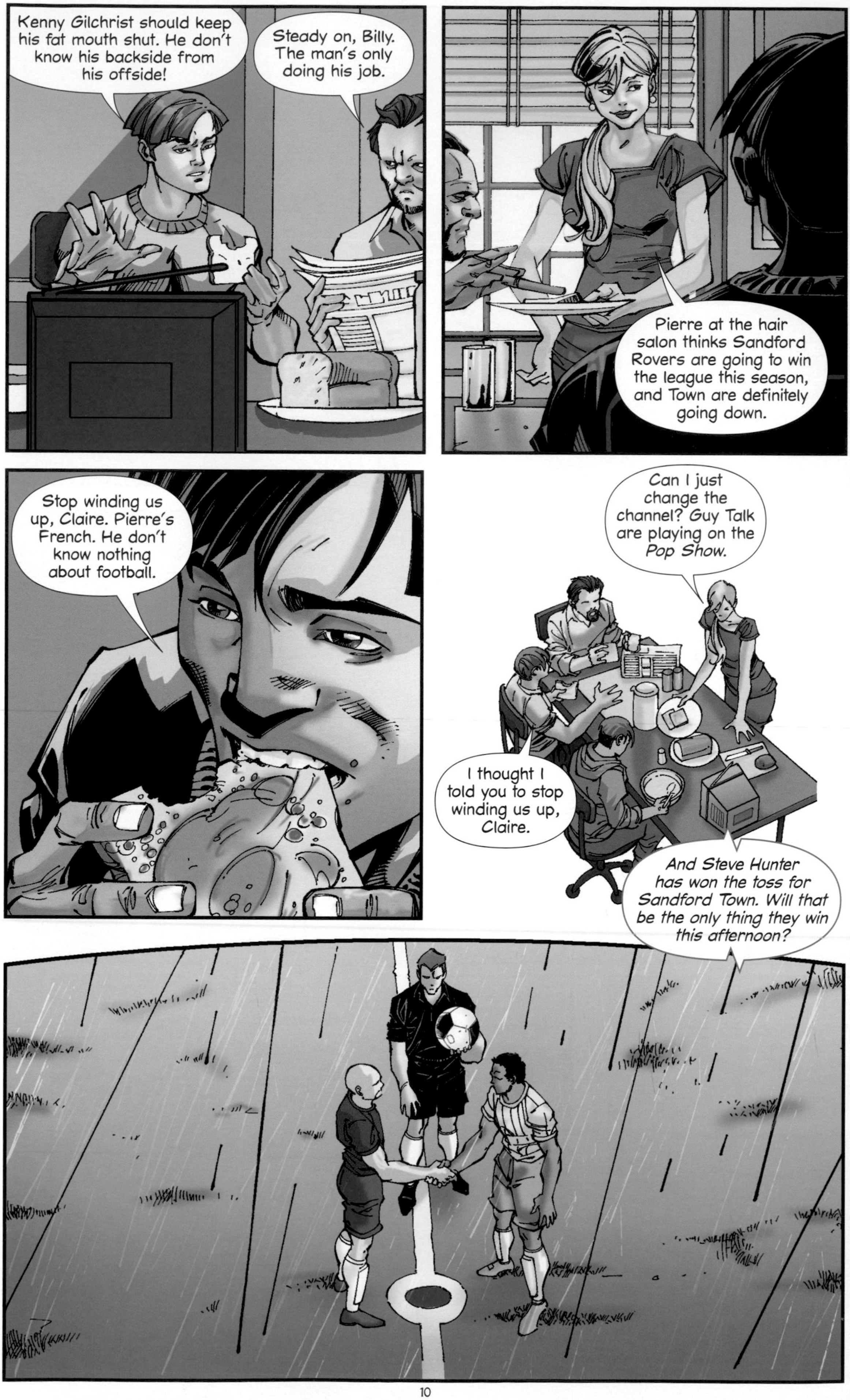
Kenny Gilchrist should keep his fat mouth shut. He don't know his backside from his offside!
Steady on, Billy. The man's only doing his job.
Pierre at the hair salon thinks Sandford Rovers are going to win the league this season, and Town are definitely going down.
Stop winding us up, Claire. Pierre's French. He don't know nothing about football.
Can I just change the channel? Guy Talk are playing on the *Pop Show*.
I thought I told you to stop winding us up, Claire.
And Steve Hunter has won the toss for Sandford Town. Will that be the only thing they win this afternoon?

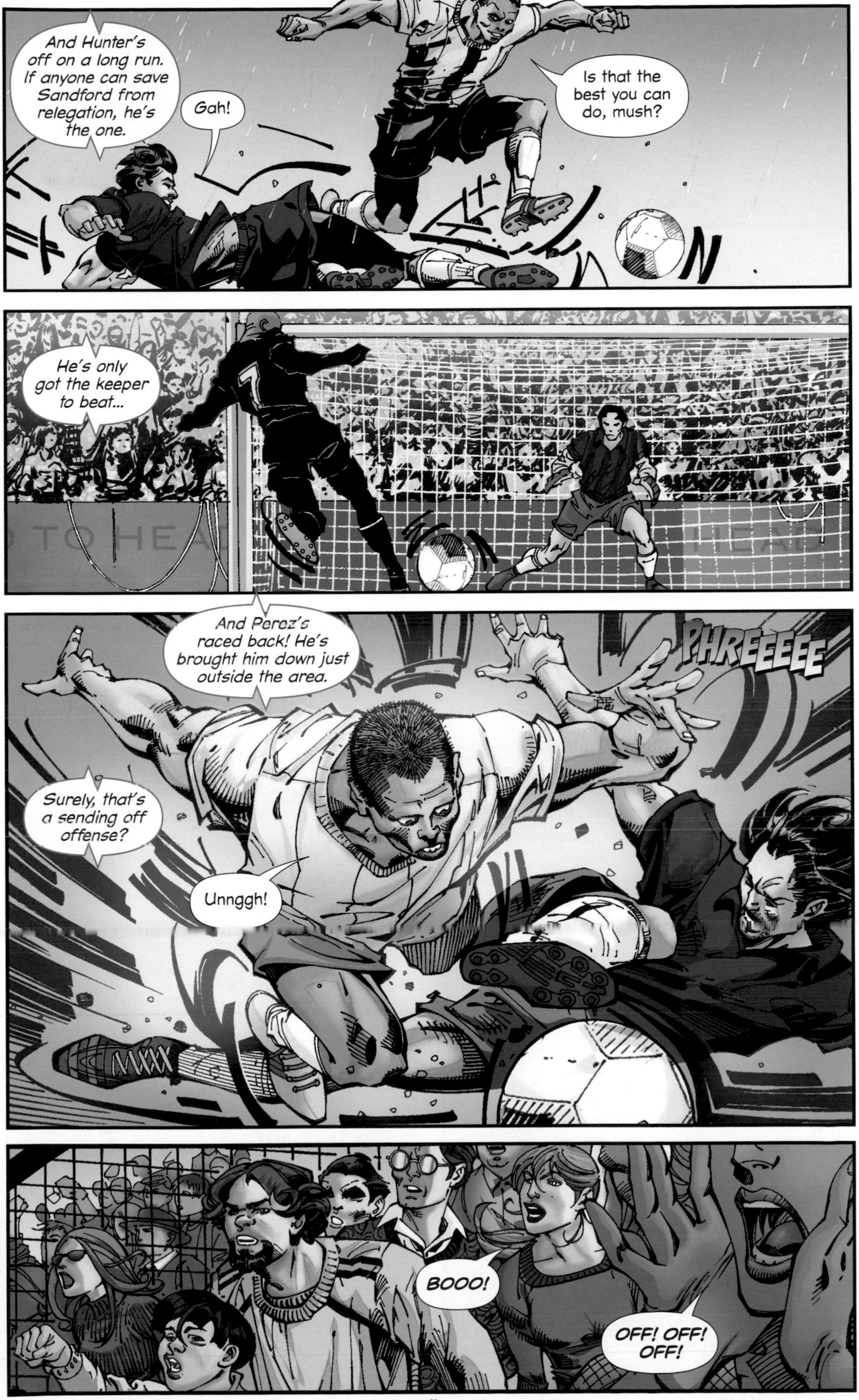

And Hunter's off on a long run. If anyone can save Sandford from relegation, he's the one.
Gah!
Is that the best you can do, mush?
He's only got the keeper to beat...
And Perez's raced back! He's brought him down just outside the area.
PHREEEEE
Surely, that's a sending off offense?
Unnggh!
BOOO!
OFF! OFF! OFF!

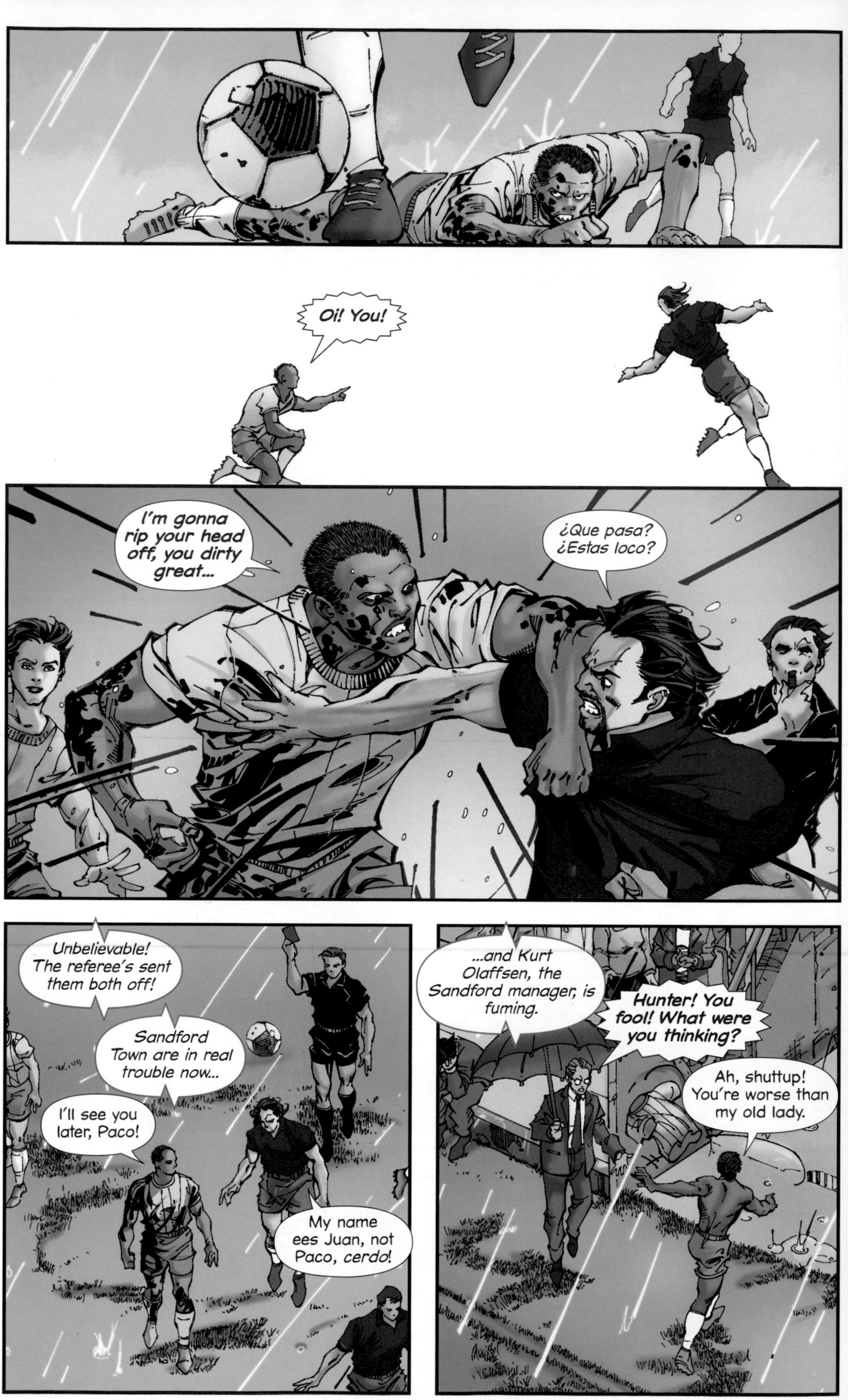

Oi! You!
I'm gonna rip your head off, you dirty great...
¿Que pasa? ¿Estas loco?
Unbelievable! The referee's sent them both off!
Sandford Town are in real trouble now...
I'll see you later, Paco!
My name ees Juan, not Paco, *cerdo*!
...and Kurt Olaffsen, the Sandford manager, is fuming.
Hunter! You fool! What were you thinking?
Ah, shuttup! You're worse than my old lady.

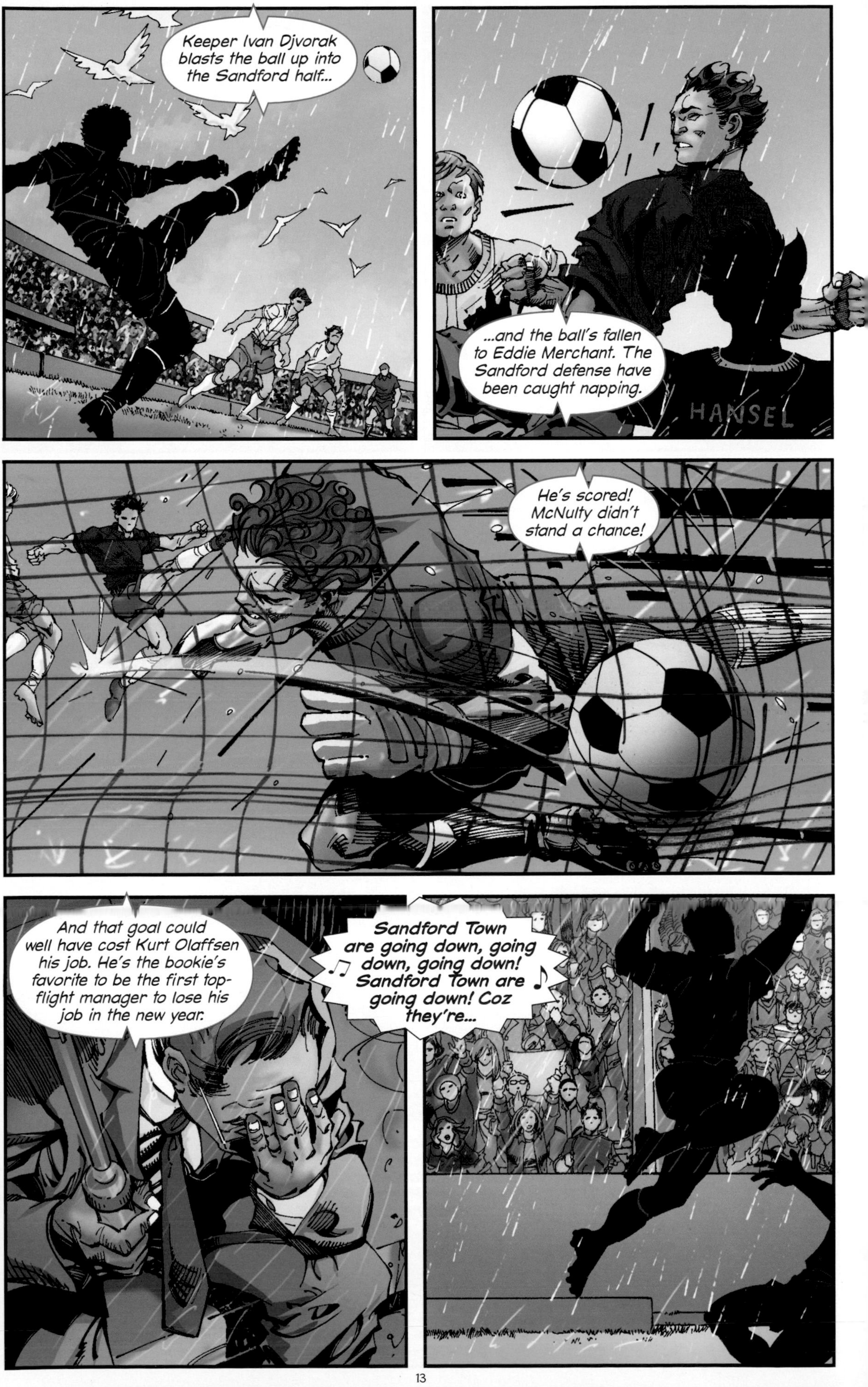
Keeper Ivan Djvorak blasts the ball up into the Sandford half...
...and the ball's fallen to Eddie Merchant. The Sandford defense have been caught napping.
HANSEL
He's scored! McNulty didn't stand a chance!
And that goal could well have cost Kurt Olaffsen his job. He's the bookie's favorite to be the first top-flight manager to lose his job in the new year.
Sandford Town are going down, going down, going down! Sandford Town are going down! Coz they're...

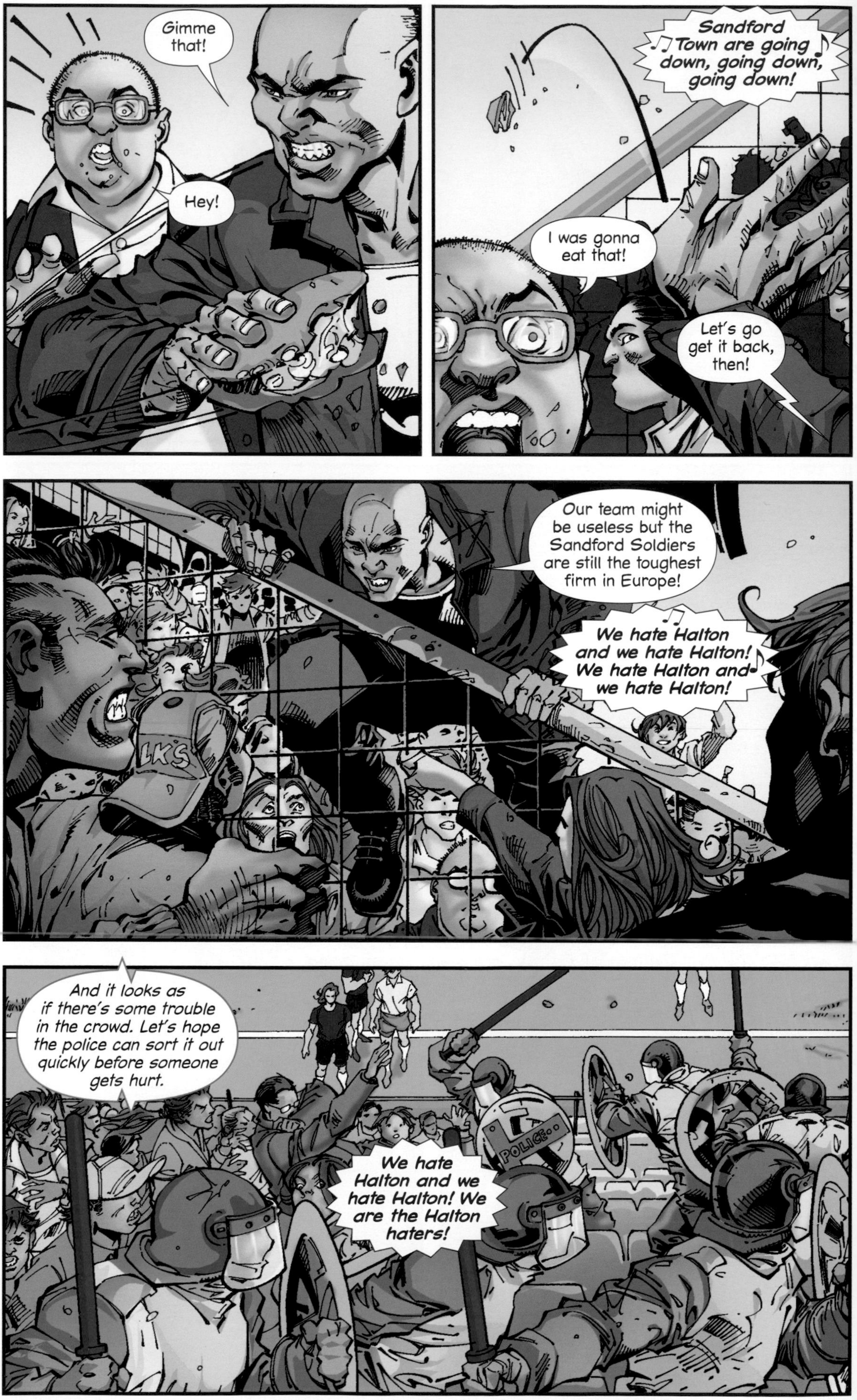
Gimme that!
Hey!
Sandford Town are going down, going down, going down!
I was gonna eat that!
Let's go get it back, then!
Our team might be useless but the Sandford Soldiers are still the toughest firm in Europe!
We hate Halton and we hate Halton! We hate Halton and we hate Halton!
LKS
And it looks as if there's some trouble in the crowd. Let's hope the police can sort it out quickly before someone gets hurt.
POLICE
We hate Halton and we hate Halton! We are the Halton haters!

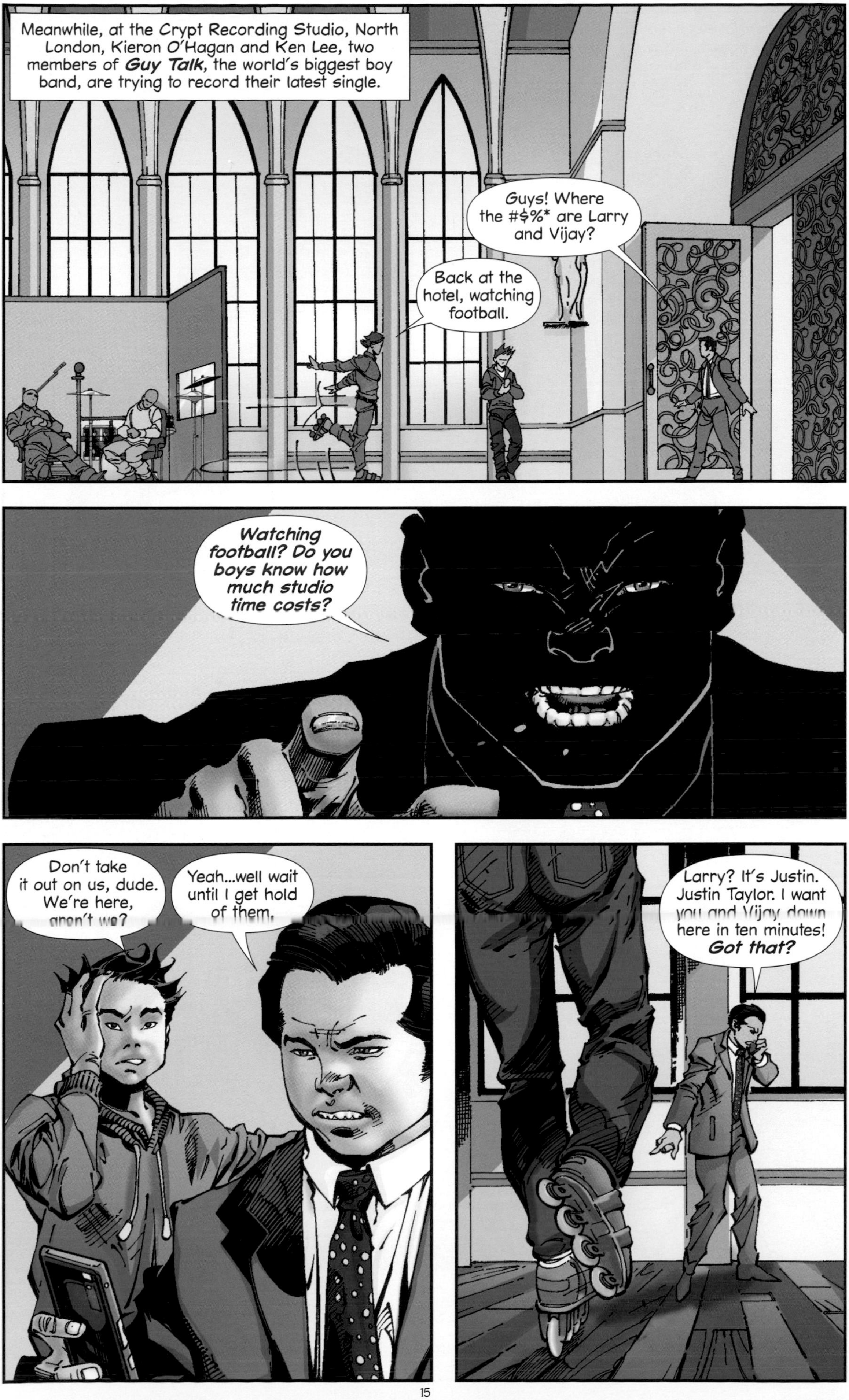
Meanwhile, at the Crypt Recording Studio, North London, Kieron O'Hagan and Ken Lee, two members of *Guy Talk*, the world's biggest boy band, are trying to record their latest single.
Guys! Where the #$%* are Larry and Vijay?
Back at the hotel, watching football.
Watching football? Do you boys know how much studio time costs?
Don't take it out on us, dude. We're here, aren't we?
Yeah...well wait until I get hold of them.
Larry? It's Justin. Justin Taylor. I want you and Vijay down here in ten minutes! *Got that?*

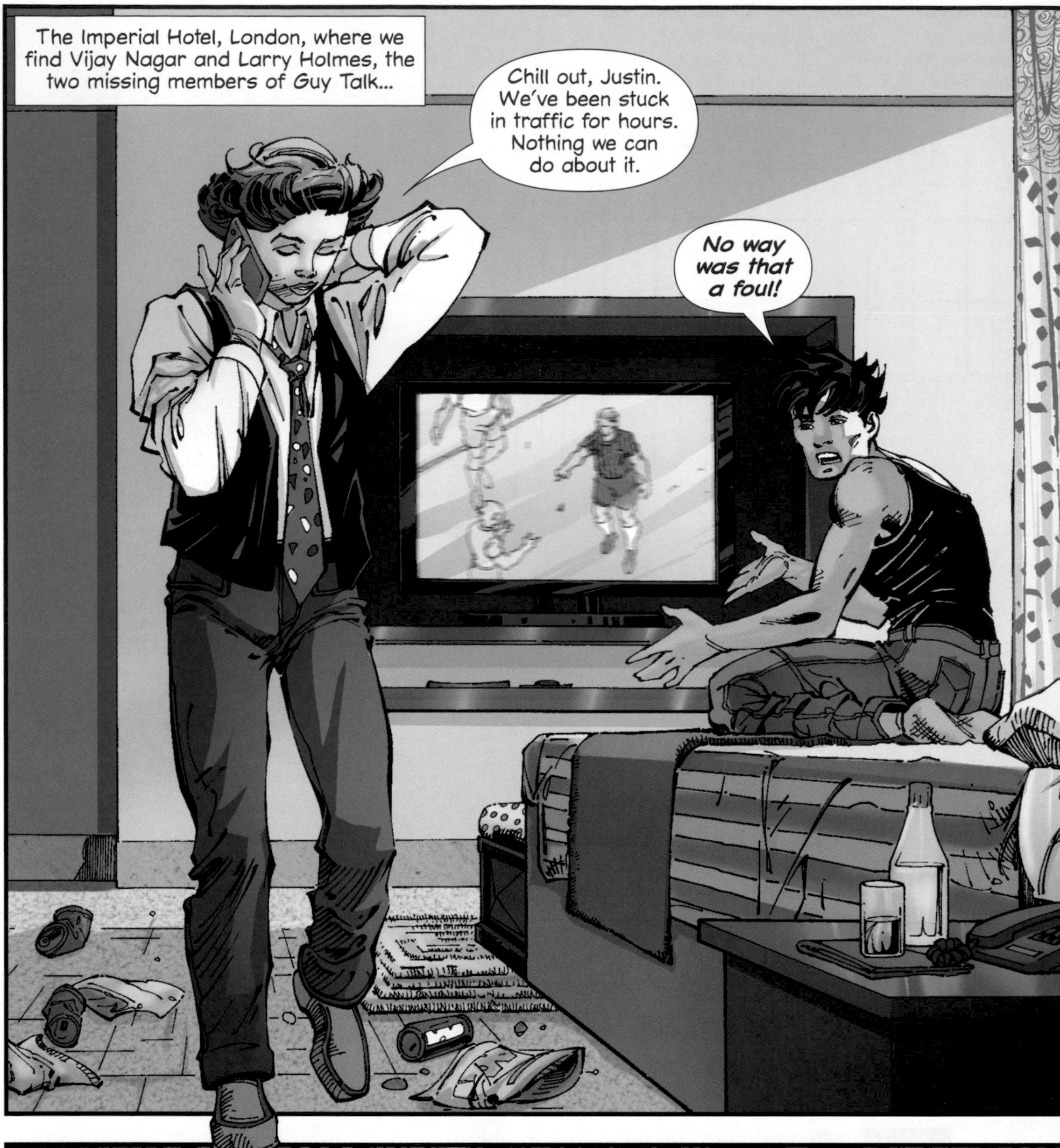
The Imperial Hotel, London, where we find Vijay Nagar and Larry Holmes, the two missing members of Guy Talk...
Chill out, Justin. We've been stuck in traffic for hours. Nothing we can do about it.
No way was that a foul!

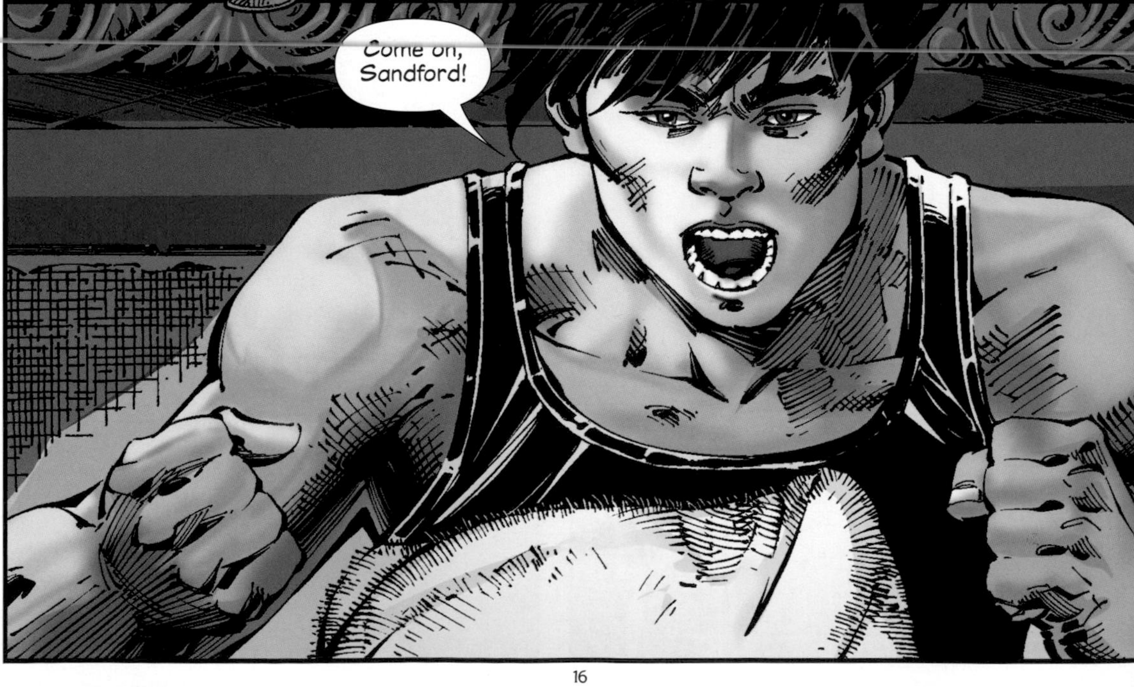
Come on, Sandford!

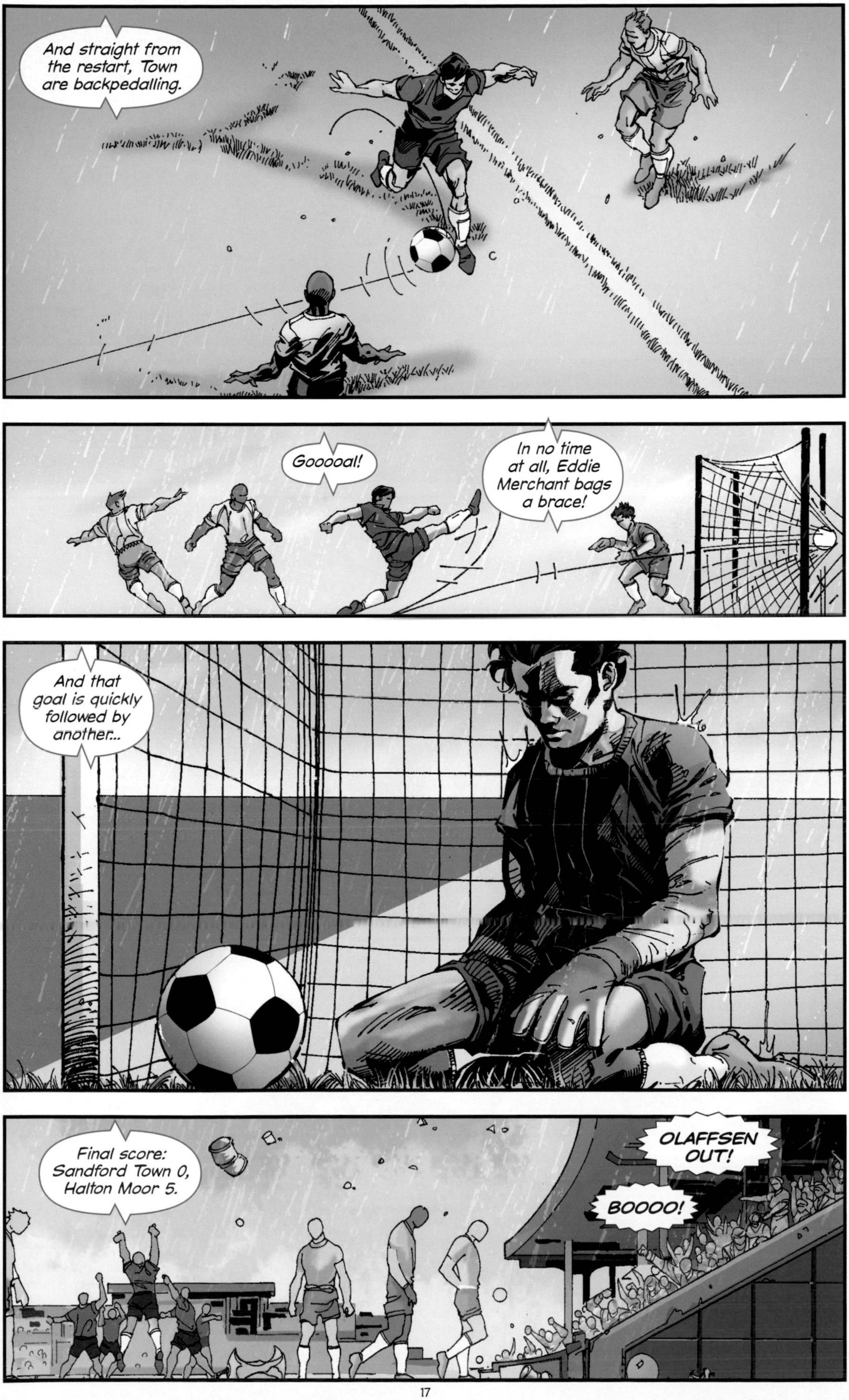
And straight from the restart, Town are backpedalling.
Goooooal!
In no time at all, Eddie Merchant bags a brace!
And that goal is quickly followed by another...
Final score: Sandford Town 0, Halton Moor 5.
OLAFFSEN OUT!
BOOOO!

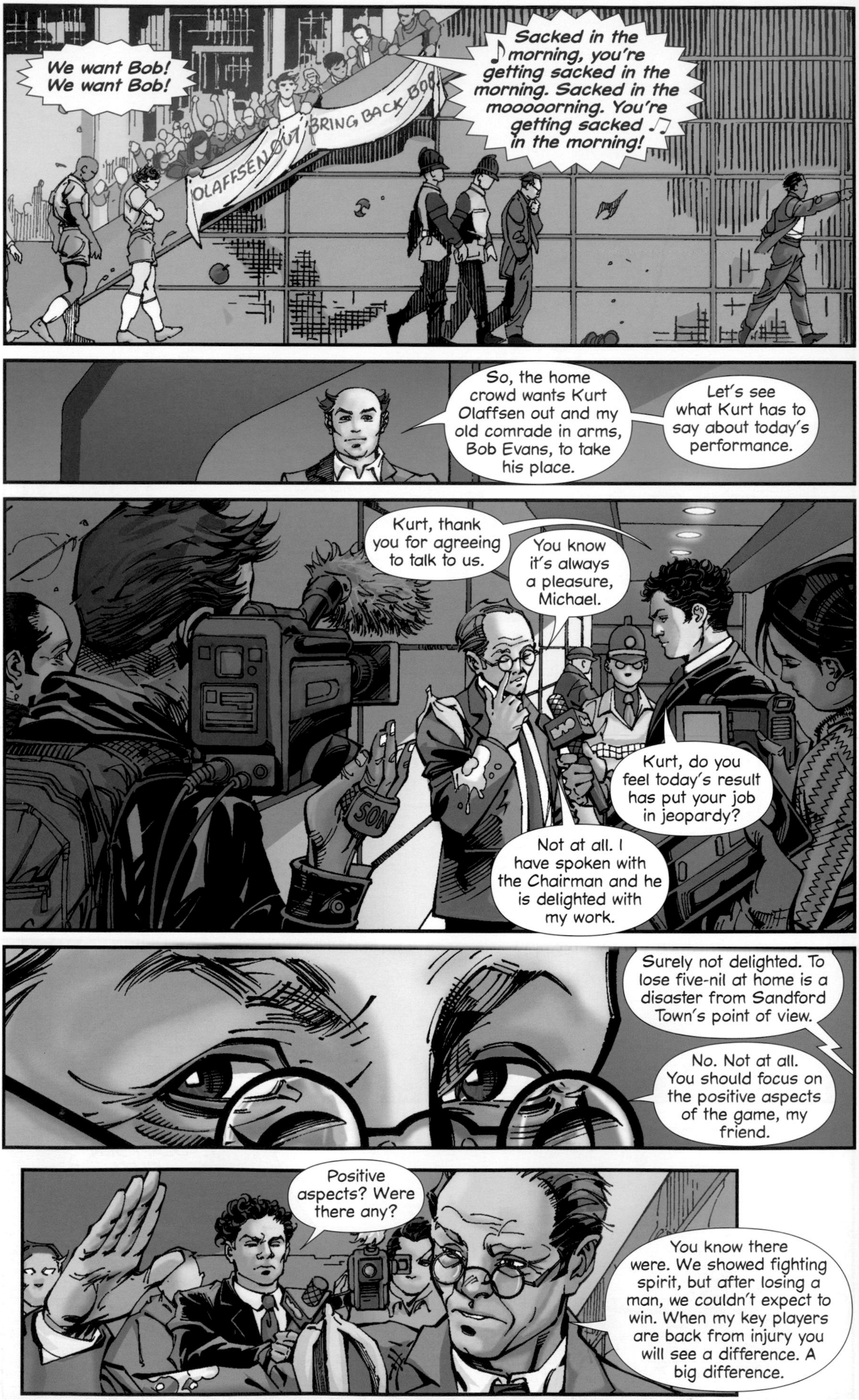
We want Bob! We want Bob!
Sacked in the morning, you're getting sacked in the morning. Sacked in the mooooorning. You're getting sacked in the morning!
OLAFFSEN OUT
BRING BACK BOB
So, the home crowd wants Kurt Olaffsen out and my old comrade in arms, Bob Evans, to take his place.
Let's see what Kurt has to say about today's performance.
Kurt, thank you for agreeing to talk to us.
You know it's always a pleasure, Michael.
Kurt, do you feel today's result has put your job in jeopardy?
Not at all. I have spoken with the Chairman and he is delighted with my work.
Surely not delighted. To lose five-nil at home is a disaster from Sandford Town's point of view.
No. Not at all. You should focus on the positive aspects of the game, my friend.
Positive aspects? Were there any?
You know there were. We showed fighting spirit, but after losing a man, we couldn't expect to win. When my key players are back from injury you will see a difference. A big difference.

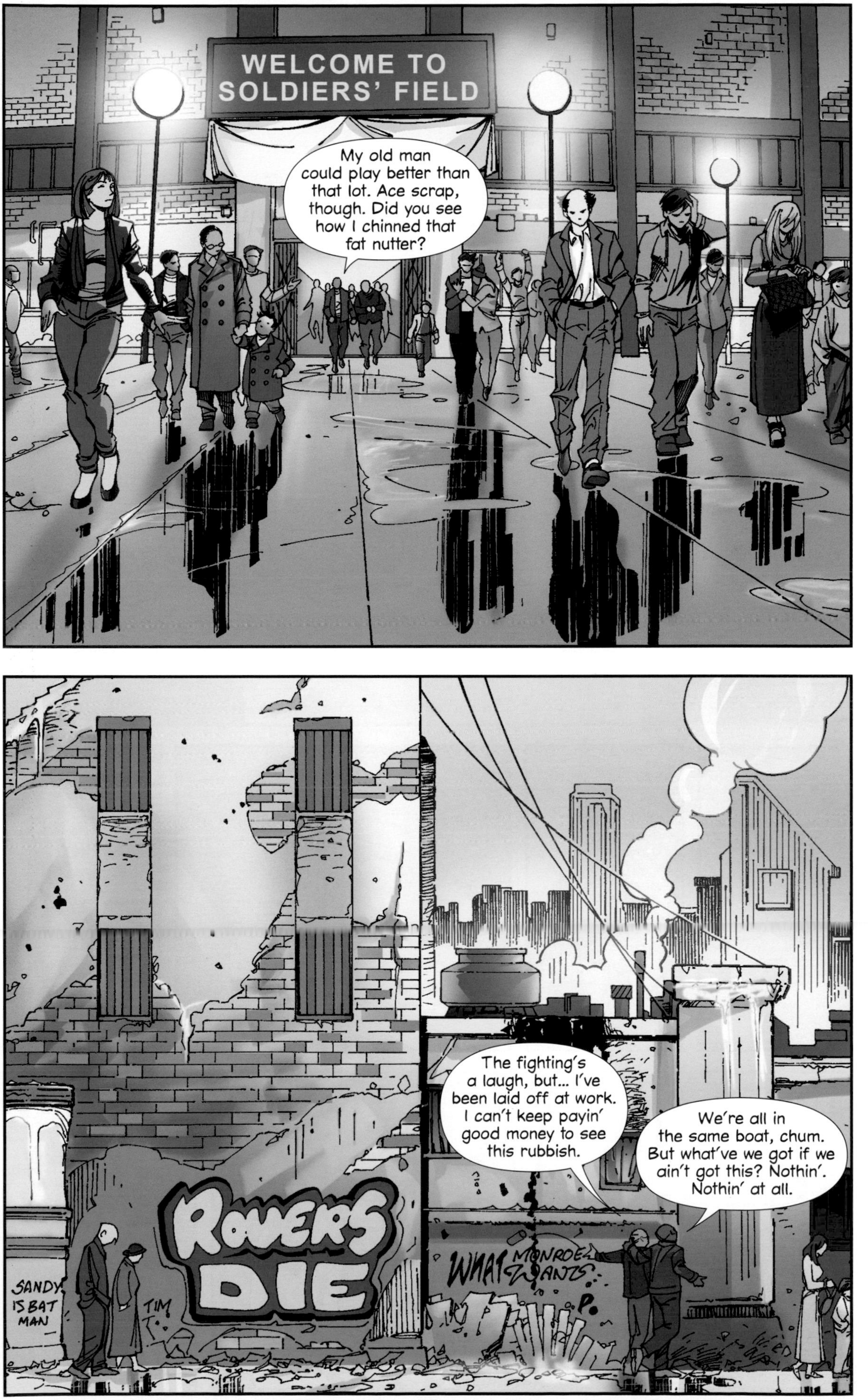
WELCOME TO SOLDIERS' FIELD
My old man could play better than that lot. Ace scrap, though. Did you see how I chinned that fat nutter?
ROVERS DIE
SANDY IS BAT MAN
TIM
WHAT MONROE WANTS
The fighting's a laugh, but... I've been laid off at work. I can't keep payin' good money to see this rubbish.
We're all in the same boat, chum. But what've we got if we ain't got this? Nothin'. Nothin' at all.

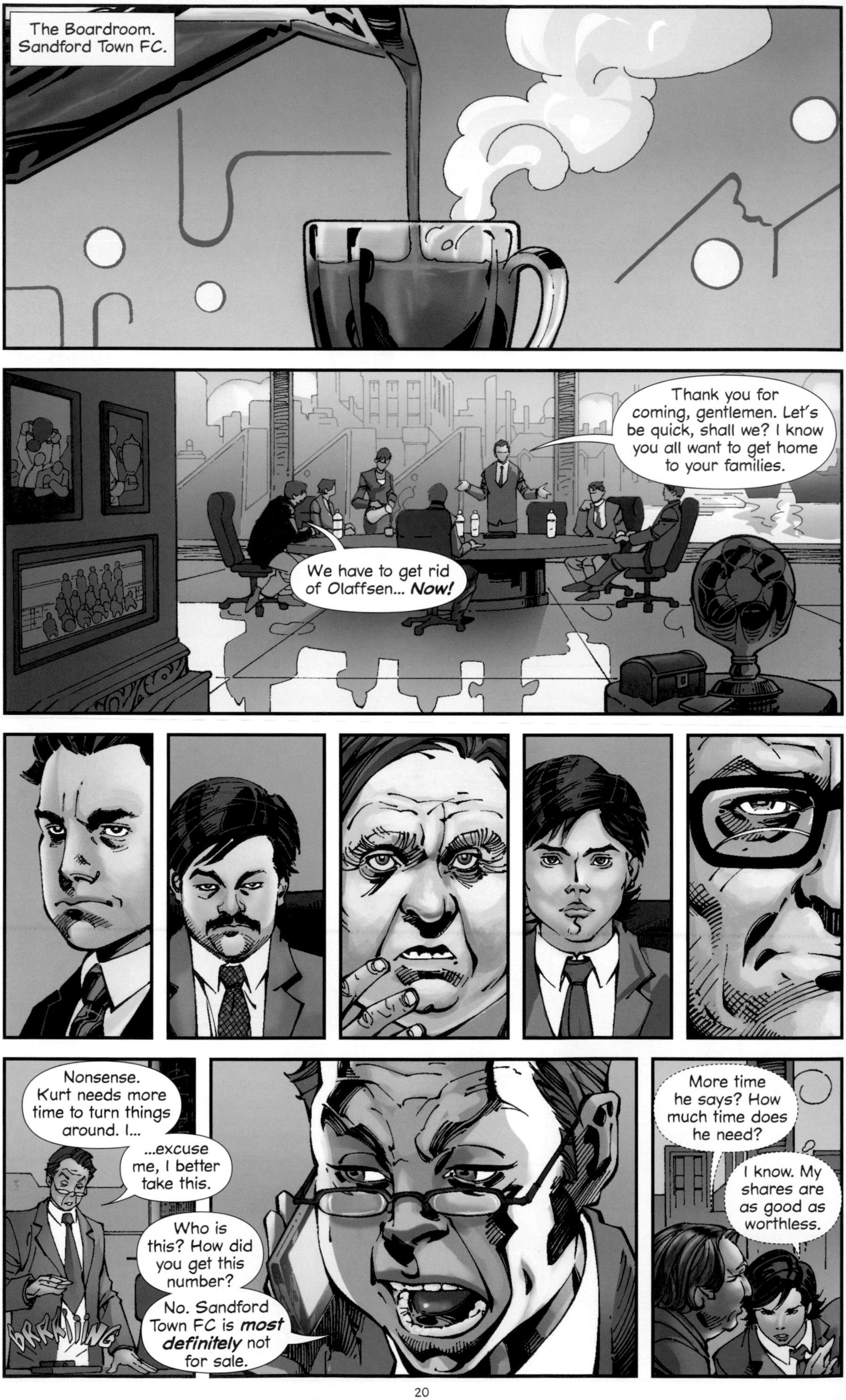

The Boardroom. Sandford Town FC.
Thank you for coming, gentlemen. Let's be quick, shall we? I know you all want to get home to your families.
We have to get rid of Olaffsen... **Now!**
Nonsense. Kurt needs more time to turn things around. I...
...excuse me, I better take this.
BRRRIIING
Who is this? How did you get this number?
No. Sandford Town FC is ***most definitely*** not for sale.
More time he says? How much time does he need?
I know. My shares are as good as worthless.

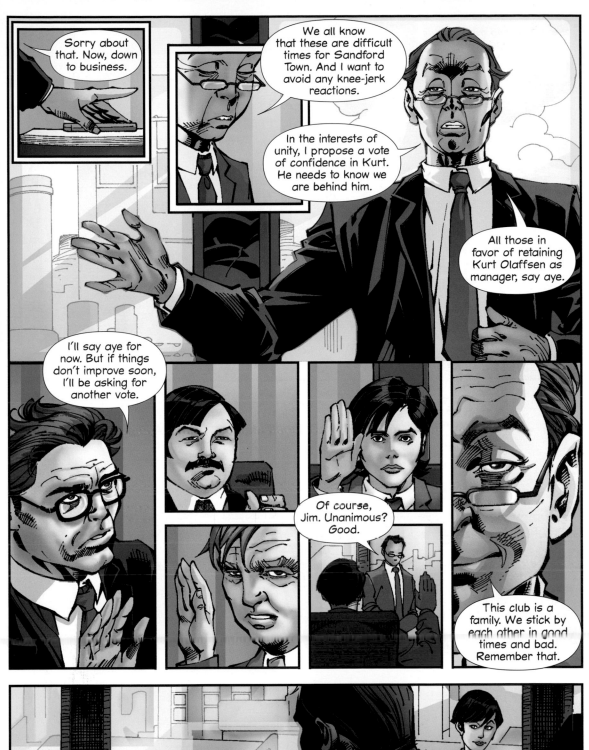

Sorry about that. Now, down to business.

We all know that these are difficult times for Sandford Town. And I want to avoid any knee-jerk reactions.

In the interests of unity, I propose a vote of confidence in Kurt. He needs to know we are behind him.

All those in favor of retaining Kurt Olaffsen as manager, say aye.

I'll say aye for now. But if things don't improve soon, I'll be asking for another vote.

Of course, Jim. Unanimous? Good.

This club is a family. We stick by each other in good times and bad. Remember that.

Jenna, would you please inform Mr. Olaffsen that he has the full backing of the board? And that we trust the dark days are now behind us?

Very good, Mr. Lydon, sir.

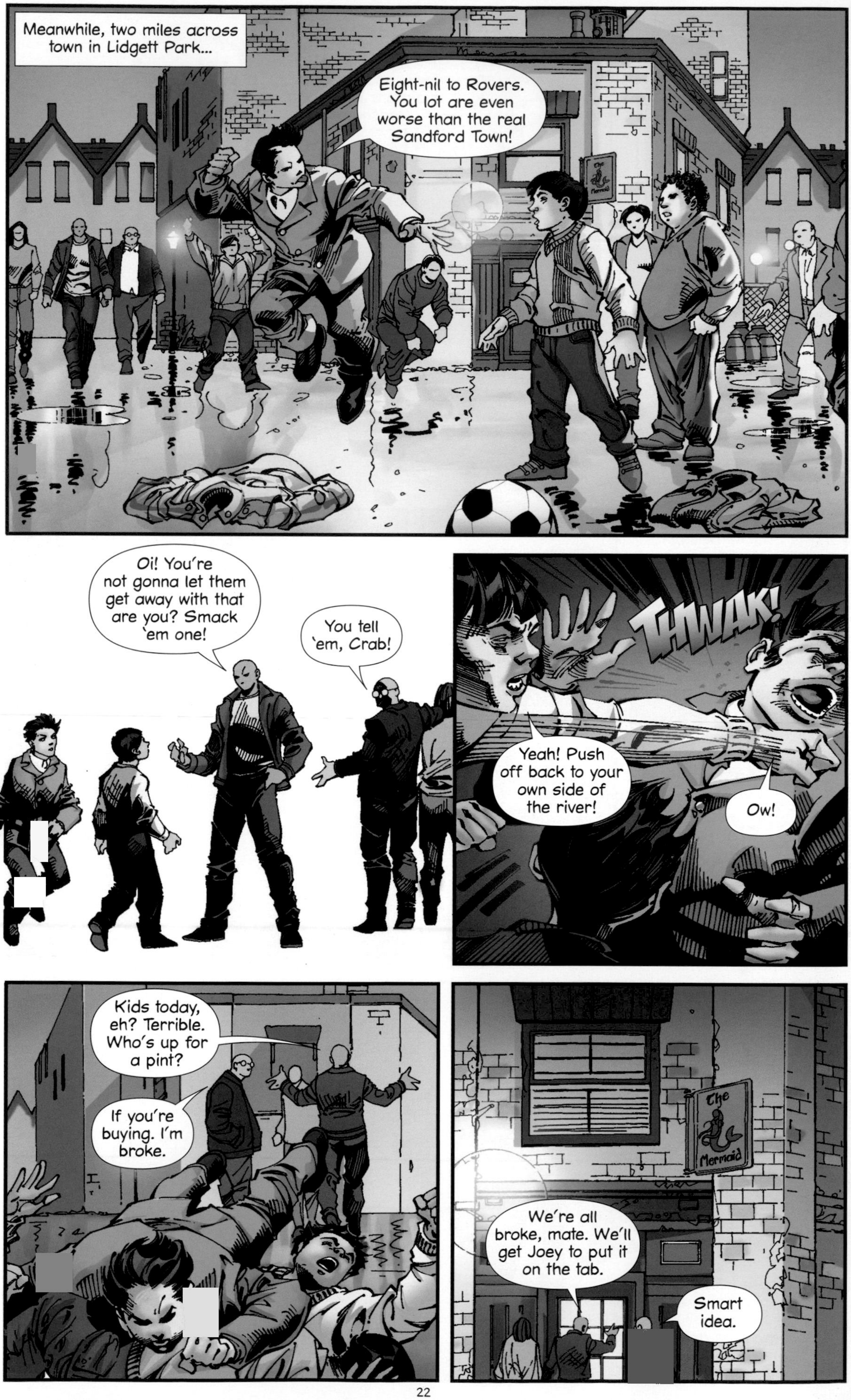
Meanwhile, two miles across town in Lidgett Park...
Eight-nil to Rovers. You lot are even worse than the real Sandford Town!
The Mermaid
Oi! You're not gonna let them get away with that are you? Smack 'em one!
You tell 'em, Crab!
THWAK!
Yeah! Push off back to your own side of the river!
Ow!
Kids today, eh? Terrible. Who's up for a pint?
If you're buying. I'm broke.
The Mermaid
We're all broke, mate. We'll get Joey to put it on the tab.
Smart idea.

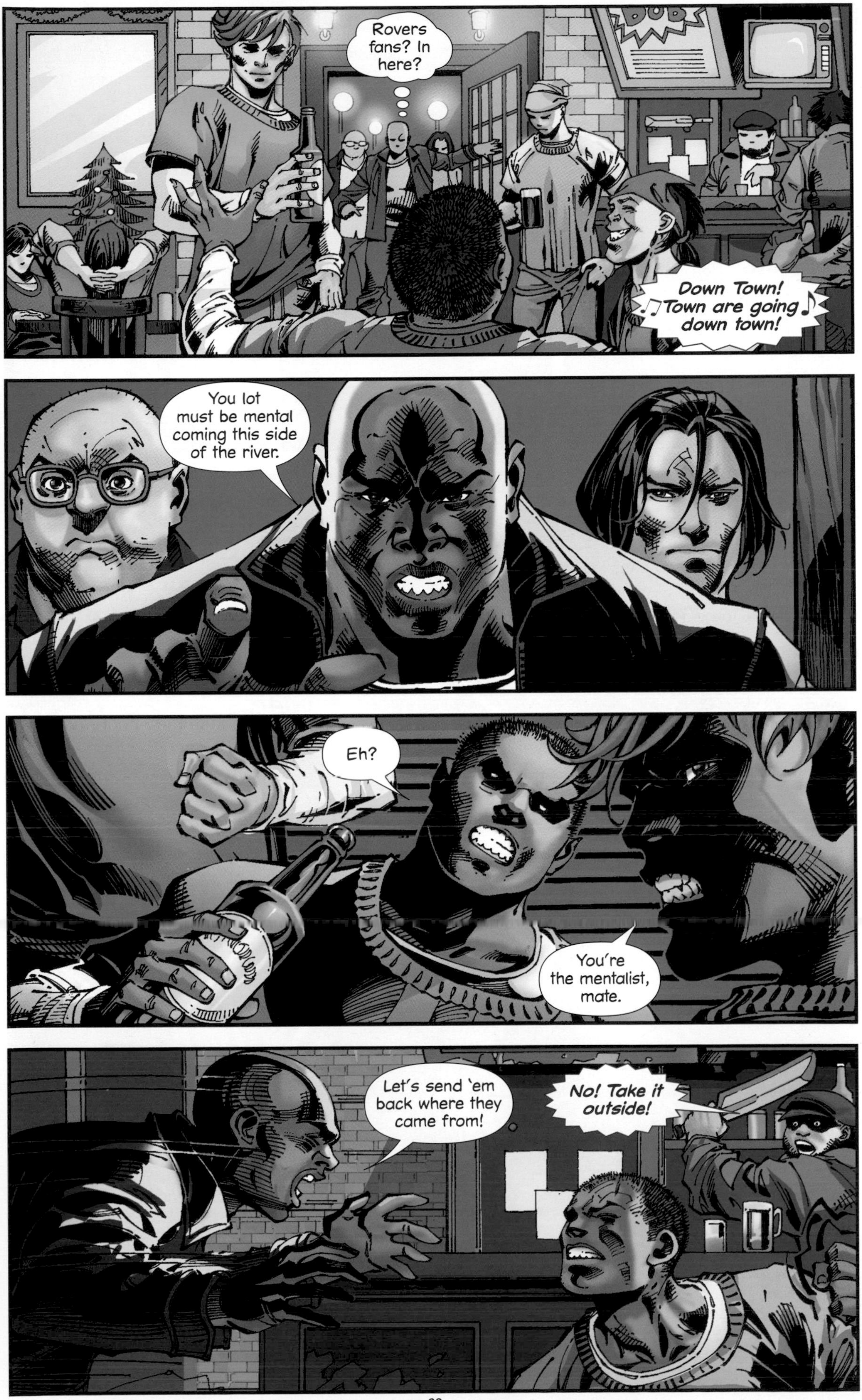
Rovers fans? In here?
Down Town! ♪Town are going♪ down town!
You lot must be mental coming this side of the river.
Eh?
You're the mentalist, mate.
Let's send 'em back where they came from!
No! Take it outside!

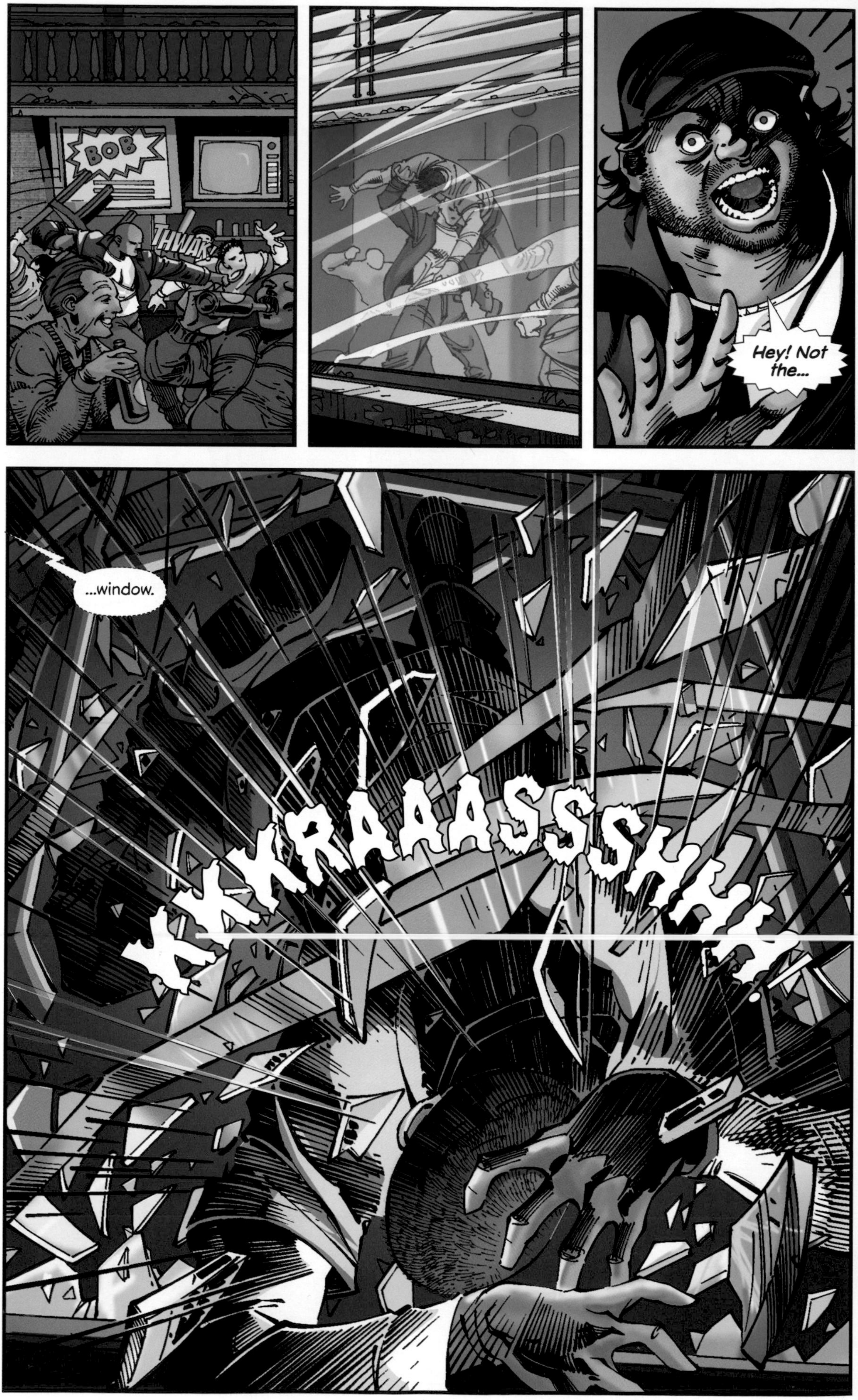
BOB
THWAK!
Hey! Not the...
...window.
KKKRAAASSSHH

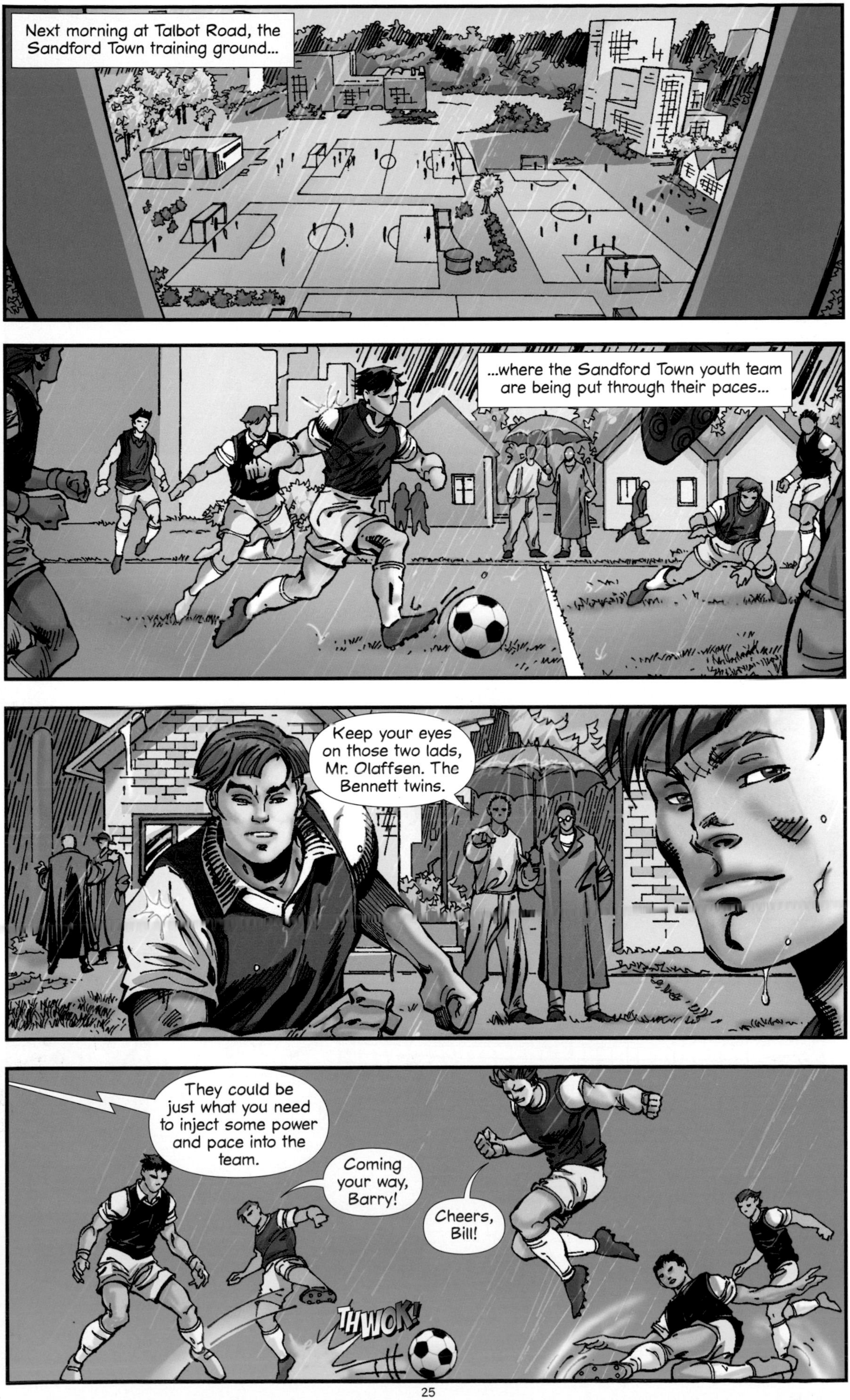
Next morning at Talbot Road, the Sandford Town training ground...
...where the Sandford Town youth team are being put through their paces...
Keep your eyes on those two lads, Mr. Olaffsen. The Bennett twins.
They could be just what you need to inject some power and pace into the team.
Coming your way, Barry!
Cheers, Bill!
THWOK!

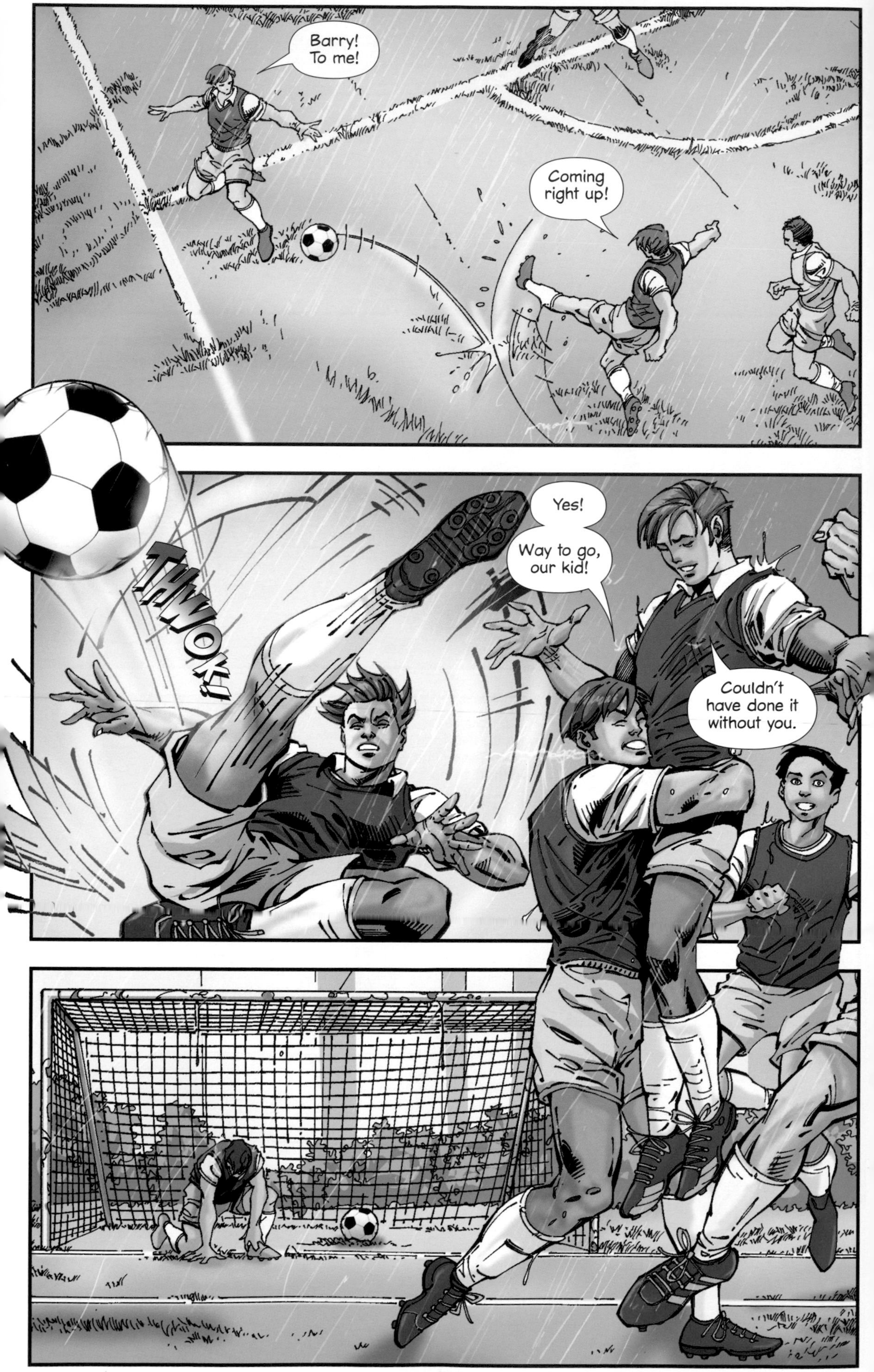
Barry!
To me!
Coming right up!
THWOK!
Yes!
Way to go, our kid!
Couldn't have done it without you.

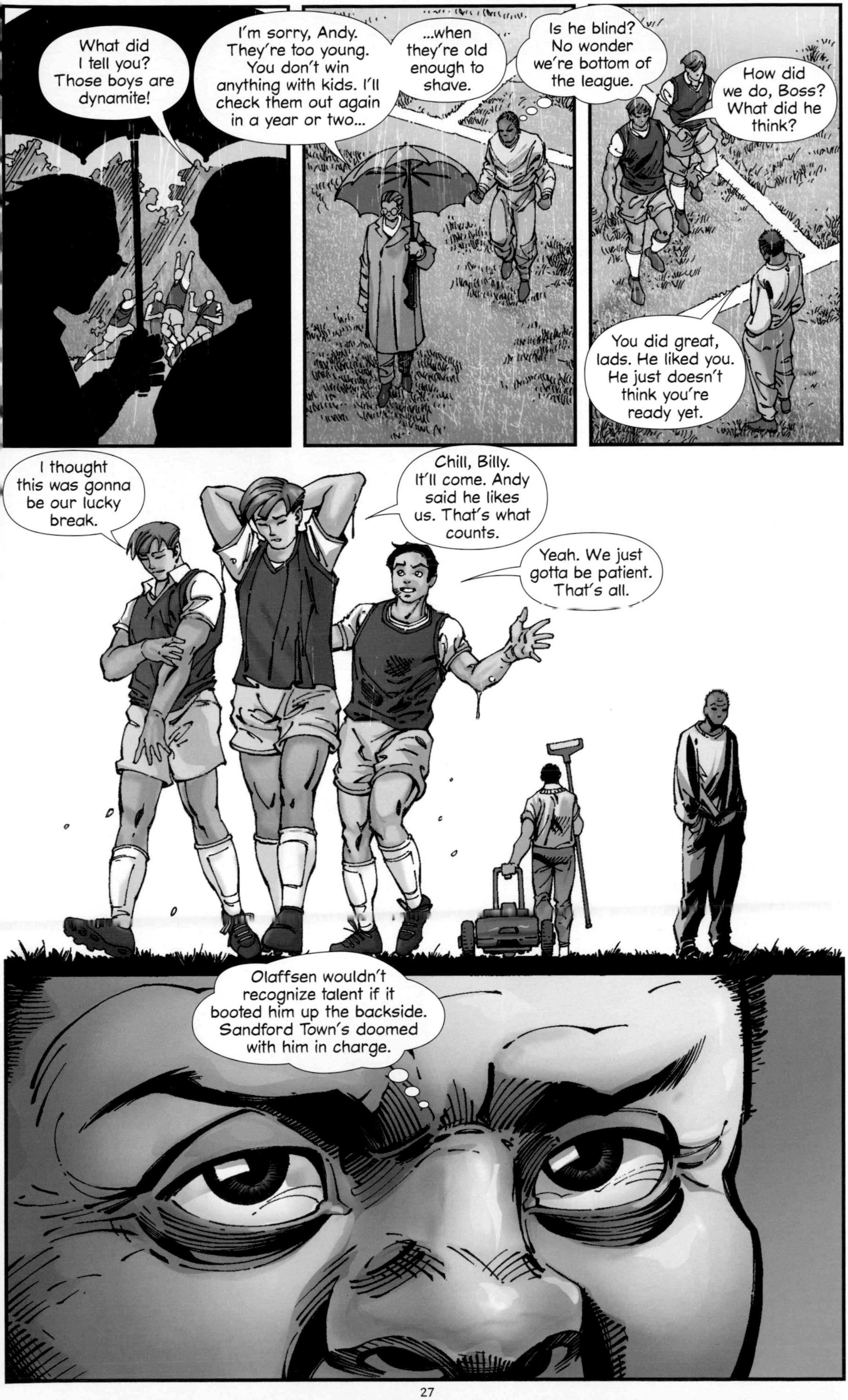
What did I tell you? Those boys are dynamite!
I'm sorry, Andy. They're too young. You don't win anything with kids. I'll check them out again in a year or two...
...when they're old enough to shave.
Is he blind? No wonder we're bottom of the league.
How did we do, Boss? What did he think?
You did great, lads. He liked you. He just doesn't think you're ready yet.
I thought this was gonna be our lucky break.
Chill, Billy. It'll come. Andy said he likes us. That's what counts.
Yeah. We just gotta be patient. That's all.
Olaffsen wouldn't recognize talent if it booted him up the backside. Sandford Town's doomed with him in charge.

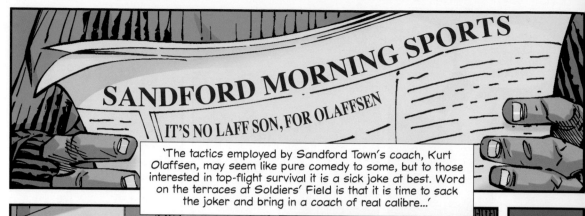

SANDFORD MORNING SPORTS

IT'S NO LAFF SON, FOR OLAFFSEN

'The tactics employed by Sandford Town's coach, Kurt Olaffsen, may seem like pure comedy to some, but to those interested in top-flight survival it is a sick joke at best. Word on the terraces at Soldiers' Field is that it is time to sack the joker and bring in a coach of real calibre...'

Hey! Yo! Claire!

Crab...are you stalking me now?

Come on, Claire. I just wanna grab a coffee or something.

Oi!

!?

Leave our sister alone, Crab.

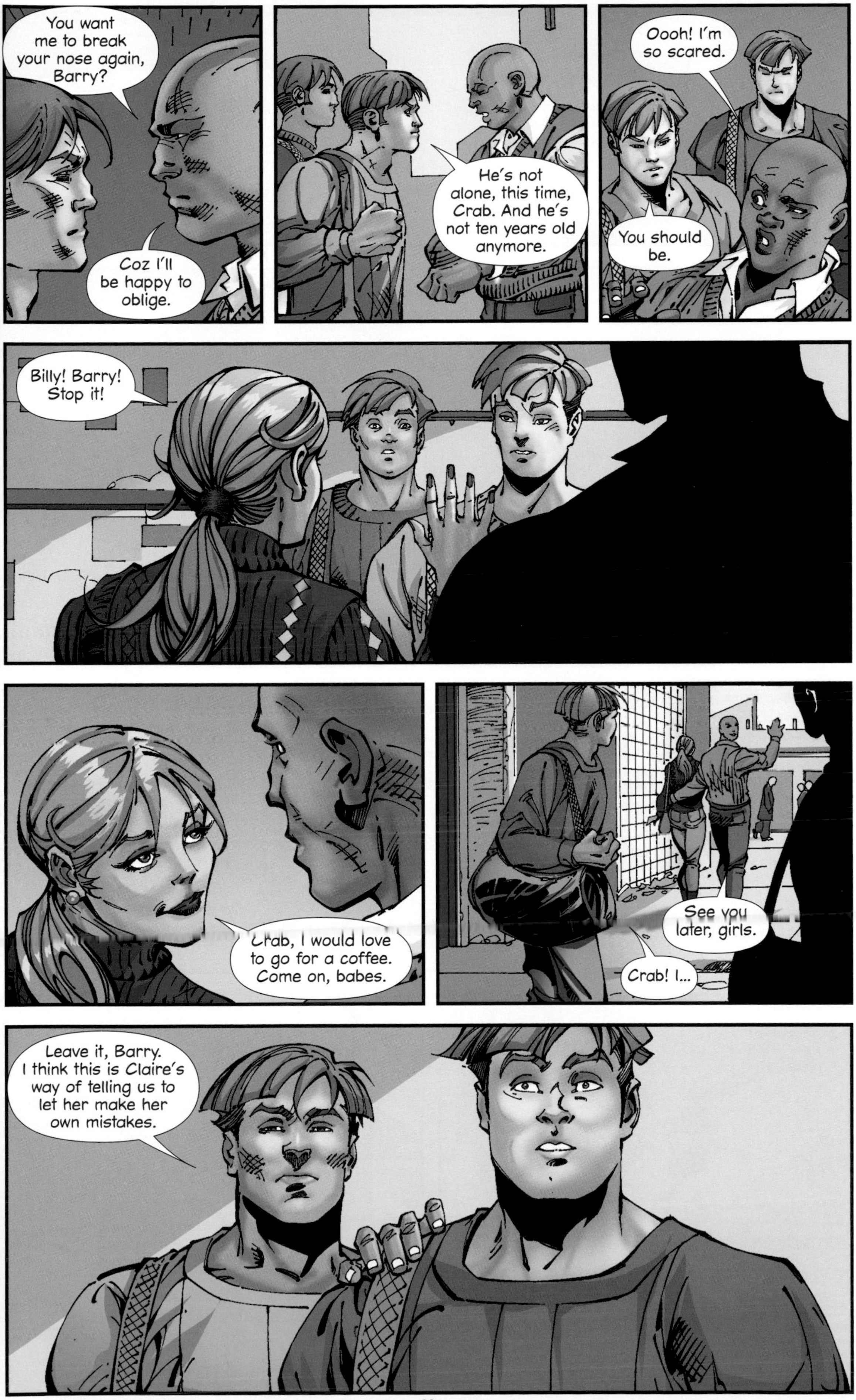
You want me to break your nose again, Barry?
Coz I'll be happy to oblige.
He's not alone, this time, Crab. And he's not ten years old anymore.
Oooh! I'm so scared.
You should be.
Billy! Barry! Stop it!
Crab, I would love to go for a coffee. Come on, babes.
See you later, girls.
Crab! I...
Leave it, Barry. I think this is Claire's way of telling us to let her make her own mistakes.

January 1. New Year's Day.

Good afternoon, and welcome to this crucial bottom-of-the-table clash between Moorfield Vale and Sandford Town.

And Davi Cordoso has been recalled to the team in place of the suspended Steve Hunter.

Cordoso will need to be sharper than that. He's given the ball away.

AWOOOOSH

THWAK!

Ooh! That was close!

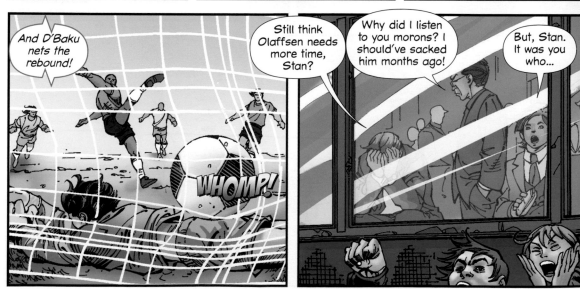

And D'Baku nets the rebound!

WHOMP!

Still think Olaffsen needs more time, Stan?

Why did I listen to you morons? I should've sacked him months ago!

But, Stan. It was you who...

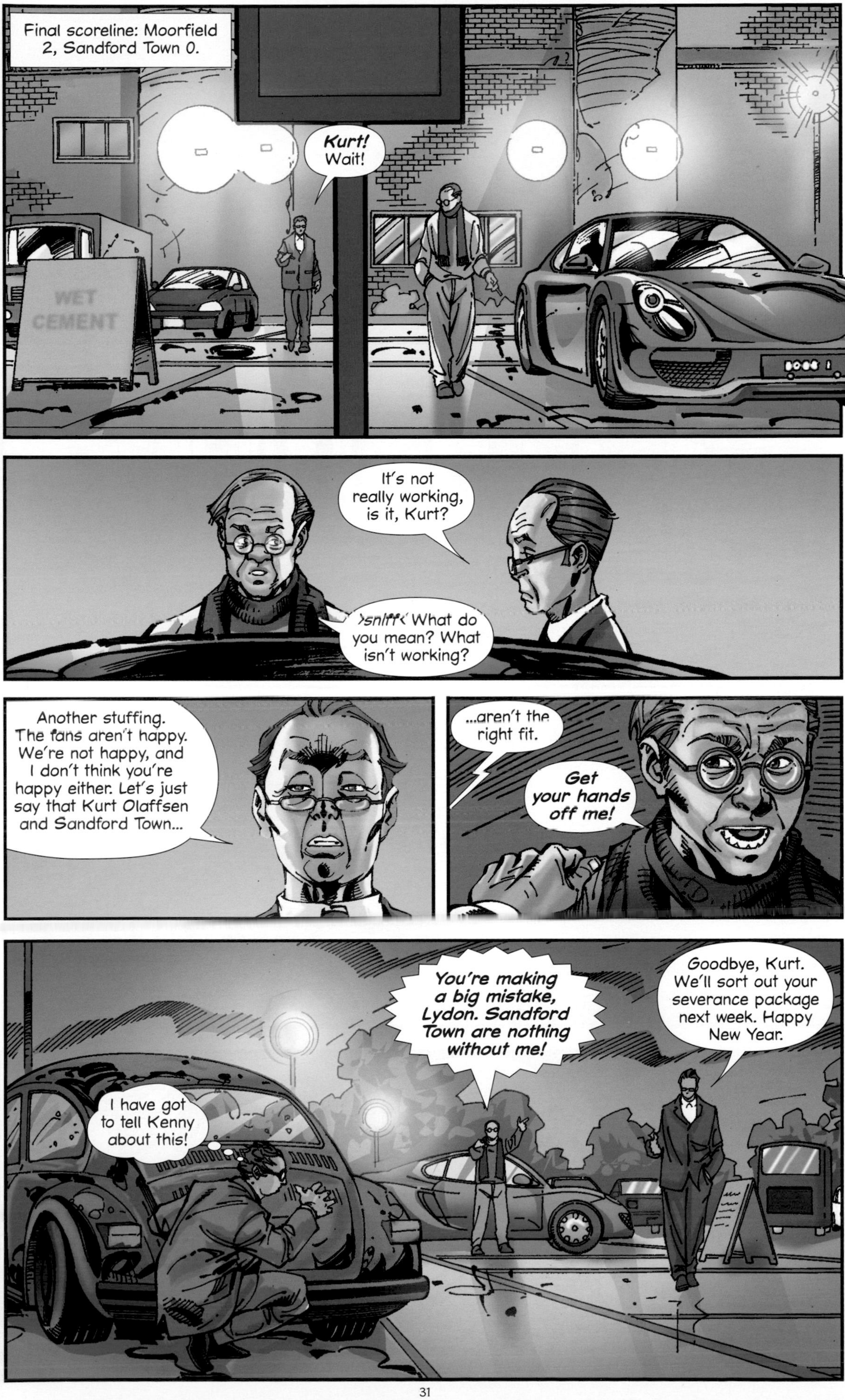
Final scoreline: Moorfield 2, Sandford Town 0.
Kurt! Wait!
WET CEMENT
It's not really working, is it, Kurt?
›sniff‹ What do you mean? What isn't working?
Another stuffing. The fans aren't happy. We're not happy, and I don't think you're happy either. Let's just say that Kurt Olaffsen and Sandford Town...
...aren't the right fit.
Get your hands off me!
I have got to tell Kenny about this!
You're making a big mistake, Lydon. Sandford Town are nothing without me!
Goodbye, Kurt. We'll sort out your severance package next week. Happy New Year.

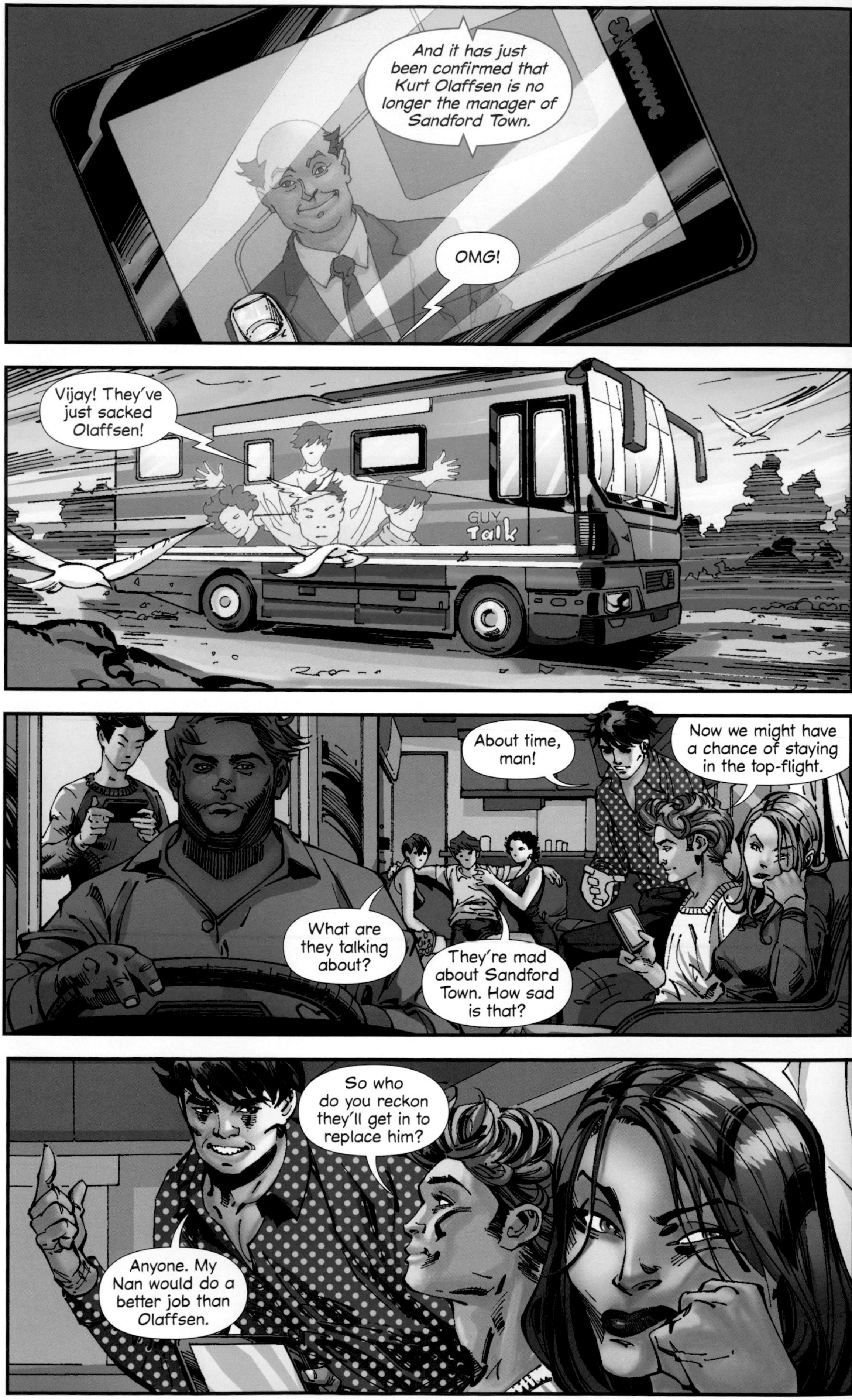
And it has just been confirmed that Kurt Olaffsen is no longer the manager of Sandford Town.
OMG!
Vijay! They've just sacked Olaffsen!
GUY Talk
About time, man!
Now we might have a chance of staying in the top-flight.
What are they talking about?
They're mad about Sandford Town. How sad is that?
So who do you reckon they'll get in to replace him?
Anyone. My Nan would do a better job than Olaffsen.

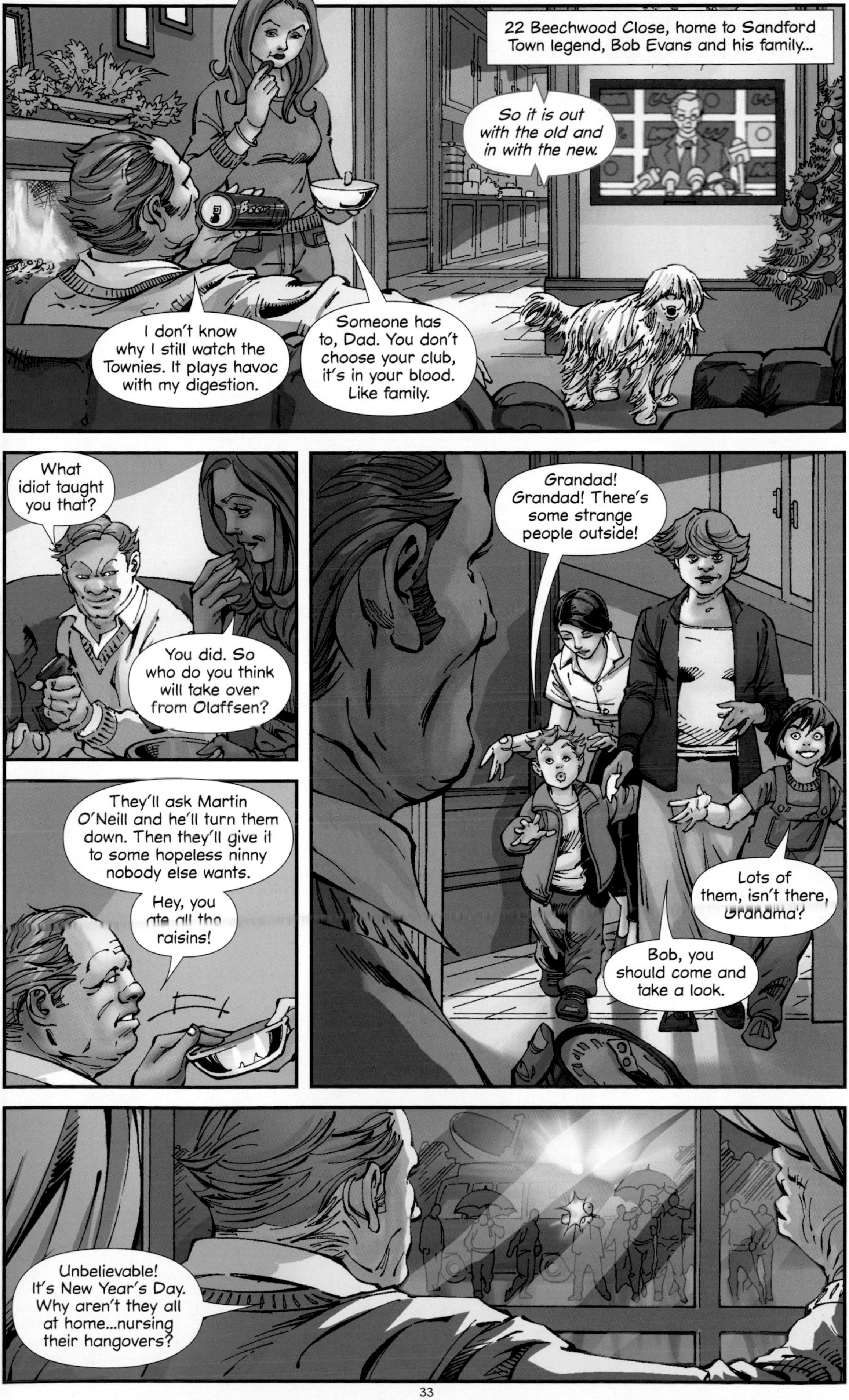
22 Beechwood Close, home to Sandford Town legend, Bob Evans and his family...
So it is out with the old and in with the new.
I don't know why I still watch the Townies. It plays havoc with my digestion.
Someone has to, Dad. You don't choose your club, it's in your blood. Like family.
What idiot taught you that?
You did. So who do you think will take over from Olaffsen?
They'll ask Martin O'Neill and he'll turn them down. Then they'll give it to some hopeless ninny nobody else wants.
Hey, you ate all the raisins!
Grandad! Grandad! There's some strange people outside!
Lots of them, isn't there, Grandma?
Bob, you should come and take a look.
Unbelievable! It's New Year's Day. Why aren't they all at home...nursing their hangovers?

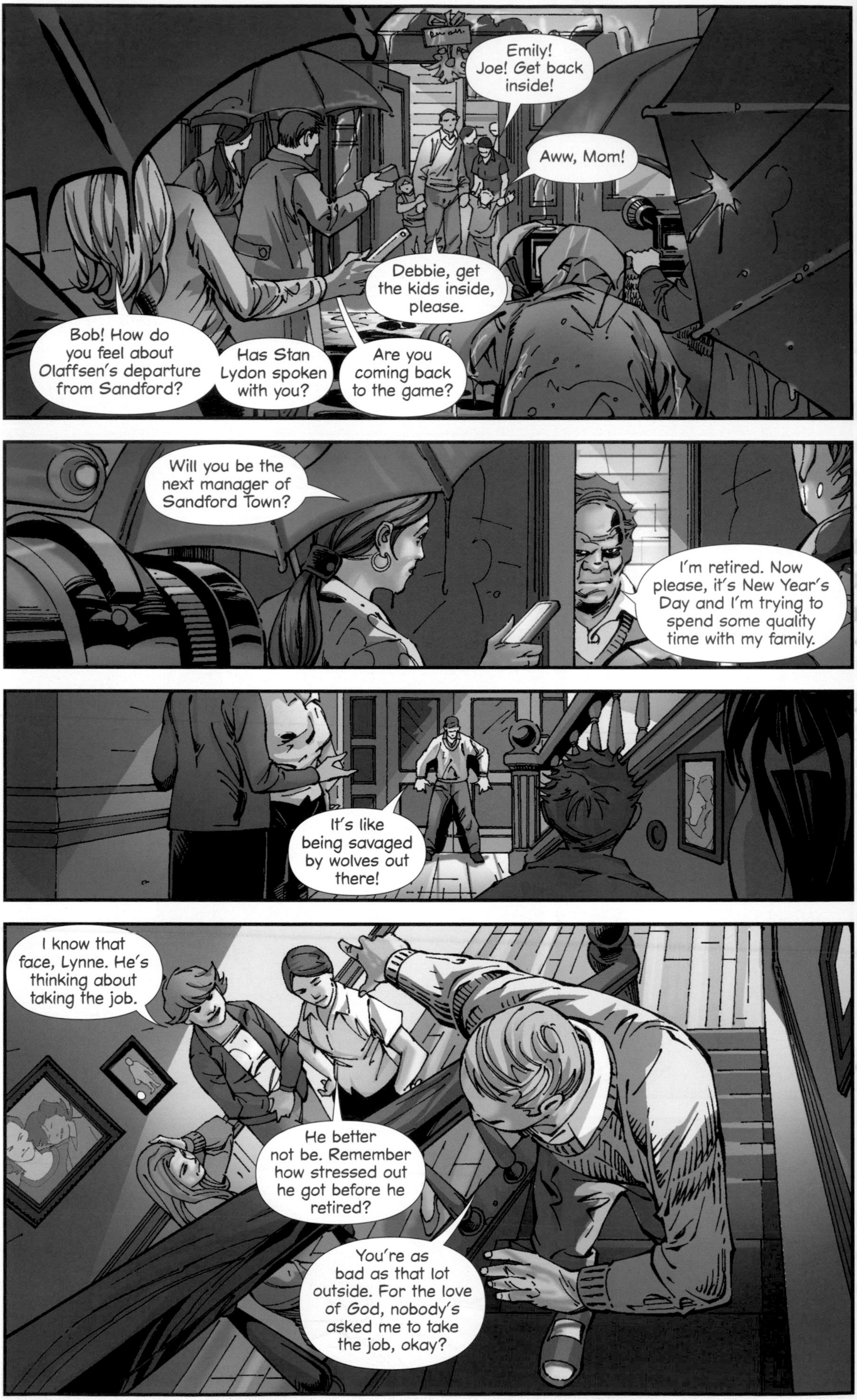
Emily! Joe! Get back inside!
Aww, Mom!
Debbie, get the kids inside, please.
Bob! How do you feel about Olaffsen's departure from Sandford?
Has Stan Lydon spoken with you?
Are you coming back to the game?
Will you be the next manager of Sandford Town?
I'm retired. Now please, it's New Year's Day and I'm trying to spend some quality time with my family.
It's like being savaged by wolves out there!
I know that face, Lynne. He's thinking about taking the job.
He better not be. Remember how stressed out he got before he retired?
You're as bad as that lot outside. For the love of God, nobody's asked me to take the job, okay?

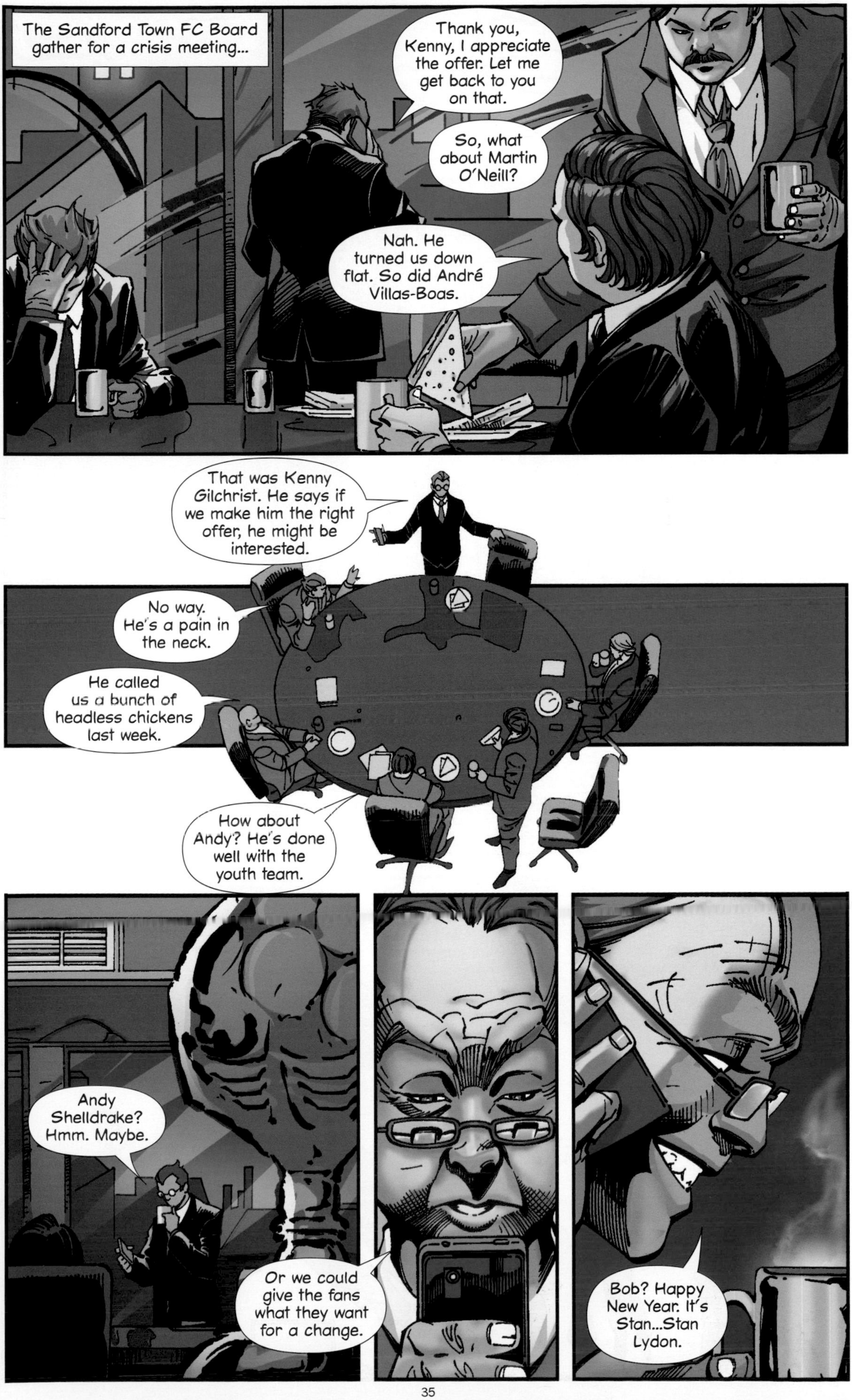
The Sandford Town FC Board gather for a crisis meeting...
Thank you, Kenny, I appreciate the offer. Let me get back to you on that.
So, what about Martin O'Neill?
Nah. He turned us down flat. So did André Villas-Boas.
That was Kenny Gilchrist. He says if we make him the right offer, he might be interested.
No way. He's a pain in the neck.
He called us a bunch of headless chickens last week.
How about Andy? He's done well with the youth team.
Andy Shelldrake? Hmm. Maybe.
Or we could give the fans what they want for a change.
Bob? Happy New Year. It's Stan...Stan Lydon.

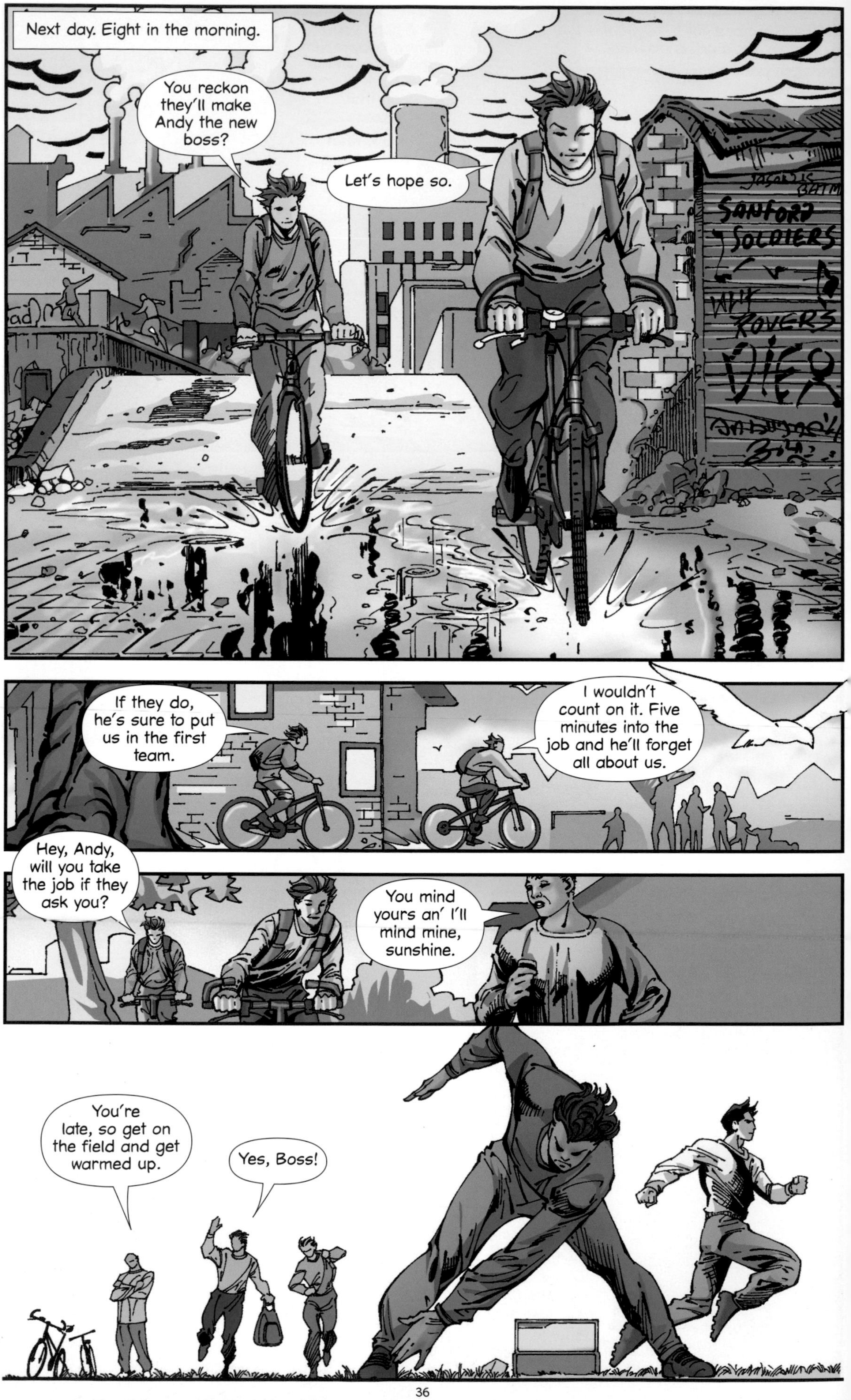
Next day. Eight in the morning.
You reckon they'll make Andy the new boss?
Let's hope so.
SANFORD SOLDIERS
ROVERS
If they do, he's sure to put us in the first team.
I wouldn't count on it. Five minutes into the job and he'll forget all about us.
Hey, Andy, will you take the job if they ask you?
You mind yours an' I'll mind mine, sunshine.
You're late, so get on the field and get warmed up.
Yes, Boss!

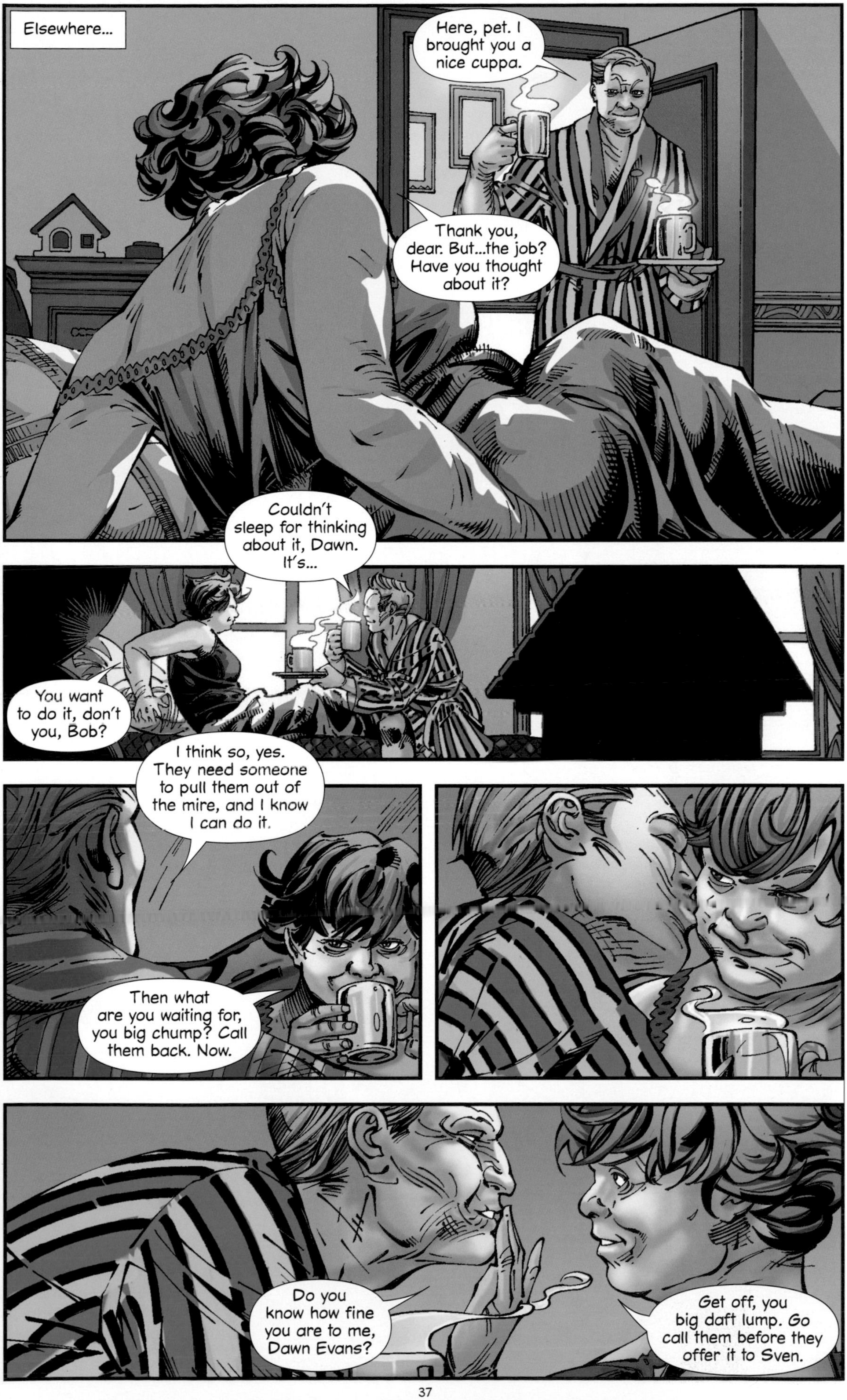
Elsewhere...
Here, pet. I brought you a nice cuppa.
Thank you, dear. But...the job? Have you thought about it?
Couldn't sleep for thinking about it, Dawn. It's...
You want to do it, don't you, Bob?
I think so, yes. They need someone to pull them out of the mire, and I know I can do it.
Then what are you waiting for, you big chump? Call them back. Now.
Do you know how fine you are to me, Dawn Evans?
Get off, you big daft lump. Go call them before they offer it to Sven.

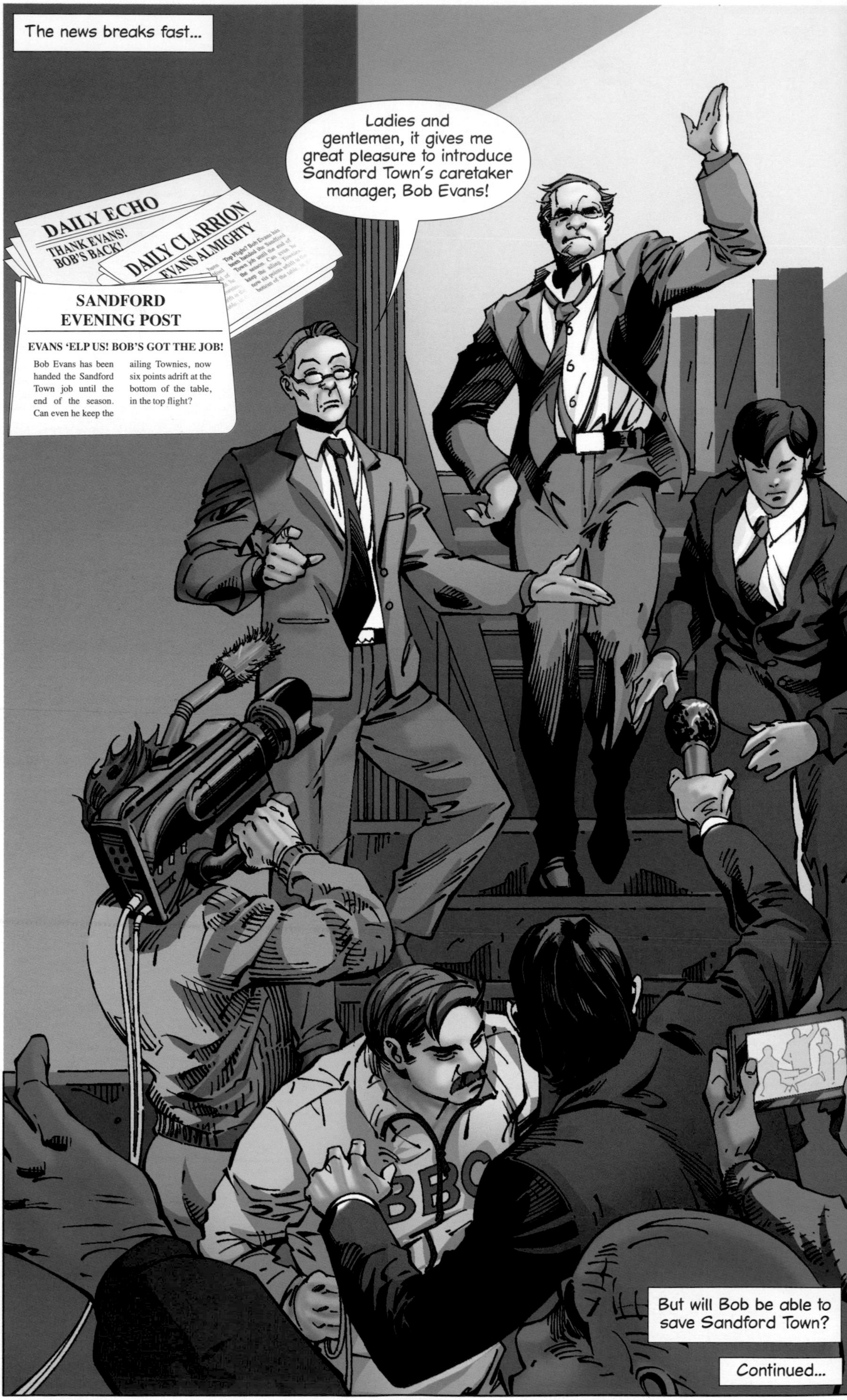
The news breaks fast...
DAILY ECHO
THANK EVANS! BOB'S BACK!
DAILY CLARRION
EVANS ALMIGHTY
SANDFORD EVENING POST
EVANS 'ELP US! BOB'S GOT THE JOB!
Bob Evans has been handed the Sandford Town job until the end of the season. Can even he keep the ailing Townies, now six points adrift at the bottom of the table, in the top flight?
Ladies and gentlemen, it gives me great pleasure to introduce Sandford Town's caretaker manager, Bob Evans!
BBC
But will Bob be able to save Sandford Town?
Continued...

Chapter 2

WHO'S WHO IN THE BEAUTIFUL GAME

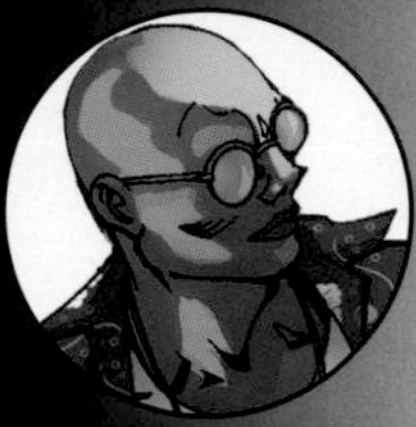

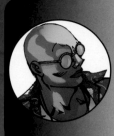

SIMON FOX
Age: 28
Owner, Euphoria night club

A successful businessman who is not choosy about how he makes his money, Foxy has been known to deal in drugs, illegal gambling, match fixing, violence...in short, everything and anything that's illegal and dodgy is his domain of expertise. He is charming when it suits him, but underneath the smooth veneer hides an unpredictable temper.

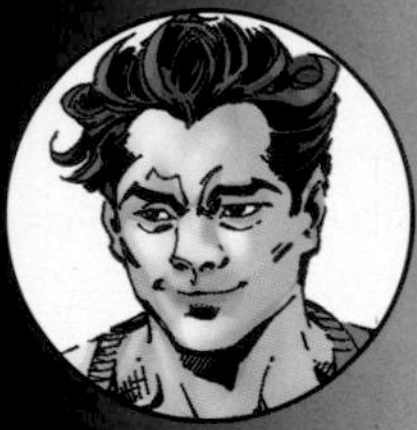

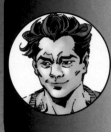

BRENDAN MCNULTY
Age: 31
Goalkeeper

Once known as 'the safest hands in soccer', McNulty is going through a crisis of confidence. McNulty played for Halton Moor where he helped them win the FA Cup and the league title, two years in a trot. This is his third season at Sandford Town and if things don't go well, it could well be his last.

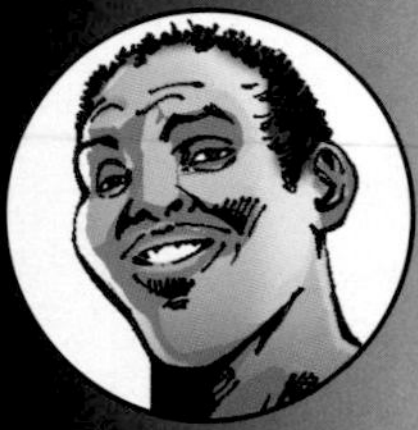

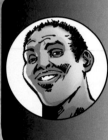

ANDY SHELDRAKE
Age: 61
Coach, Sandford Town Youth Academy

Snapped up as a teenager, Andy has spent his whole career at Sandford Town. The former left back was a part of the 'golden generation' that included Kenny Gilchrist and Bob Evans, back in the 1970s. Like Bob, Andy was also injured in the 1983 Swiss coach disaster that destroyed the team and put an end to his playing career.

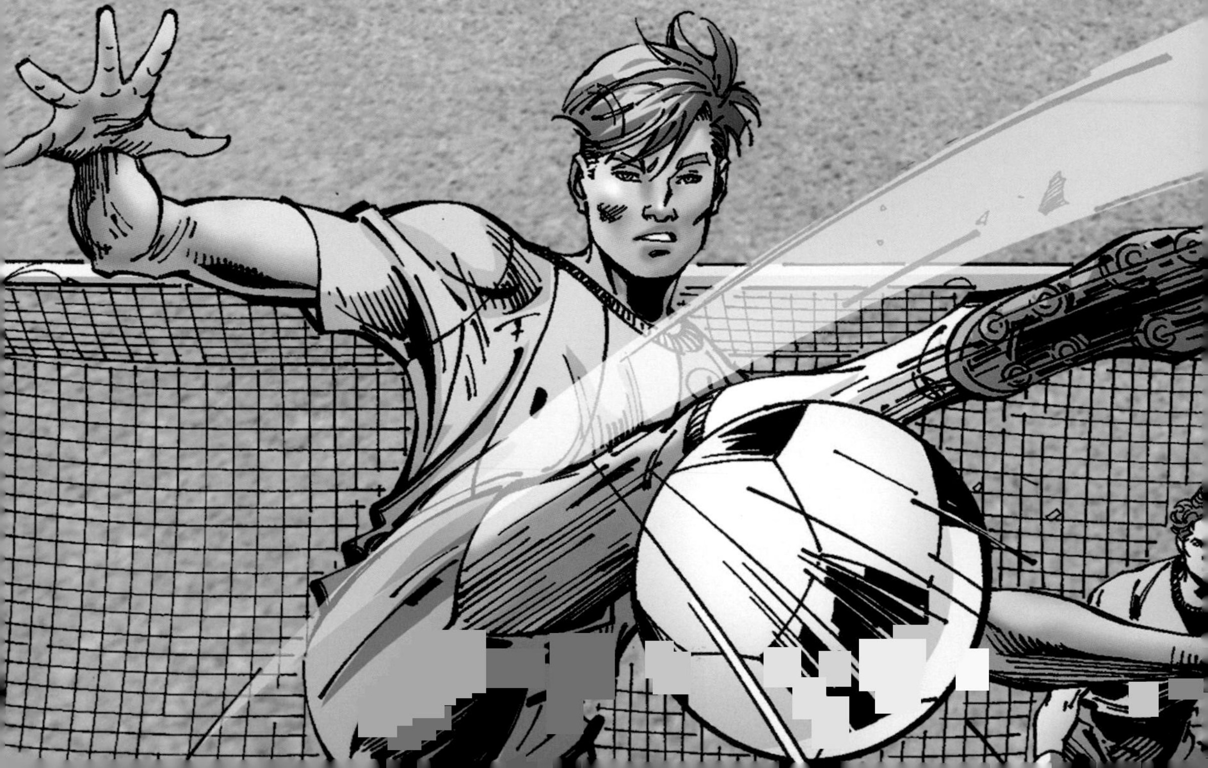

Chapter 2 A FRESH START

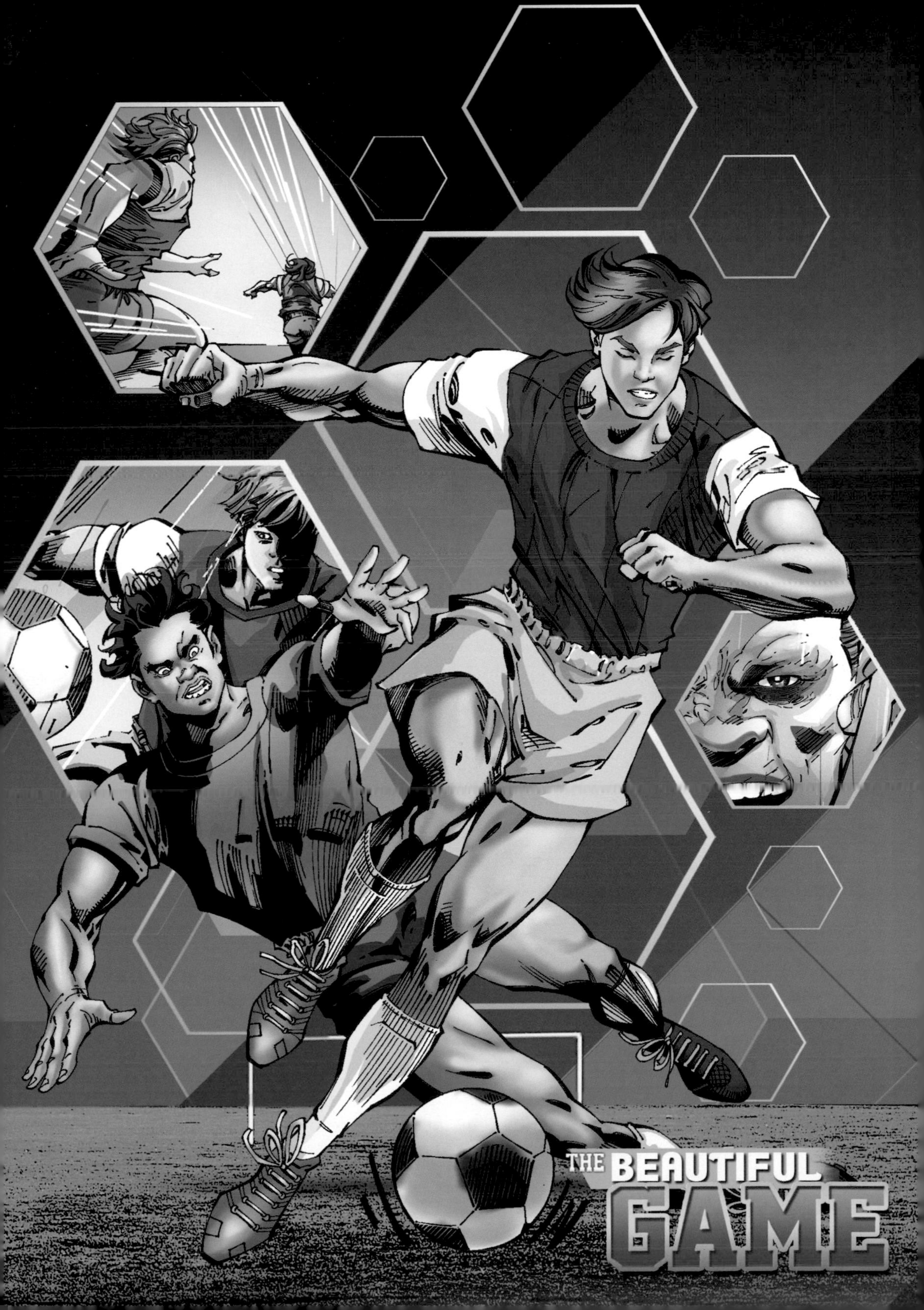
THE BEAUTIFUL GAME

SANDFORD EVENING POST

'Evans 'elp him. *Can Bob Evans turn his club's fortunes around? Sure.*

FA CUP GLORY

Bob Evans's first match in charge is a game Sandford is expected to win, against Division 2 leaders, Rothwell FC, in the third round of the FA Cup this weekend, but as the man himself says, 'There are no easy games in football'.

If Evans is to save Town from almost certain relegation, he will certainly be hoping to make a few canny buys during the January transfer window and bring some fresh new blood into his ailing team. But the biggest problem facing the new manager is that all of football knows that Sandford Town don't have a huge pot of gold to spend on new players, and facing almost certain relegation, it is highly unlikely that 'star' players will be queuing up to sign a contract. Will Evans be forced to look to the club's still highly acclaimed youth academy?

For now, it remains to be seen whether the man who took Latvia to the semi-finals of the World Cup in 1998 can save Sandford Town from the drop.

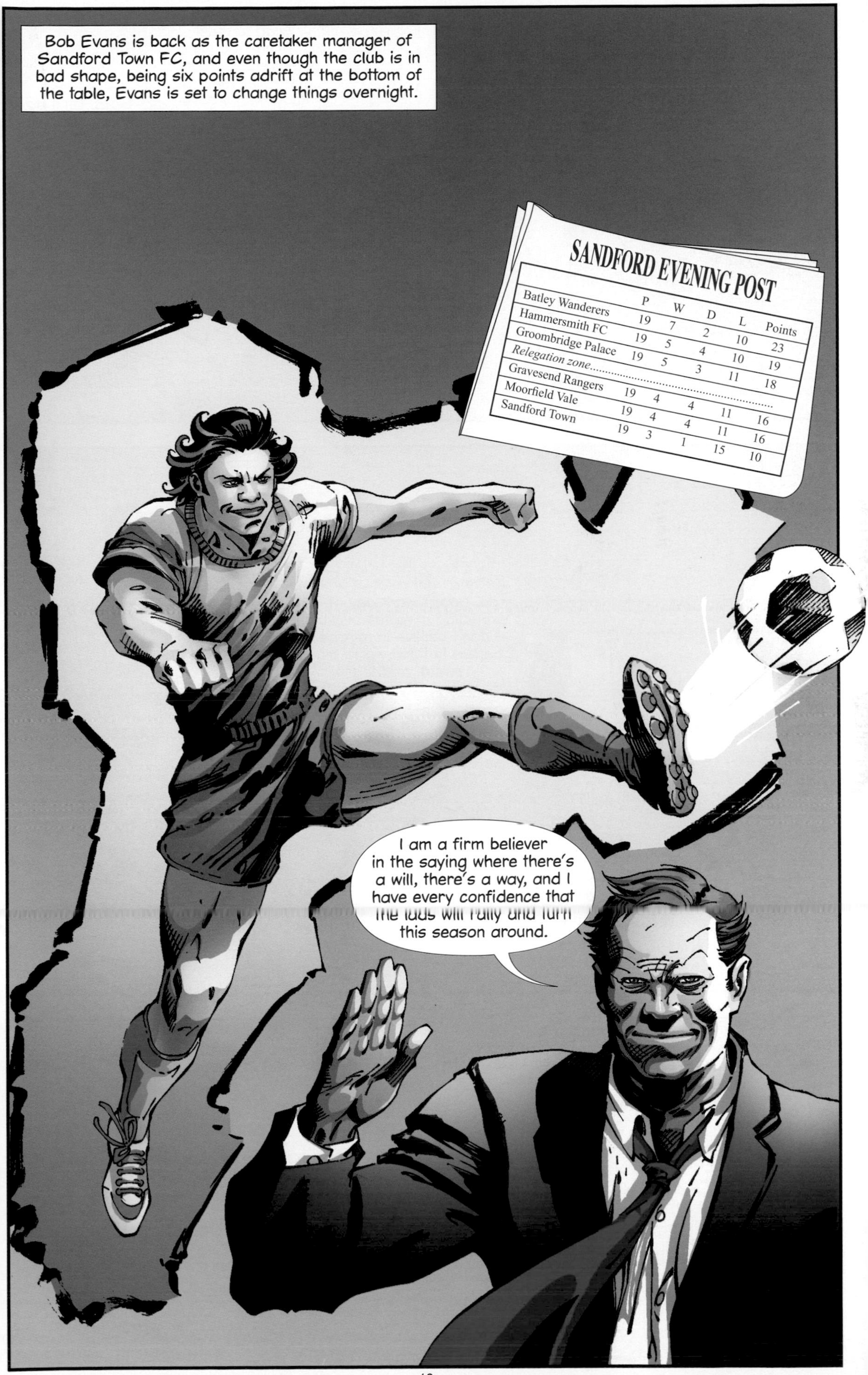
Bob Evans is back as the caretaker manager of Sandford Town FC, and even though the club is in bad shape, being six points adrift at the bottom of the table, Evans is set to change things overnight.
SANDFORD EVENING POST
P W D L Points
Batley Wanderers 19 7 2 10 23
Hammersmith FC 19 5 4 10 19
Groombridge Palace 19 5 3 11 18
Relegation zone..
Gravesend Rangers 19 4 4 11 16
Moorfield Vale 19 4 4 11 16
Sandford Town 19 3 1 15 10
I am a firm believer in the saying where there's a will, there's a way, and I have every confidence that the lads will rally and turn this season around.

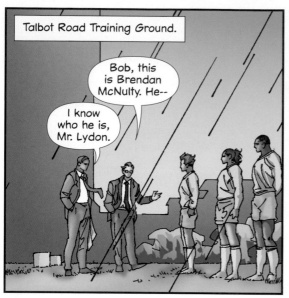

Talbot Road Training Ground.

Bob, this is Brendan McNulty. He--

I know who he is, Mr. Lydon.

Glad to meet you, Bren. You need to command your area more. Let the lads know who's boss.

Aye...yes, Boss. I...I'll do my best.

I'll keep this brief, coz we've all got a lot of work to do. I don't want any of you expecting miracles overnight. I don't believe in miracles. I believe in hard work, blood, sweat, and tears.

Great, he's expecting us to break down and cry like babies.

Shh...

Was there something you wanted to say, Steven?

Err...no, Boss.

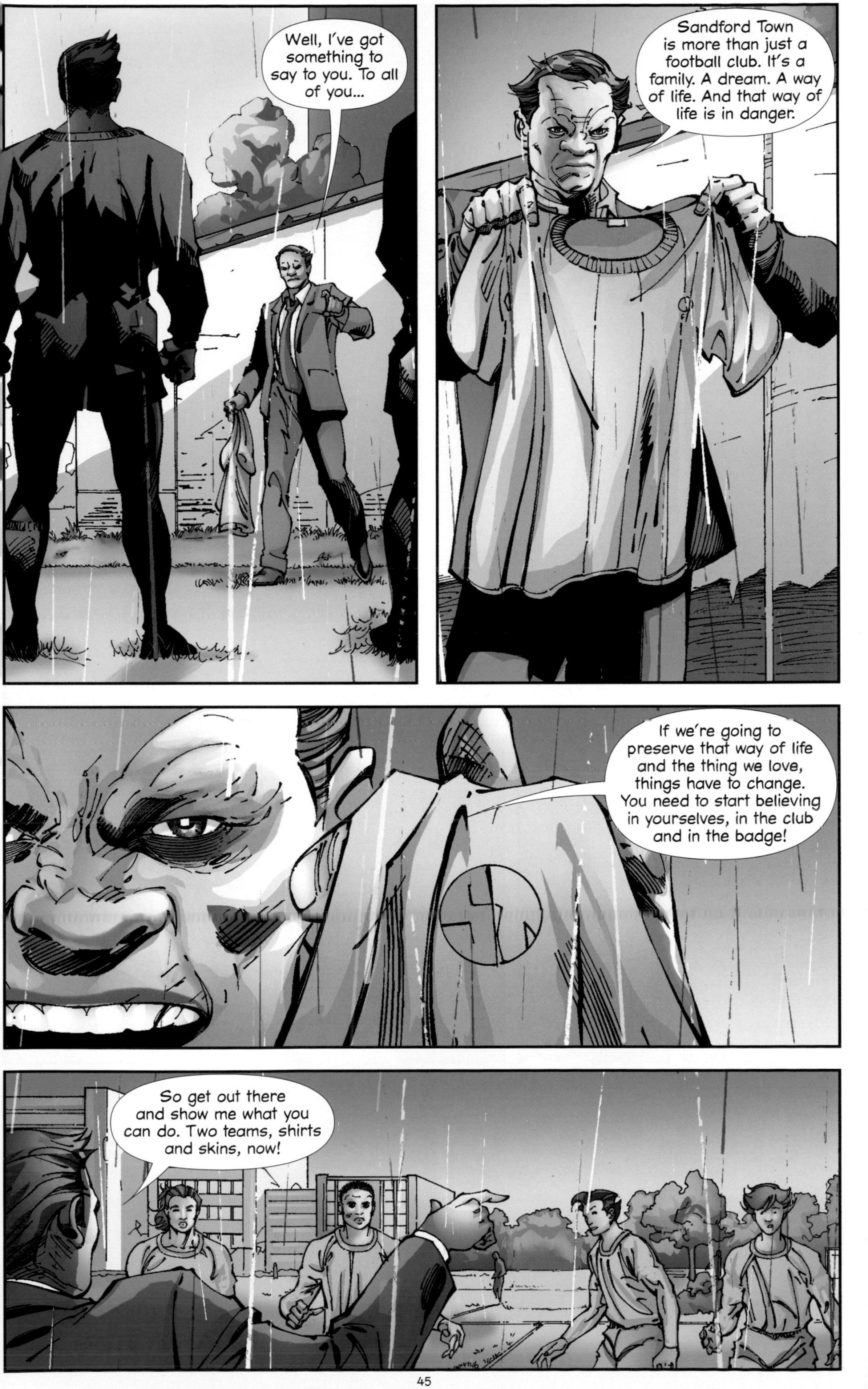
Well, I've got something to say to you. To all of you...
Sandford Town is more than just a football club. It's a family. A dream. A way of life. And that way of life is in danger.
If we're going to preserve that way of life and the thing we love, things have to change. You need to start believing in yourselves, in the club and in the badge!
So get out there and show me what you can do. Two teams, shirts and skins, now!

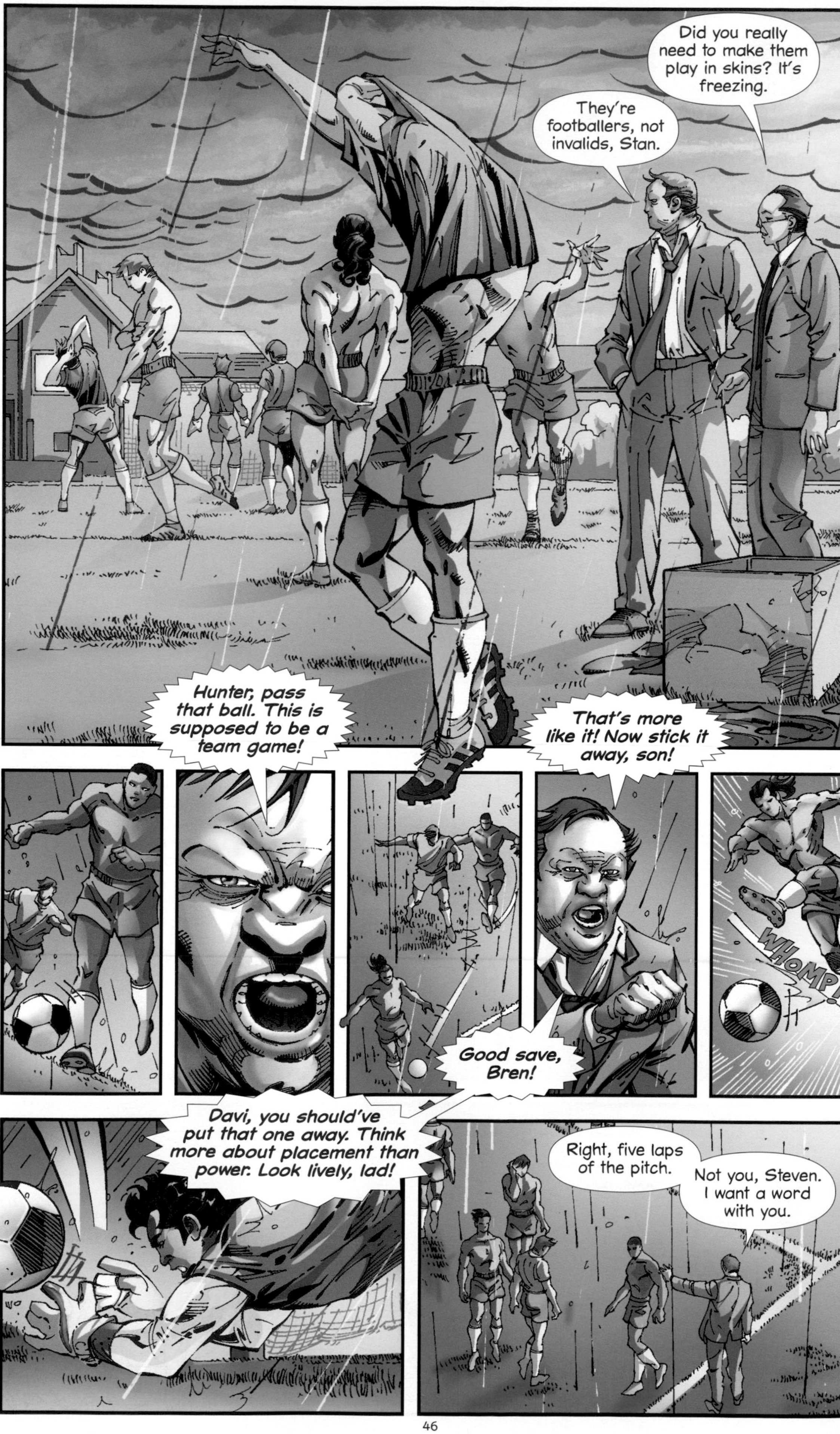

Did you really need to make them play in skins? It's freezing.
They're footballers, not invalids, Stan.
Hunter, pass that ball. This is supposed to be a team game!
That's more like it! Now stick it away, son!
Good save, Bren!
WHOMP!
Davi, you should've put that one away. Think more about placement than power. Look lively, lad!
Right, five laps of the pitch.
Not you, Steven. I want a word with you.

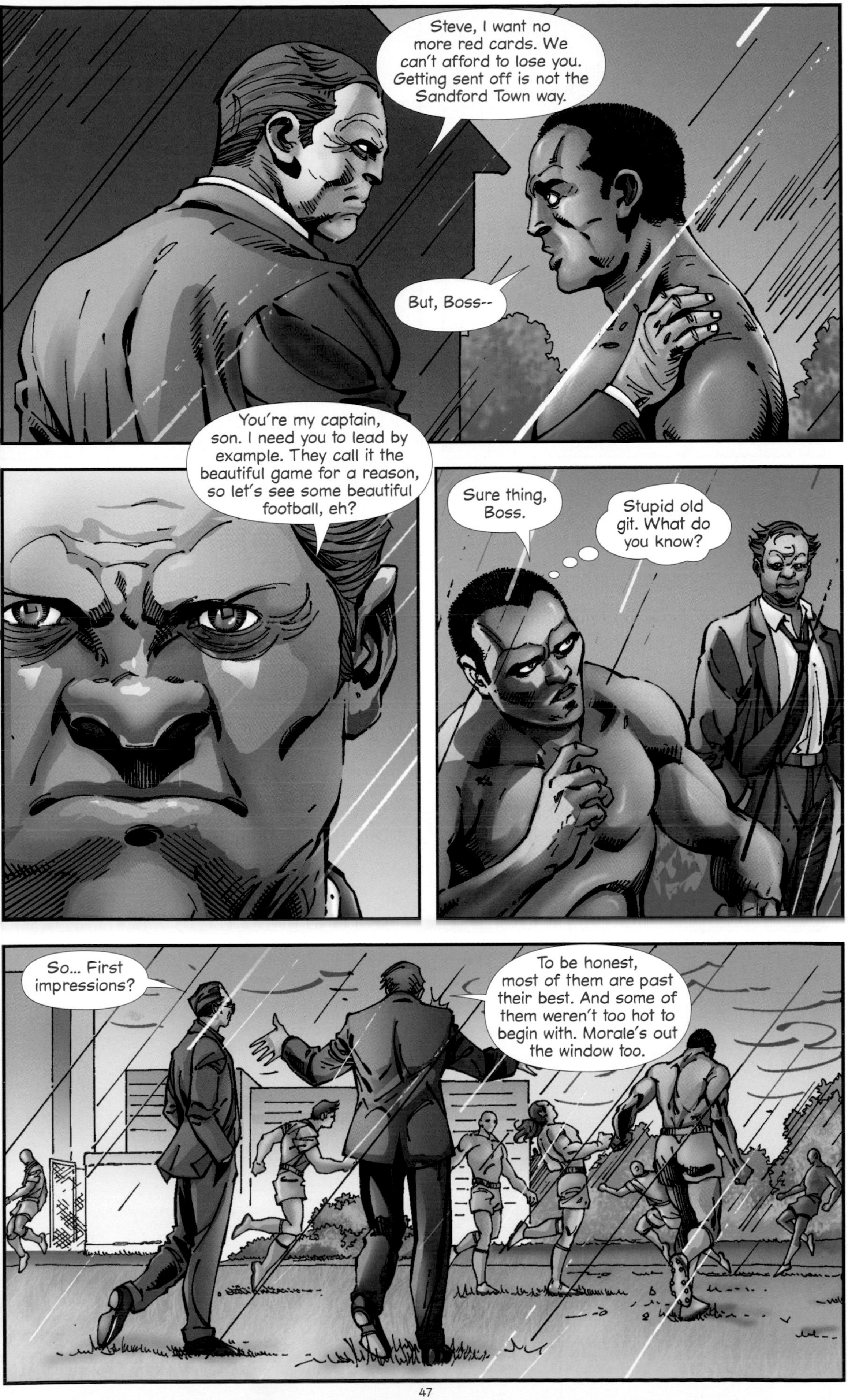
Steve, I want no more red cards. We can't afford to lose you. Getting sent off is not the Sandford Town way.
But, Boss--
You're my captain, son. I need you to lead by example. They call it the beautiful game for a reason, so let's see some beautiful football, eh?
Sure thing, Boss.
Stupid old git. What do you know?
So... First impressions?
To be honest, most of them are past their best. And some of them weren't too hot to begin with. Morale's out the window too.

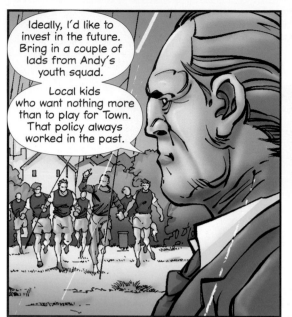

Ideally, I'd like to invest in the future. Bring in a couple of lads from Andy's youth squad.

Local kids who want nothing more than to play for Town. That policy always worked in the past.

But there's no time to mollycoddle youngsters, so I'd like to bring in an experienced playmaker while the transfer window's open.

Sorry, Bob. Not an option. One of our creditors just called in a loan. Things were already tight, but we over-stretched ourselves paying Olaffsen off.

Take a look around. Sandford's a dump. No jobs, no money. The only thing people round here can take pride in is their football team. Can you give them that pride, Bob?

I'll have to, won't I?

What have I let myself in for this time?

Right, places to be, people to see. I'll catch up with you later, Bob.

I'll look forward to it.

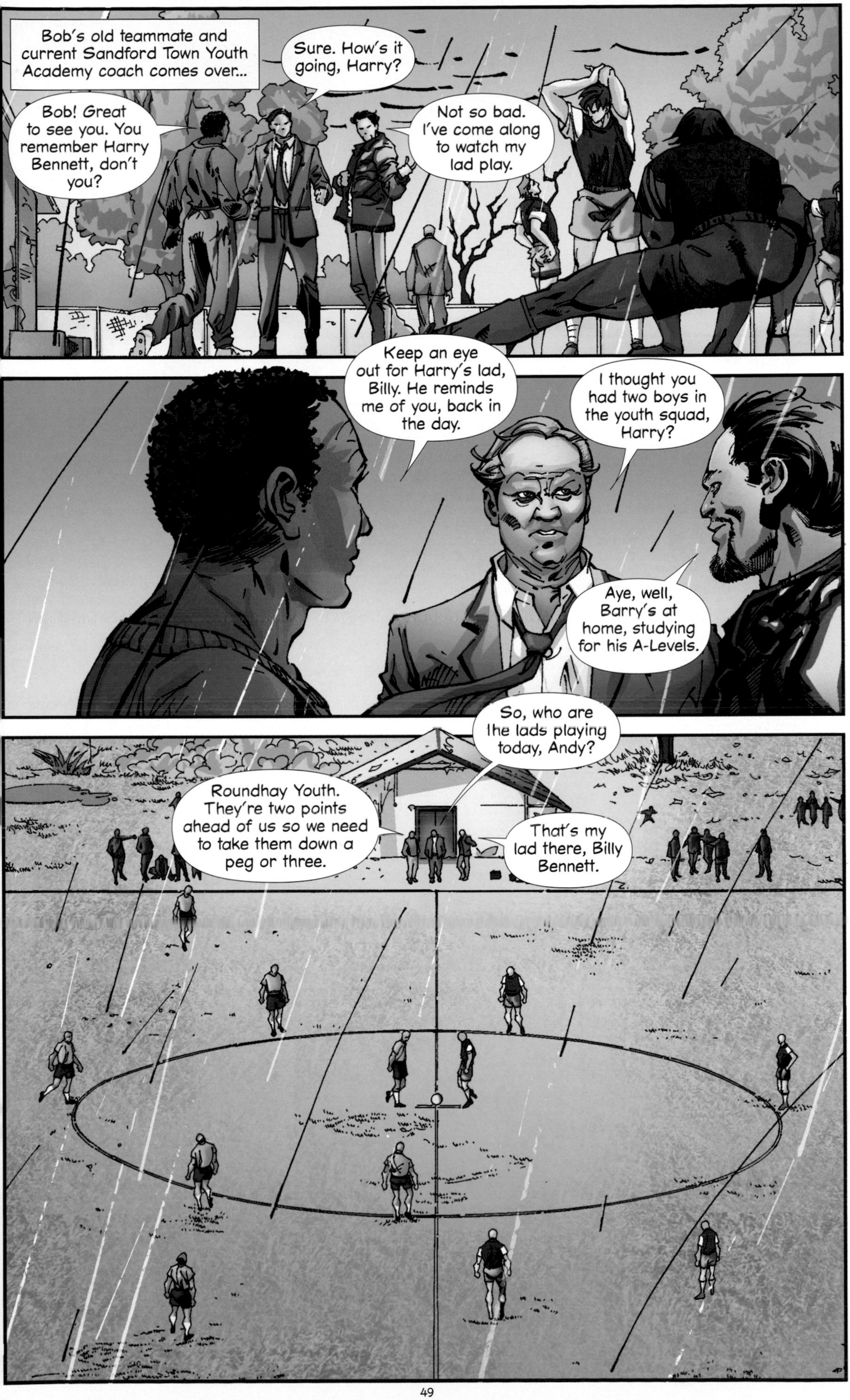
Bob's old teammate and current Sandford Town Youth Academy coach comes over...
Bob! Great to see you. You remember Harry Bennett, don't you?
Sure. How's it going, Harry?
Not so bad. I've come along to watch my lad play.
Keep an eye out for Harry's lad, Billy. He reminds me of you, back in the day.
I thought you had two boys in the youth squad, Harry?
Aye, well, Barry's at home, studying for his A-Levels.
So, who are the lads playing today, Andy?
Roundhay Youth. They're two points ahead of us so we need to take them down a peg or three.
That's my lad there, Billy Bennett.

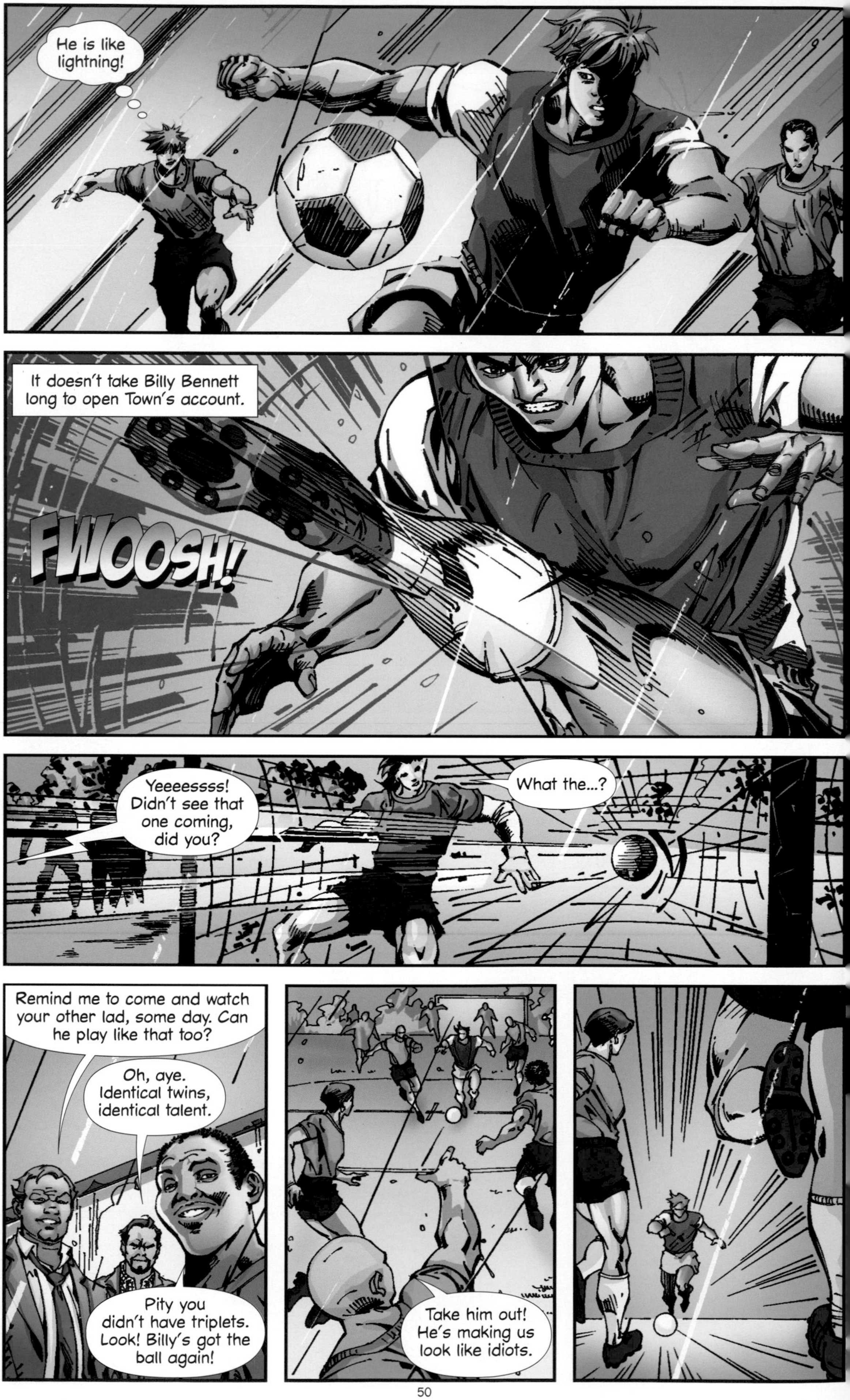
He is like lightning!
It doesn't take Billy Bennett long to open Town's account.
FWOOSH!
Yeeeessss! Didn't see that one coming, did you?
What the...?
Remind me to come and watch your other lad, some day. Can he play like that too?
Oh, aye. Identical twins, identical talent.
Pity you didn't have triplets. Look! Billy's got the ball again!
Take him out! He's making us look like idiots.

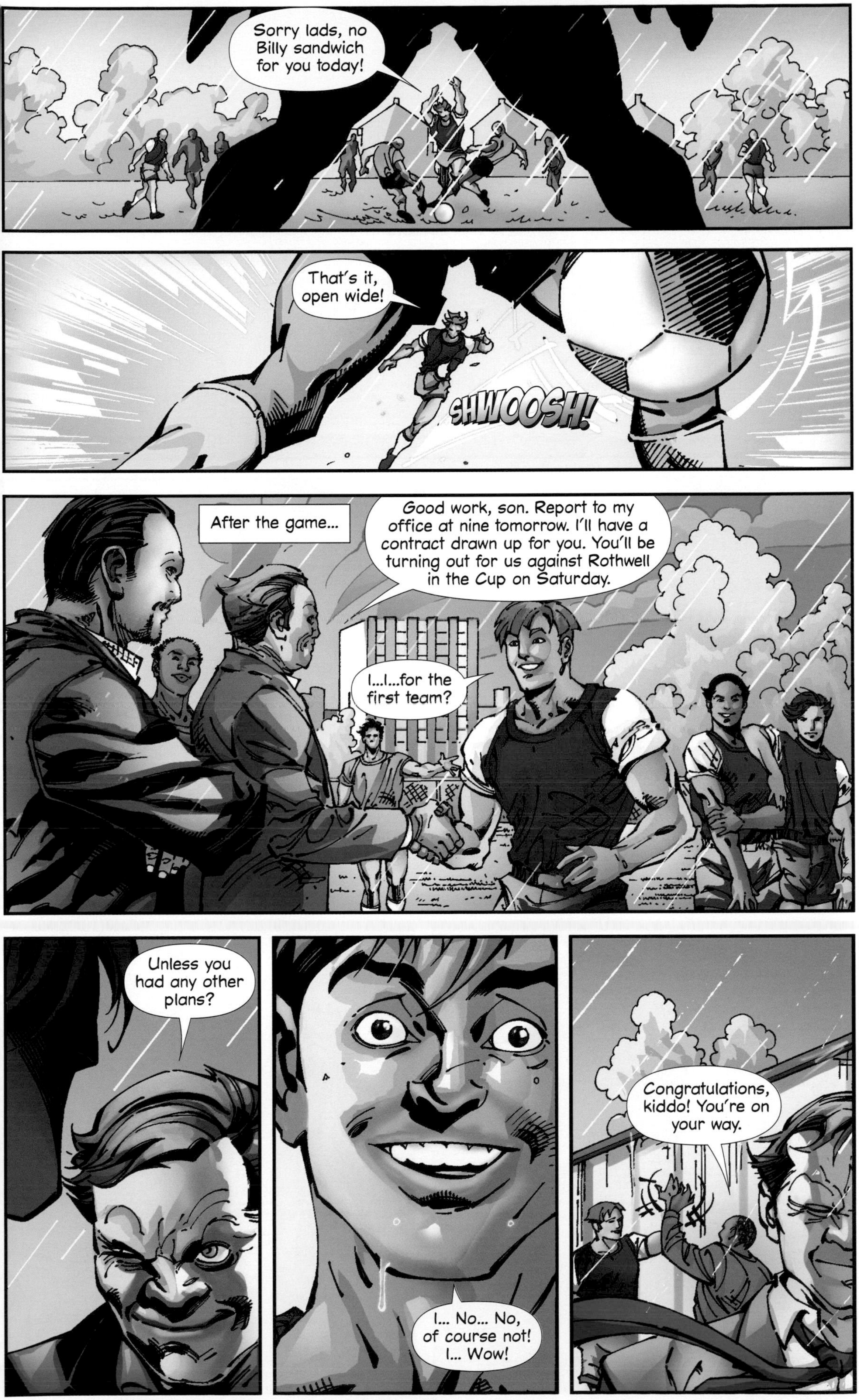
Sorry lads, no Billy sandwich for you today!
That's it, open wide!
SHWOOSH!
After the game...
Good work, son. Report to my office at nine tomorrow. I'll have a contract drawn up for you. You'll be turning out for us against Rothwell in the Cup on Saturday.
I...I...for the first team?
Unless you had any other plans?
I... No... No, of course not! I... Wow!
Congratulations, kiddo! You're on your way.

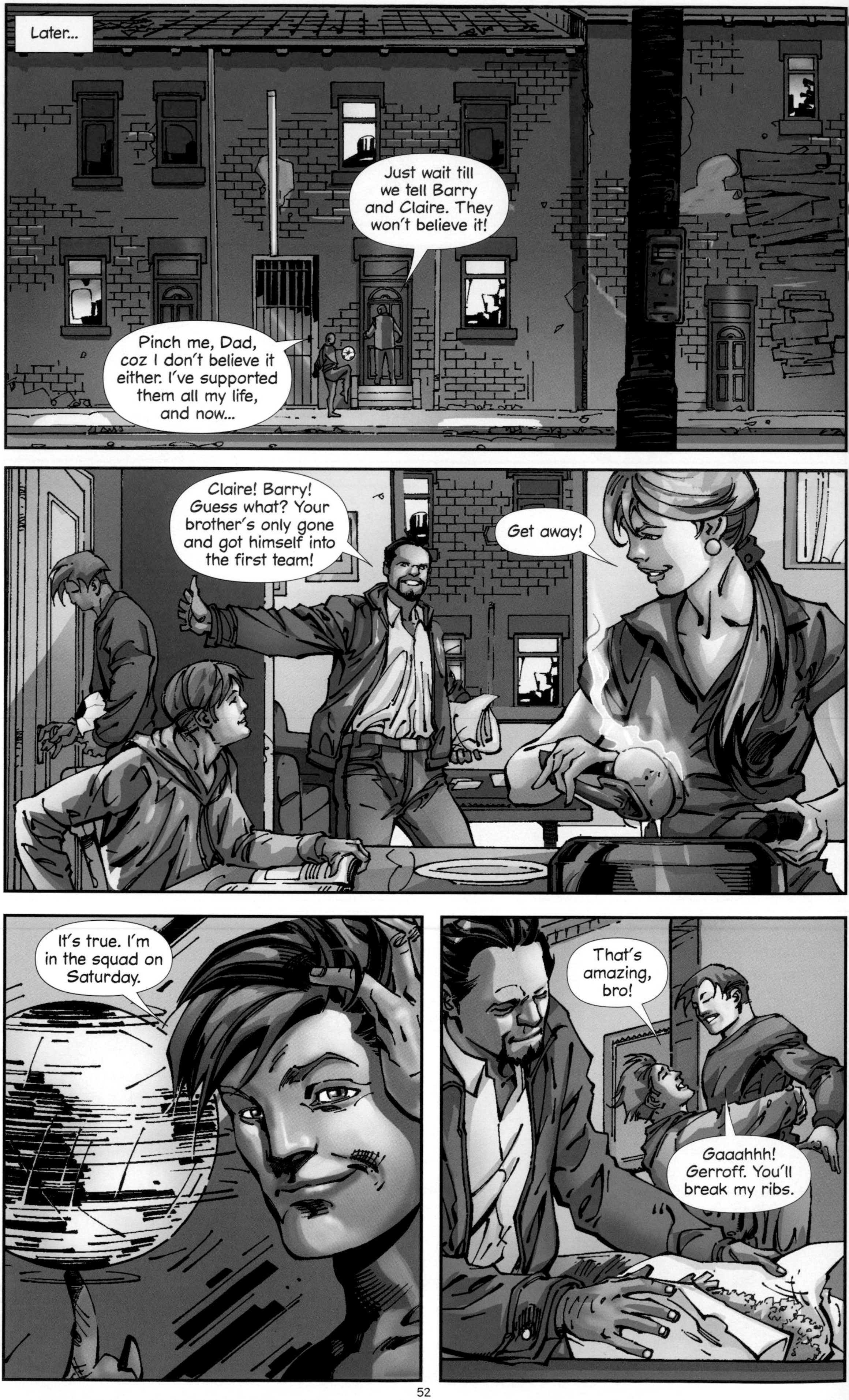
Later...
Just wait till we tell Barry and Claire. They won't believe it!
Pinch me, Dad, coz I don't believe it either. I've supported them all my life, and now...
Claire! Barry! Guess what? Your brother's only gone and got himself into the first team!
Get away!
It's true. I'm in the squad on Saturday.
That's amazing, bro!
Gaaahhh! Gerroff. You'll break my ribs.

This time next year, you'll be playing for England.

Where are you going, Billy? It's dinner time.

Just out for a quick pint to celebrate with the lads.

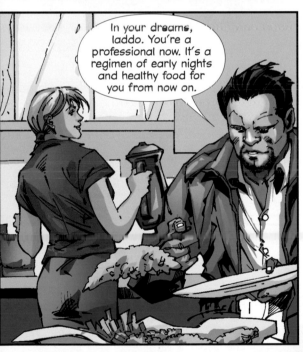

In your dreams, laddo. You're a professional now. It's a regimen of early nights and healthy food for you from now on.

You call fish and chips healthy?

It's fish, ain't it? Brain food. A footballer has to use his brains as well as his body, Claire.

CHOMP!

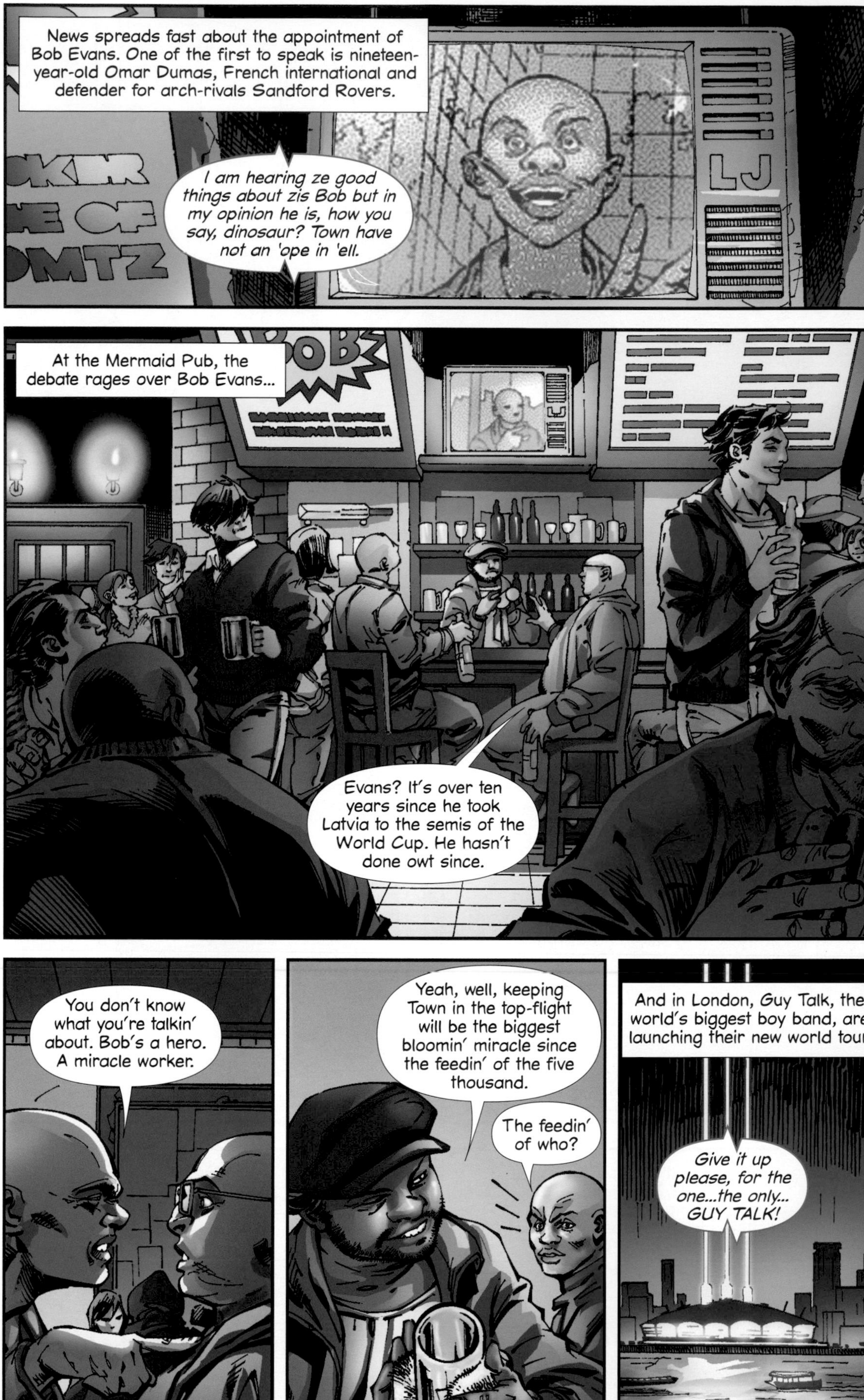
News spreads fast about the appointment of Bob Evans. One of the first to speak is nineteen-year-old Omar Dumas, French international and defender for arch-rivals Sandford Rovers.
I am hearing ze good things about zis Bob but in my opinion he is, how you say, dinosaur? Town have not an 'ope in 'ell.
LJ
At the Mermaid Pub, the debate rages over Bob Evans...
BOB
Evans? It's over ten years since he took Latvia to the semis of the World Cup. He hasn't done owt since.
You don't know what you're talkin' about. Bob's a hero. A miracle worker.
Yeah, well, keeping Town in the top-flight will be the biggest bloomin' miracle since the feedin' of the five thousand.
The feedin' of who?
And in London, Guy Talk, the world's biggest boy band, are launching their new world tour.
Give it up please, for the one...the only... GUY TALK!

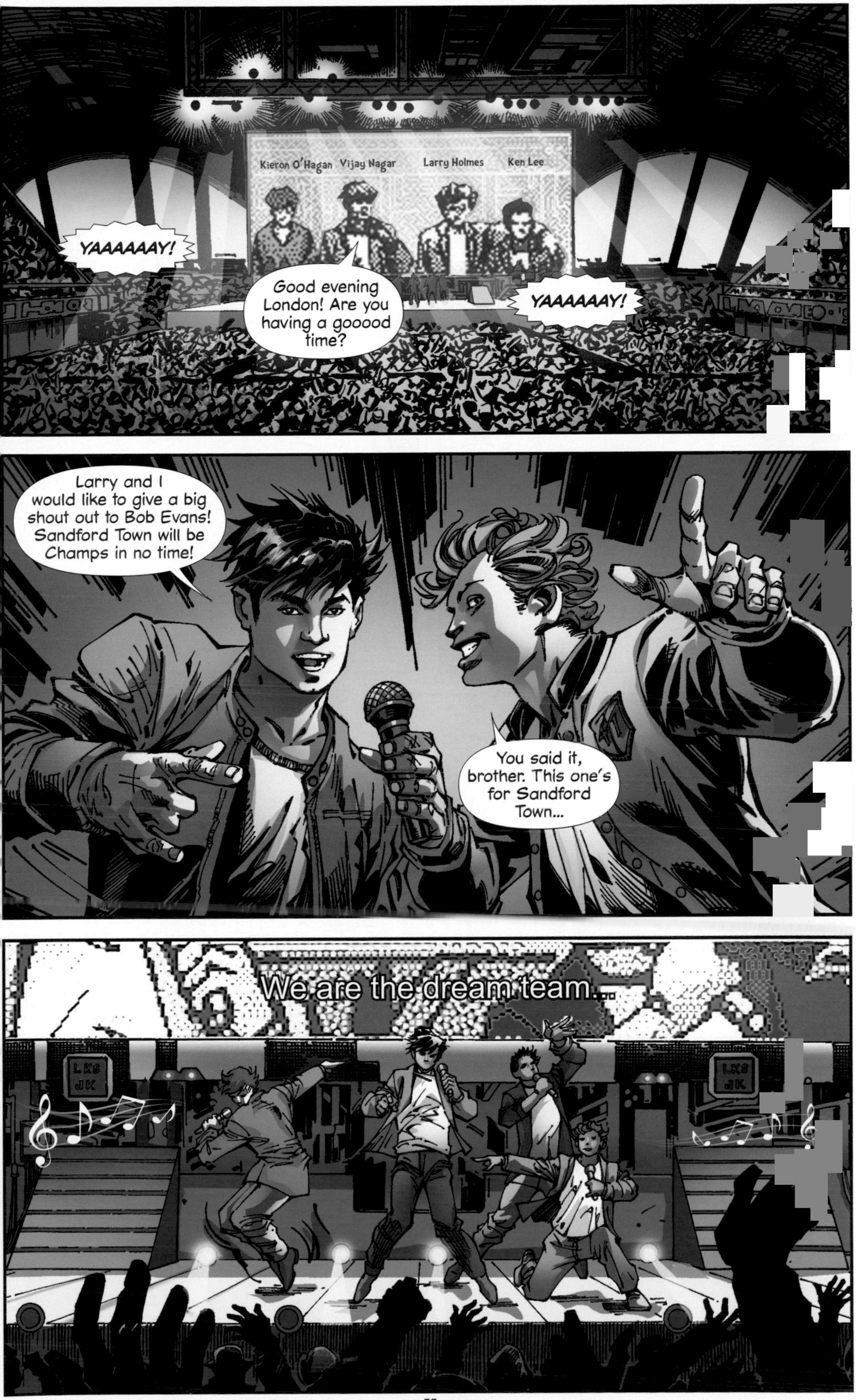
Kieron O'Hagan
Vijay Nagar
Larry Holmes
Ken Lee
YAAAAAAY!
Good evening London! Are you having a gooood time?
YAAAAAAY!
Larry and I would like to give a big shout out to Bob Evans! Sandford Town will be Champs in no time!
You said it, brother. This one's for Sandford Town...
We are the dream team...

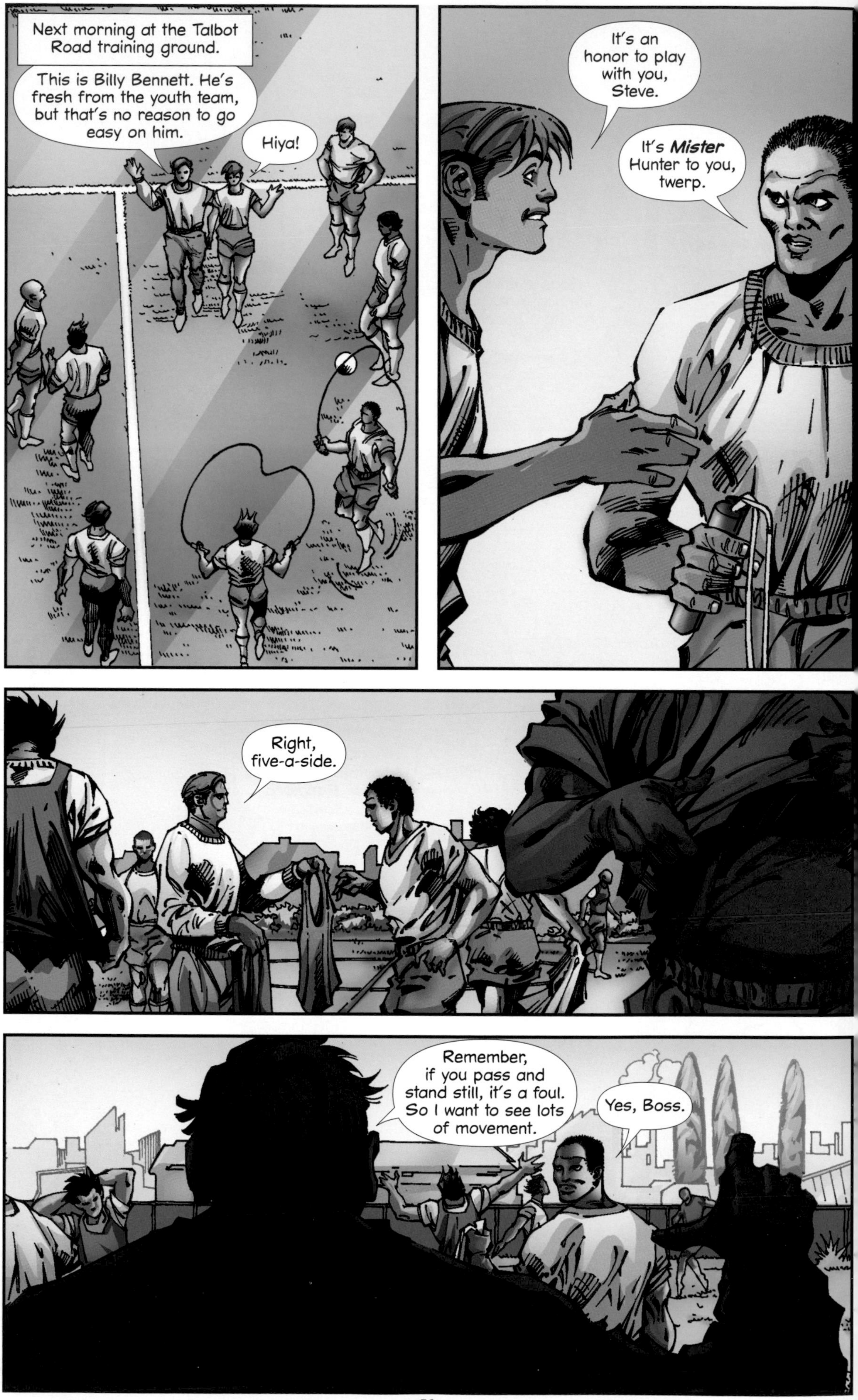
Next morning at the Talbot Road training ground.
This is Billy Bennett. He's fresh from the youth team, but that's no reason to go easy on him.
Hiya!
It's an honor to play with you, Steve.
It's **Mister** Hunter to you, twerp.
Right, five-a-side.
Remember, if you pass and stand still, it's a foul. So I want to see lots of movement.
Yes, Boss.

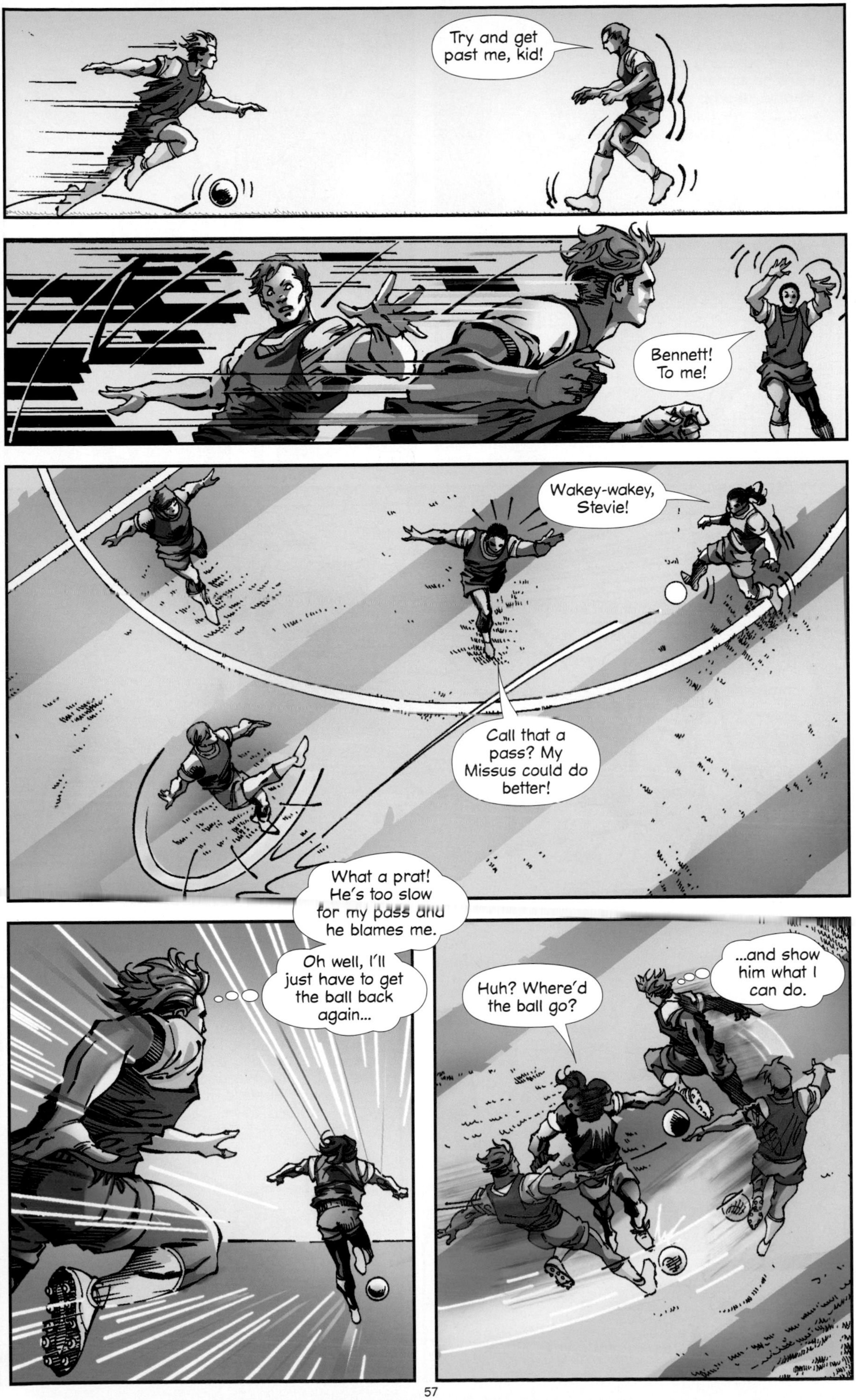
Try and get past me, kid!
Bennett! To me!
Wakey-wakey, Stevie!
Call that a pass? My Missus could do better!
What a prat! He's too slow for my pass and he blames me.
Oh well, I'll just have to get the ball back again...
Huh? Where'd the ball go?
...and show him what I can do.

McNulty always comes out early. Here he comes. Ready...steady...

To me! To me! Are you blind?

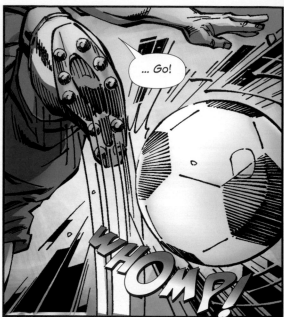

... Go!

WHOMP!

Aww... come on!

Nice work, kid!

Cheers!

By the end of the session, Billy had chalked up three more goals, but not everyone was delighted with the newcomer's performance.

Don't get too big-headed, sonny. Just do as you're told and pass the ball to me. We don't like glory hunters at Sandford Town.

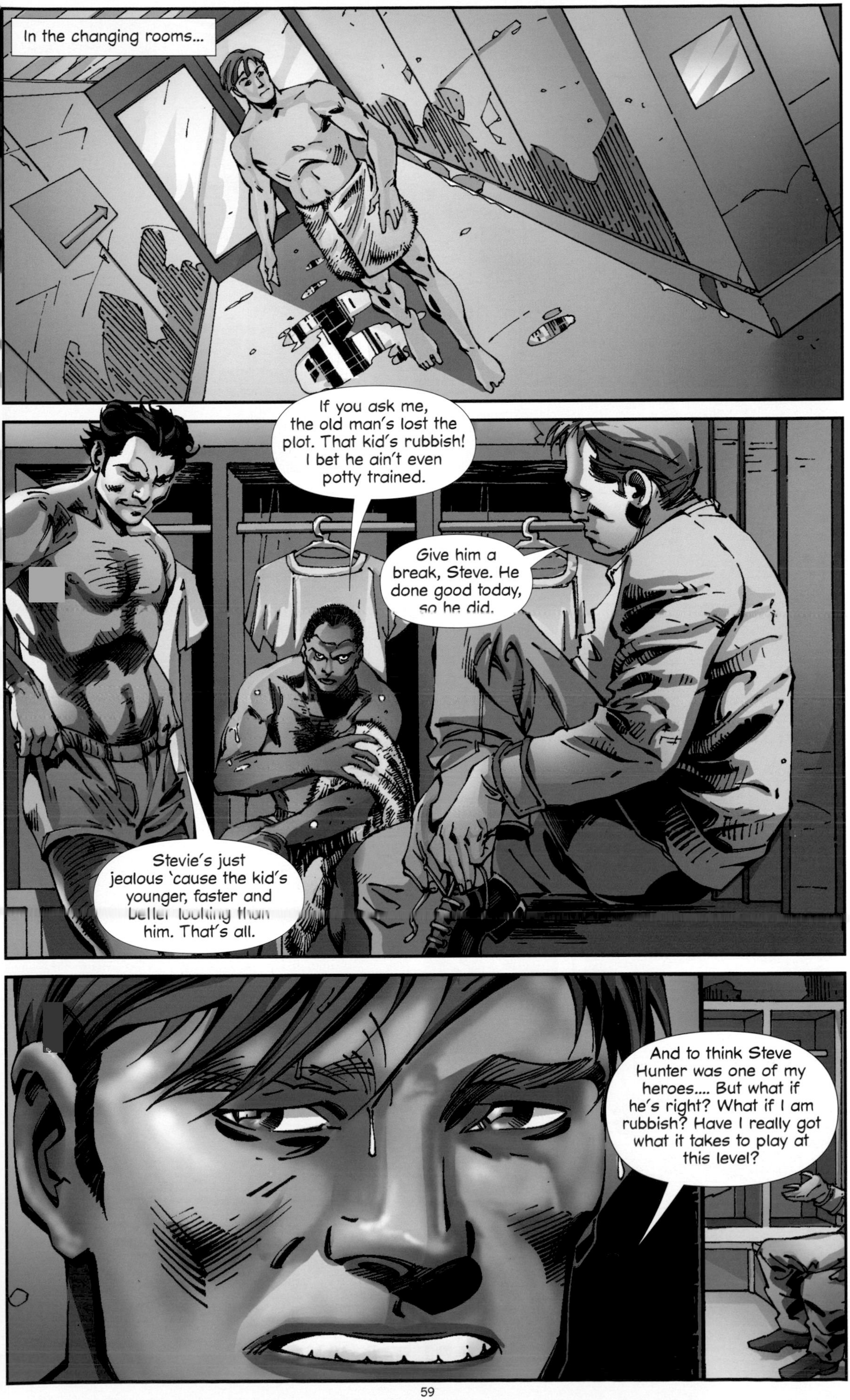
In the changing rooms...
If you ask me, the old man's lost the plot. That kid's rubbish! I bet he ain't even potty trained.
Give him a break, Steve. He done good today, so he did.
Stevie's just jealous 'cause the kid's younger, faster and better looking than him. That's all.
And to think Steve Hunter was one of my heroes.... But what if he's right? What if I am rubbish? Have I really got what it takes to play at this level?

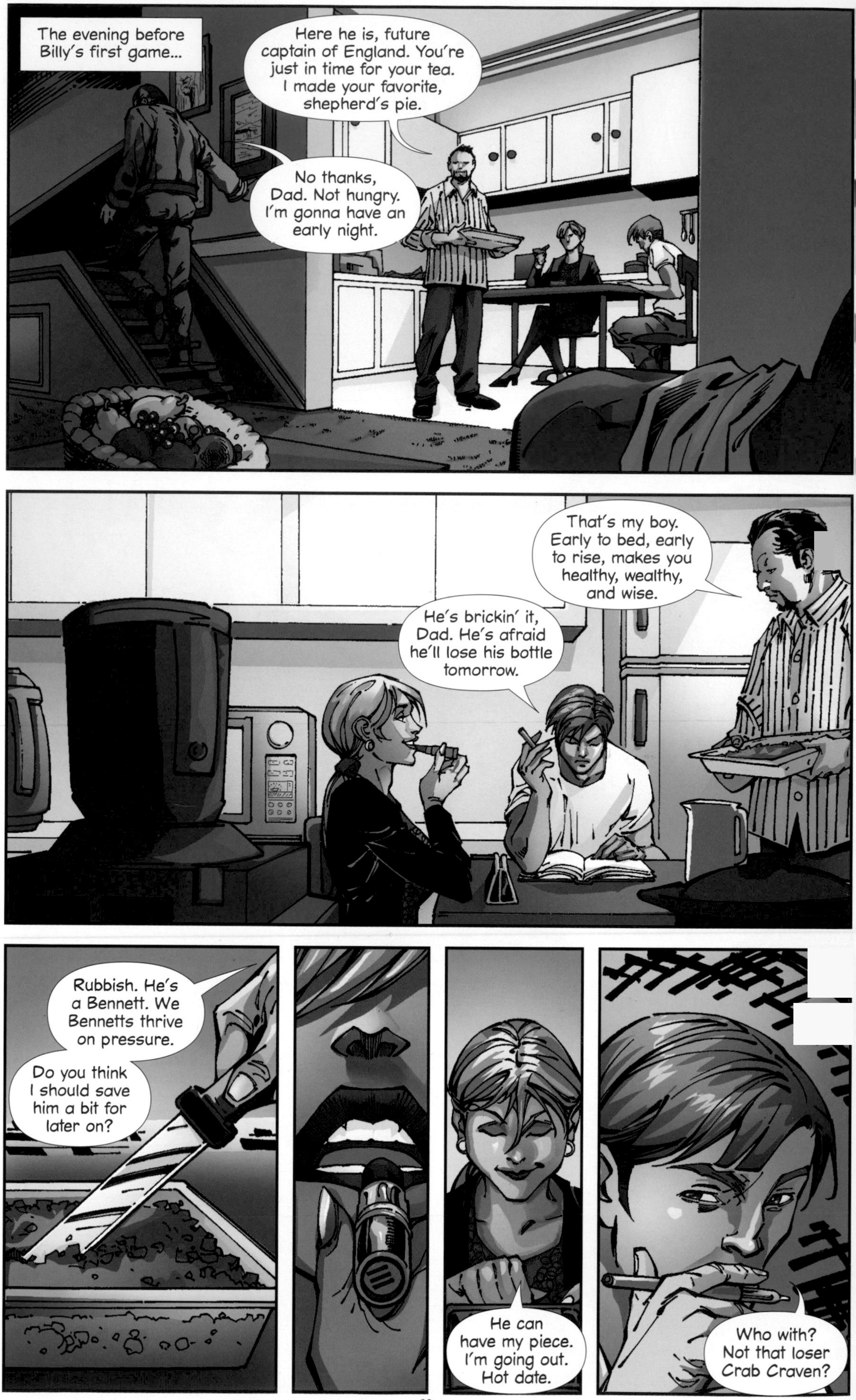
The evening before Billy's first game...
Here he is, future captain of England. You're just in time for your tea. I made your favorite, shepherd's pie.
No thanks, Dad. Not hungry. I'm gonna have an early night.
That's my boy. Early to bed, early to rise, makes you healthy, wealthy, and wise.
He's brickin' it, Dad. He's afraid he'll lose his bottle tomorrow.
Rubbish. He's a Bennett. We Bennetts thrive on pressure.
Do you think I should save him a bit for later on?
He can have my piece. I'm going out. Hot date.
Who with? Not that loser Crab Craven?

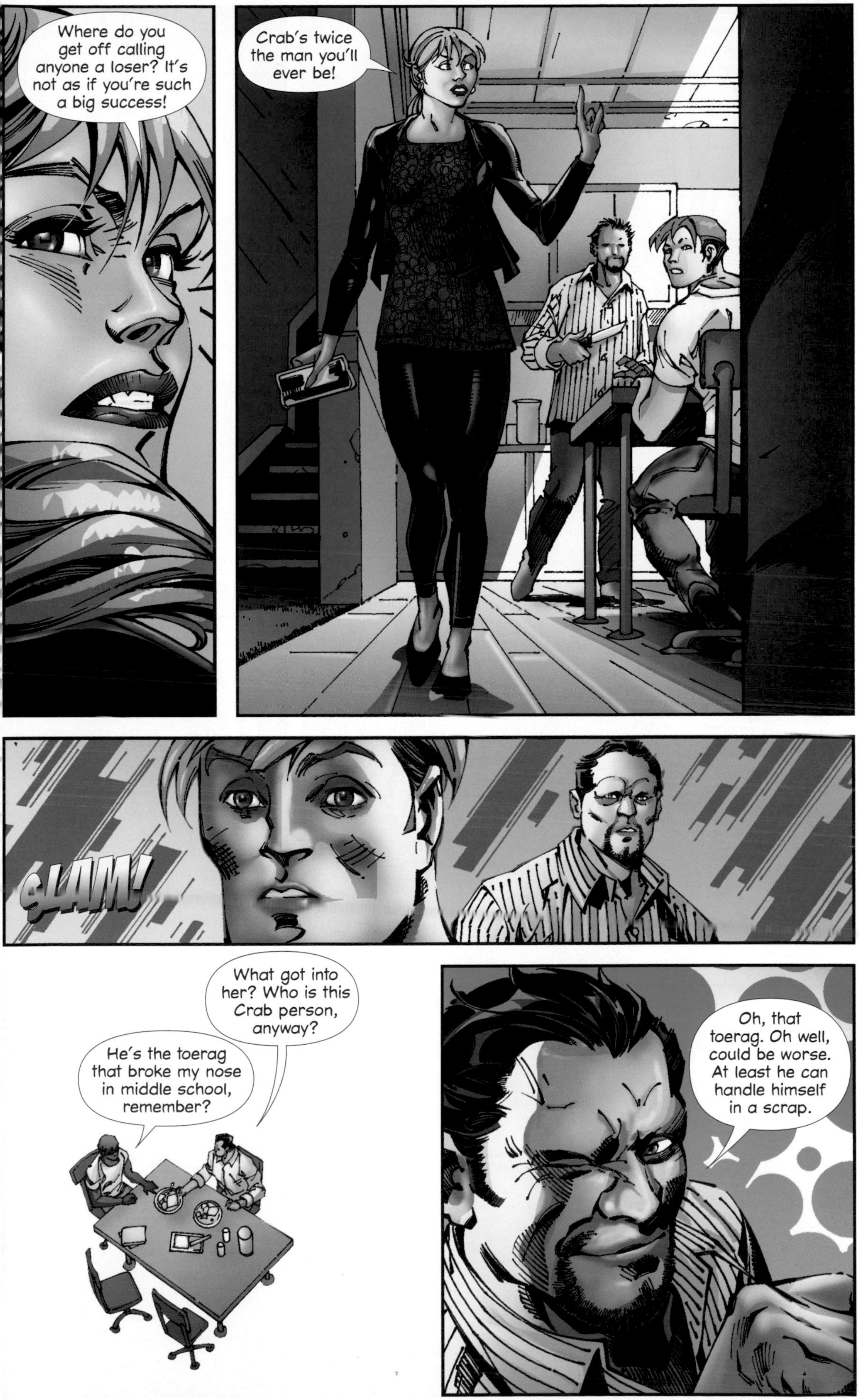
Where do you get off calling anyone a loser? It's not as if you're such a big success!
Crab's twice the man you'll ever be!
SLAM!
What got into her? Who is this Crab person, anyway?
He's the toerag that broke my nose in middle school, remember?
Oh, that toerag. Oh well, could be worse. At least he can handle himself in a scrap.

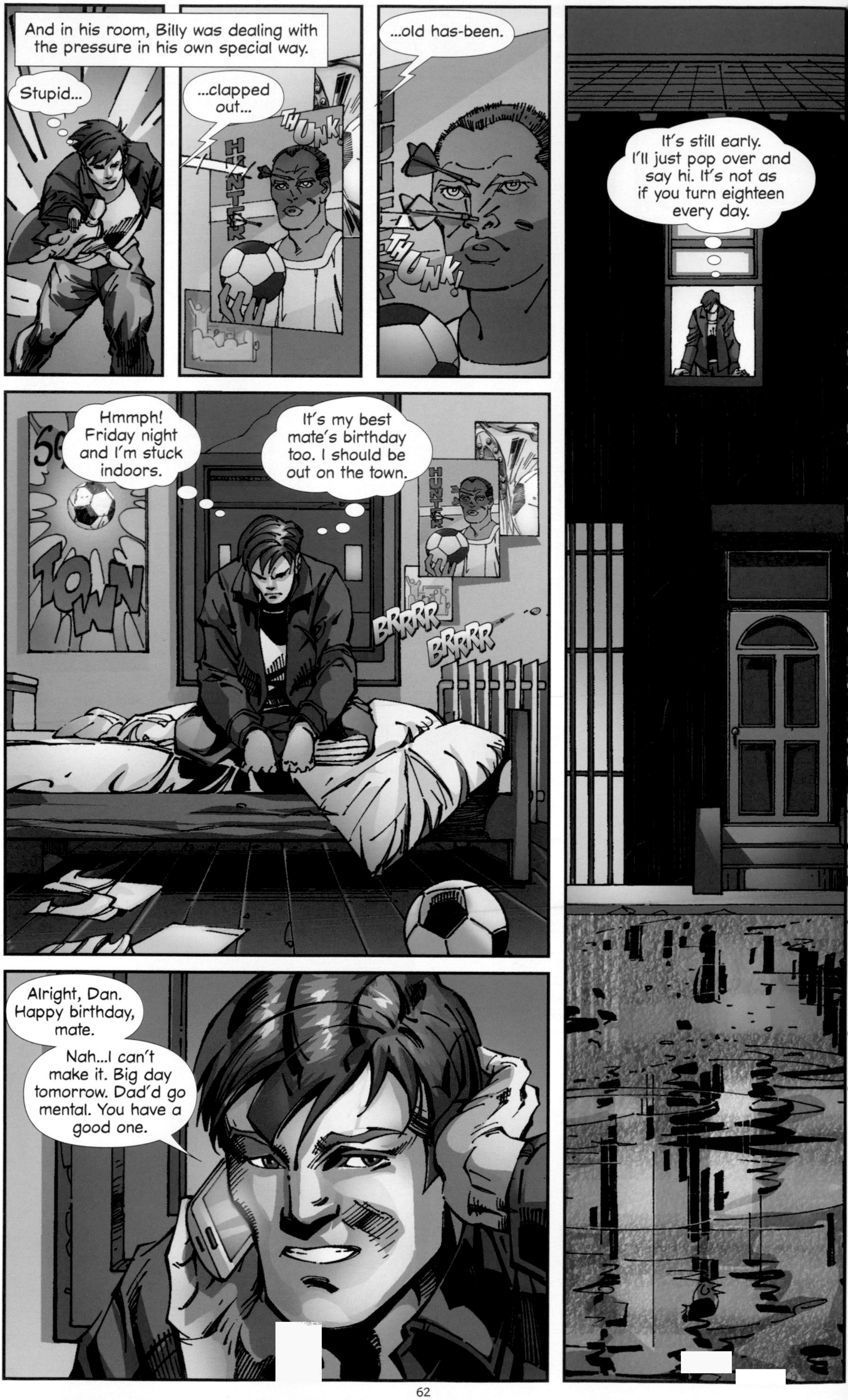
And in his room, Billy was dealing with the pressure in his own special way.
Stupid...
...clapped out...
THUNK!
...old has-been.
THUNK!
Hmmph! Friday night and I'm stuck indoors.
It's my best mate's birthday too. I should be out on the town.
BRRRR
BRRRR
Alright, Dan. Happy birthday, mate.
Nah...I can't make it. Big day tomorrow. Dad'd go mental. You have a good one.
It's still early. I'll just pop over and say hi. It's not as if you turn eighteen every day.

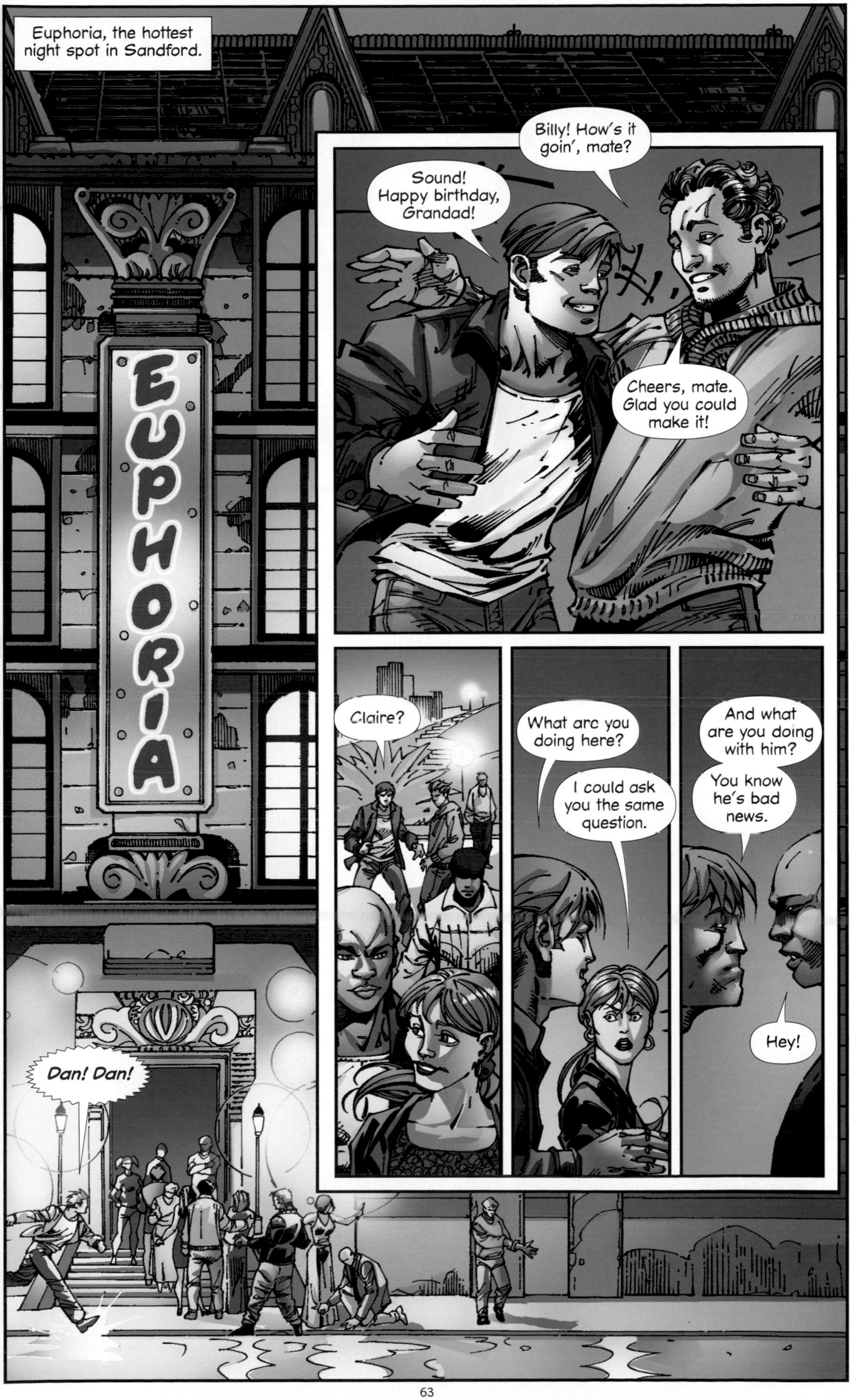
Euphoria, the hottest night spot in Sandford.
EUPHORIA
Billy! How's it goin', mate?
Sound! Happy birthday, Grandad!
Cheers, mate. Glad you could make it!
Dan! Dan!
Claire?
What are you doing here?
I could ask you the same question.
And what are you doing with him?
You know he's bad news.
Hey!

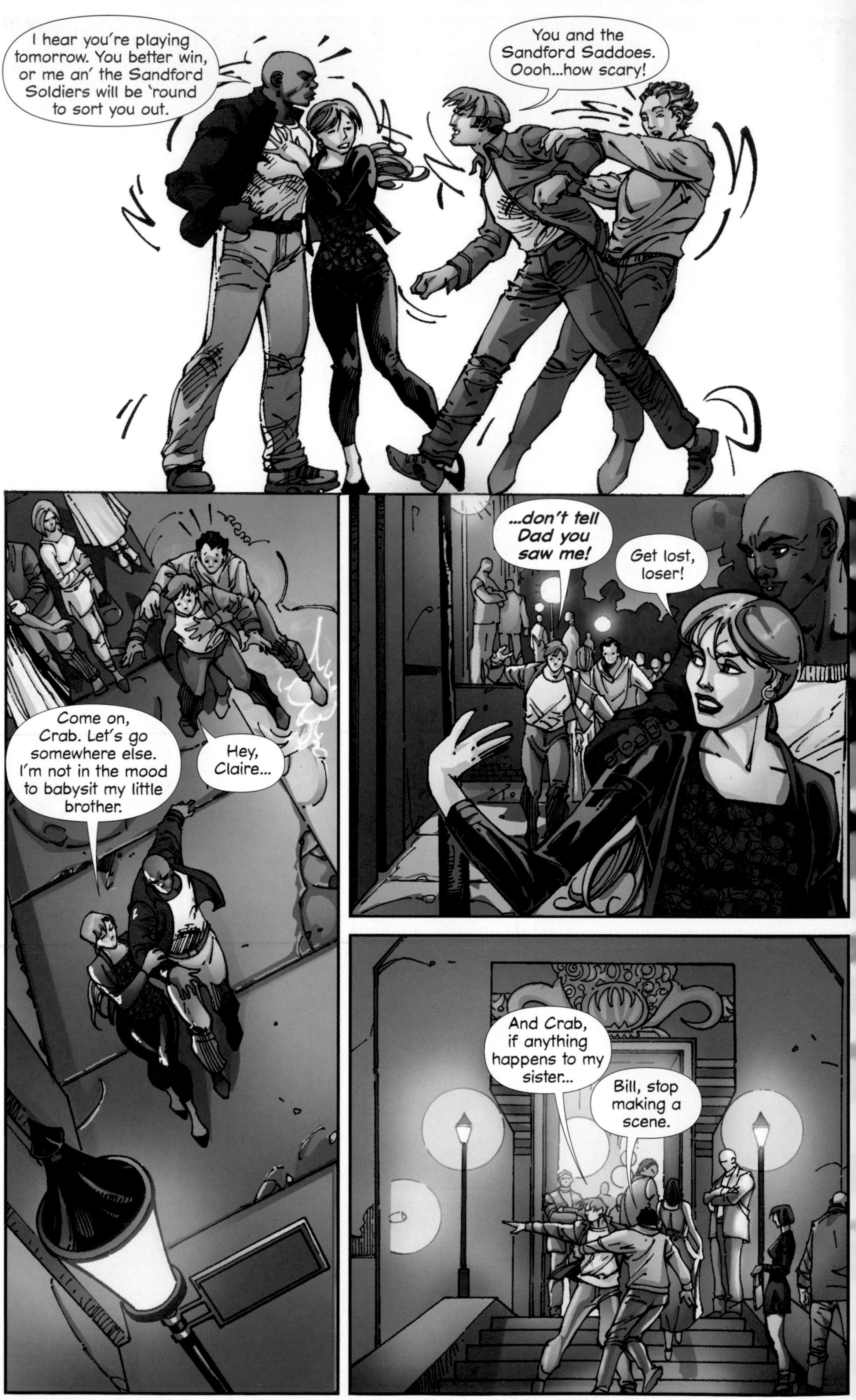

I hear you're playing tomorrow. You better win, or me an' the Sandford Soldiers will be 'round to sort you out.
You and the Sandford Saddoes. Oooh...how scary!
Come on, Crab. Let's go somewhere else. I'm not in the mood to babysit my little brother.
Hey, Claire...
...don't tell Dad you saw me!
Get lost, loser!
And Crab, if anything happens to my sister...
Bill, stop making a scene.

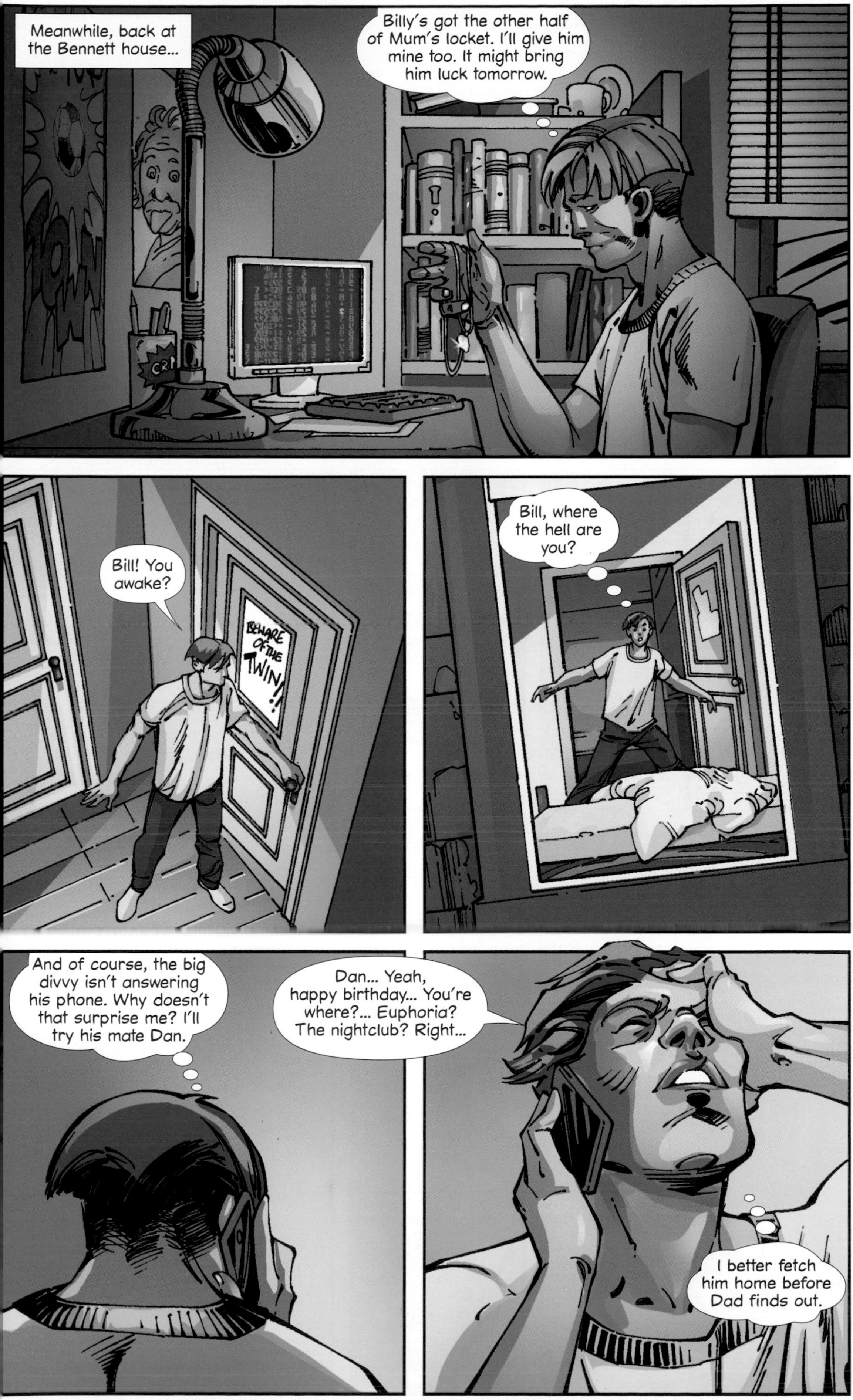
Meanwhile, back at the Bennett house...
Billy's got the other half of Mum's locket. I'll give him mine too. It might bring him luck tomorrow.
BEWARE OF THE TWIN!!
Bill! You awake?
Bill, where the hell are you?
And of course, the big divvy isn't answering his phone. Why doesn't that surprise me? I'll try his mate Dan.
Dan... Yeah, happy birthday... You're where?... Euphoria? The nightclub? Right...
I better fetch him home before Dad finds out.

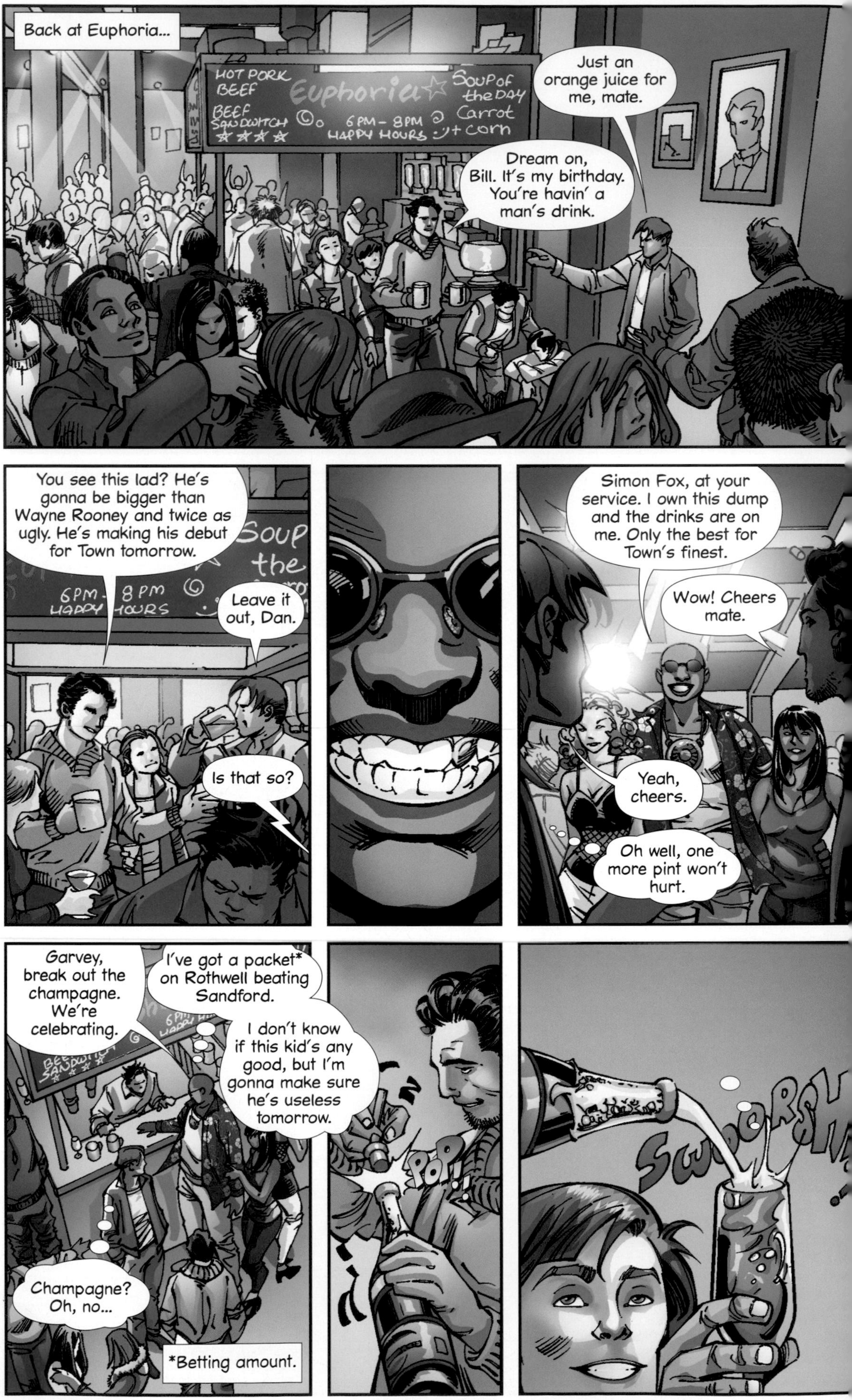

Back at Euphoria...
HOT PORK BEEF
BEEF SANDWITCH
Euphoria
6PM – 8PM HAPPY HOURS
SOUP OF the DAY Carrot + corn
Just an orange juice for me, mate.
Dream on, Bill. It's my birthday. You're havin' a man's drink.
You see this lad? He's gonna be bigger than Wayne Rooney and twice as ugly. He's making his debut for Town tomorrow.
Leave it out, Dan.
Is that so?
Simon Fox, at your service. I own this dump and the drinks are on me. Only the best for Town's finest.
Wow! Cheers mate.
Yeah, cheers.
Oh well, one more pint won't hurt.
Garvey, break out the champagne. We're celebrating.
I've got a packet* on Rothwell beating Sandford.
I don't know if this kid's any good, but I'm gonna make sure he's useless tomorrow.
Champagne? Oh, no...
*Betting amount.
POP!

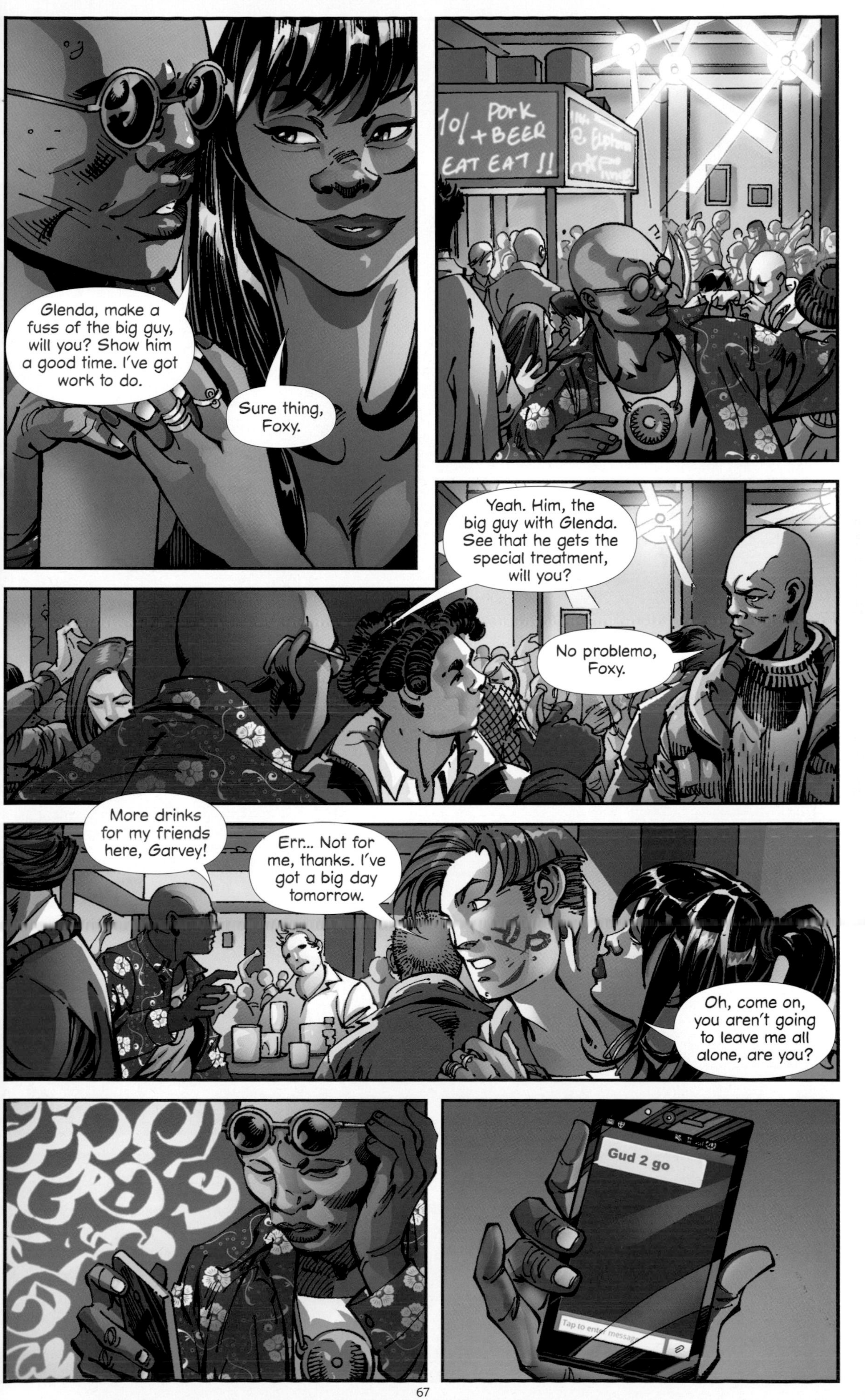
Glenda, make a fuss of the big guy, will you? Show him a good time. I've got work to do.
Sure thing, Foxy.
10/ PORK + BEER EAT EAT !!
Yeah. Him, the big guy with Glenda. See that he gets the special treatment, will you?
No problemo, Foxy.
More drinks for my friends here, Garvey!
Err... Not for me, thanks. I've got a big day tomorrow.
Oh, come on, you aren't going to leave me all alone, are you?
Gud 2 go

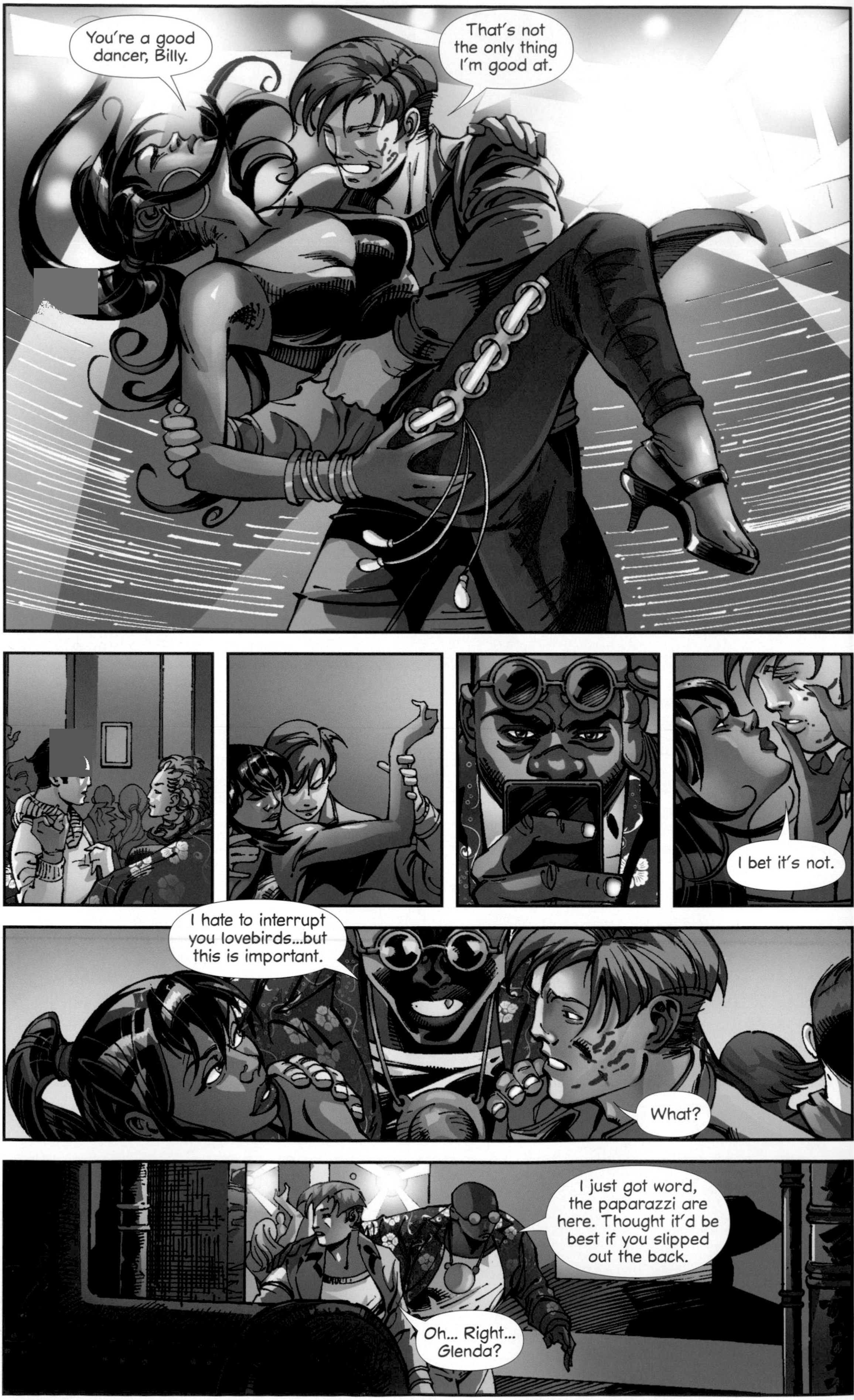

You're a good dancer, Billy.
That's not the only thing I'm good at.
I bet it's not.
I hate to interrupt you lovebirds...but this is important.
What?
I just got word, the paparazzi are here. Thought it'd be best if you slipped out the back.
Oh... Right... Glenda?

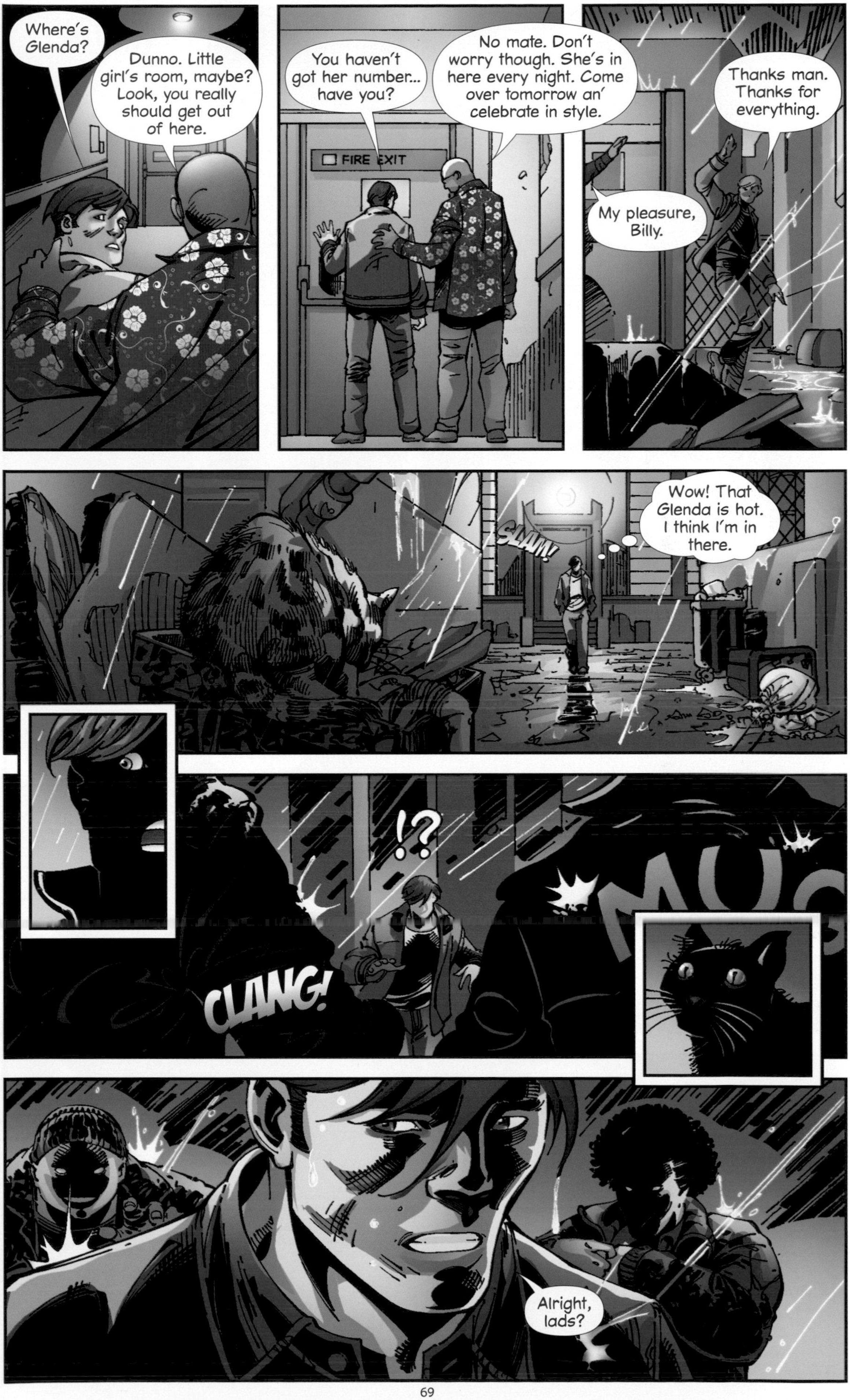
Where's Glenda?
Dunno. Little girl's room, maybe? Look, you really should get out of here.
You haven't got her number... have you?
FIRE EXIT
No mate. Don't worry though. She's in here every night. Come over tomorrow an' celebrate in style.
Thanks man. Thanks for everything.
My pleasure, Billy.
SLAM!
Wow! That Glenda is hot. I think I'm in there.
!?
CLANG!
Alright, lads?

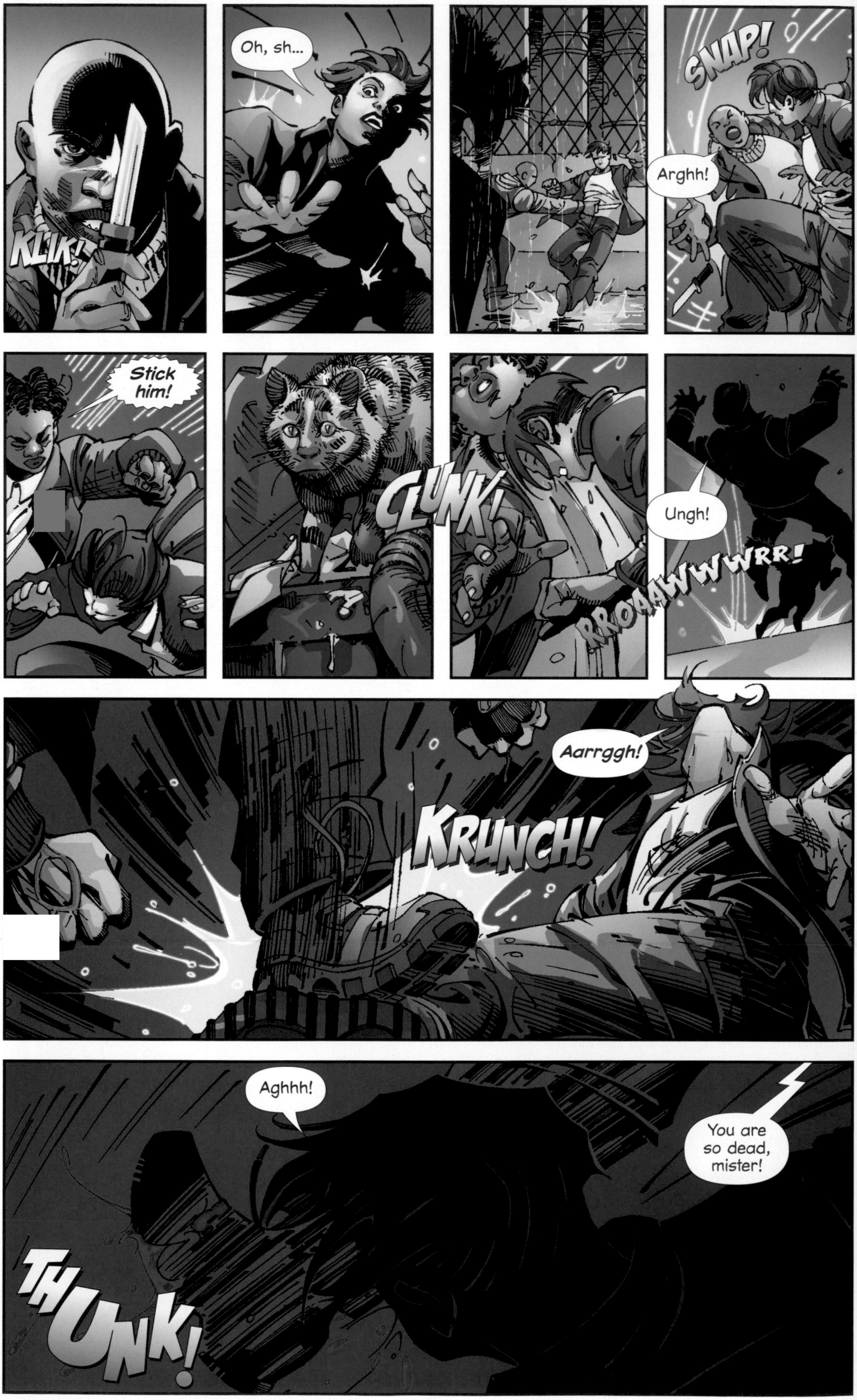
KLIK!
Oh, sh...
SNAP!
Arghh!
Stick him!
CLUNK!
Ungh!
RROAAWWWRR!
Aarrggh!
KRUNCH!
Aghhh!
You are so dead, mister!
THUNK!

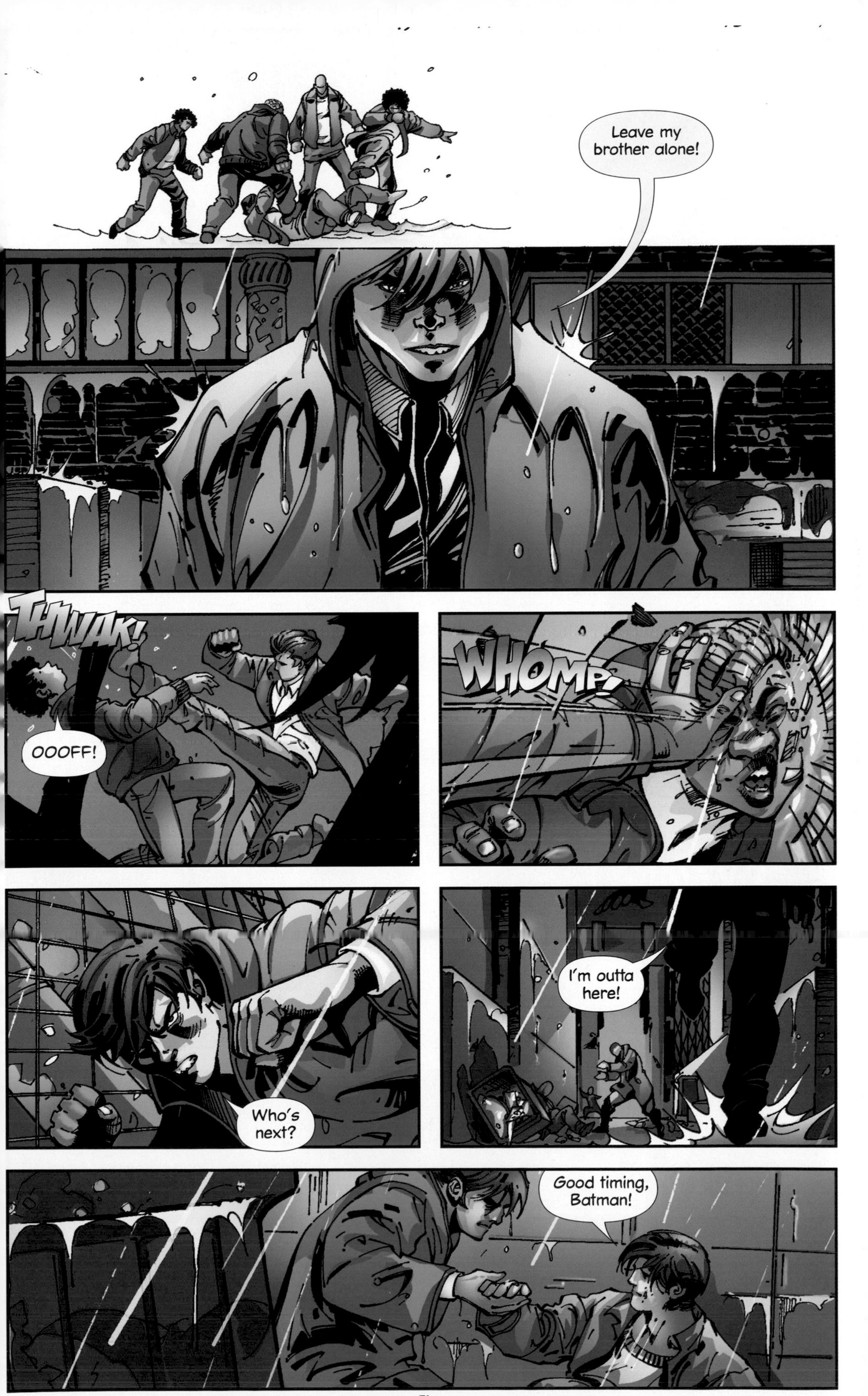
Leave my brother alone!
THWAK!
OOOFF!
WHOMP!
Who's next?
I'm outta here!
Good timing, Batman!

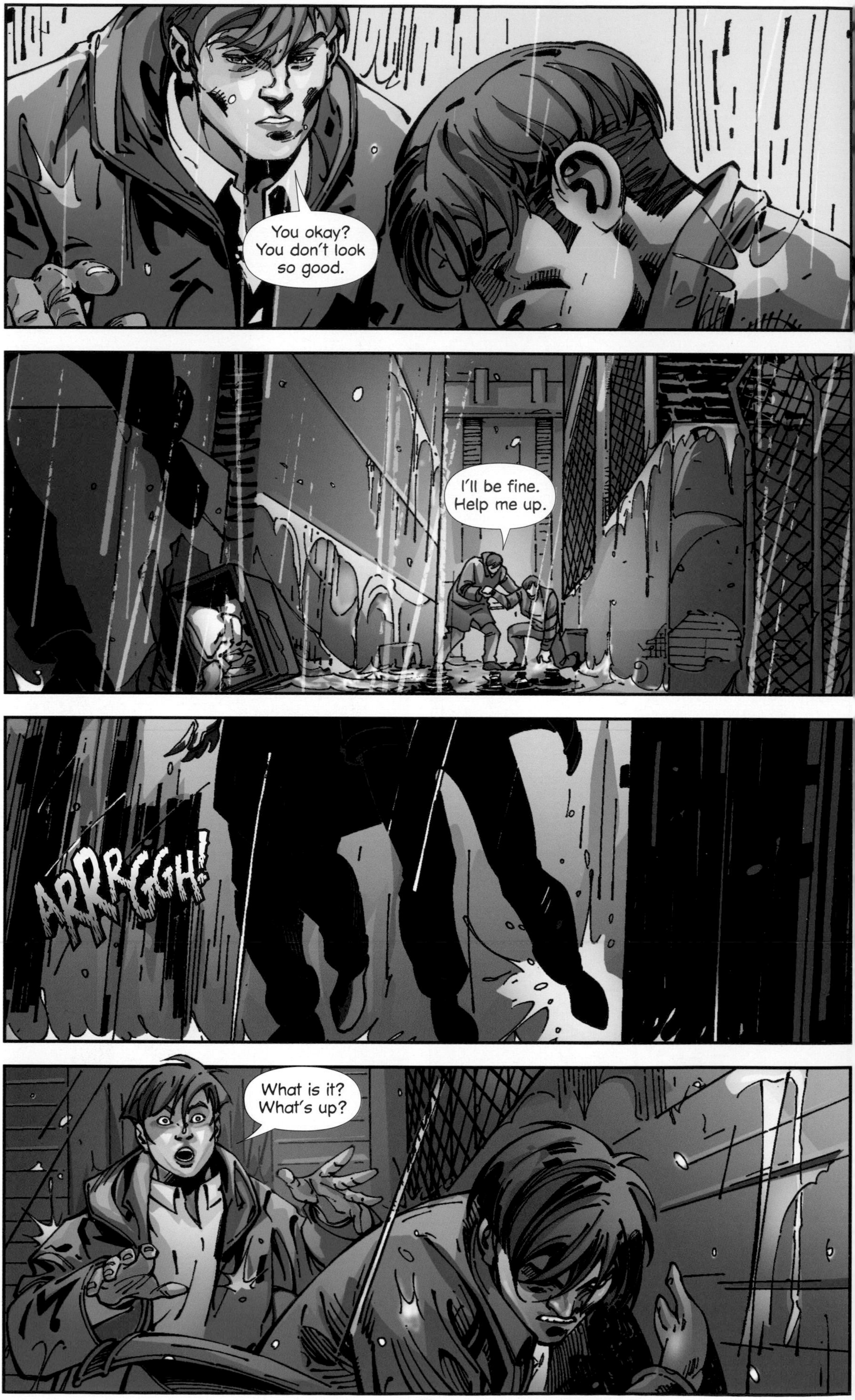
You okay? You don't look so good.
I'll be fine. Help me up.
ARRRGGH!
What is it? What's up?

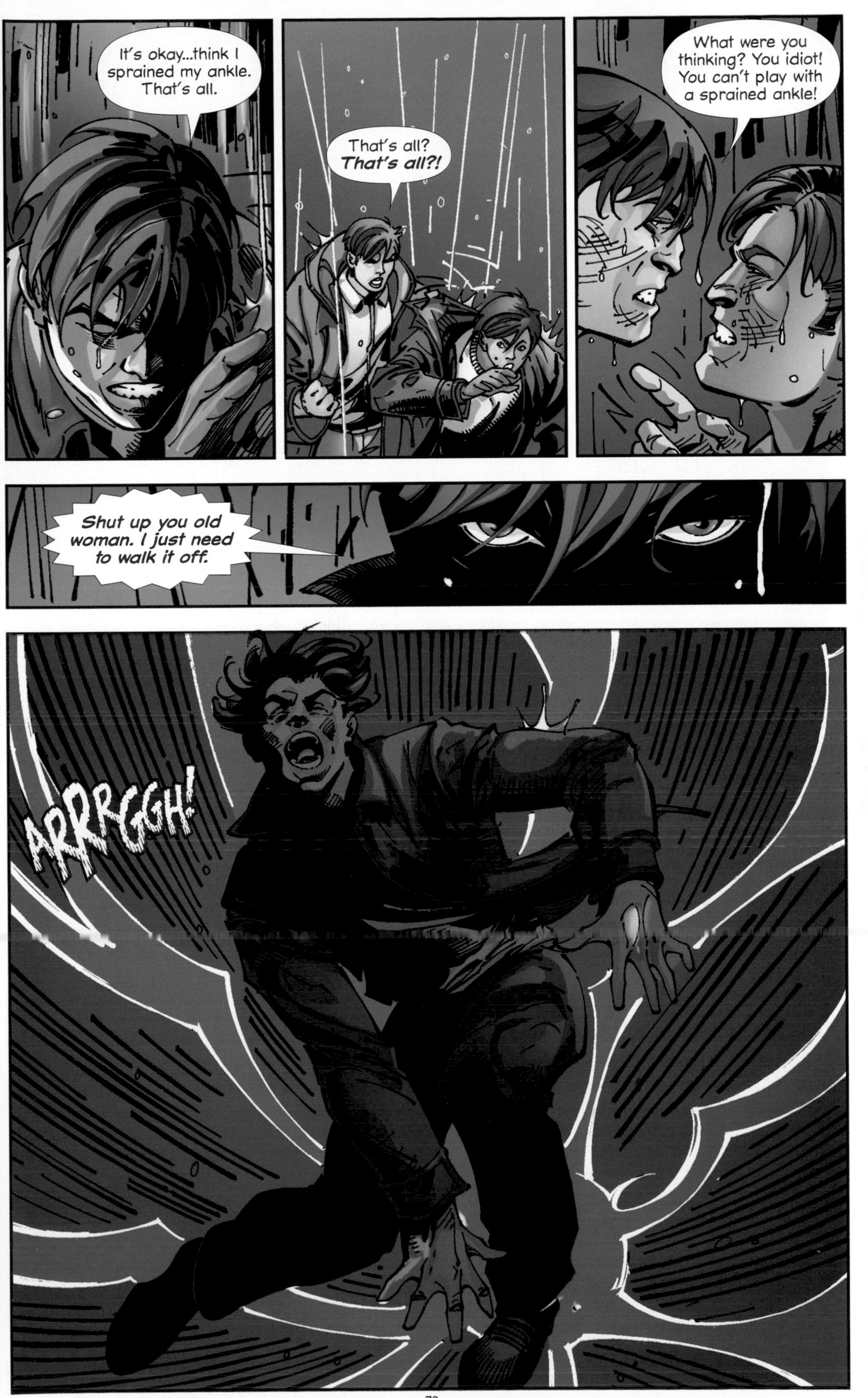

It's okay...think I sprained my ankle. That's all.
That's all? That's all?!
What were you thinking? You idiot! You can't play with a sprained ankle!
Shut up you old woman. I just need to walk it off.
ARRRGGH!

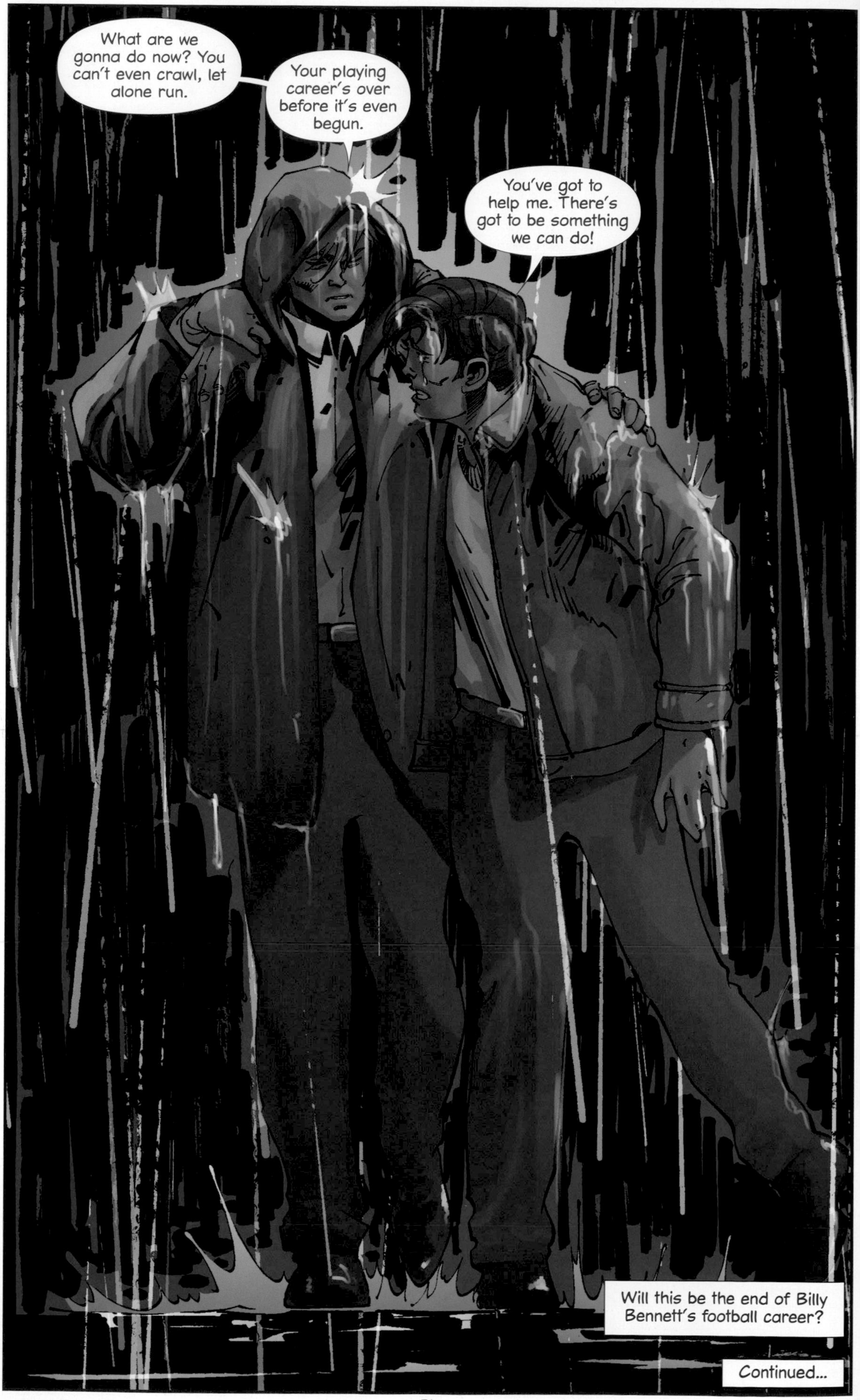
What are we gonna do now? You can't even crawl, let alone run.
Your playing career's over before it's even begun.
You've got to help me. There's got to be something we can do!
Will this be the end of Billy Bennett's football career?
Continued...

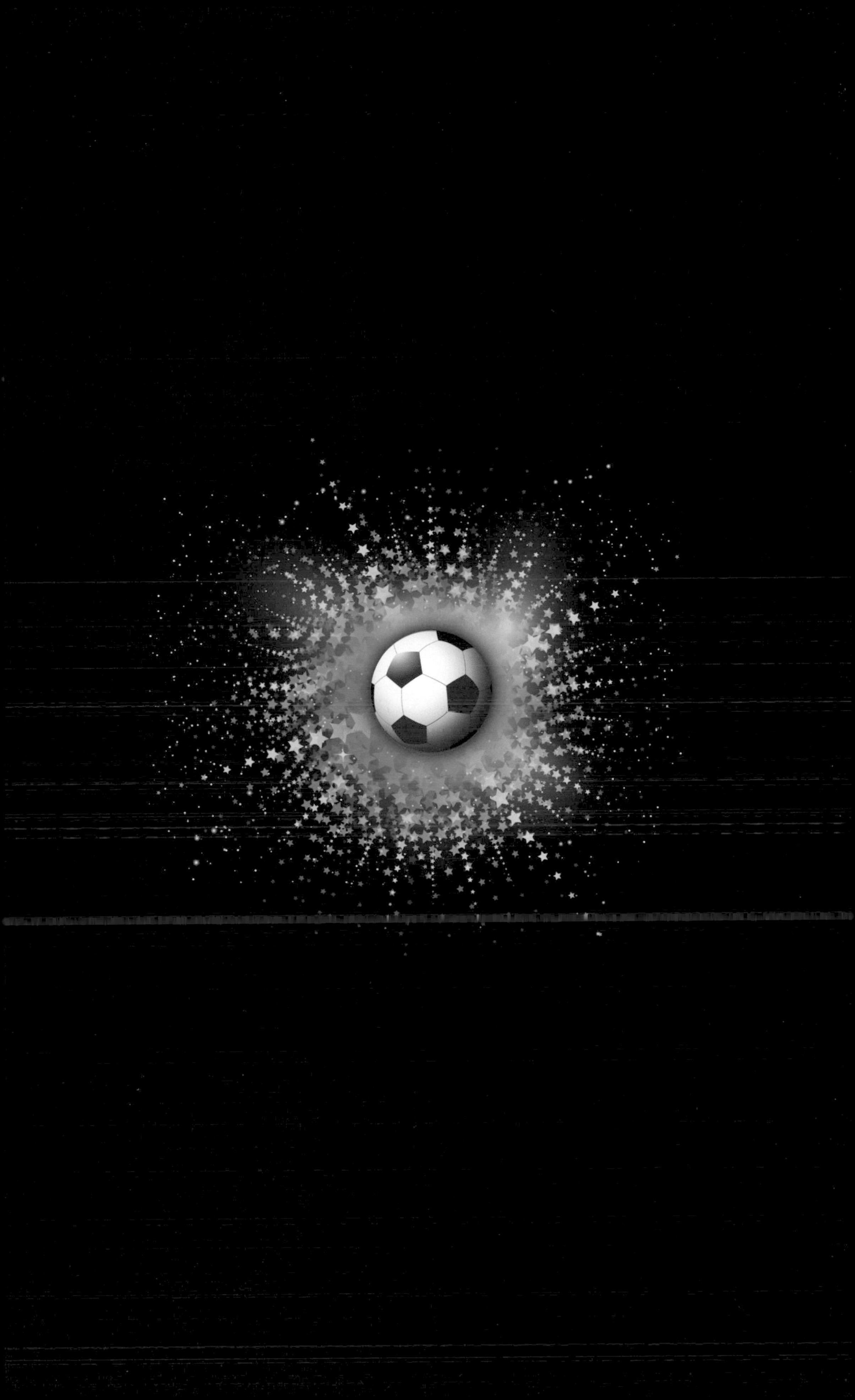

Chapter 3

WHO'S WHO IN THE BEAUTIFUL GAME

SHARON HUNTER

Age: 31
Wife of Steven Hunter

The eldest child of first-generation Jamaican immigrant parents, Sharon has had a tough childhood with the family barely managing to make ends meet. Now, she is practically the first lady of the Sandford Football Wives club, and has developed a taste for the good life.

RAVI KATDARE

Age: 18
Football player

Ravi was born to Indian immigrant parents in England. When Ravi chose football over medicine as his future career, he was labeled as the 'black sheep' of the family. However, the support of his friends—especially Billy and Barry Bennett—and the rest of the team at Sandford Town Youth has made things a bit easier for him.

SANDFORD ROVERS

Football club

Arch-rival of Town, Sandford's second club—Sandford Rovers—was formed in 1892. Sandford Rovers was started by a breakaway group of Town players. Over the last couple years, the Rovers have upped their game considerably, especially ever since their caretaker manager, Jonny Magnanti appointed Garry Bowers as the captain of the team.

Chapter 3 YOUNG BLOOD

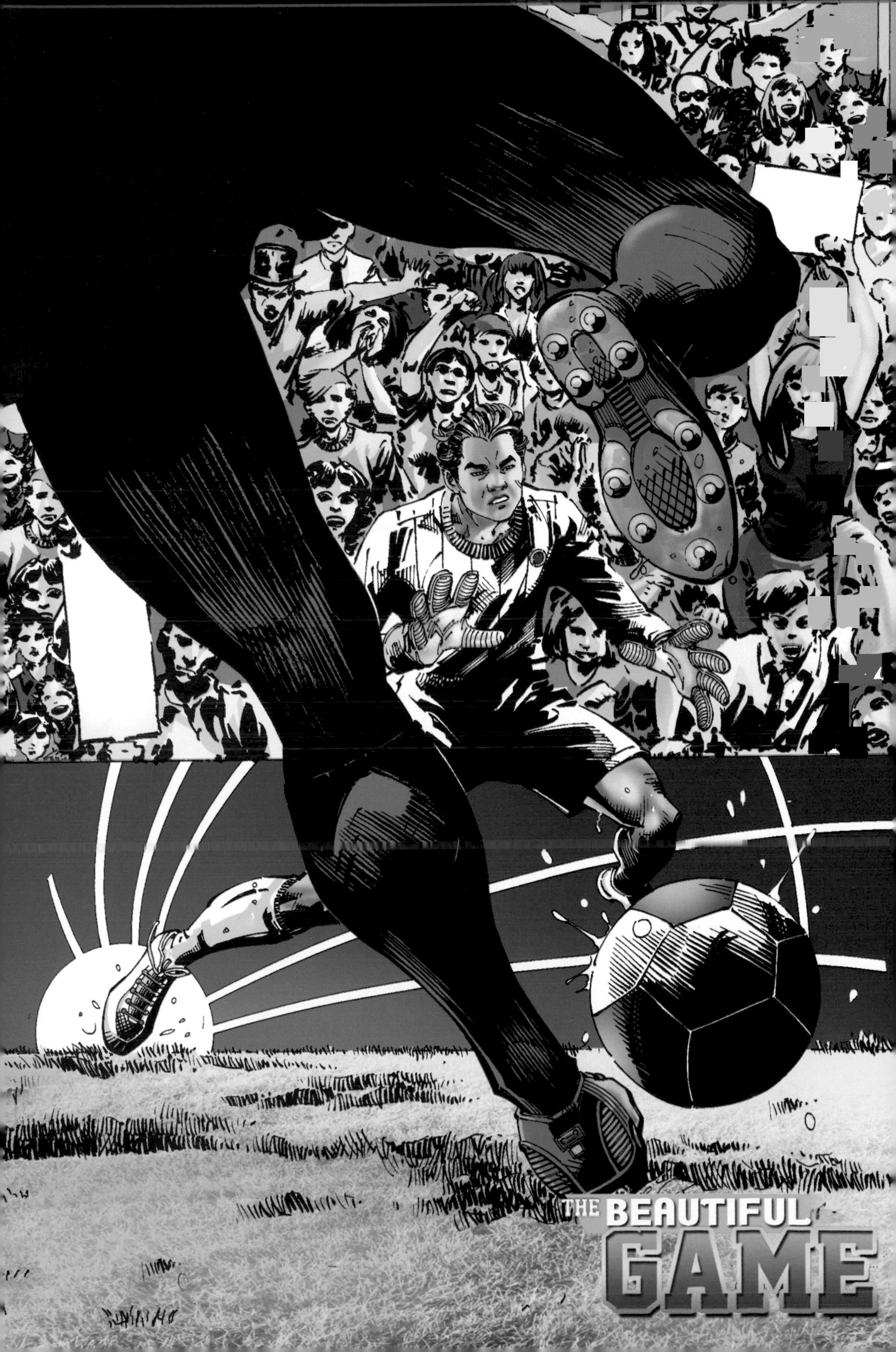
THE BEAUTIFUL GAME

SANDFORD EVENING POST

SANDFORD YOUTH: ANSWER TO A PRAYER?

In an attempt to salvage the team's position and place, Evans has inducted new blood into the squad. Local star, Billy Bennett of the Sandford Town Youth Academy is his first recruit. According to youth team coach Andy Shelldrake, 'Billy Bennett is the Bob Evans of today. Watch out for him'.

Evans, a firm believer of change, is wasting no time in putting the young lad to the test. Bennett will be debuting in the upcoming match between Sandford Town and Rothwell FC in the third round of the FA Cup. Sounds like a trial by fire, but if Shelldrake is right about Billy's talent then he might just be the miracle that Sandford Town have been praying for.

Can Bob Evans turn his club's fortunes around?

LOCAL YOUTH JOINS THE BIG LEAGUE

Star player of the local football youth team, Billy Bennett, has joined Sandford Town FC. A local lad, Billy caught Evans's eye during a practice match and was immediately offered a chance to join the team.

With the team's future and Evans's expectations resting on his shoulders, there is a lot of pressure on young Billy.

The weekend match will decide whether or not Evans's decision was a prudent one. But one thing is for sure, Billy Bennett will have to bring his 'A' game to ensure a spot in the team.

Billy Bennett, *the new kid on the block.*

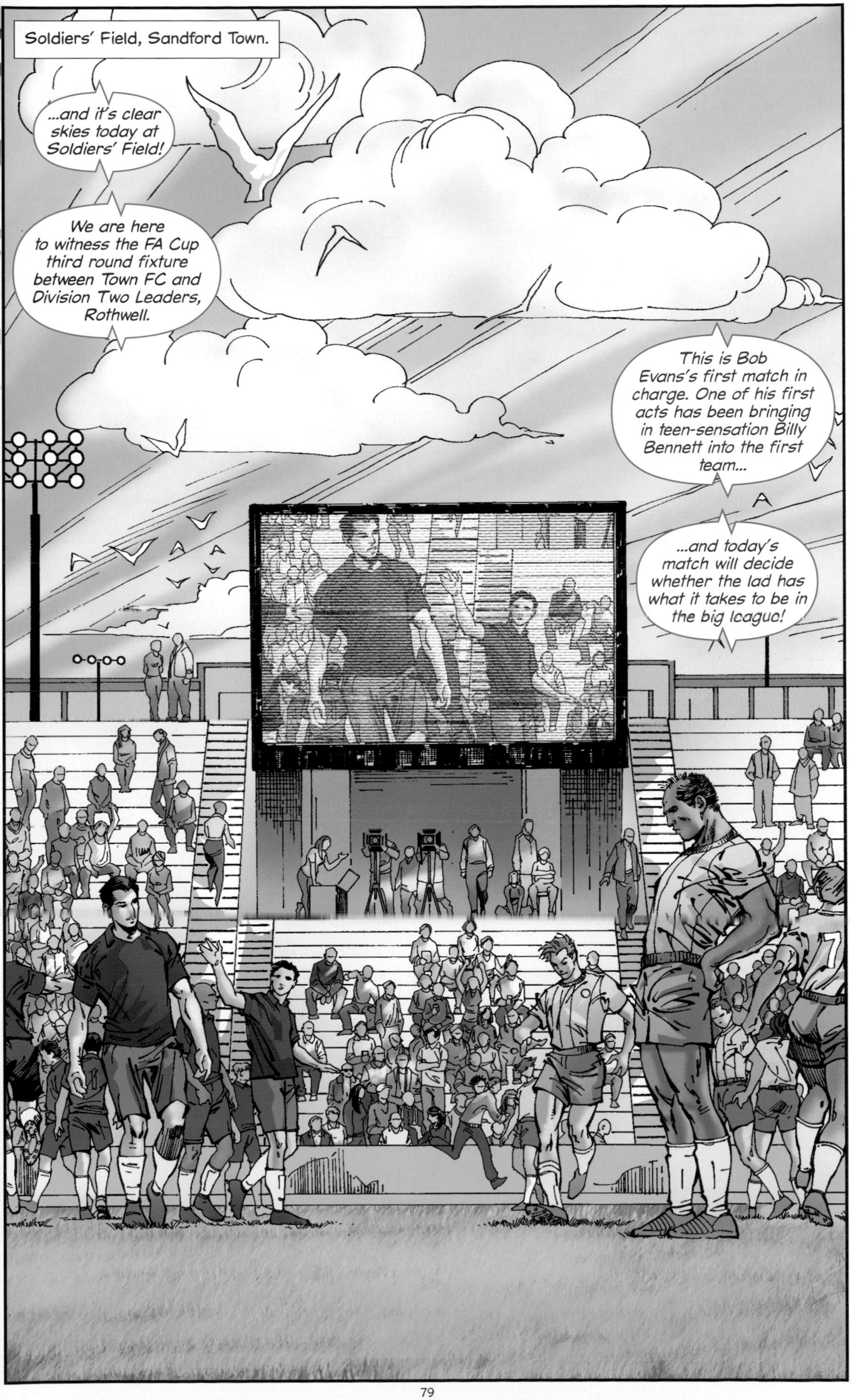
Soldiers' Field, Sandford Town.
...and it's clear skies today at Soldiers' Field!
We are here to witness the FA Cup third round fixture between Town FC and Division Two Leaders, Rothwell.
This is Bob Evans's first match in charge. One of his first acts has been bringing in teen-sensation Billy Bennett into the first team...
...and today's match will decide whether the lad has what it takes to be in the big league!

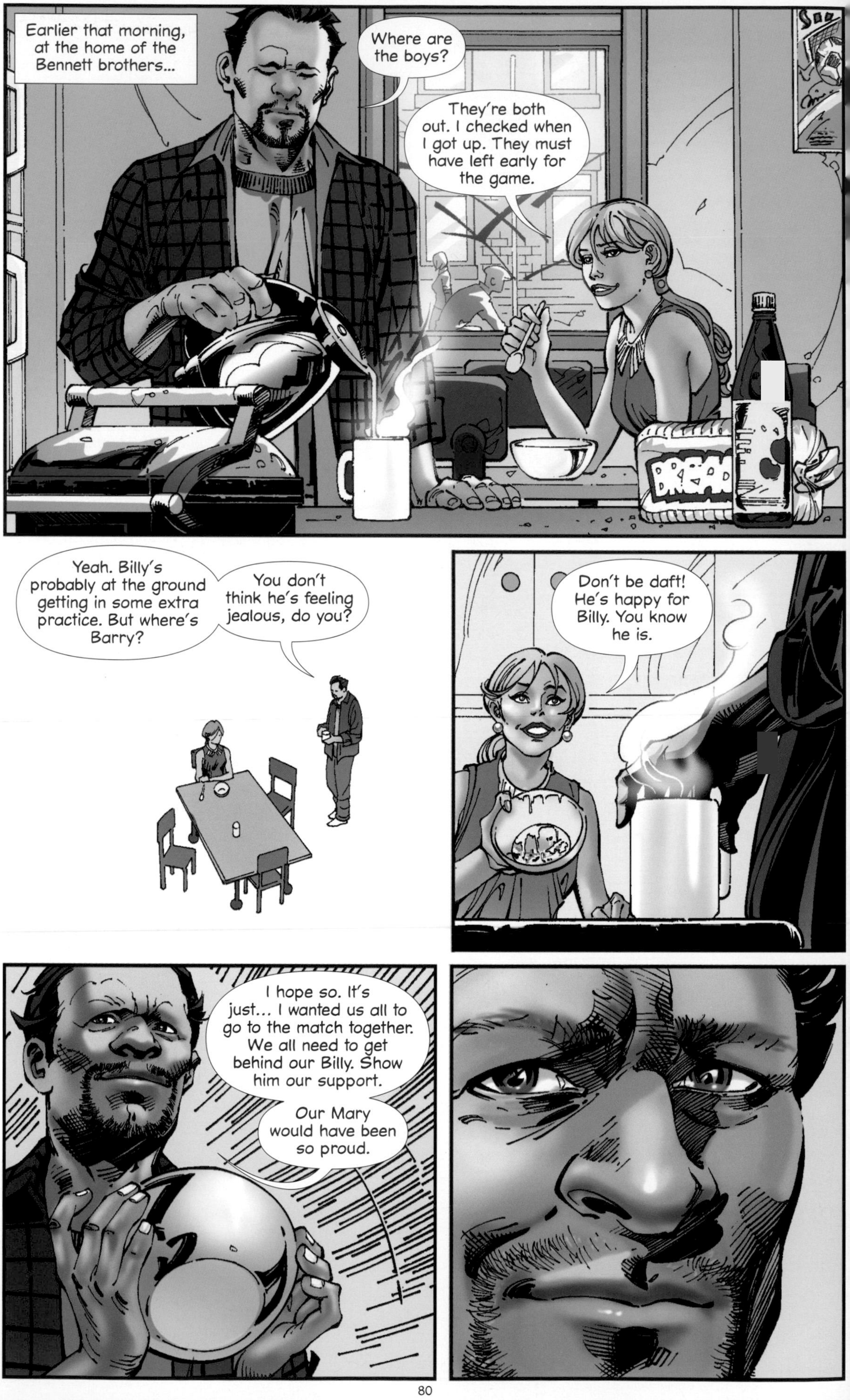
Earlier that morning, at the home of the Bennett brothers...
Where are the boys?
They're both out. I checked when I got up. They must have left early for the game.
Yeah. Billy's probably at the ground getting in some extra practice. But where's Barry?
You don't think he's feeling jealous, do you?
Don't be daft! He's happy for Billy. You know he is.
I hope so. It's just... I wanted us all to go to the match together. We all need to get behind our Billy. Show him our support.
Our Mary would have been so proud.

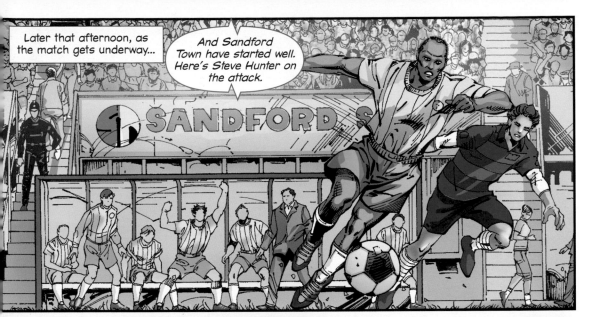

Later that afternoon, as the match gets underway...

And Sandford Town have started well. Here's Steve Hunter on the attack.

And Hunter nearly made the Rothwell defense pay for that lapse of judgment!

Blast!

THUD!

But Rothwell are quick to counter attack.

It's little Pablo Tortazo, he's...

Goooaaal!

And we have a couple of celebrity Sandford fans in the stadium. Larry Holmes and Vijay Nagar from Guy Talk don't look too happy with their team's performance...

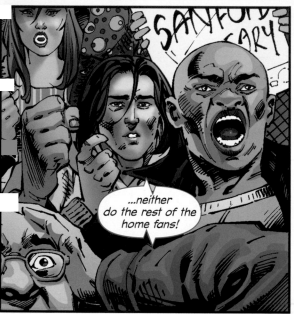

...neither do the rest of the home fans!

And Bob Evans looks furious. Rothwell may well be in a lower league, but they're outplaying Sandford today.

Get warmed up, son. I'm putting you on straight after the break.

Yes, Boss.

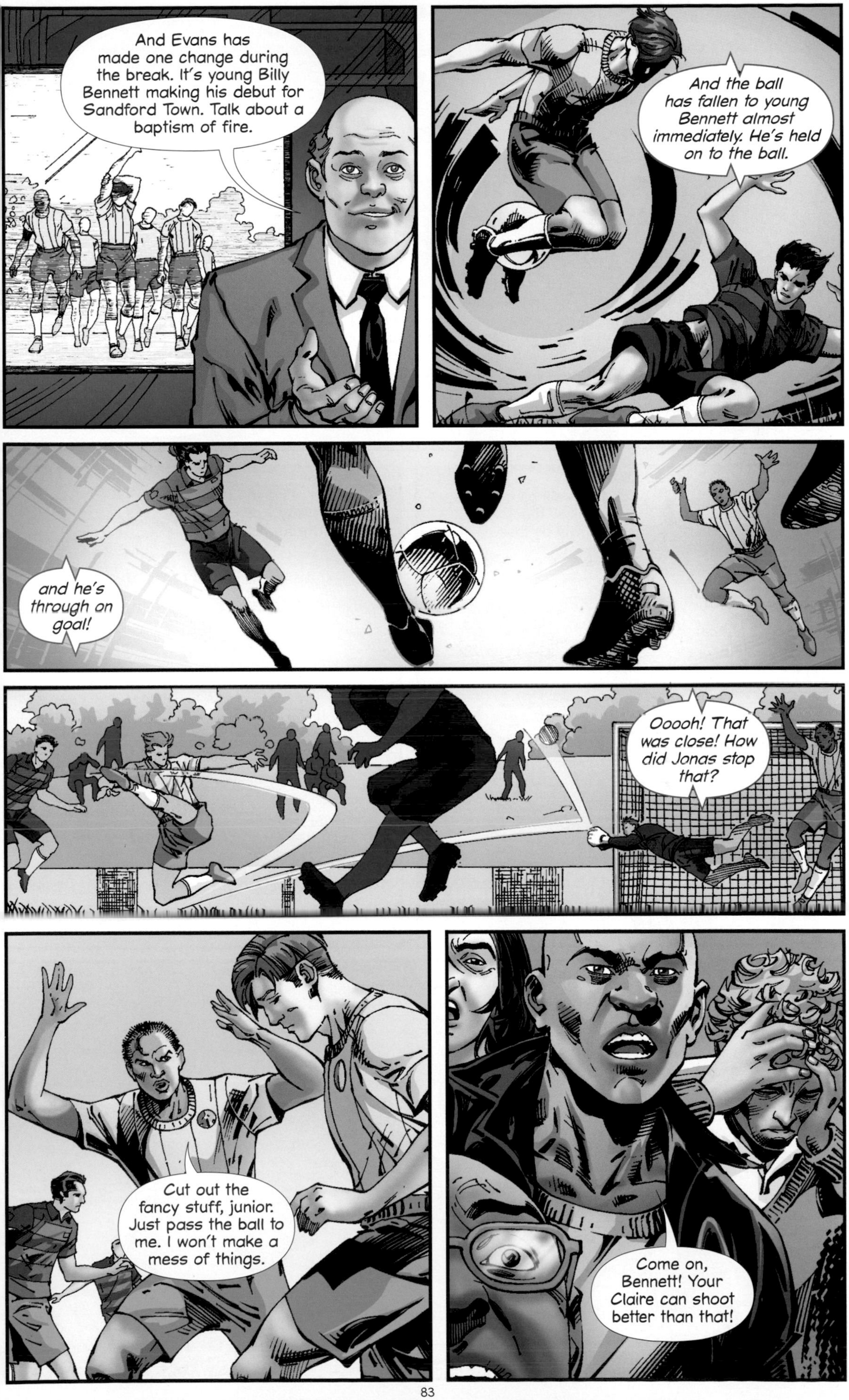
And Evans has made one change during the break. It's young Billy Bennett making his debut for Sandford Town. Talk about a baptism of fire.
And the ball has fallen to young Bennett almost immediately. He's held on to the ball.
and he's through on goal!
Ooooh! That was close! How did Jonas stop that?
Cut out the fancy stuff, junior. Just pass the ball to me. I won't make a mess of things.
Come on, Bennett! Your Claire can shoot better than that!

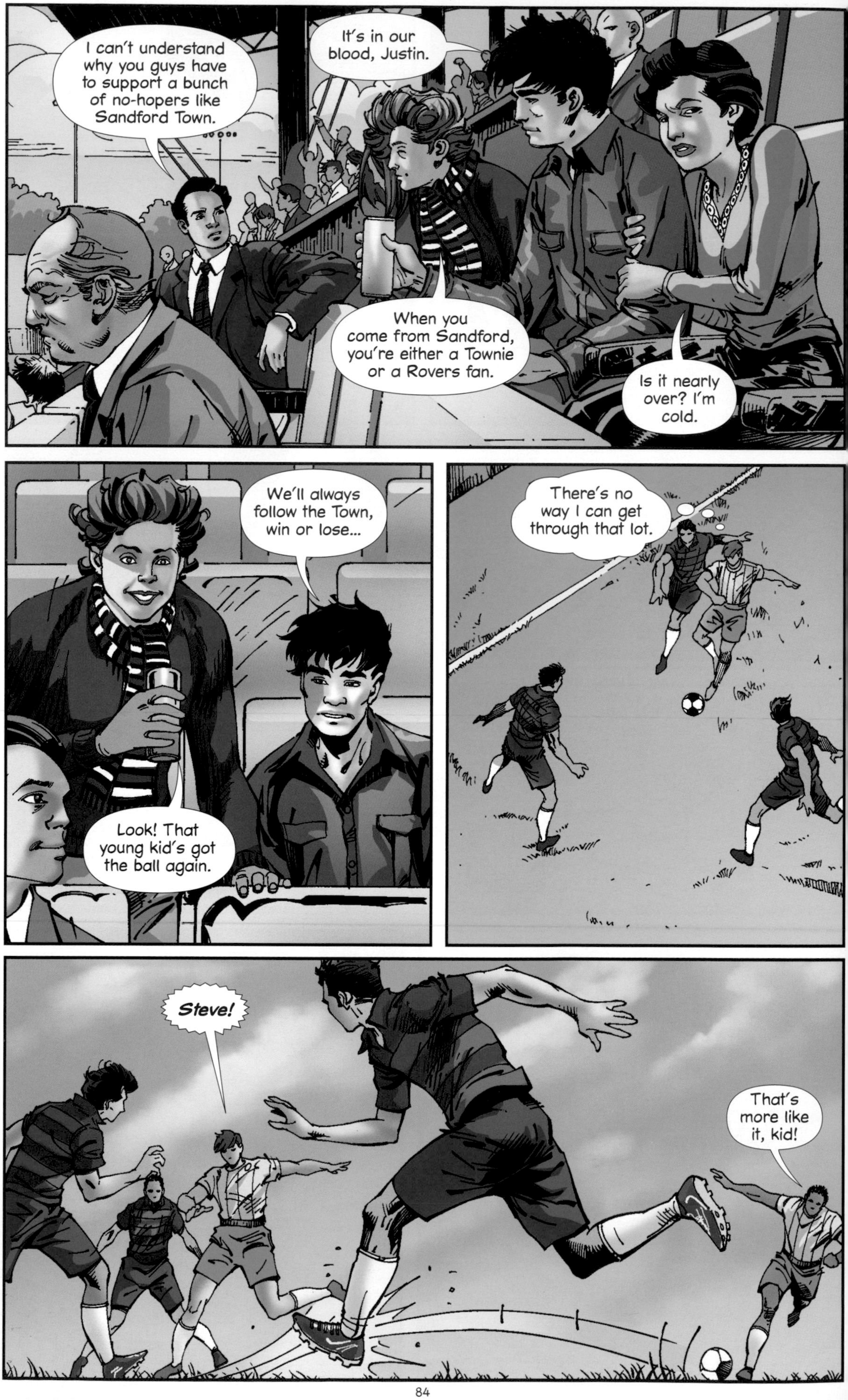
I can't understand why you guys have to support a bunch of no-hopers like Sandford Town.
It's in our blood, Justin.
When you come from Sandford, you're either a Townie or a Rovers fan.
Is it nearly over? I'm cold.
We'll always follow the Town, win or lose...
Look! That young kid's got the ball again.
There's no way I can get through that lot.
Steve!
That's more like it, kid!

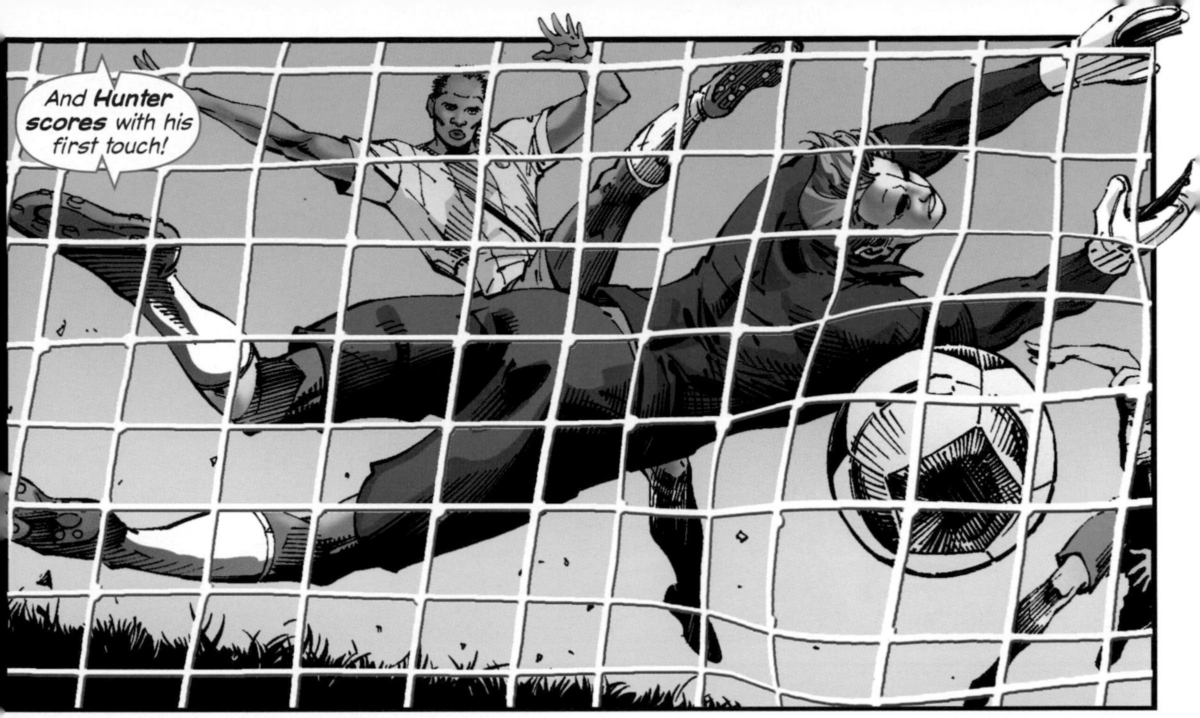
And **Hunter** **scores** with his first touch!

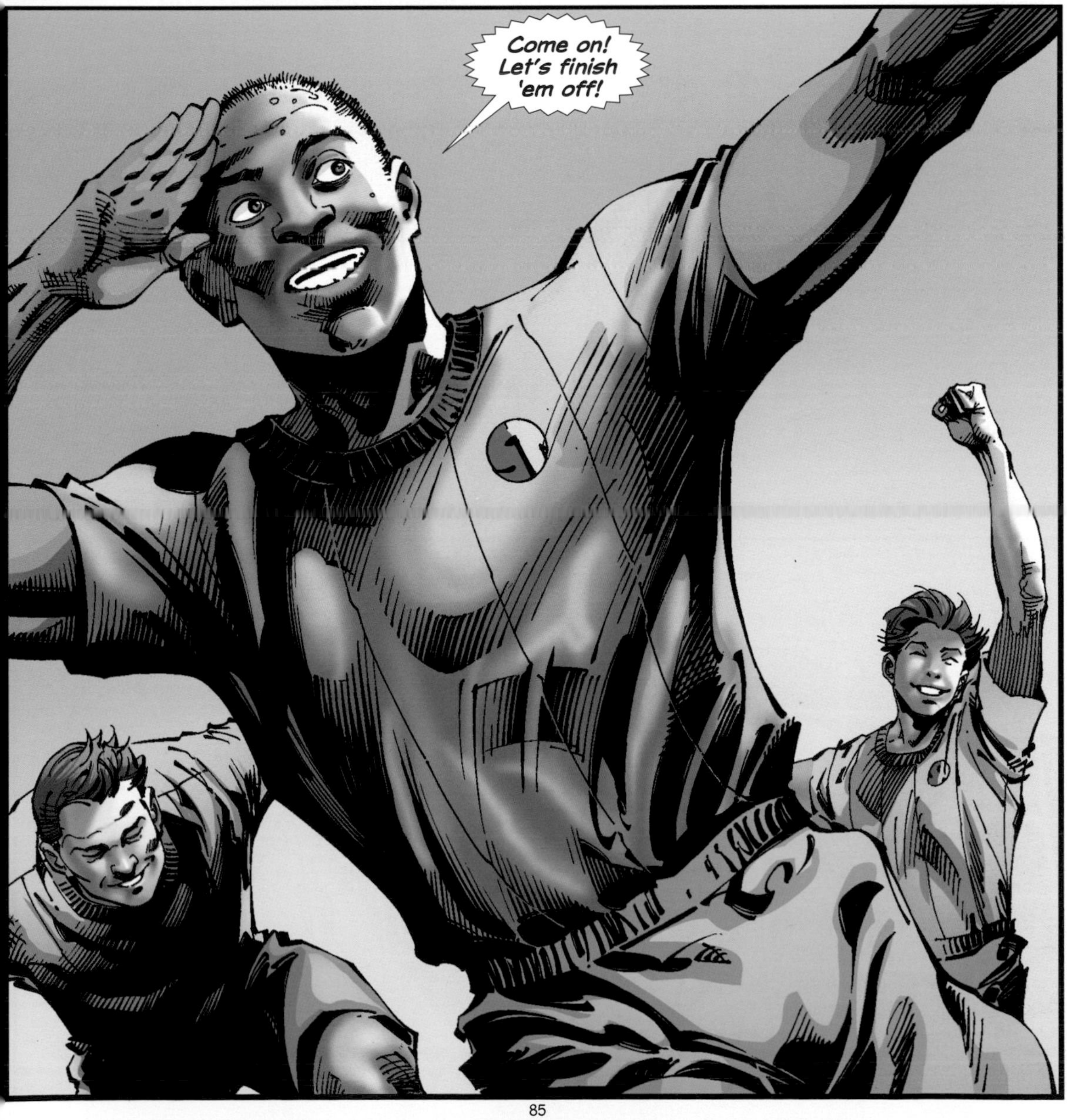
Come on! Let's finish 'em off!

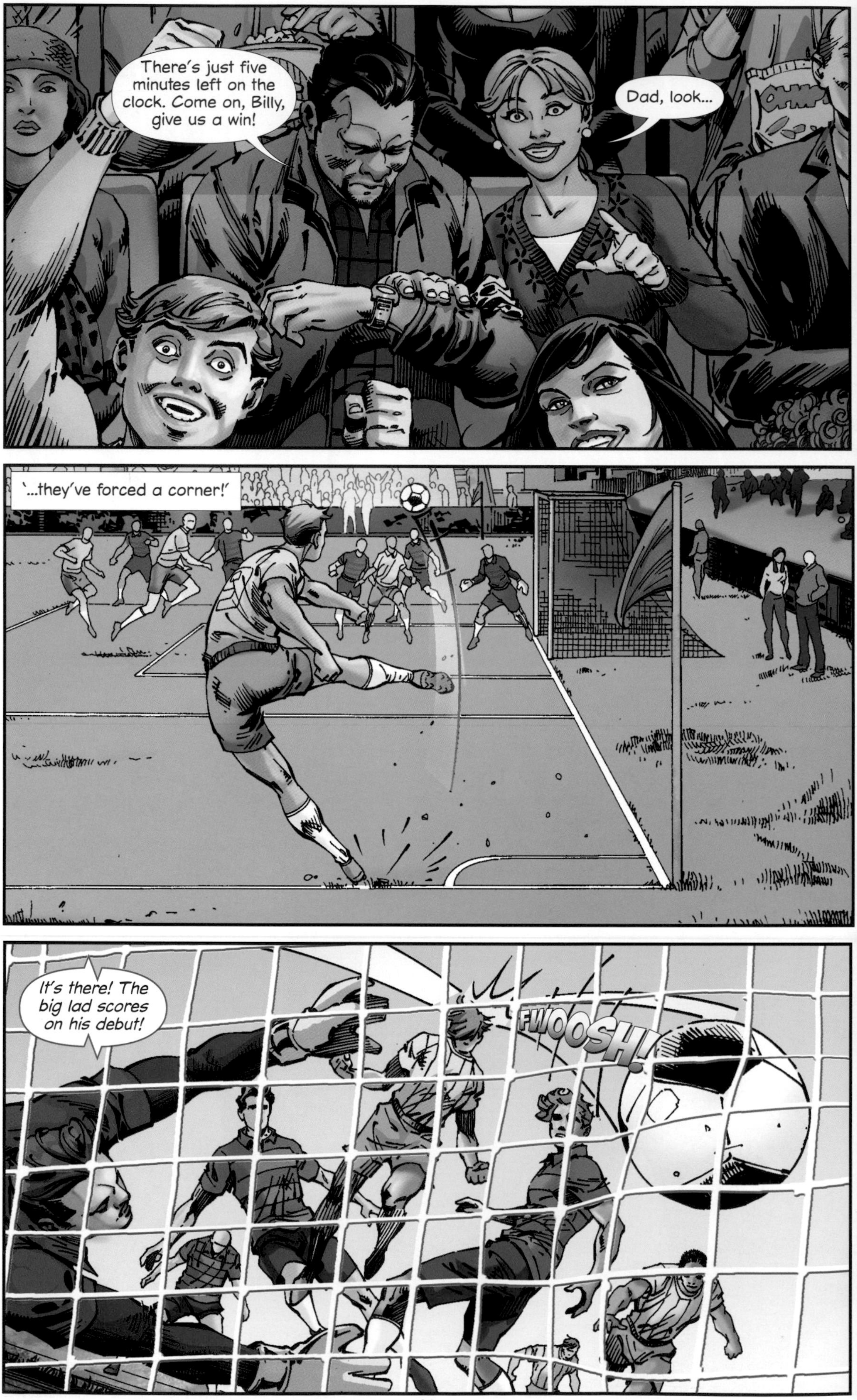
There's just five minutes left on the clock. Come on, Billy, give us a win!
Dad, look...
'...they've forced a corner!'
It's there! The big lad scores on his debut!
FWOOSH!

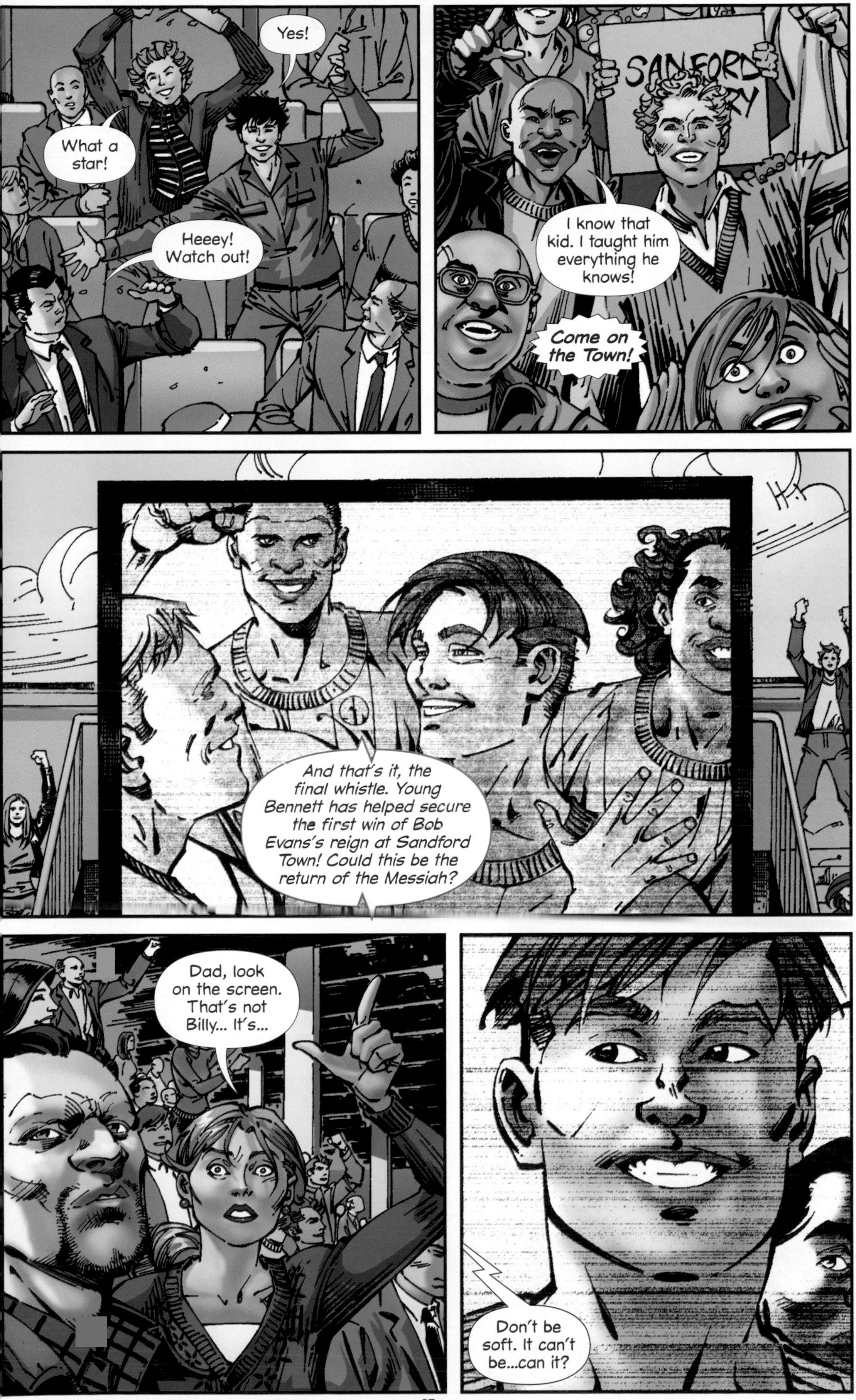
Yes!
What a star!
Heeey! Watch out!
SANFORD
I know that kid. I taught him everything he knows!
Come on the Town!
And that's it, the final whistle. Young Bennett has helped secure the first win of Bob Evans's reign at Sandford Town! Could this be the return of the Messiah?
Dad, look on the screen. That's not Billy... It's...
Don't be soft. It can't be...can it?

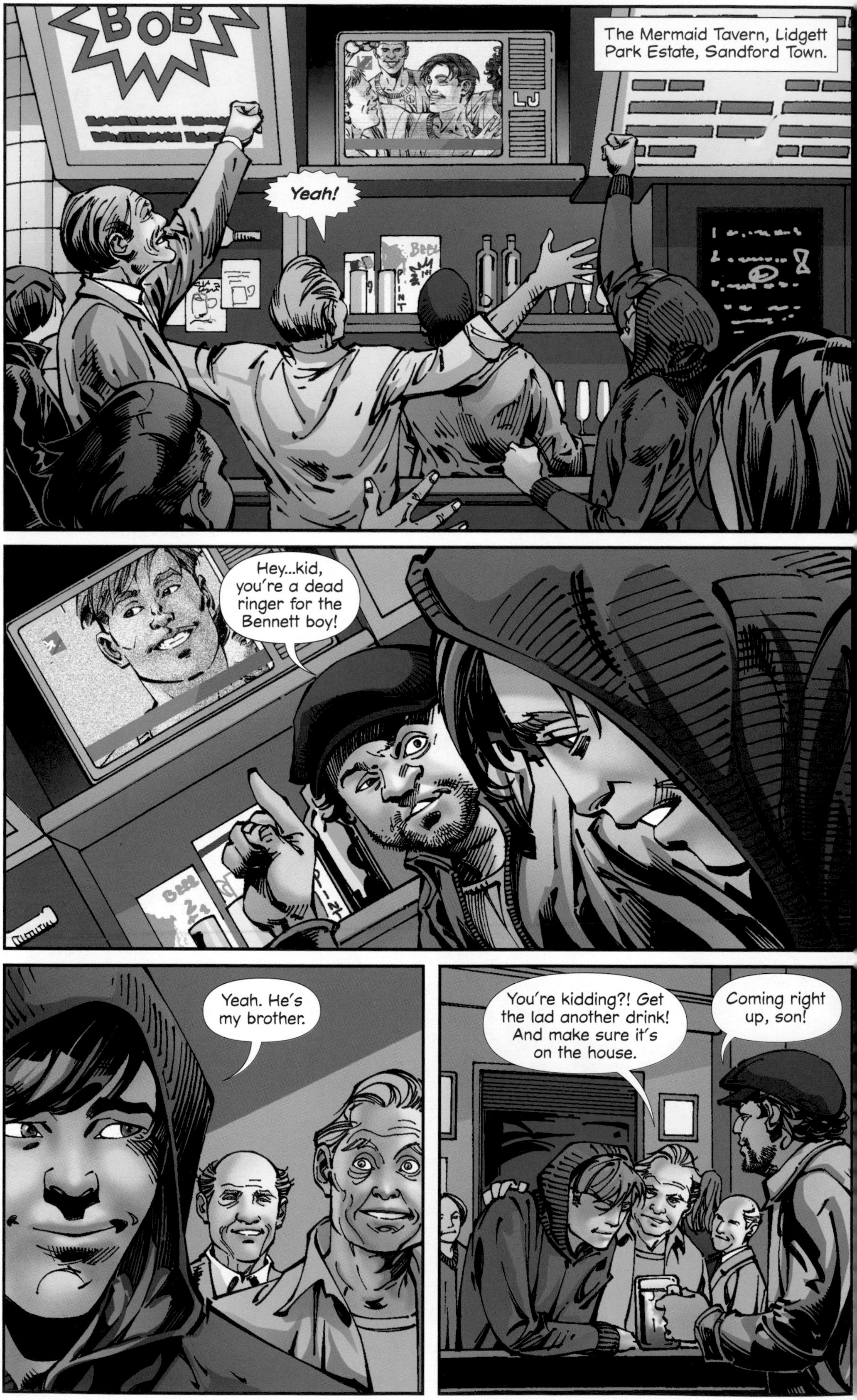
BOB
The Mermaid Tavern, Lidgett Park Estate, Sandford Town.
LJ
Yeah!
Hey...kid, you're a dead ringer for the Bennett boy!
Yeah. He's my brother.
You're kidding?! Get the lad another drink! And make sure it's on the house.
Coming right up, son!

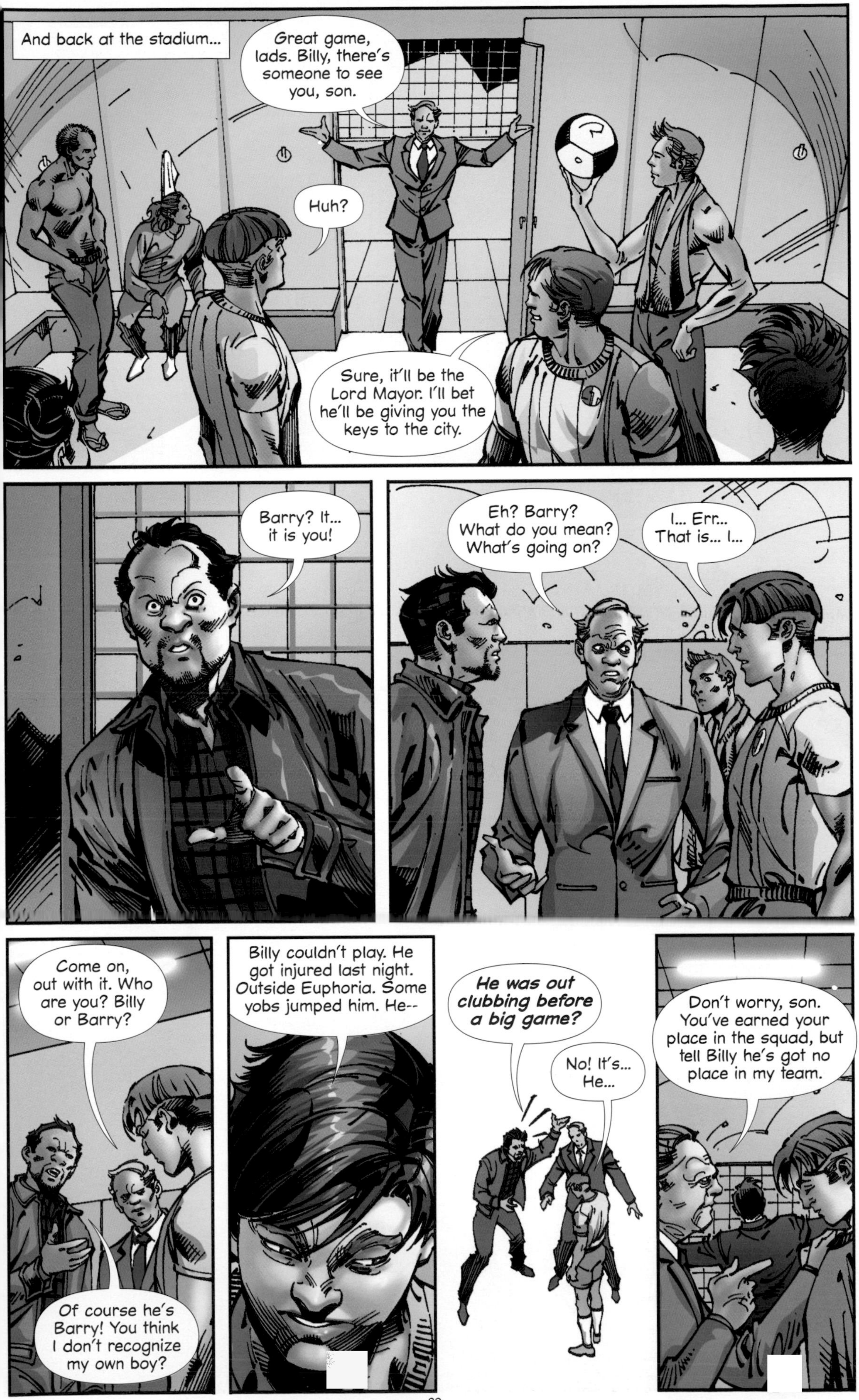
And back at the stadium...
Great game, lads. Billy, there's someone to see you, son.
Huh?
Sure, it'll be the Lord Mayor. I'll bet he'll be giving you the keys to the city.
Barry? It... it is you!
Eh? Barry? What do you mean? What's going on?
I... Err... That is... I...
Come on, out with it. Who are you? Billy or Barry?
Of course he's Barry! You think I don't recognize my own boy?
Billy couldn't play. He got injured last night. Outside Euphoria. Some yobs jumped him. He--
He was out clubbing before a big game?
No! It's... He...
Don't worry, son. You've earned your place in the squad, but tell Billy he's got no place in my team.

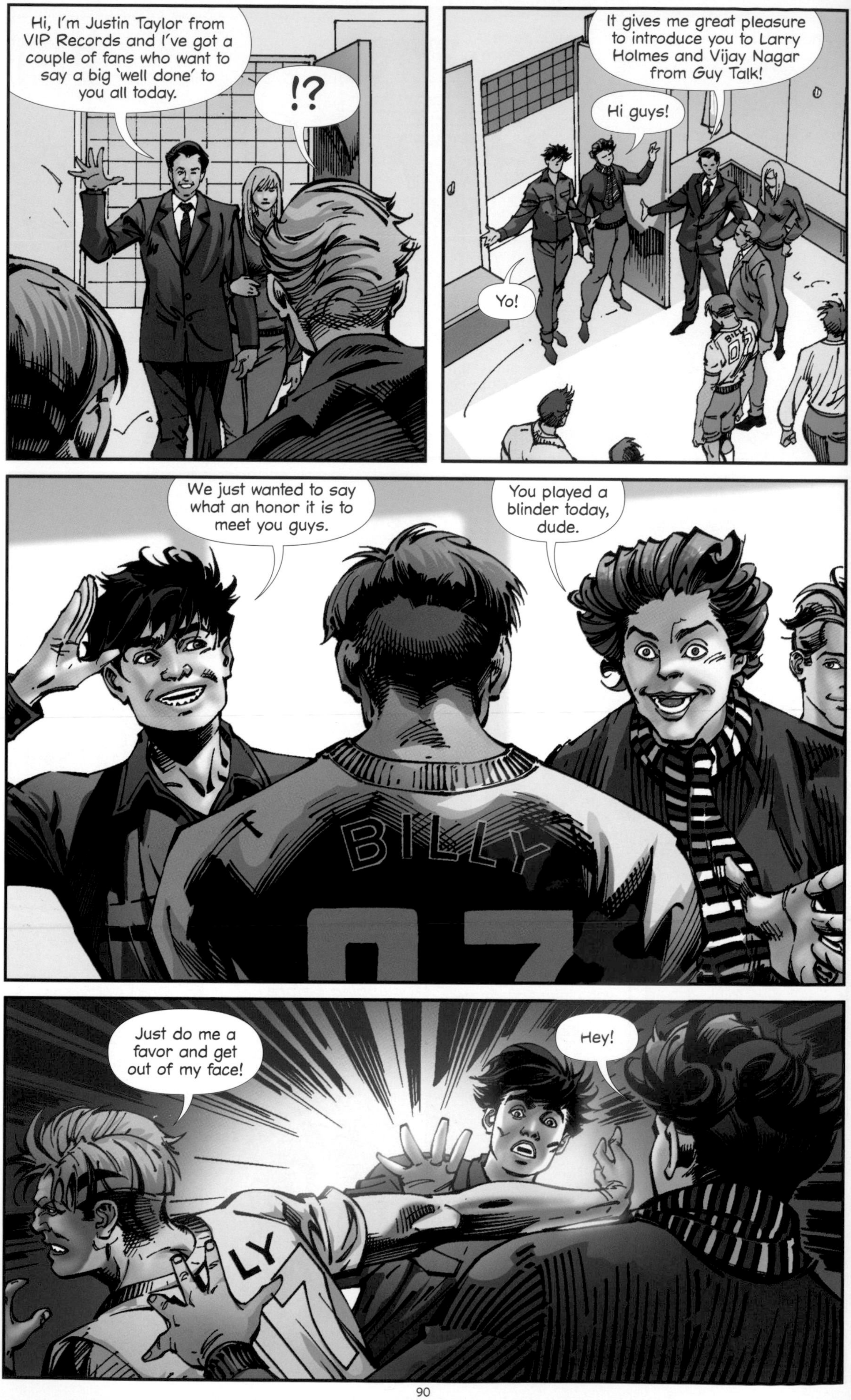
Hi, I'm Justin Taylor from VIP Records and I've got a couple of fans who want to say a big 'well done' to you all today.
!?
It gives me great pleasure to introduce you to Larry Holmes and Vijay Nagar from Guy Talk!
Hi guys!
Yo!
We just wanted to say what an honor it is to meet you guys.
You played a blinder today, dude.
BILLY
Just do me a favor and get out of my face!
Hey!

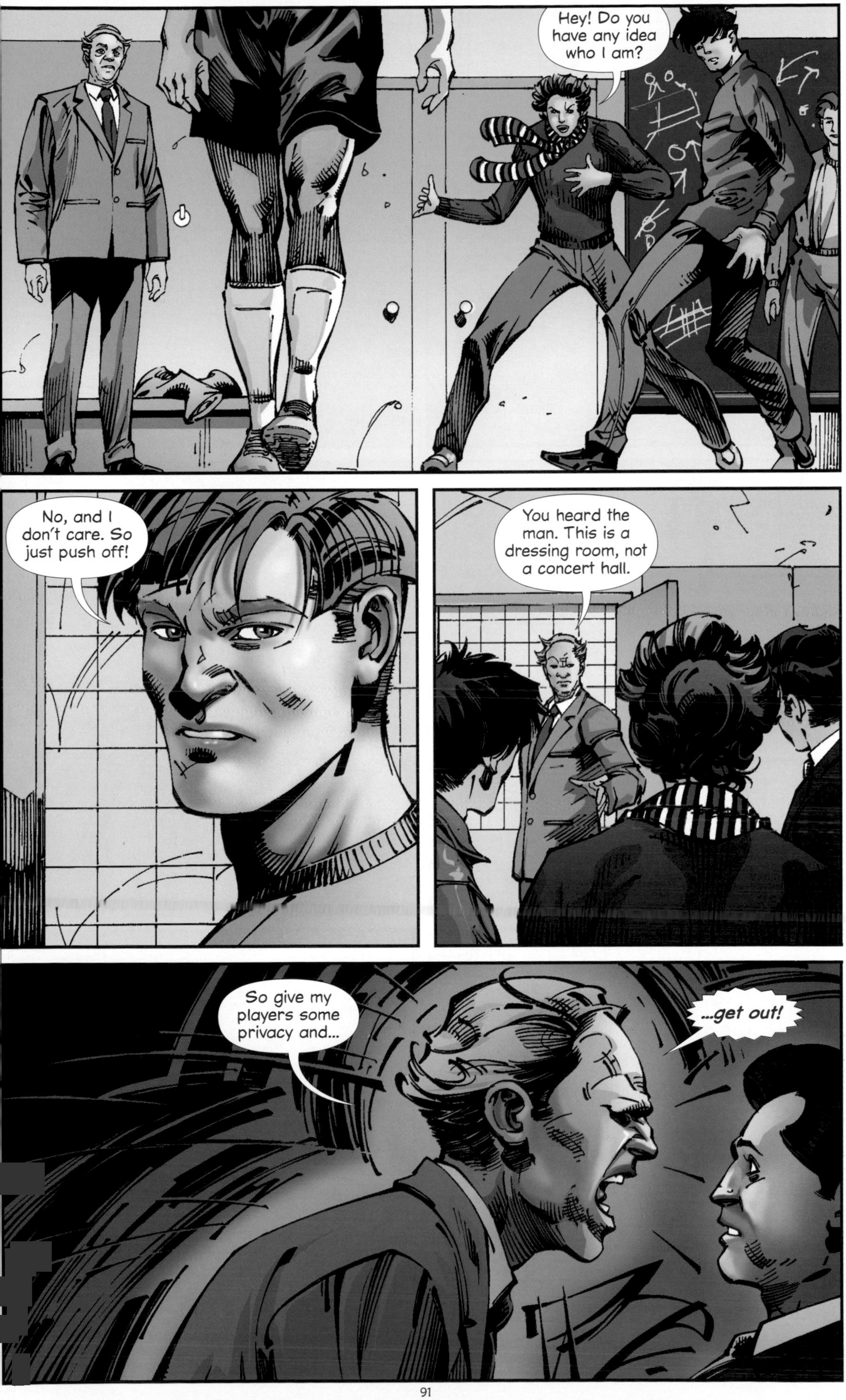
Hey! Do you have any idea who I am?
No, and I don't care. So just push off!
You heard the man. This is a dressing room, not a concert hall.
So give my players some privacy and...
...get out!

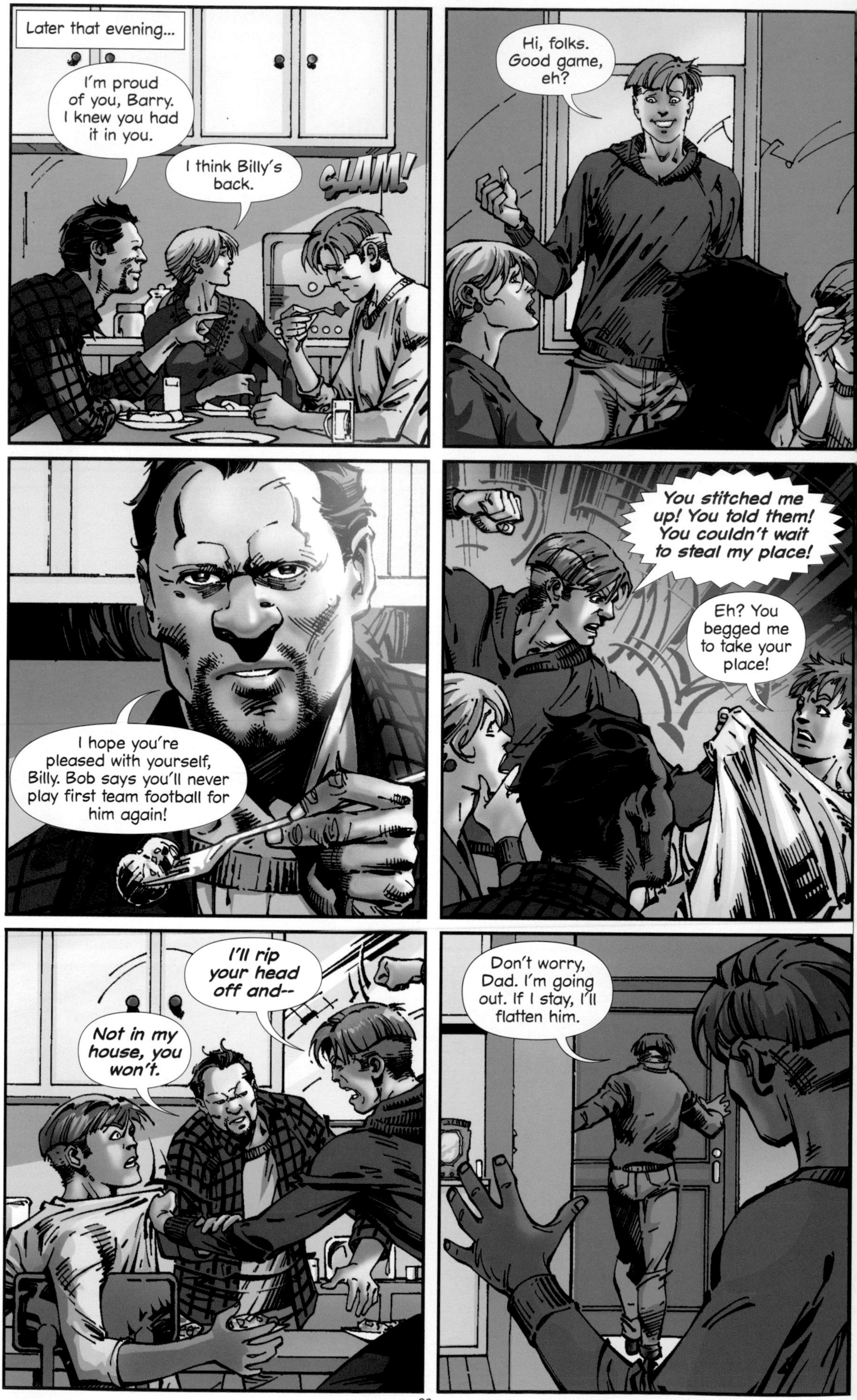
Later that evening...
I'm proud of you, Barry. I knew you had it in you.
I think Billy's back.
SLAM!
Hi, folks. Good game, eh?
I hope you're pleased with yourself, Billy. Bob says you'll never play first team football for him again!
You stitched me up! You told them! You couldn't wait to steal my place!
Eh? You begged me to take your place!
I'll rip your head off and--
Not in my house, you won't.
Don't worry, Dad. I'm going out. If I stay, I'll flatten him.

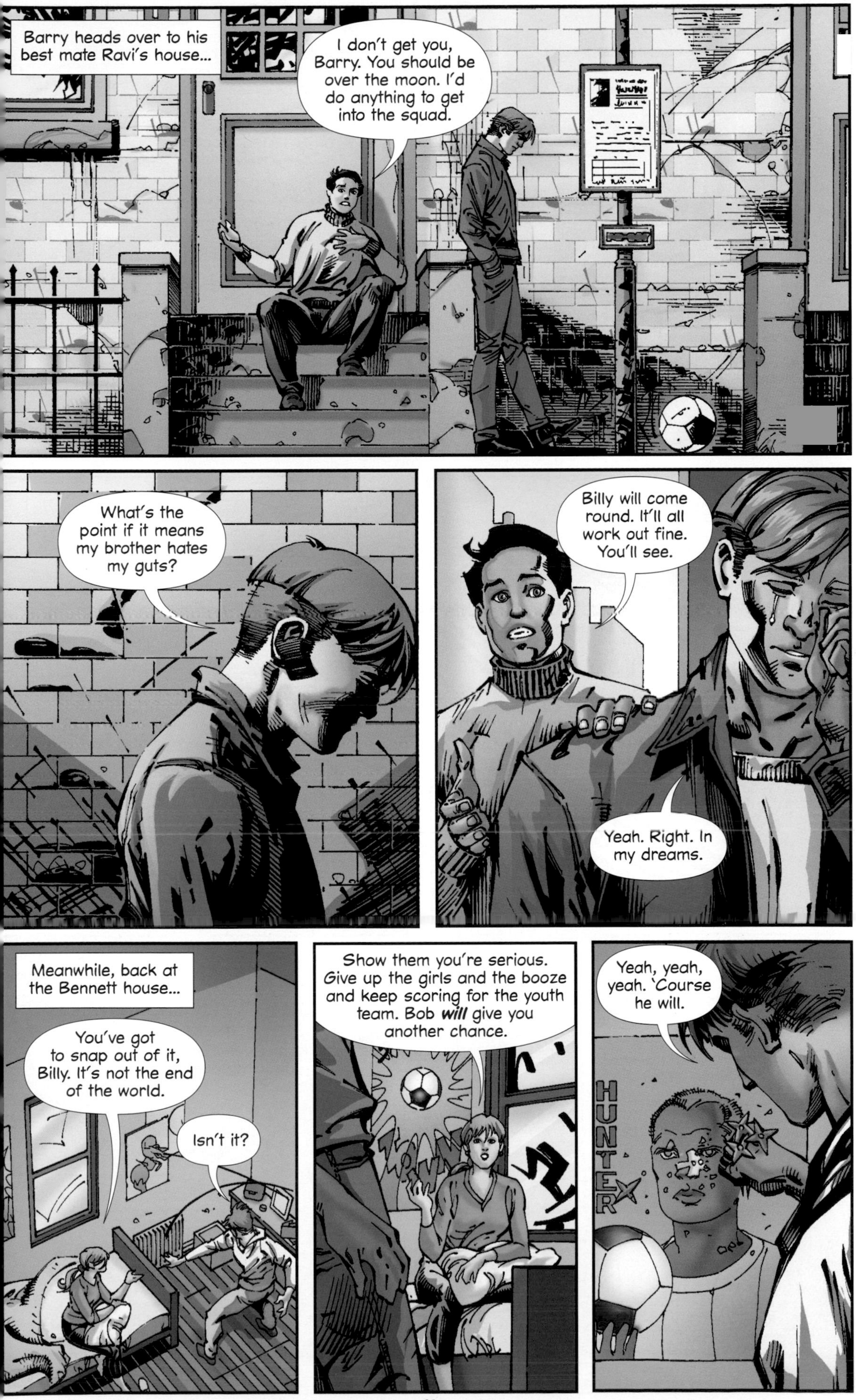
Barry heads over to his best mate Ravi's house...
I don't get you, Barry. You should be over the moon. I'd do anything to get into the squad.
What's the point if it means my brother hates my guts?
Billy will come round. It'll all work out fine. You'll see.
Yeah. Right. In my dreams.
Meanwhile, back at the Bennett house...
You've got to snap out of it, Billy. It's not the end of the world.
Isn't it?
Show them you're serious. Give up the girls and the booze and keep scoring for the youth team. Bob **will** give you another chance.
Yeah, yeah, yeah. 'Course he will.
HUNTER

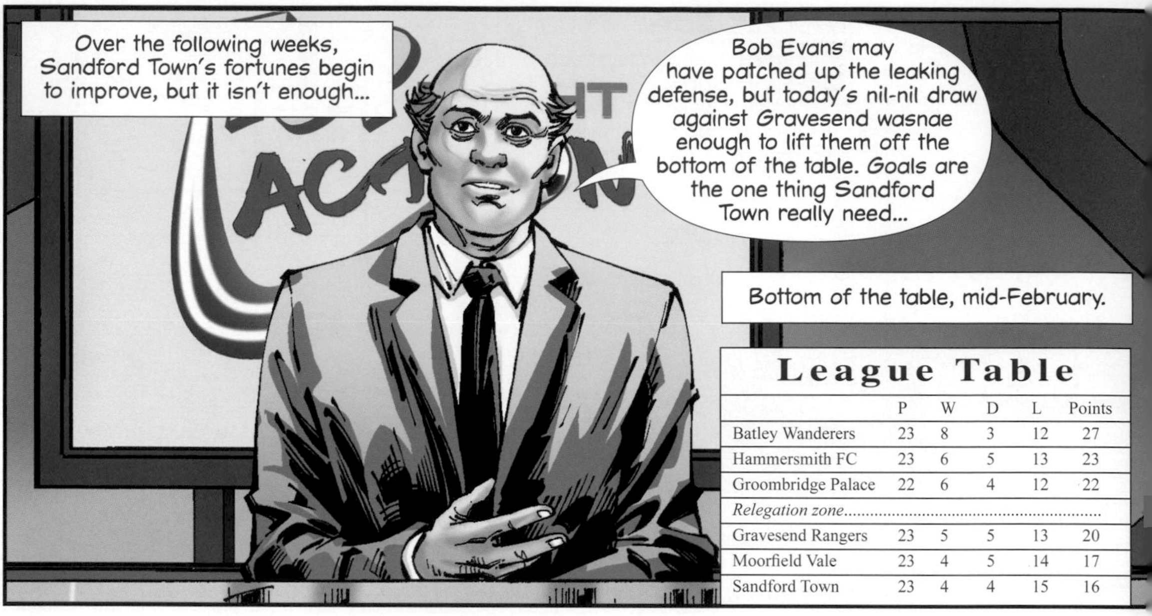

Over the following weeks, Sandford Town's fortunes begin to improve, but it isn't enough...
Bob Evans may have patched up the leaking defense, but today's nil-nil draw against Gravesend wasnae enough to lift them off the bottom of the table. Goals are the one thing Sandford Town really need...
Bottom of the table, mid-February.

League Table

	P	W	D	L	Points
Batley Wanderers	23	8	3	12	27
Hammersmith FC	23	6	5	13	23
Groombridge Palace	22	6	4	12	22
Relegation zone............					
Gravesend Rangers	23	5	5	13	20
Moorfield Vale	23	4	5	14	17
Sandford Town	23	4	4	15	16

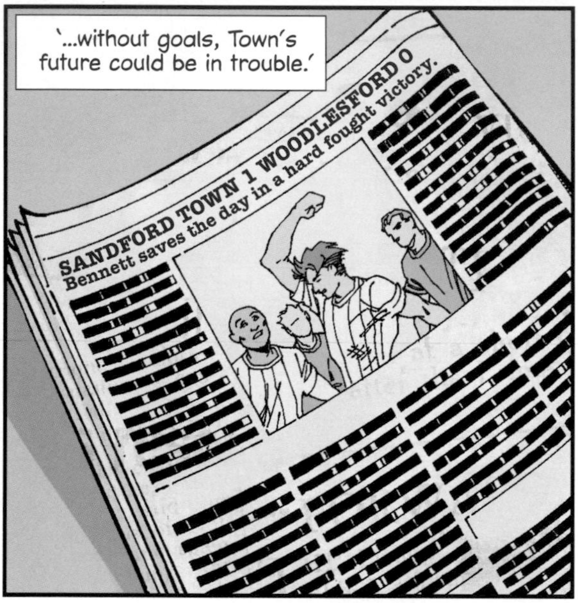

'...without goals, Town's future could be in trouble.'
SANDFORD TOWN 1 WOODLESFORD 0
Bennett saves the day in a hard fought victory.

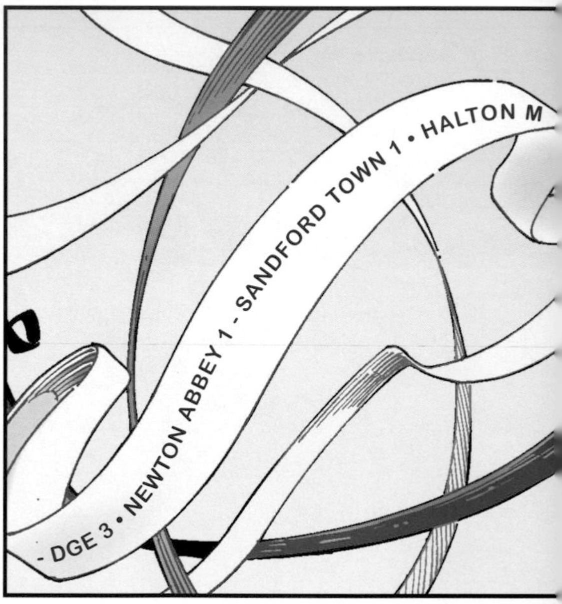

- DGE 3 • NEWTON ABBEY 1 - SANDFORD TOWN 1 • HALTON M

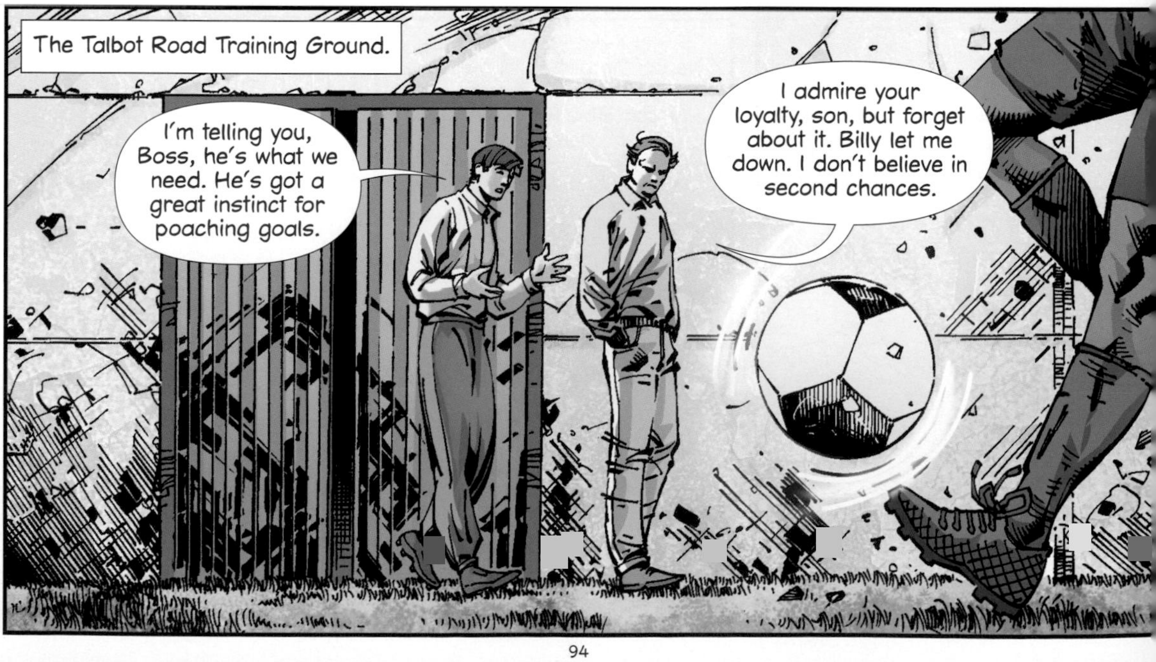

The Talbot Road Training Ground.
I'm telling you, Boss, he's what we need. He's got a great instinct for poaching goals.
I admire your loyalty, son, but forget about it. Billy let me down. I don't believe in second chances.

During the time, Billy takes his sister's advice and continues scoring for the youth team.

That's his third. What a hat trick!

PEEEEP!

Great game, mate!

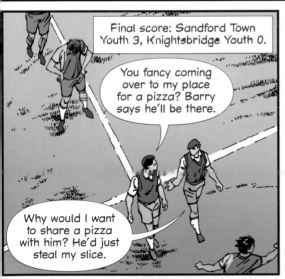

Final score: Sandford Town Youth 3, Knightsbridge Youth 0.

You fancy coming over to my place for a pizza? Barry says he'll be there.

Why would I want to share a pizza with him? He'd just steal my slice.

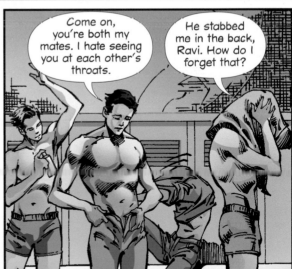

Come on, you're both my mates. I hate seeing you at each other's throats.

He stabbed me in the back, Ravi. How do I forget that?

Good game today, Billy.

Cheers, Andy.

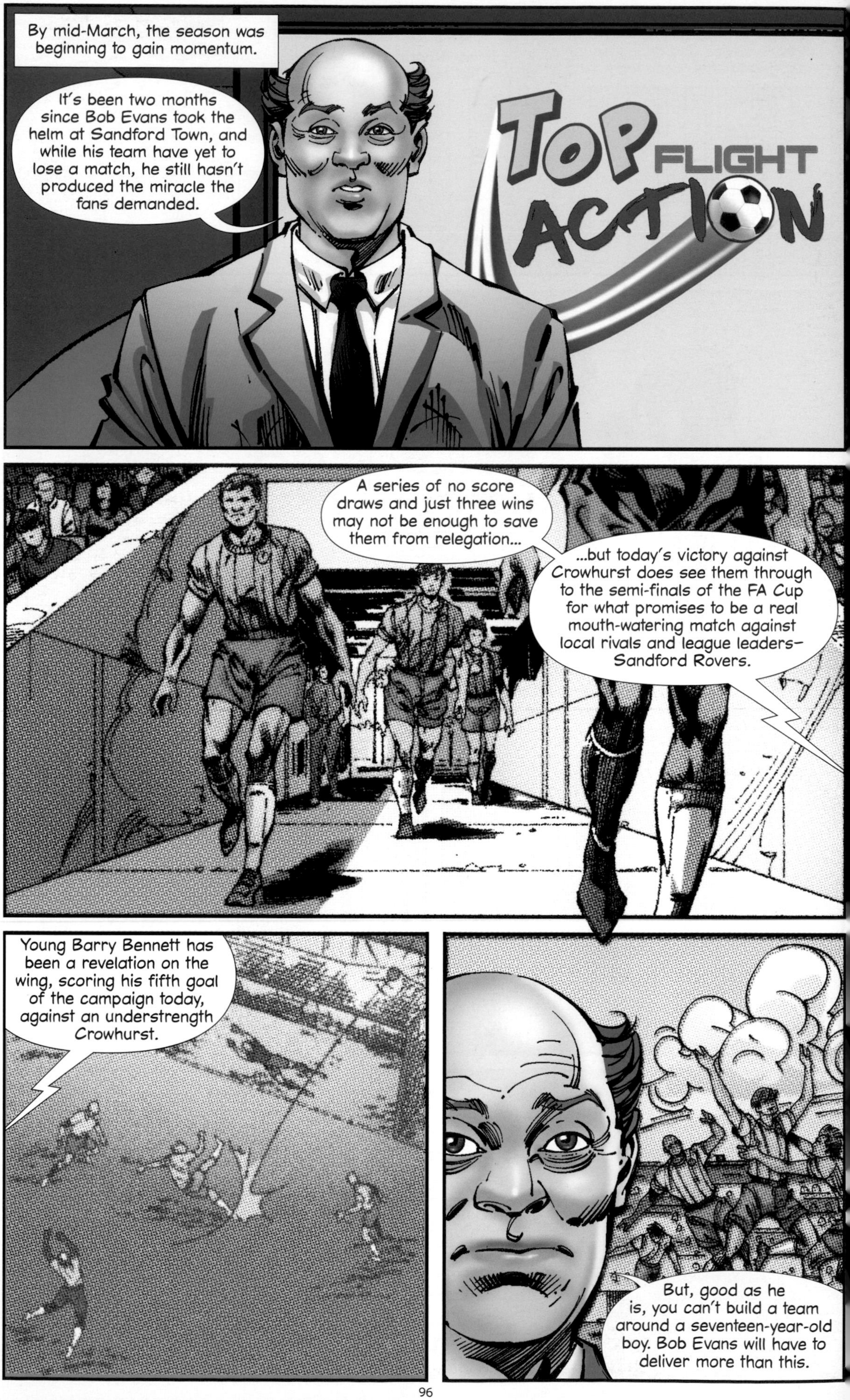
By mid-March, the season was beginning to gain momentum.
It's been two months since Bob Evans took the helm at Sandford Town, and while his team have yet to lose a match, he still hasn't produced the miracle the fans demanded.
TOP FLIGHT ACTION
A series of no score draws and just three wins may not be enough to save them from relegation...
...but today's victory against Crowhurst does see them through to the semi-finals of the FA Cup for what promises to be a real mouth-watering match against local rivals and league leaders– Sandford Rovers.
Young Barry Bennett has been a revelation on the wing, scoring his fifth goal of the campaign today, against an understrength Crowhurst.
But, good as he is, you can't build a team around a seventeen-year-old boy. Bob Evans will have to deliver more than this.

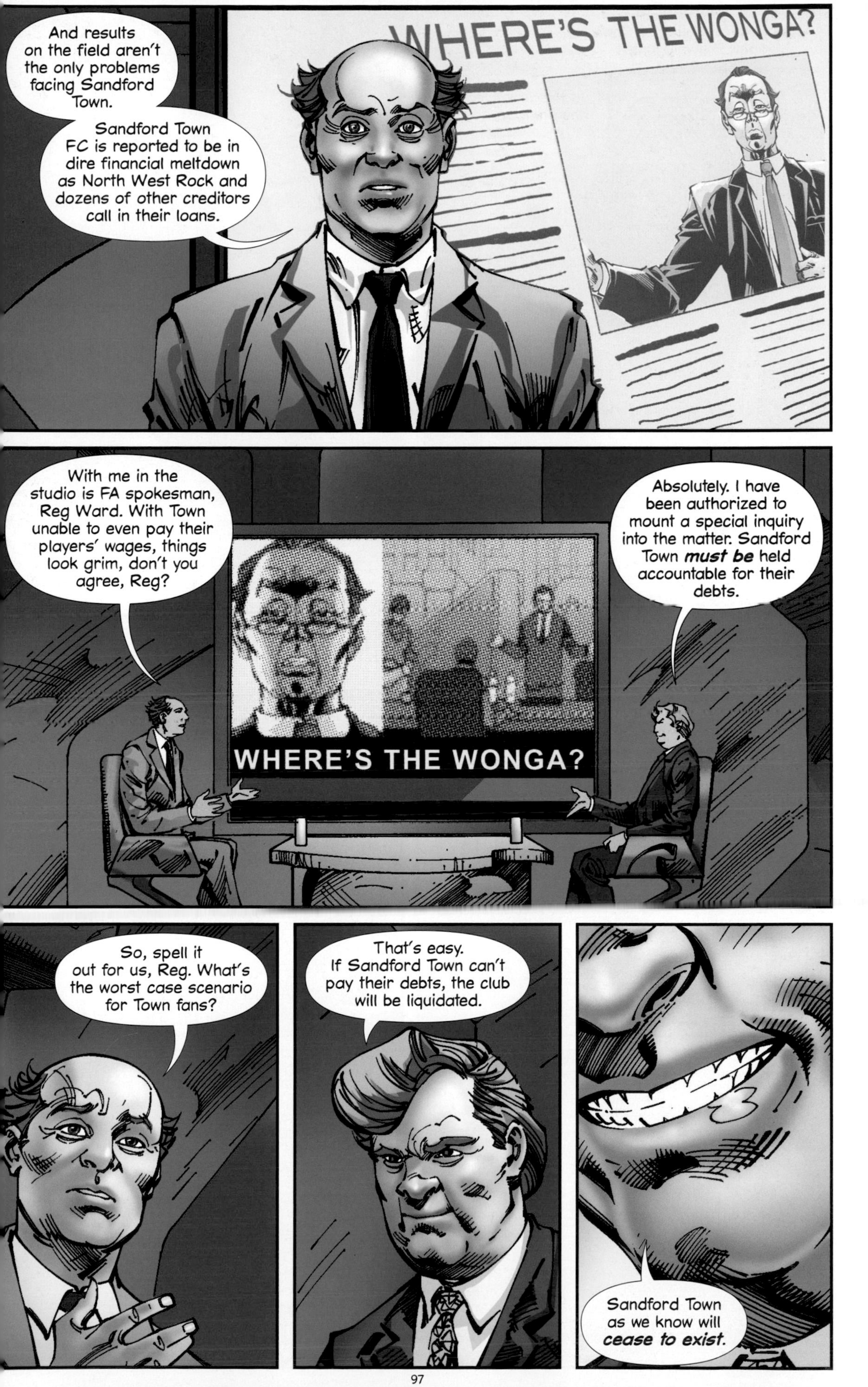

WHERE'S THE WONGA?
And results on the field aren't the only problems facing Sandford Town.
Sandford Town FC is reported to be in dire financial meltdown as North West Rock and dozens of other creditors call in their loans.
With me in the studio is FA spokesman, Reg Ward. With Town unable to even pay their players' wages, things look grim, don't you agree, Reg?
WHERE'S THE WONGA?
Absolutely. I have been authorized to mount a special inquiry into the matter. Sandford Town *must be* held accountable for their debts.
So, spell it out for us, Reg. What's the worst case scenario for Town fans?
That's easy. If Sandford Town can't pay their debts, the club will be liquidated.
Sandford Town as we know will *cease to exist*.

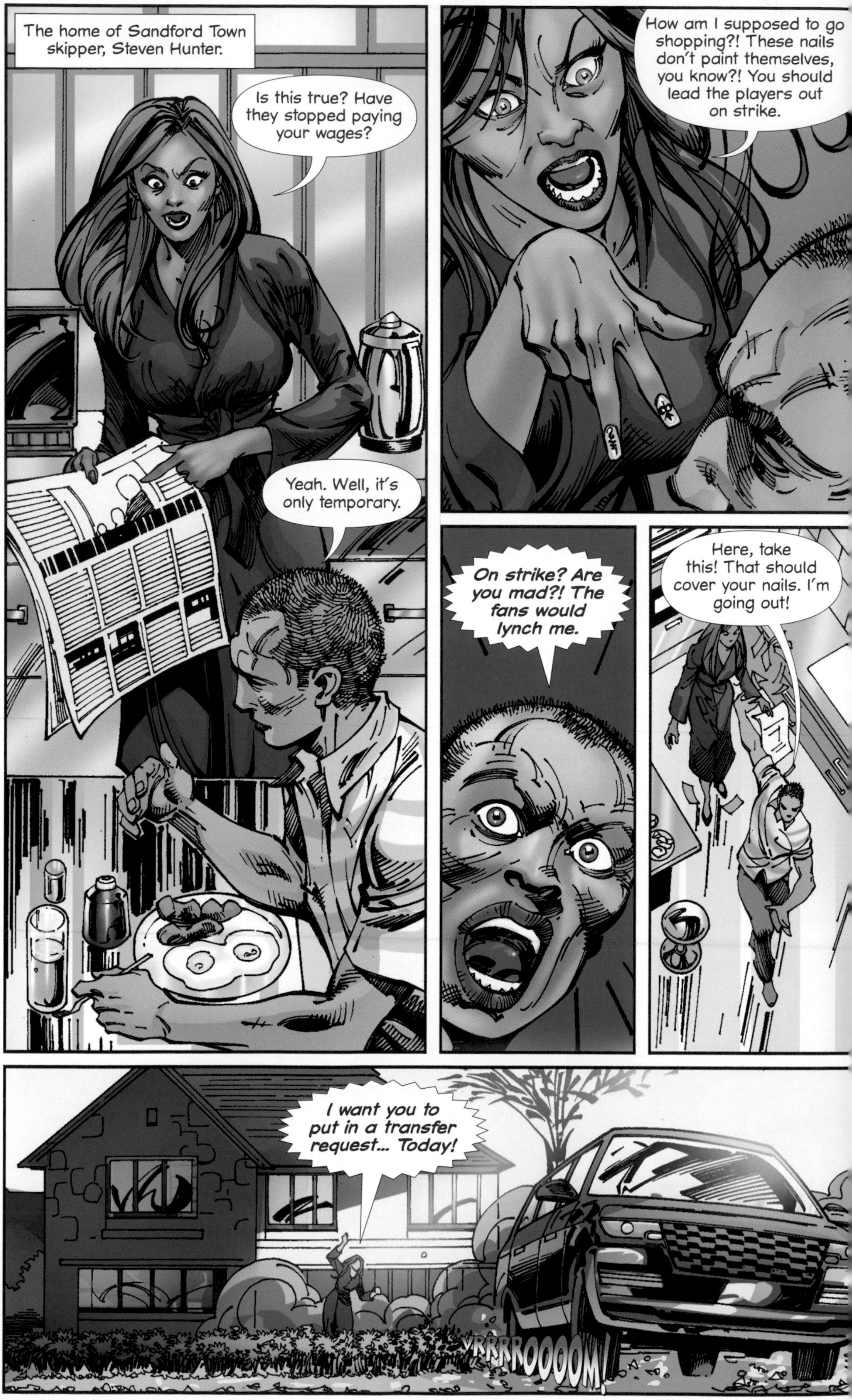
The home of Sandford Town skipper, Steven Hunter.
Is this true? Have they stopped paying your wages?
Yeah. Well, it's only temporary.
How am I supposed to go shopping?! These nails don't paint themselves, you know?! You should lead the players out on strike.
On strike? Are you mad?! The fans would lynch me.
Here, take this! That should cover your nails. I'm going out!
I want you to put in a transfer request... Today!
VRRRROOOOM!

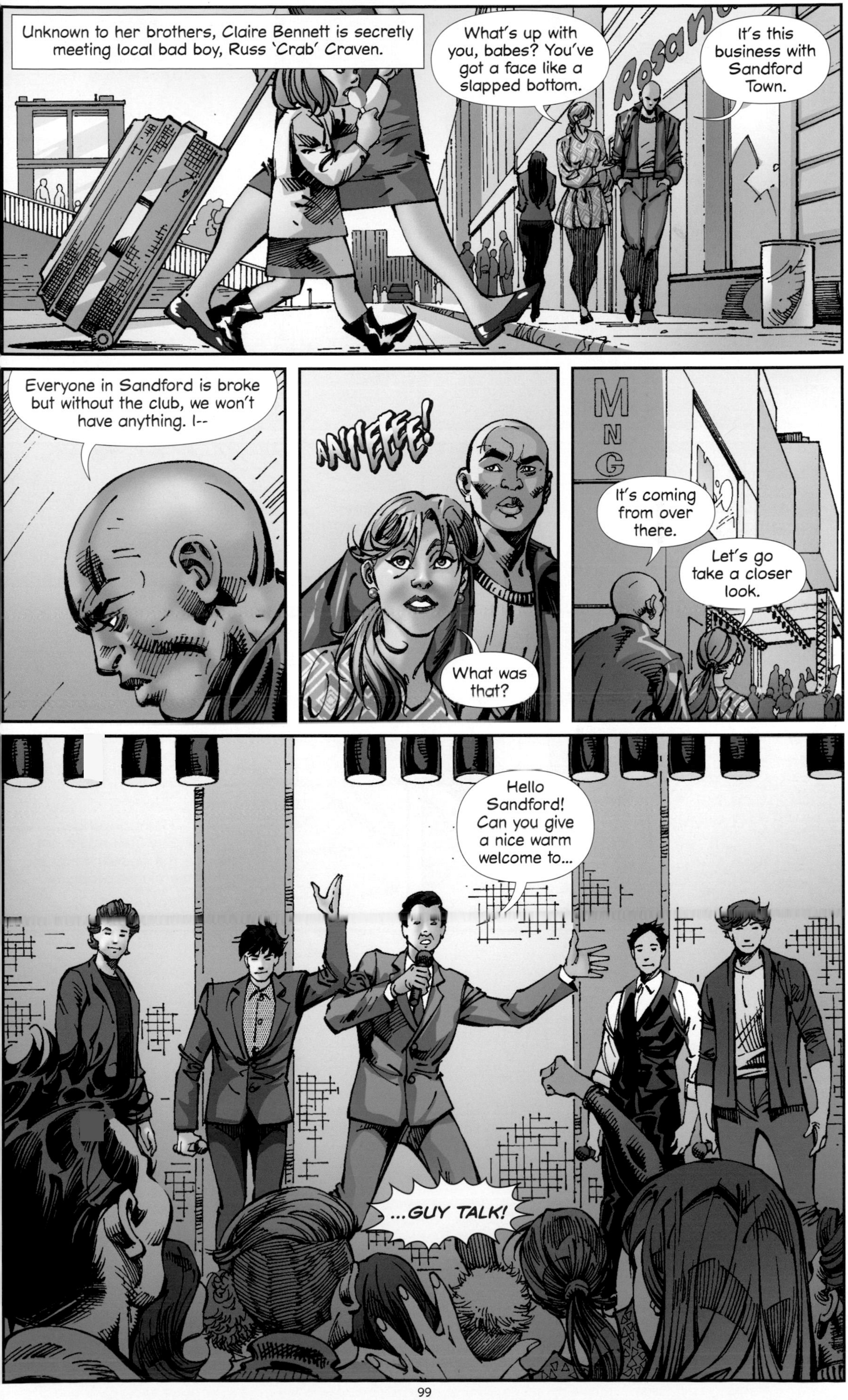
Unknown to her brothers, Claire Bennett is secretly meeting local bad boy, Russ 'Crab' Craven.
What's up with you, babes? You've got a face like a slapped bottom.
It's this business with Sandford Town.
Everyone in Sandford is broke but without the club, we won't have anything. I--
AAIIEEEE!
What was that?
It's coming from over there.
Let's go take a closer look.
Hello Sandford! Can you give a nice warm welcome to...
...GUY TALK!

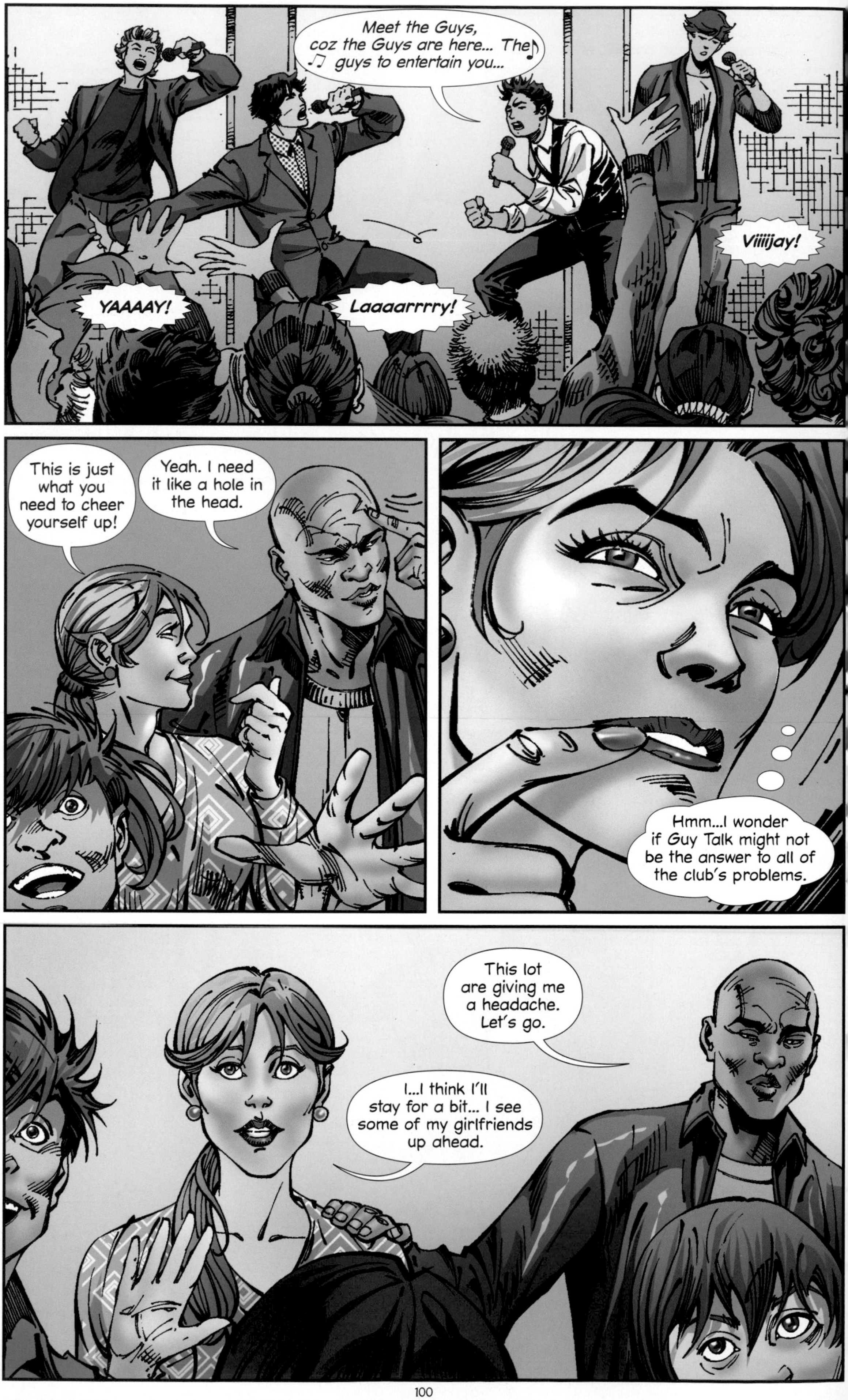
Meet the Guys, coz the Guys are here... The♪ ♫ guys to entertain you...
YAAAAY!
Laaaarrrry!
Viiiijay!
This is just what you need to cheer yourself up!
Yeah. I need it like a hole in the head.
Hmm...I wonder if Guy Talk might not be the answer to all of the club's problems.
This lot are giving me a headache. Let's go.
I...I think I'll stay for a bit... I see some of my girlfriends up ahead.

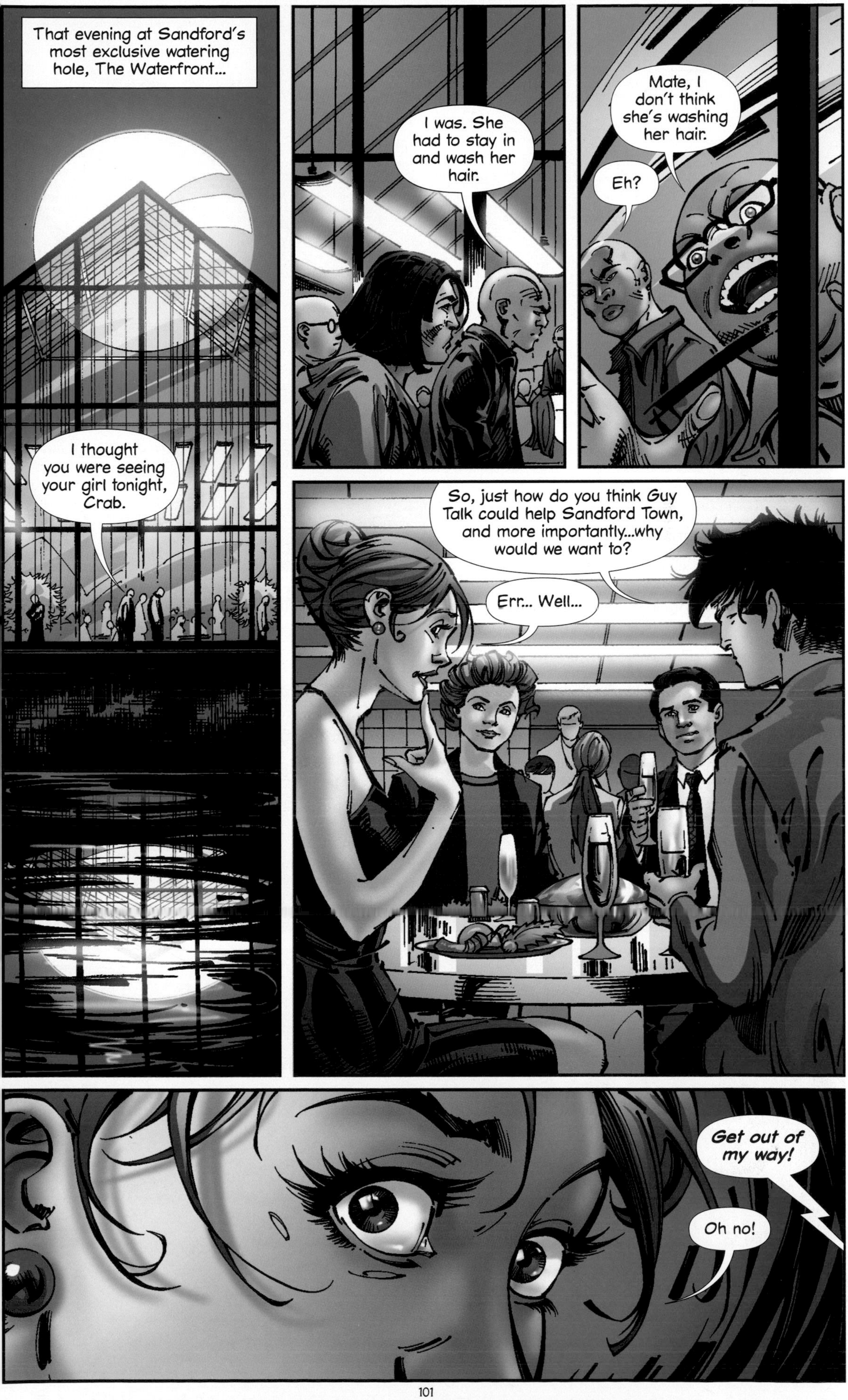
That evening at Sandford's most exclusive watering hole, The Waterfront...
I thought you were seeing your girl tonight, Crab.
I was. She had to stay in and wash her hair.
Mate, I don't think she's washing her hair.
Eh?
So, just how do you think Guy Talk could help Sandford Town, and more importantly...why would we want to?
Err... Well...
Get out of my way!
Oh no!

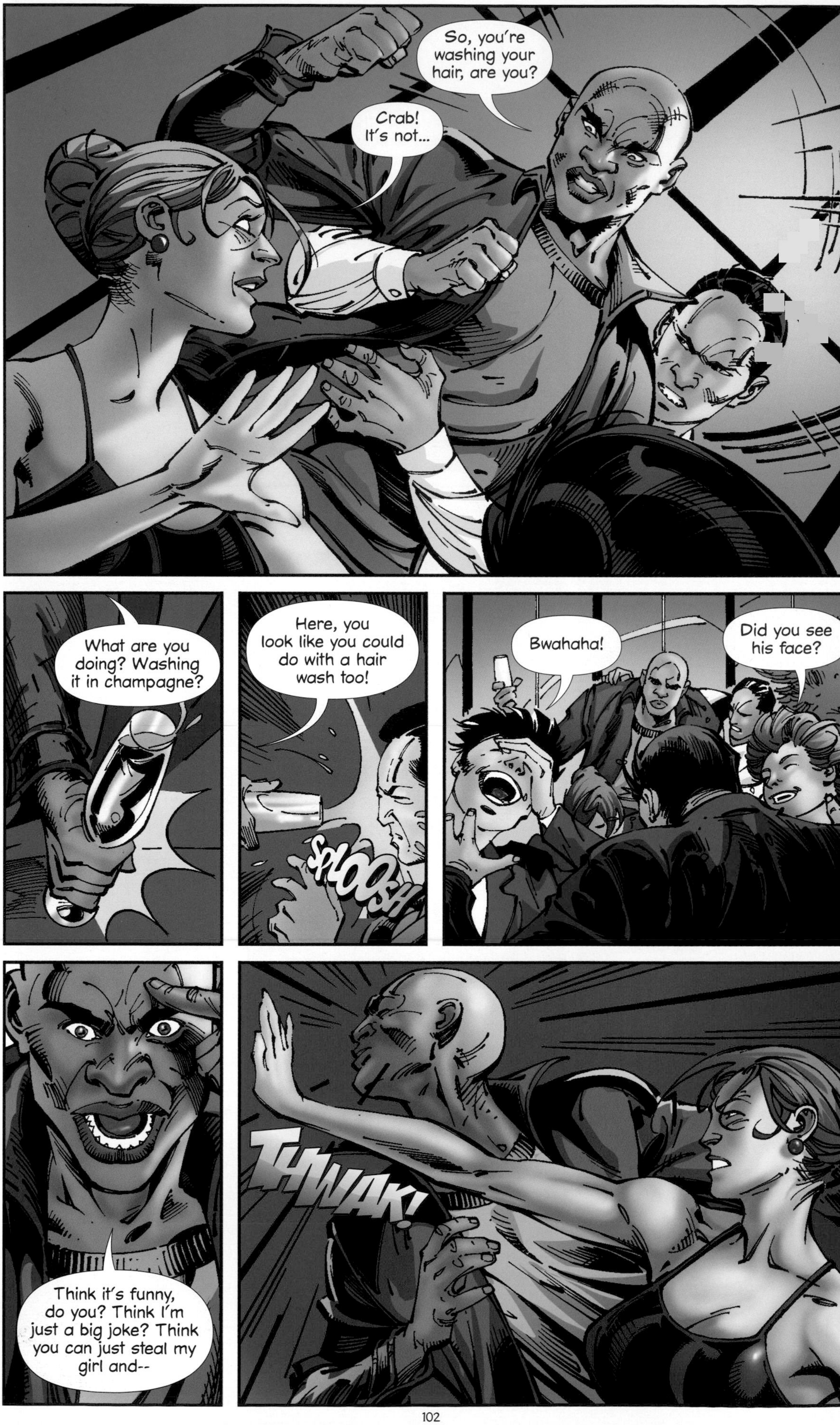
So, you're washing your hair, are you?
Crab! It's not...
What are you doing? Washing it in champagne?
Here, you look like you could do with a hair wash too!
SPLOOSH
Bwahaha!
Did you see his face?
Think it's funny, do you? Think I'm just a big joke? Think you can just steal my girl and--
THWAK!

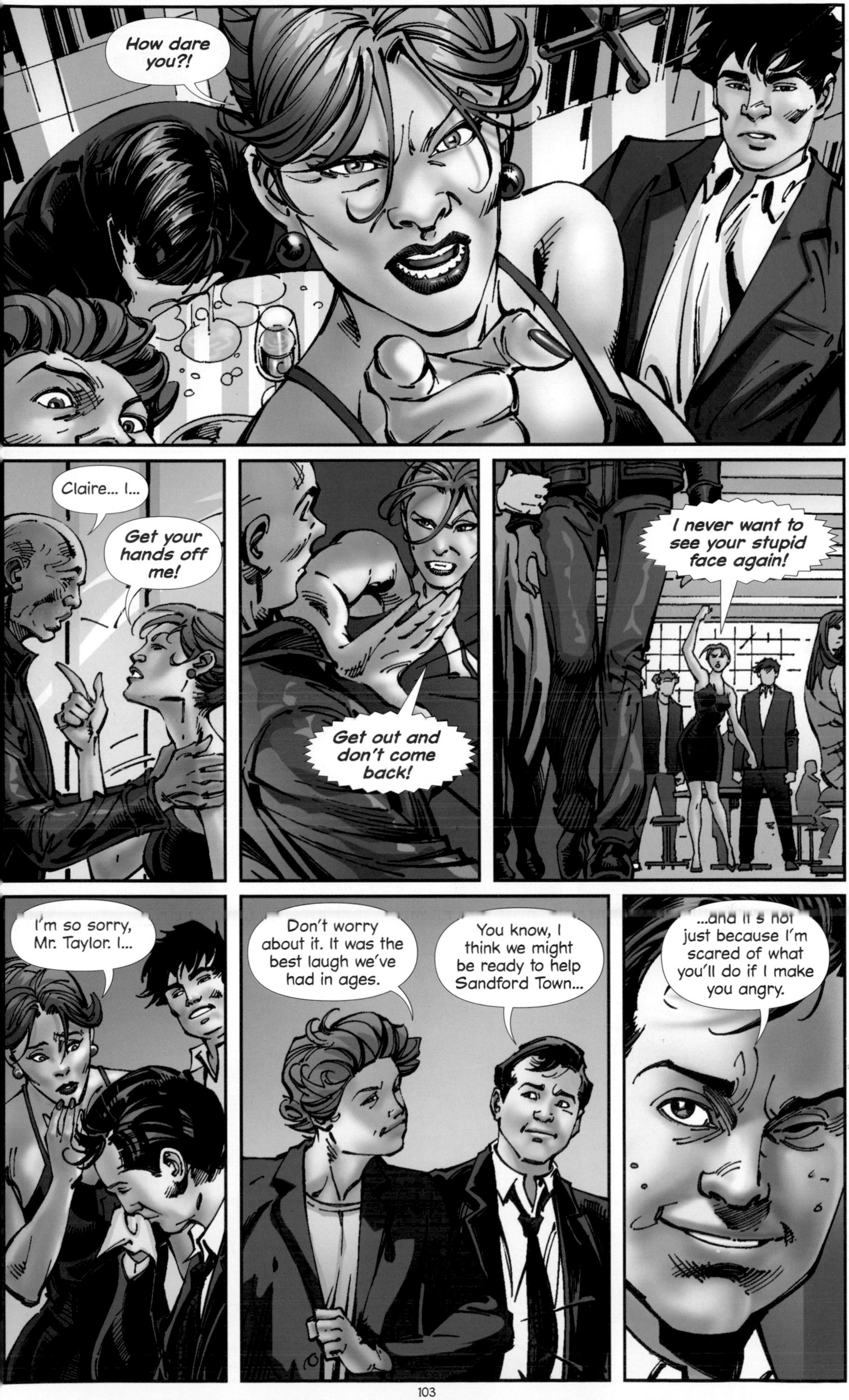
How dare you?!
Claire... I...
Get your hands off me!
Get out and don't come back!
I never want to see your stupid face again!
I'm so sorry, Mr. Taylor. I...
Don't worry about it. It was the best laugh we've had in ages.
You know, I think we might be ready to help Sandford Town...
...and it's not just because I'm scared of what you'll do if I make you angry.

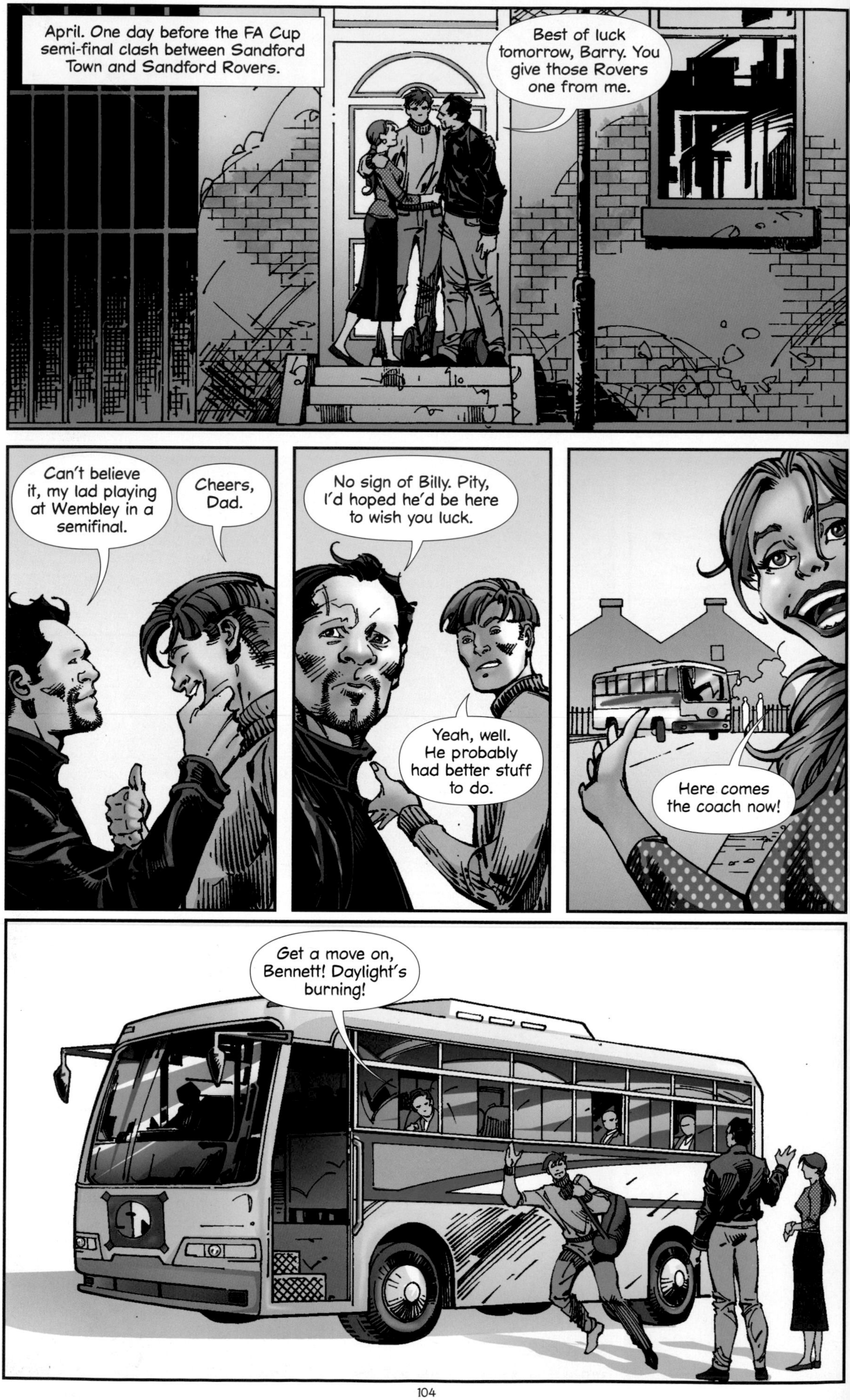
April. One day before the FA Cup semi-final clash between Sandford Town and Sandford Rovers.
Best of luck tomorrow, Barry. You give those Rovers one from me.
Can't believe it, my lad playing at Wembley in a semifinal.
Cheers, Dad.
No sign of Billy. Pity, I'd hoped he'd be here to wish you luck.
Yeah, well. He probably had better stuff to do.
Here comes the coach now!
Get a move on, Bennett! Daylight's burning!

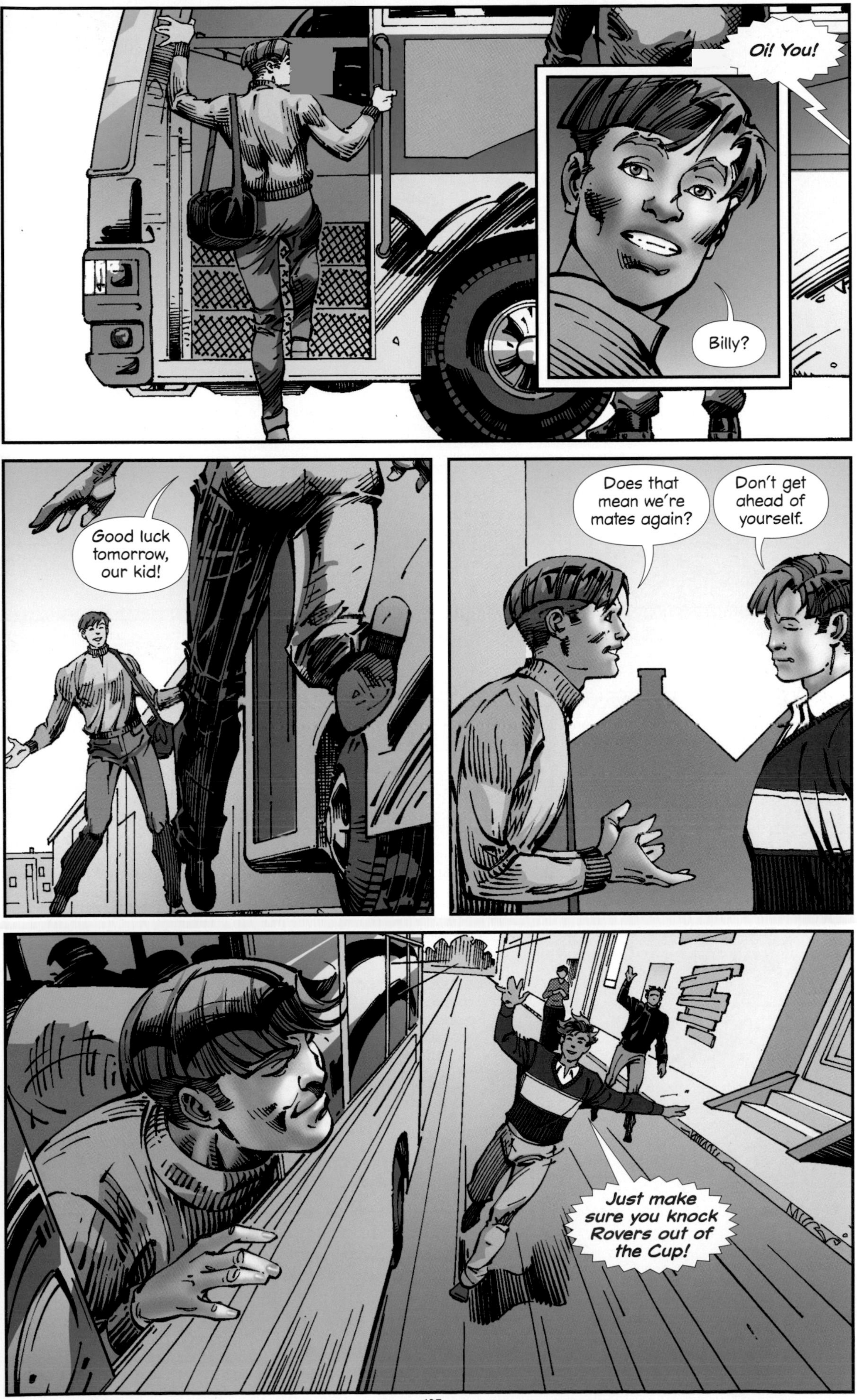
Oi! You!
Billy?
Good luck tomorrow, our kid!
Does that mean we're mates again?
Don't get ahead of yourself.
Just make sure you knock Rovers out of the Cup!

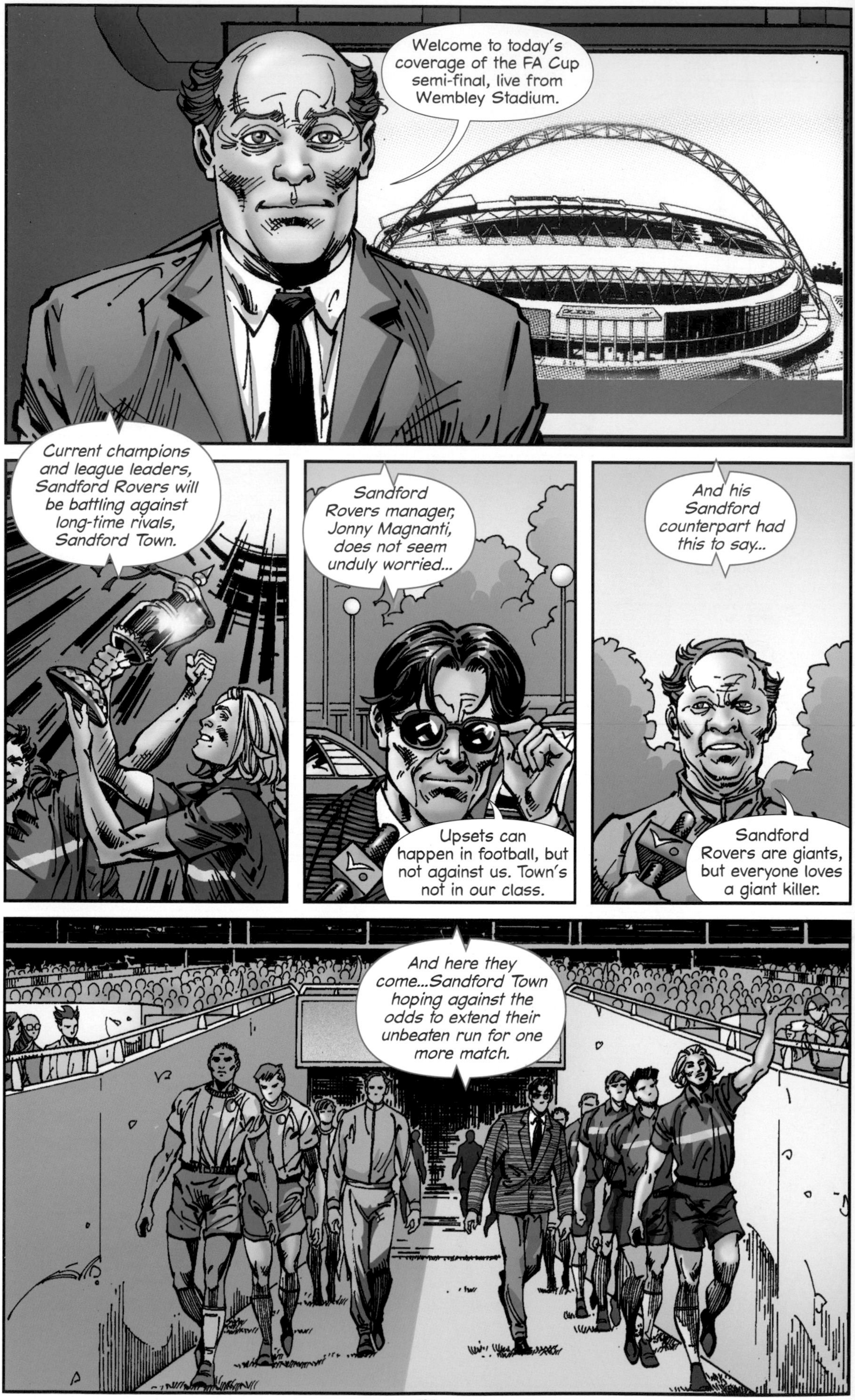
Welcome to today's coverage of the FA Cup semi-final, live from Wembley Stadium.
Current champions and league leaders, Sandford Rovers will be battling against long-time rivals, Sandford Town.
Sandford Rovers manager, Jonny Magnanti, does not seem unduly worried...
Upsets can happen in football, but not against us. Town's not in our class.
And his Sandford counterpart had this to say...
Sandford Rovers are giants, but everyone loves a giant killer.
And here they come...Sandford Town hoping against the odds to extend their unbeaten run for one more match.

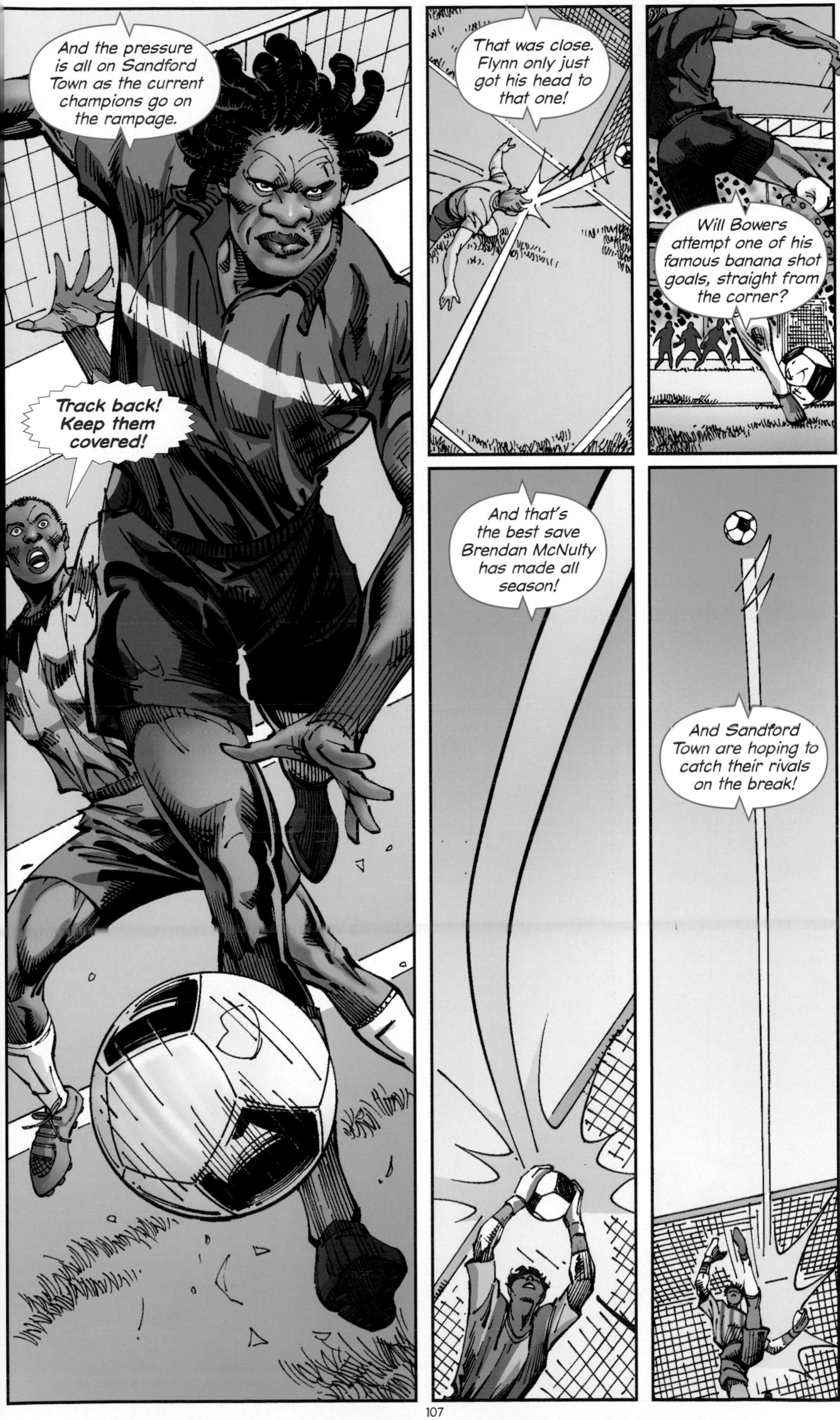
And the pressure is all on Sandford Town as the current champions go on the rampage.
Track back! Keep them covered!
That was close. Flynn only just got his head to that one!
Will Bowers attempt one of his famous banana shot goals, straight from the corner?
And that's the best save Brendan McNulty has made all season!
And Sandford Town are hoping to catch their rivals on the break!

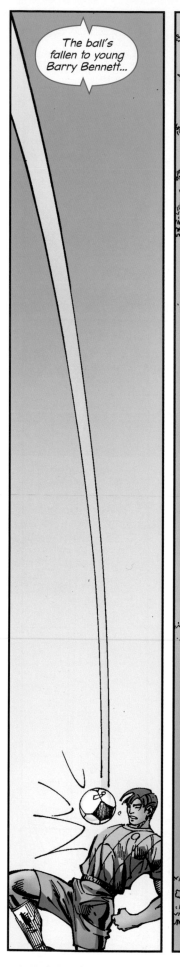

The ball's fallen to young Barry Bennett...

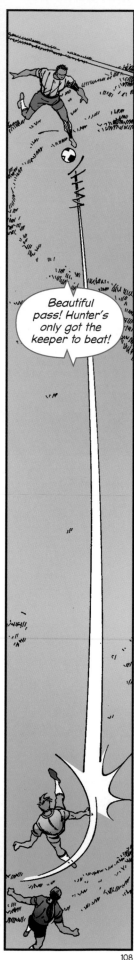

Beautiful pass! Hunter's only got the keeper to beat!

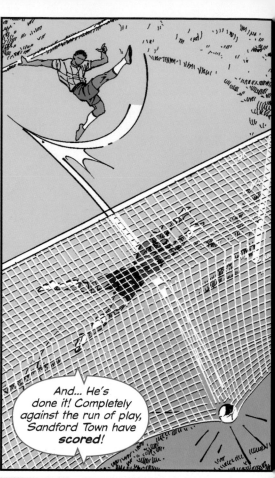

And... He's done it! Completely against the run of play, Sandford Town have **scored**!

Great ball, kid! Let's give them hell!

Wow! Steve Hunter actually behaving like a human being.

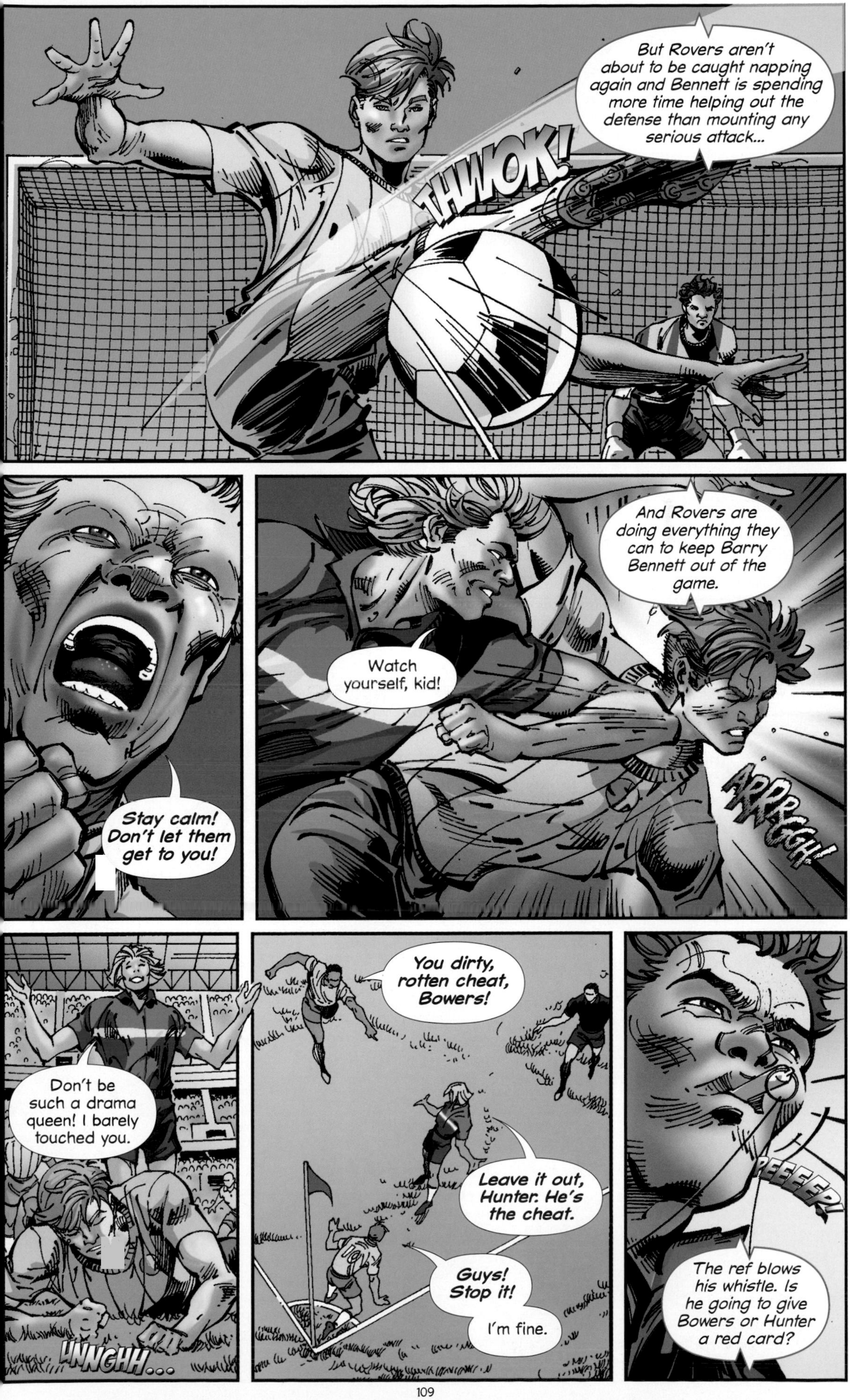
But Rovers aren't about to be caught napping again and Bennett is spending more time helping out the defense than mounting any serious attack...
THWOK!
Stay calm! Don't let them get to you!
And Rovers are doing everything they can to keep Barry Bennett out of the game.
Watch yourself, kid!
ARRRGH!
Don't be such a drama queen! I barely touched you.
UNNGHH...
You dirty, rotten cheat, Bowers!
Leave it out, Hunter. He's the cheat.
Guys! Stop it!
I'm fine.
PEEEEEP!
The ref blows his whistle. Is he going to give Bowers or Hunter a red card?

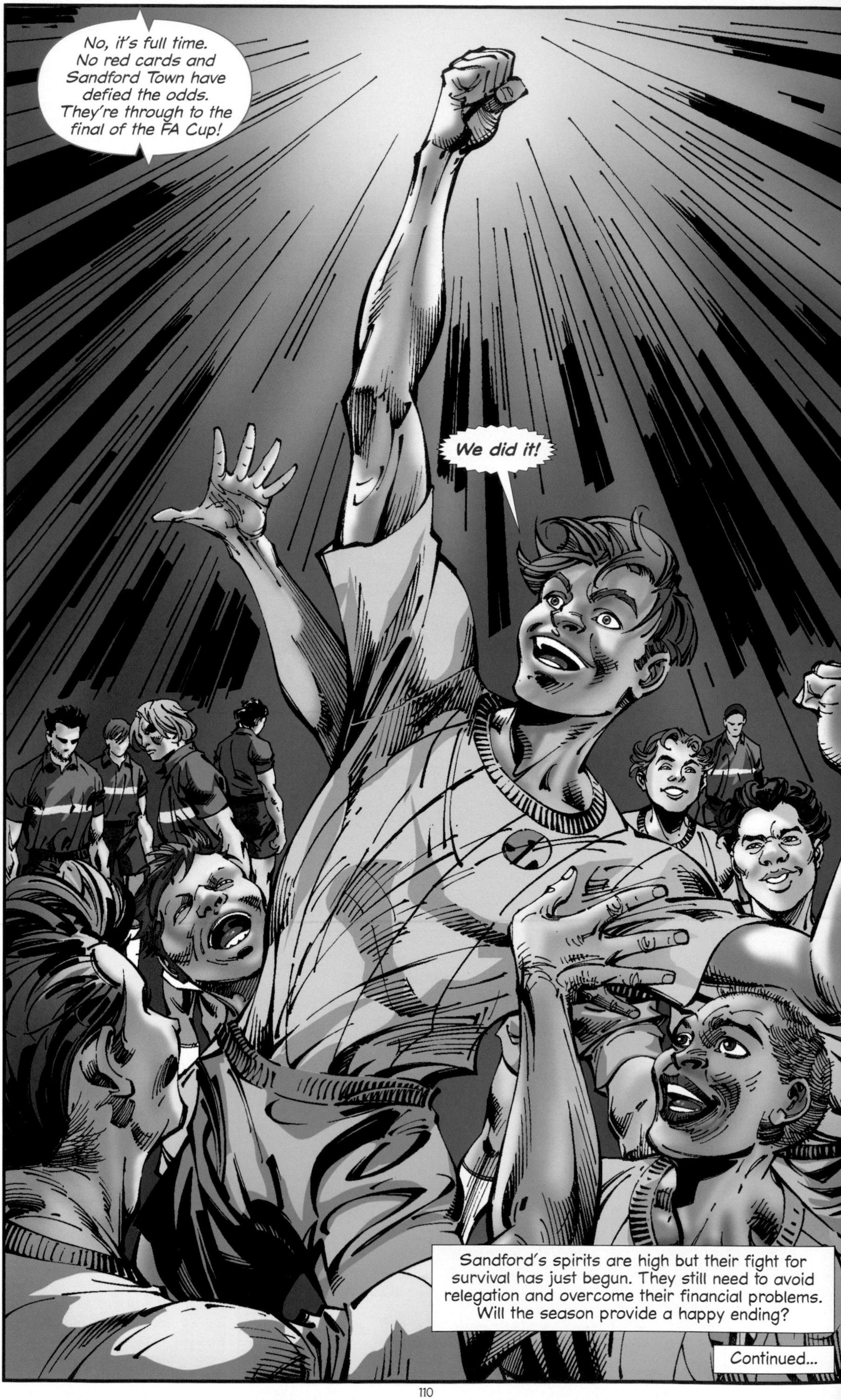
No, it's full time. No red cards and Sandford Town have defied the odds. They're through to the final of the FA Cup!
We did it!
Sandford's spirits are high but their fight for survival has just begun. They still need to avoid relegation and overcome their financial problems. Will the season provide a happy ending?
Continued...

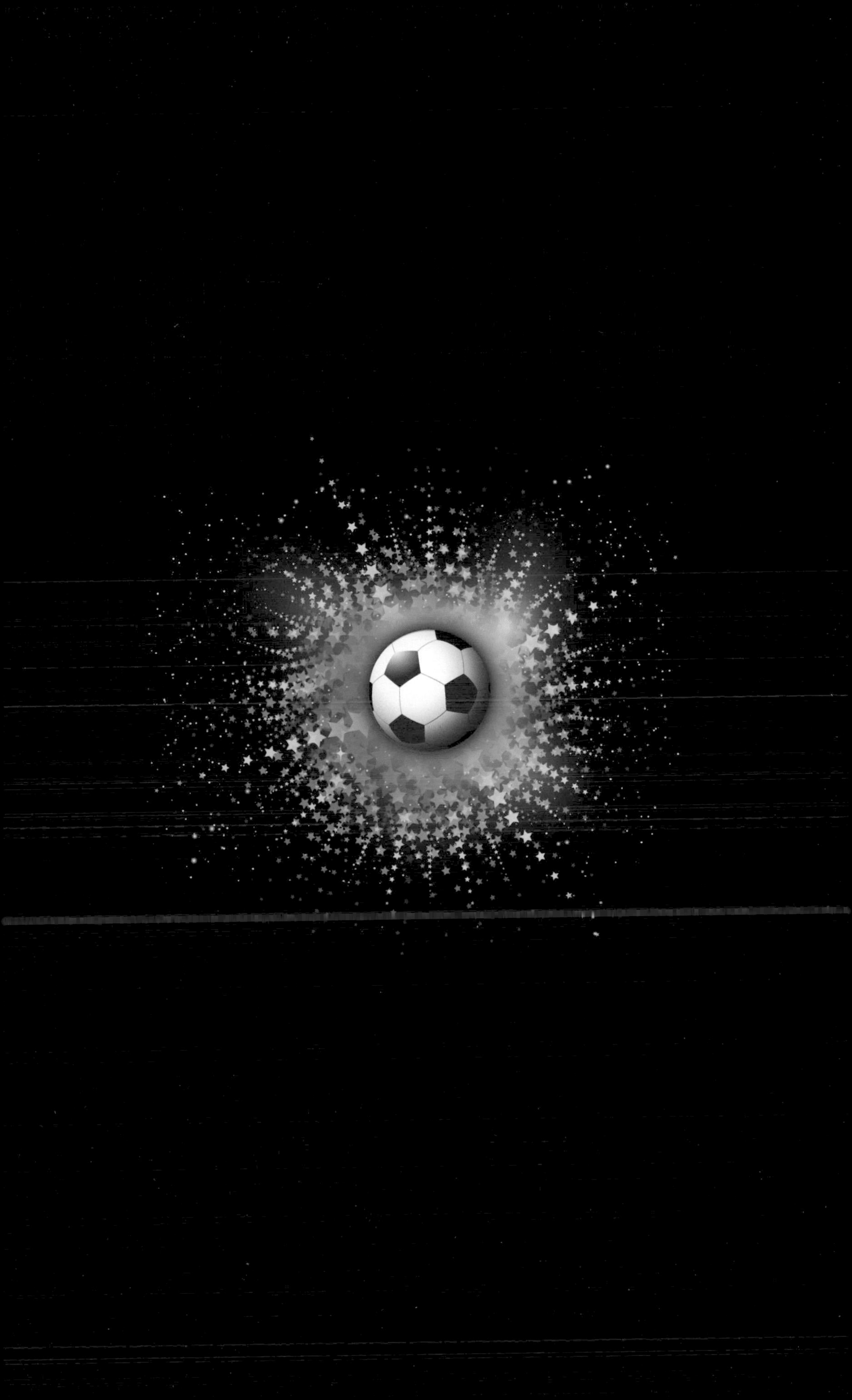

SANDFORD EVENING POST

TOWN FC FOR FA FINALS

That clinching feeling. *See you on Saturday, boys!*

SANDFORD TOWN-1
SANDFORD ROVERS-0

Sandford Town fans have something to cheer about in a season that has otherwise been dismal for them as they head into the FA Cup finals by beating arch-rivals Sandford Rovers. They will now meet Halton Moor in Wembley on Saturday. Clearly, pulling former Sandford Town legend Bob Evans out of retirement to manage the squad has proved to be the right decision.

But Town FC's biggest problems are far from over. The club is still fighting in the league to stay in the top-flight and avoid relegation. On top of that, unless they can manage to gather some real cash real soon, the club may not even exist anymore.

With some fresh blood in the side, and under Evans's steady hand, we can expect more success with Sandford Town. For the time being, the big match is on Saturday.

GUY TALK NEW ALBUM SOON?

Boy band Guy Talk has toured the country recently and is currently performing a series of concerts at their hometown. Their concerts have featured a couple of new songs, such as 'Gimme over' and 'Love undone'. Fans love the two songs and we believe they will be part of their new album that is expected any time now.

Chapter 4 SURVIVAL

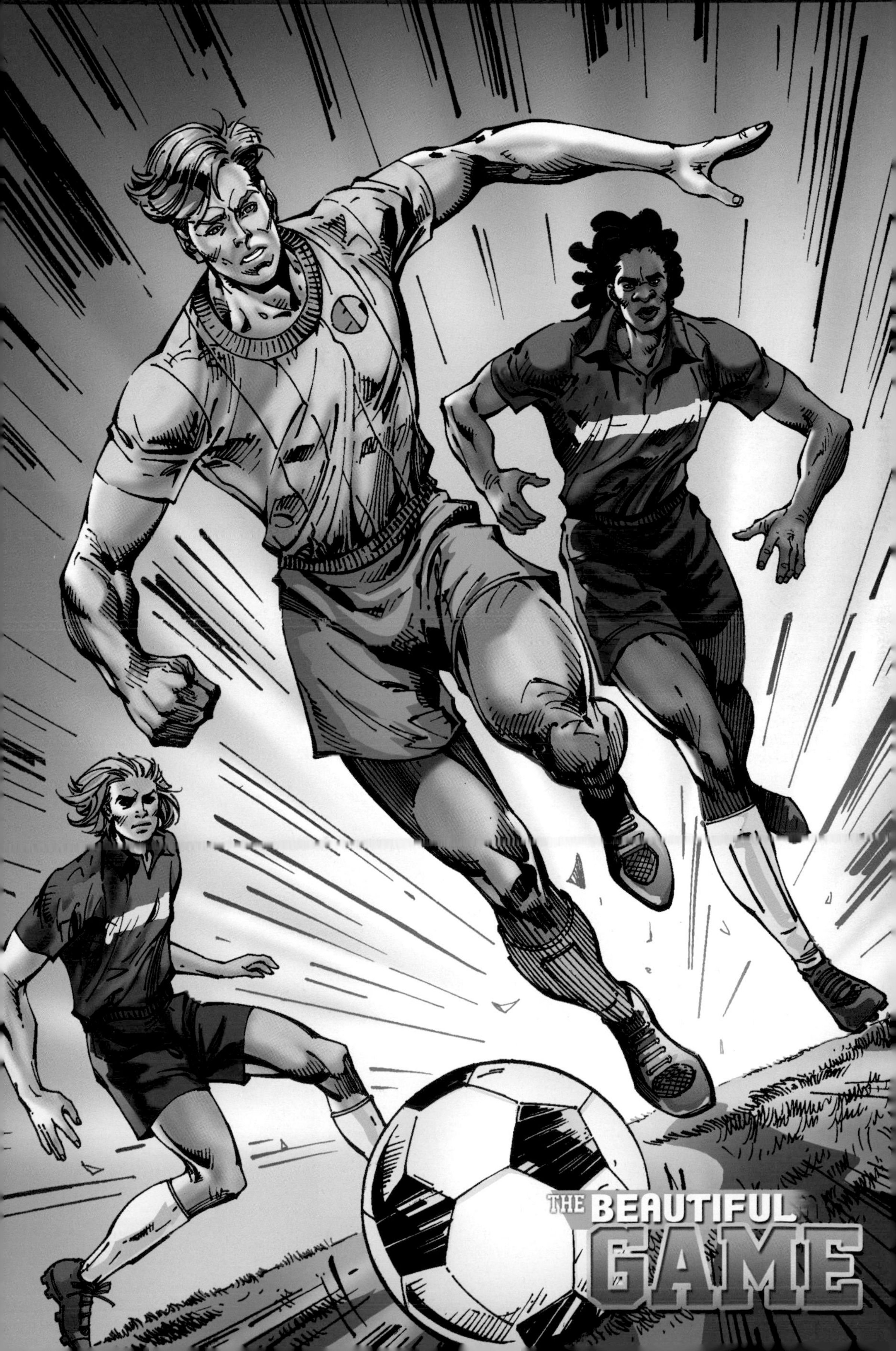
THE BEAUTIFUL
GAME

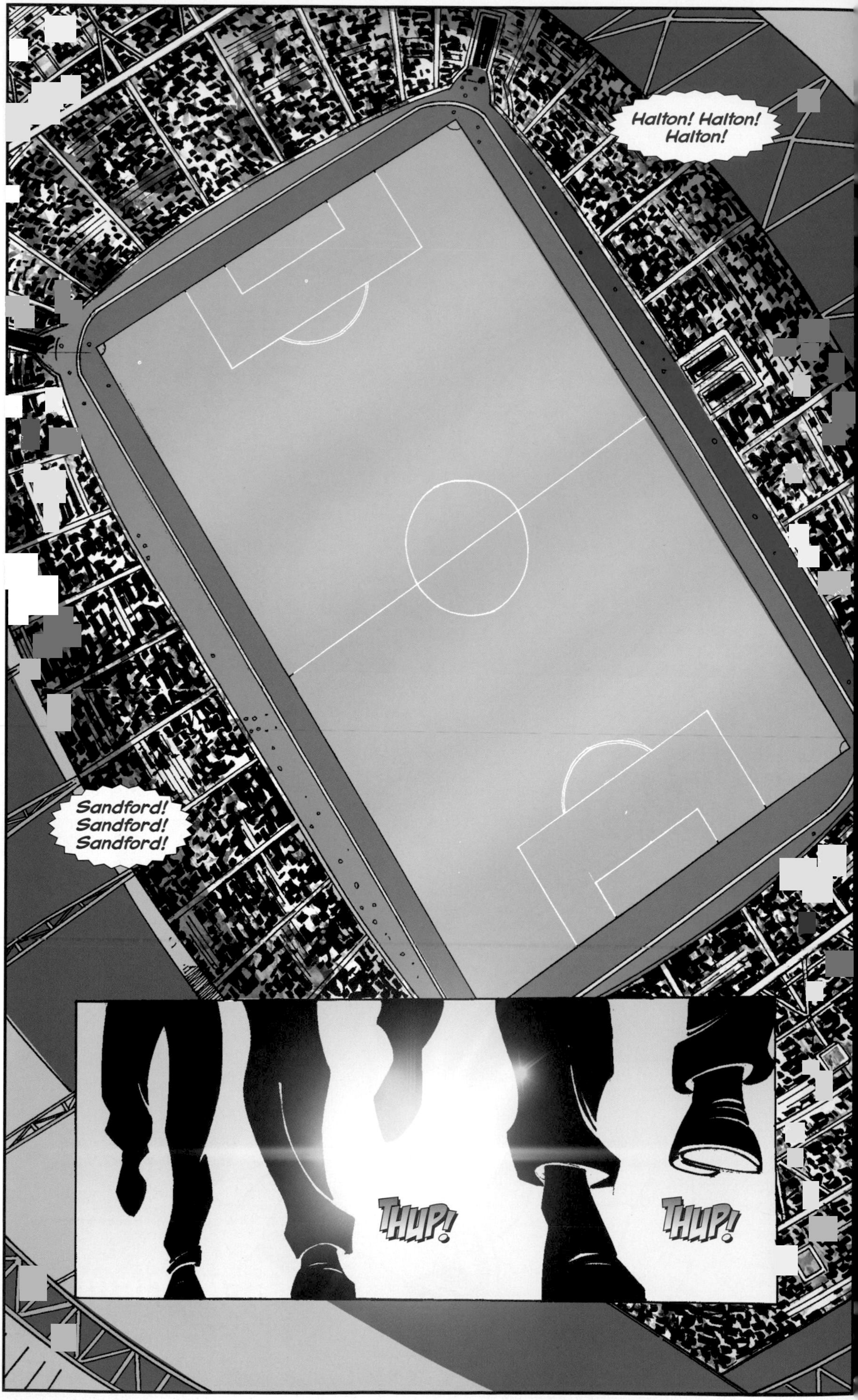
Halton! Halton! Halton!
Sandford! Sandford! Sandford!
THUP!
THUP!

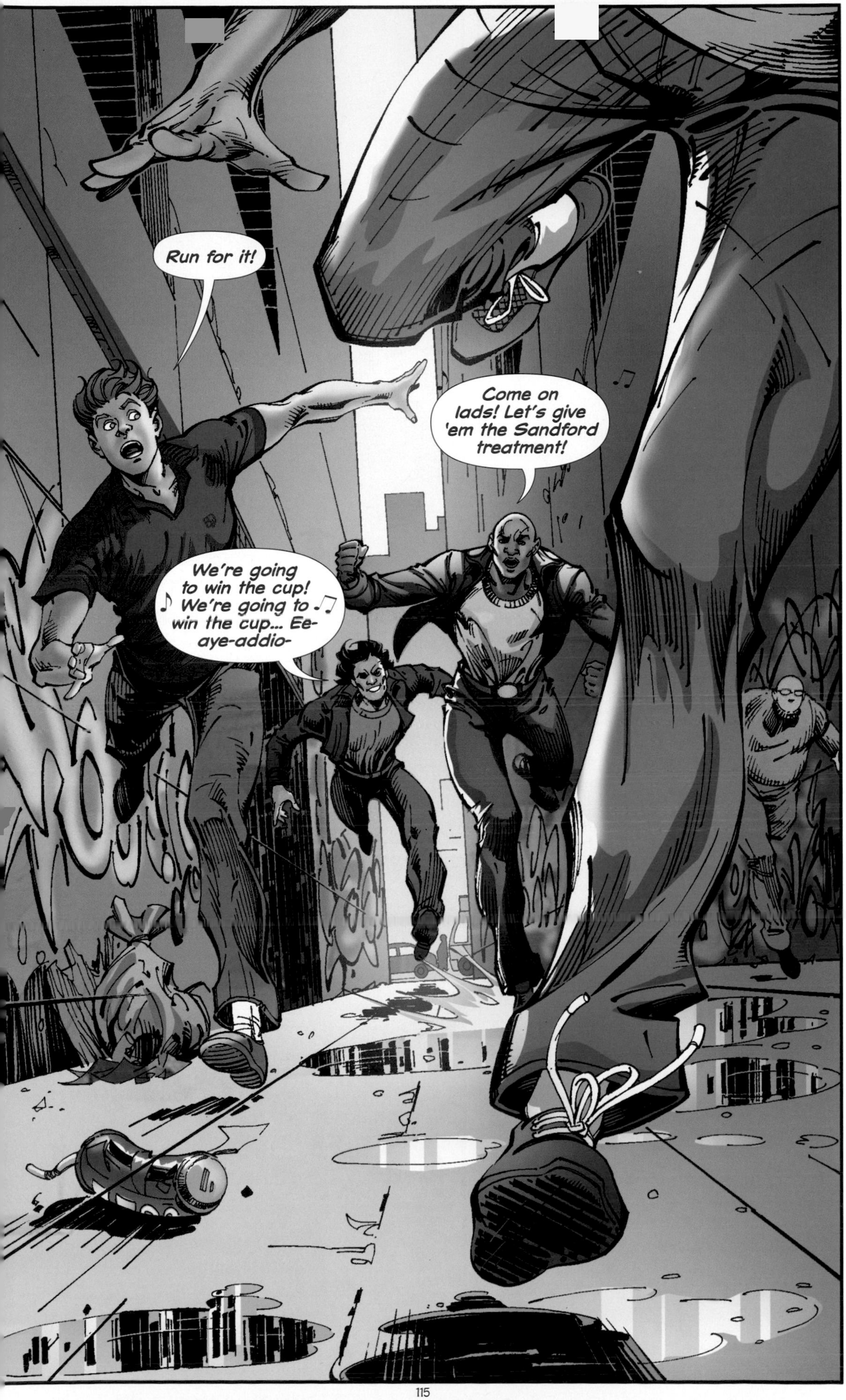
Run for it!
Come on lads! Let's give 'em the Sandford treatment!
We're going to win the cup! ♪ We're going to win the cup... Ee-aye-addio-

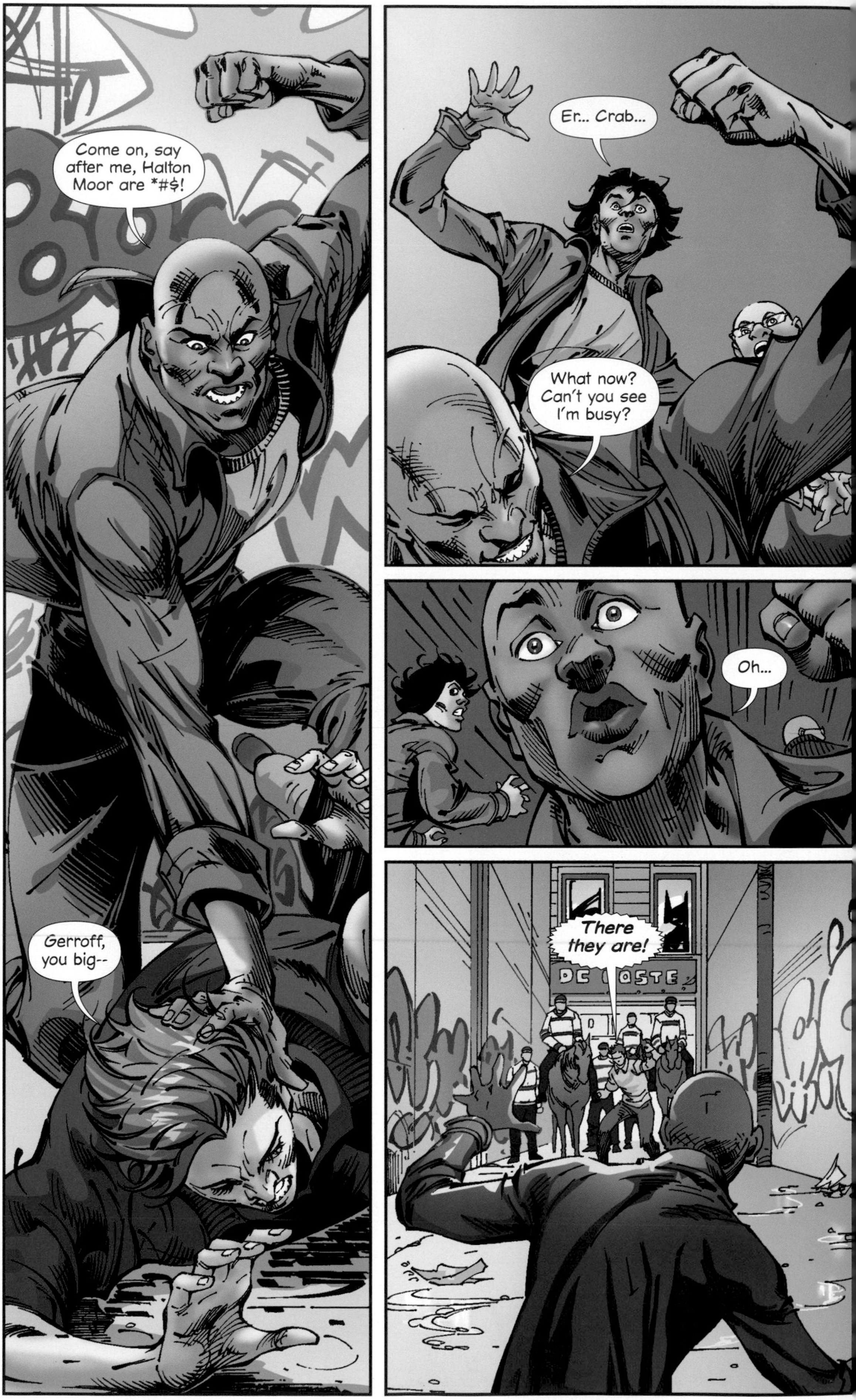
Come on, say after me, Halton Moor are *#$!
Gerroff, you big--
Er... Crab...
What now? Can't you see I'm busy?
Oh...
There they are!
DC OSTE

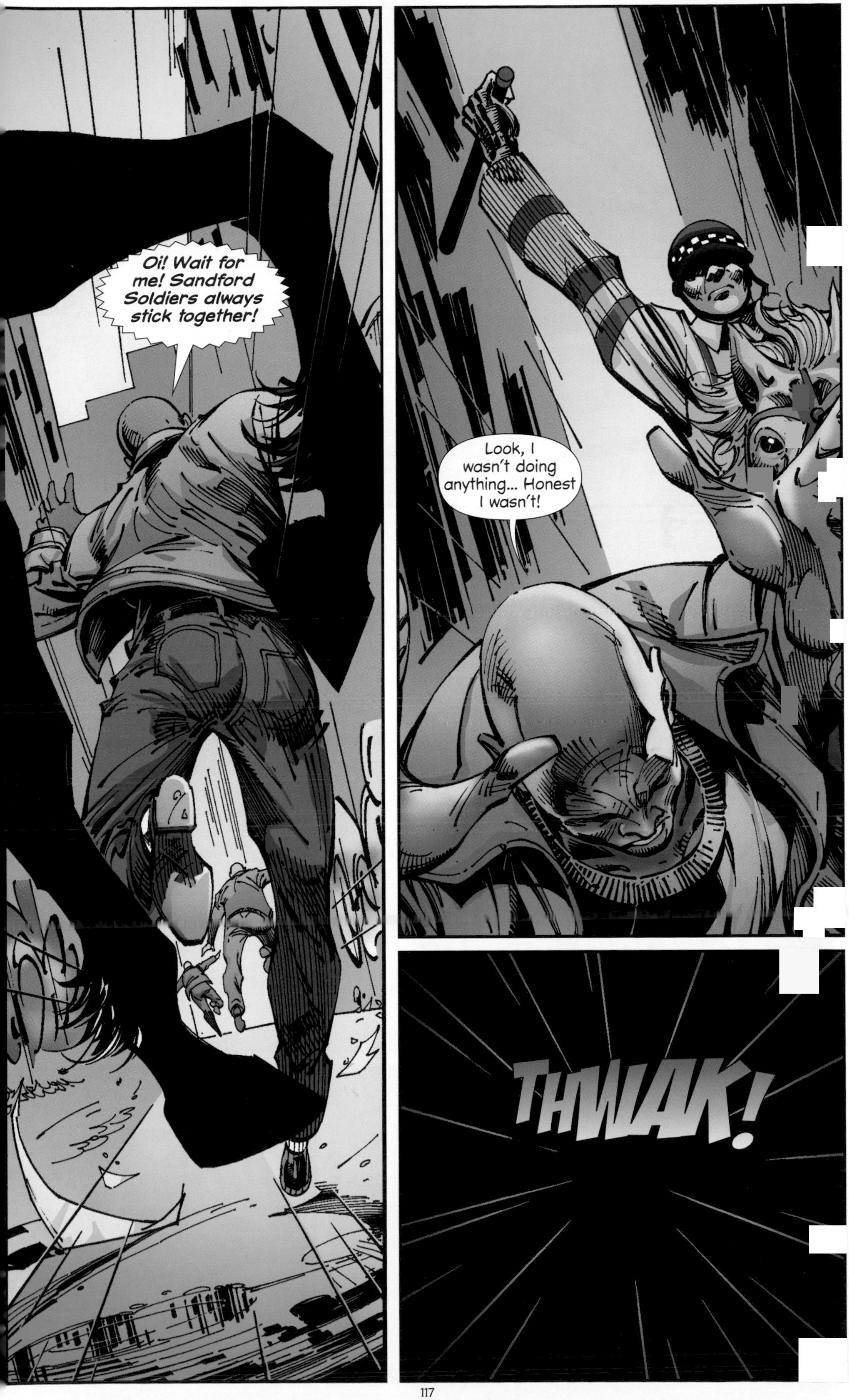
Oi! Wait for me! Sandford Soldiers always stick together!
Look, I wasn't doing anything... Honest I wasn't!
THWAK!

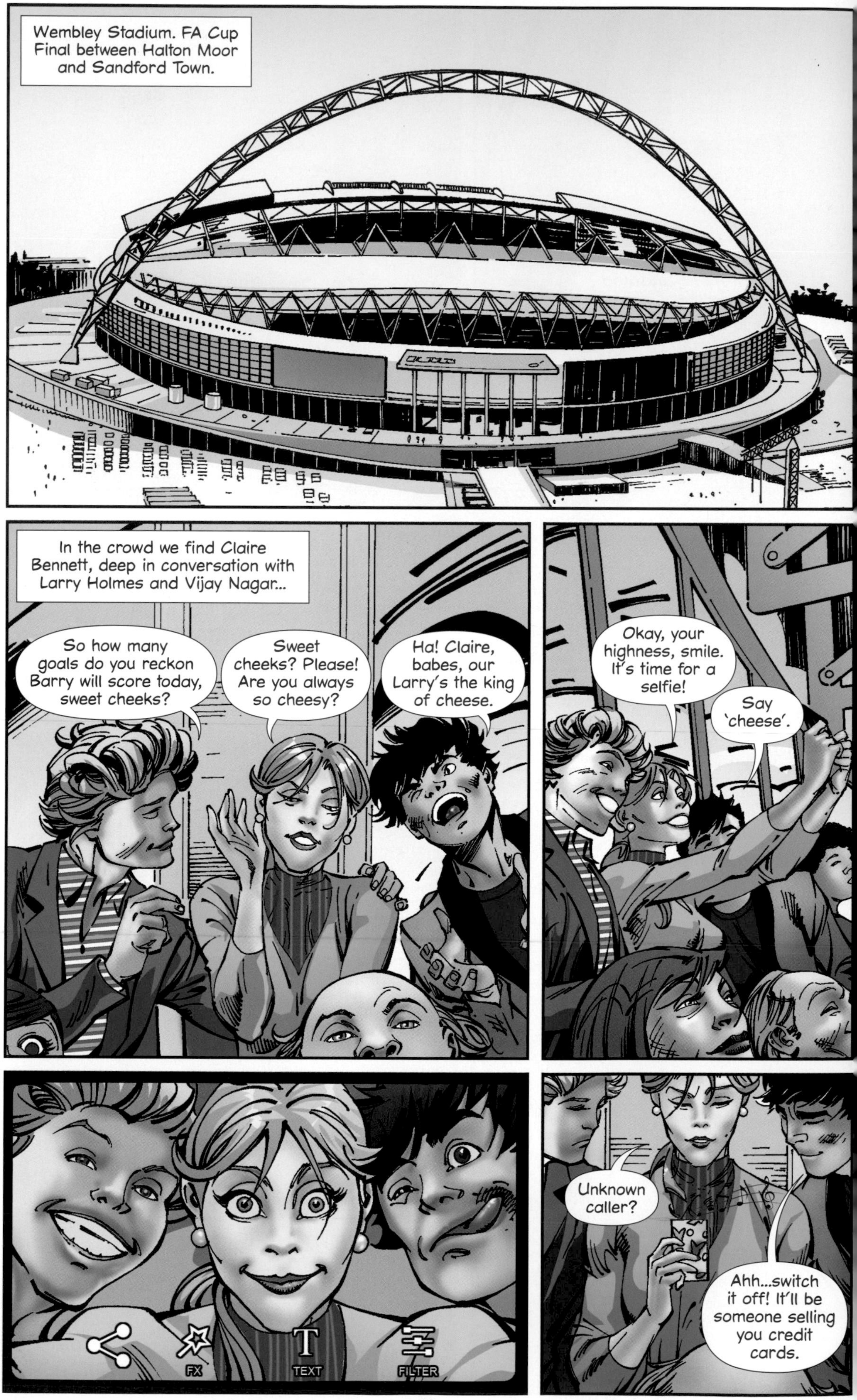

Wembley Stadium. FA Cup Final between Halton Moor and Sandford Town.
In the crowd we find Claire Bennett, deep in conversation with Larry Holmes and Vijay Nagar...
So how many goals do you reckon Barry will score today, sweet cheeks?
Sweet cheeks? Please! Are you always so cheesy?
Ha! Claire, babes, our Larry's the king of cheese.
Okay, your highness, smile. It's time for a selfie!
Say 'cheese'.
FX
TEXT
FILTER
Unknown caller?
Ahh...switch it off! It'll be someone selling you credit cards.

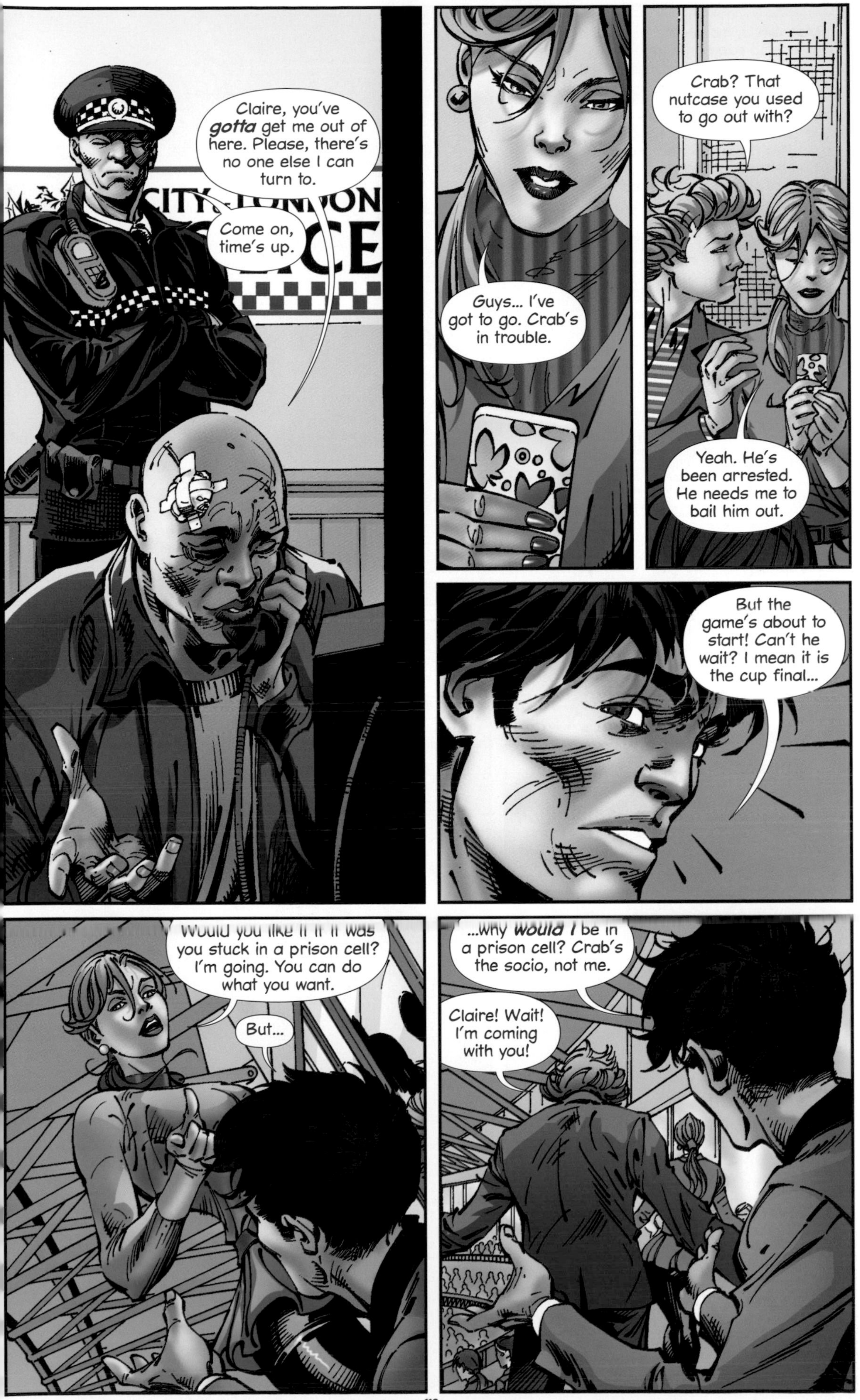

Claire, you've *gotta* get me out of here. Please, there's no one else I can turn to.
CITY LONDON
Come on, time's up.
Guys... I've got to go. Crab's in trouble.
Crab? That nutcase you used to go out with?
Yeah. He's been arrested. He needs me to bail him out.
But the game's about to start! Can't he wait? I mean it is the cup final...
Would you like it if it was you stuck in a prison cell? I'm going. You can do what you want.
But...
...why *would I* be in a prison cell? Crab's the socio, not me.
Claire! Wait! I'm coming with you!

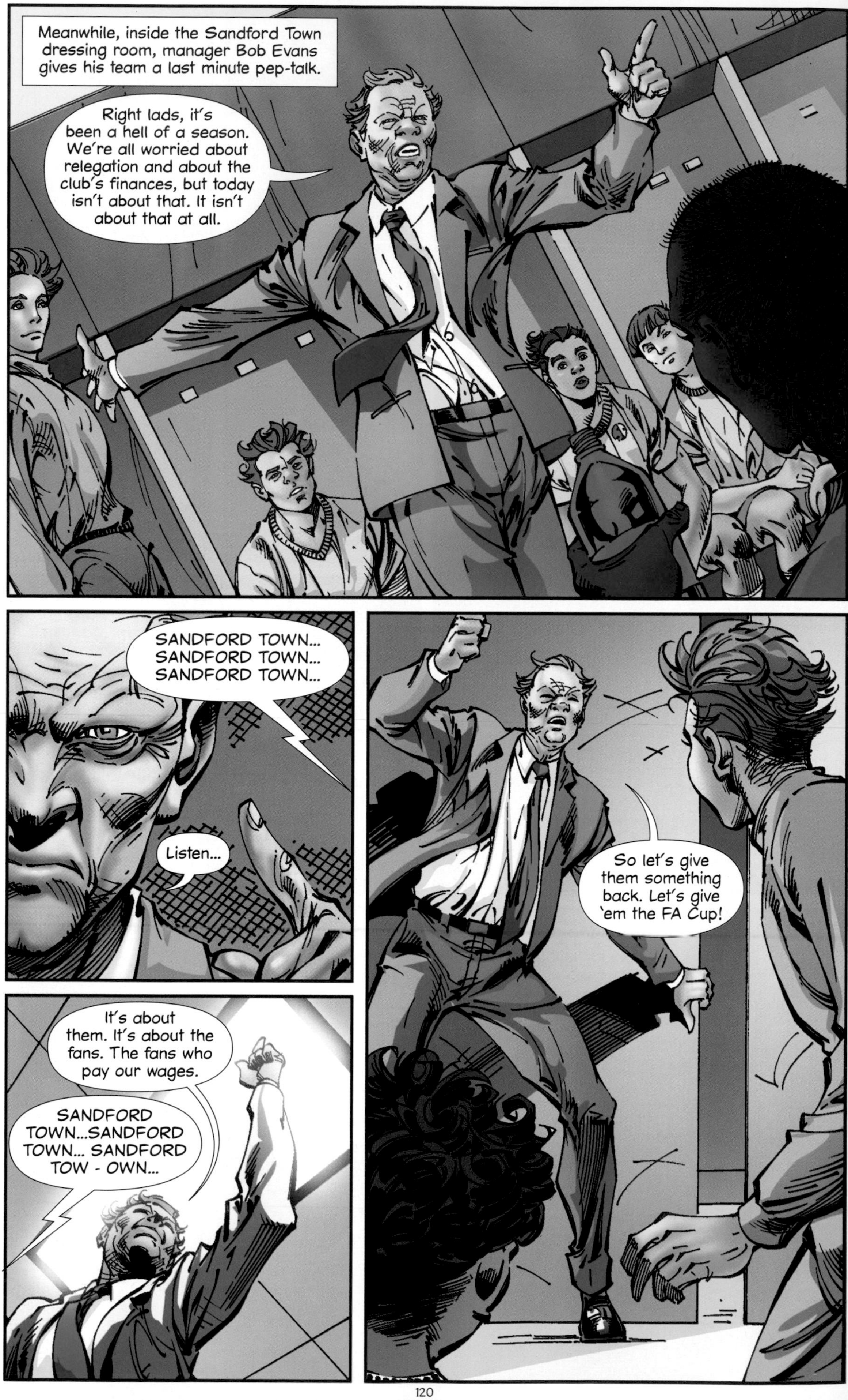
Meanwhile, inside the Sandford Town dressing room, manager Bob Evans gives his team a last minute pep-talk.
Right lads, it's been a hell of a season. We're all worried about relegation and about the club's finances, but today isn't about that. It isn't about that at all.
SANDFORD TOWN... SANDFORD TOWN... SANDFORD TOWN...
Listen...
It's about them. It's about the fans. The fans who pay our wages.
SANDFORD TOWN...SANDFORD TOWN... SANDFORD TOW - OWN...
So let's give them something back. Let's give 'em the FA Cup!

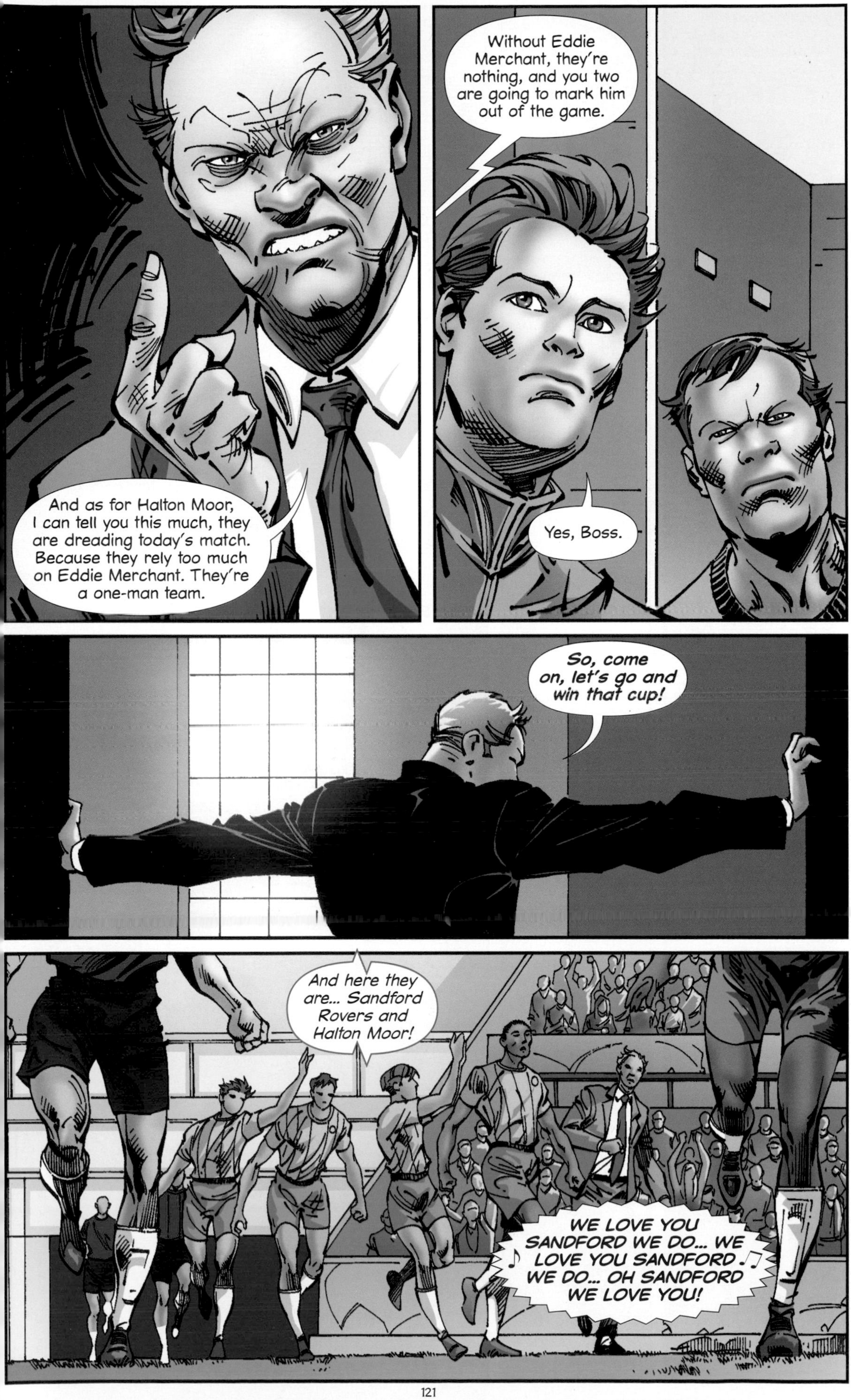
And as for Halton Moor, I can tell you this much, they are dreading today's match. Because they rely too much on Eddie Merchant. They're a one-man team.
Without Eddie Merchant, they're nothing, and you two are going to mark him out of the game.
Yes, Boss.
So, come on, let's go and win that cup!
And here they are... Sandford Rovers and Halton Moor!
WE LOVE YOU SANDFORD WE DO... WE LOVE YOU SANDFORD WE DO... OH SANDFORD WE LOVE YOU!

And both sides seem to be sizing each other up in the opening minutes...

And Sandford seem content to just keep the ball away from Halton Moor.

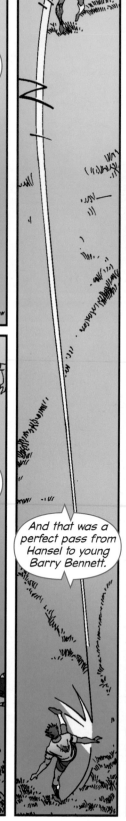

And that was a perfect pass from Hansel to young Barry Bennett.

And Hunter's through on goal...

...and that has **got to** be a penalty.

And there's a history of bad blood between Steve Hunter and Juan Perez...

Take it easy, Steve. Don't get yourself sent off, mate.

Alright, alright! I know.

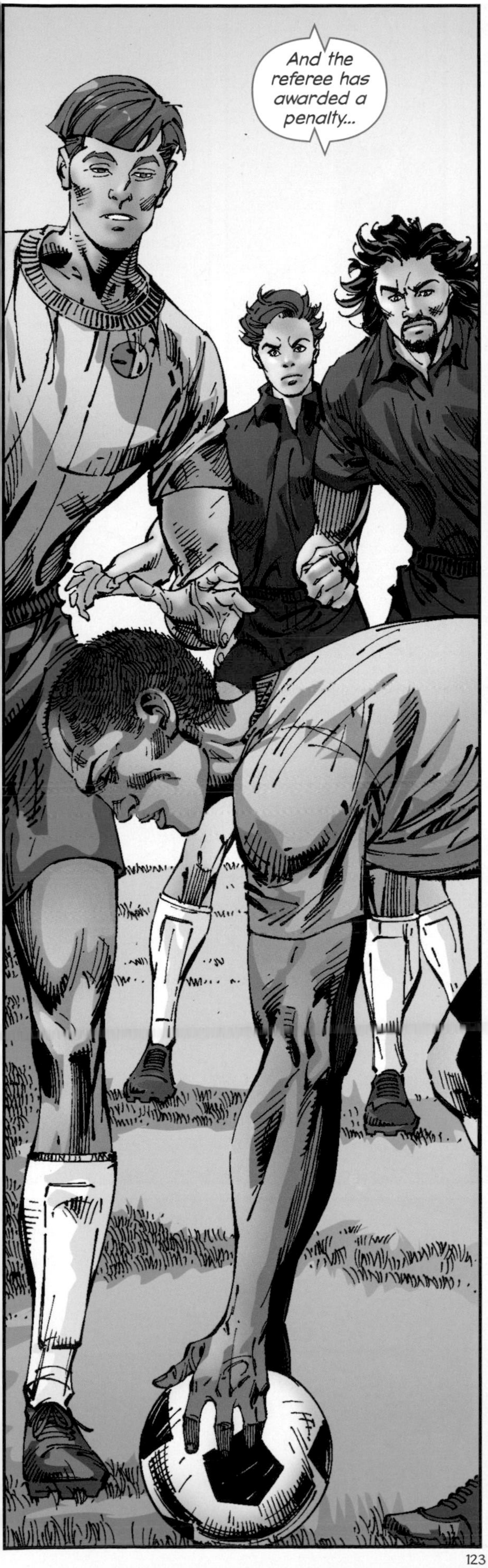
And the referee has awarded a penalty...

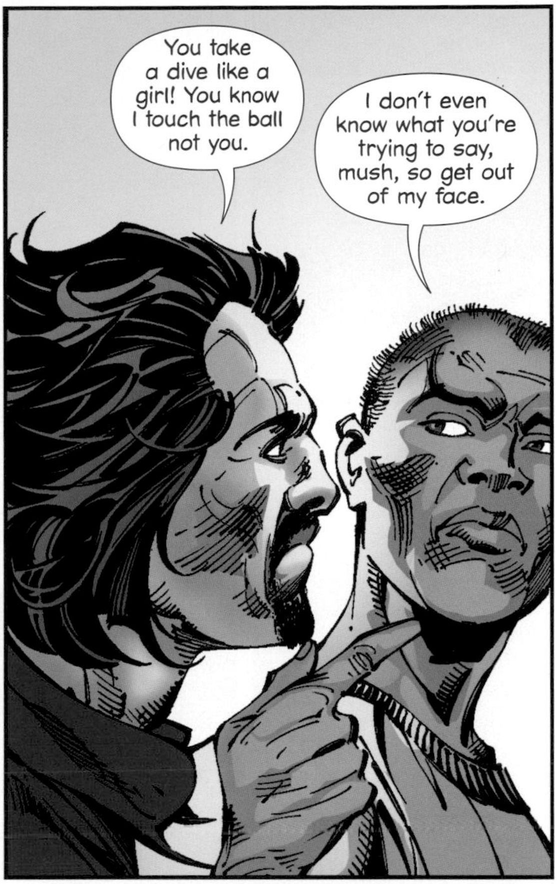
You take a dive like a girl! You know I touch the ball not you.
I don't even know what you're trying to say, mush, so get out of my face.

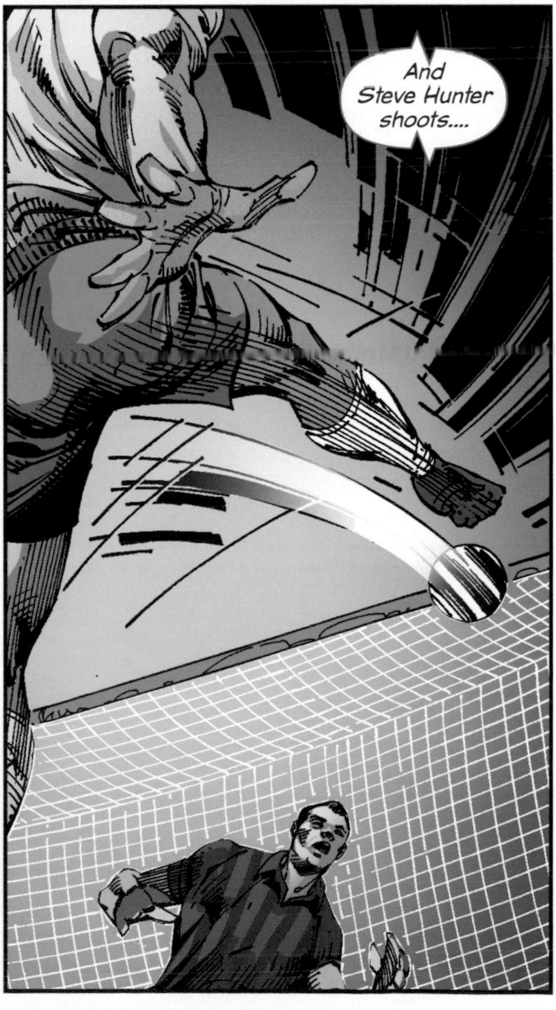
And Steve Hunter shoots....

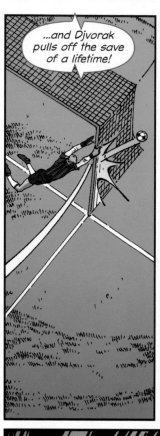

...and Djvorak pulls off the save of a lifetime!

It's Cordoso to take the corner kick...

...and Djvorak makes it look so easy.

...Halton Moor have caught the Sandford defense on the back pedal.

Eddie Merchant shoots!

And McNulty doesn't stand a chance!

Halton Moor 1 Sandford Town 0

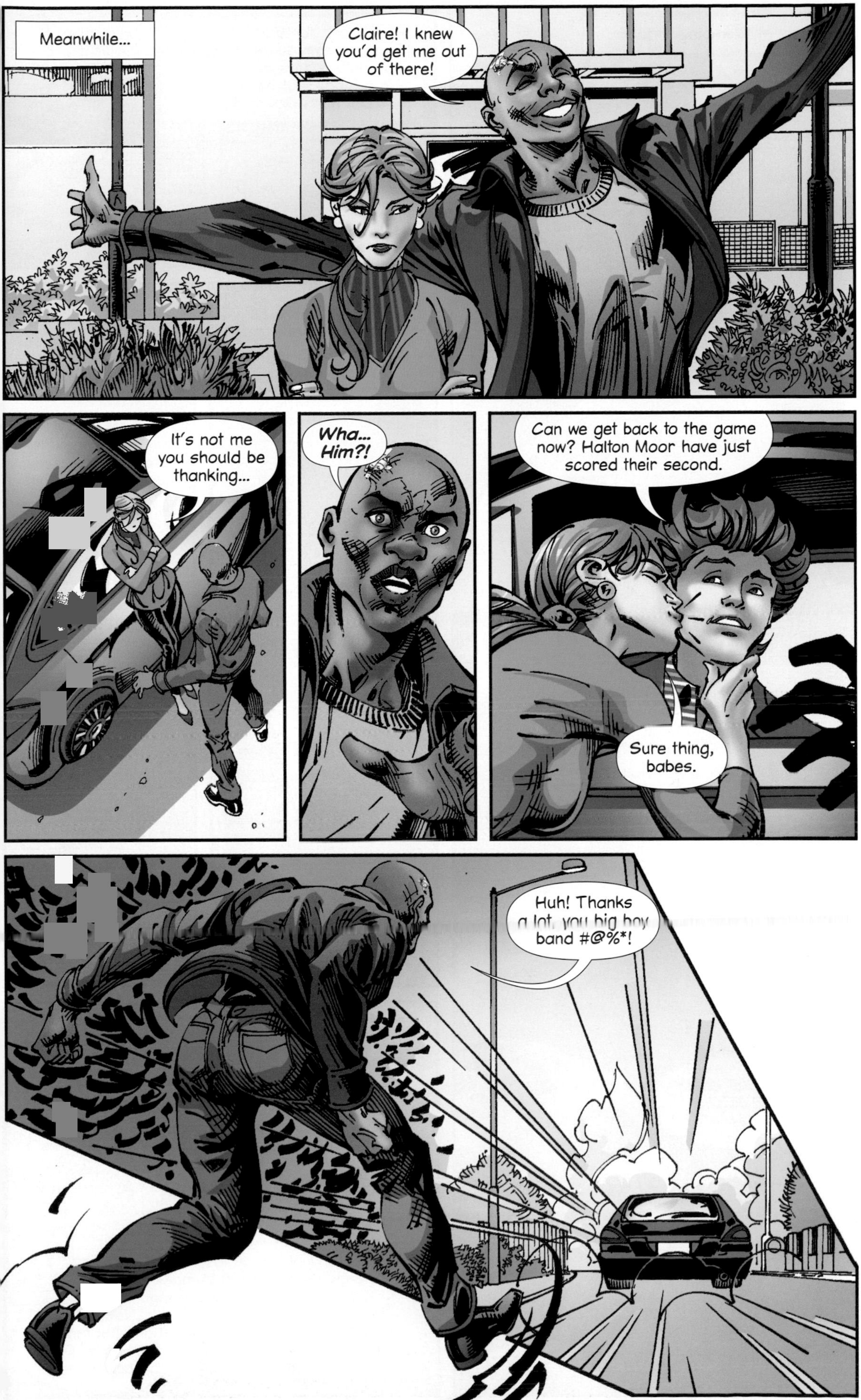
Meanwhile...
Claire! I knew you'd get me out of there!
It's not me you should be thanking...
Wha... Him?!
Can we get back to the game now? Halton Moor have just scored their second.
Sure thing, babes.
Huh! Thanks a lot, you big boy band #@%*!

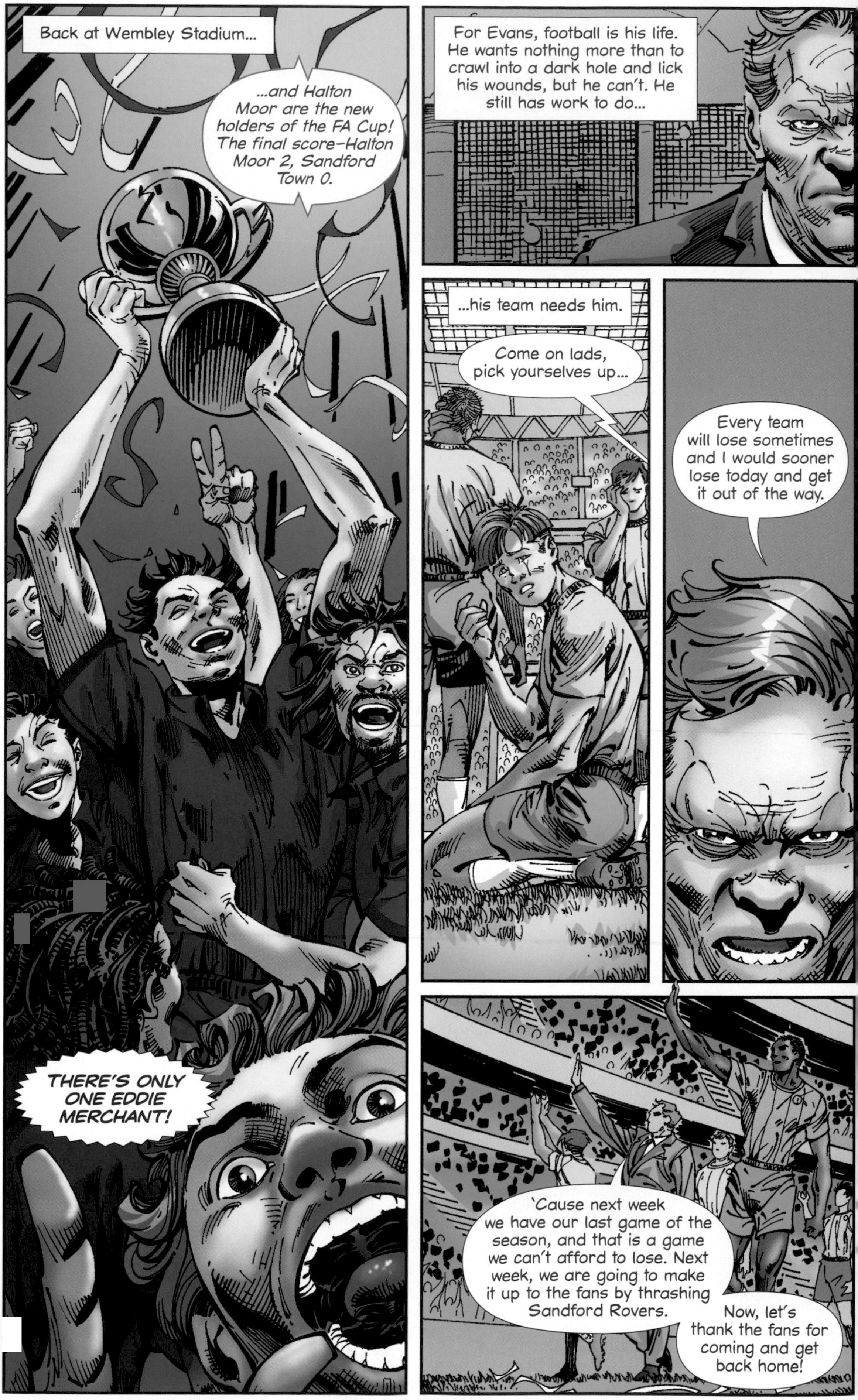
Back at Wembley Stadium...
...and Halton Moor are the new holders of the FA Cup! The final score–Halton Moor 2, Sandford Town 0.
THERE'S ONLY ONE EDDIE MERCHANT!
For Evans, football is his life. He wants nothing more than to crawl into a dark hole and lick his wounds, but he can't. He still has work to do...
...his team needs him.
Come on lads, pick yourselves up...
Every team will lose sometimes and I would sooner lose today and get it out of the way.
'Cause next week we have our last game of the season, and that is a game we can't afford to lose. Next week, we are going to make it up to the fans by thrashing Sandford Rovers.
Now, let's thank the fans for coming and get back home!

Well, Halton Moor have won the cup and Sandford Town look devastated, but they'll have to pull themselves together for next week's final game of the season against arch-rivals, Sandford Rovers.

Top Spots

	P	W	D	L	Points
Sandford Rovers	37	22	11	4	77
Halton Moor	37	22	10	5	76
Knightsbridge	37	19	12	6	69

A look at the top and bottom of the table will show you just how crucial this match is. A win for Rovers will clinch the title for them, and send Sandford Town crashing out of the top-flight.

Danger Zone

	P	W	D	L	Points
Hammersmith	37	9	13	15	40
Relegation Zone...					
Sandford Town	37	9	13	15	40
Gravesend Rangers	37	7	11	19	32
Moorfield Vale	37	6	12	19	30

At the Mermaid Tavern, where Billy has been watching the match.

We haven't got a hope in hell.

'Course we have. Today was just a hiccup. We'll smash Rovers, no probs.

If we win our last game against Rovers, and Hammersmith lose or draw, we're safe. If Hammersmith win, then we have to win by at least six goals. Easy peasey lemon squeezey!

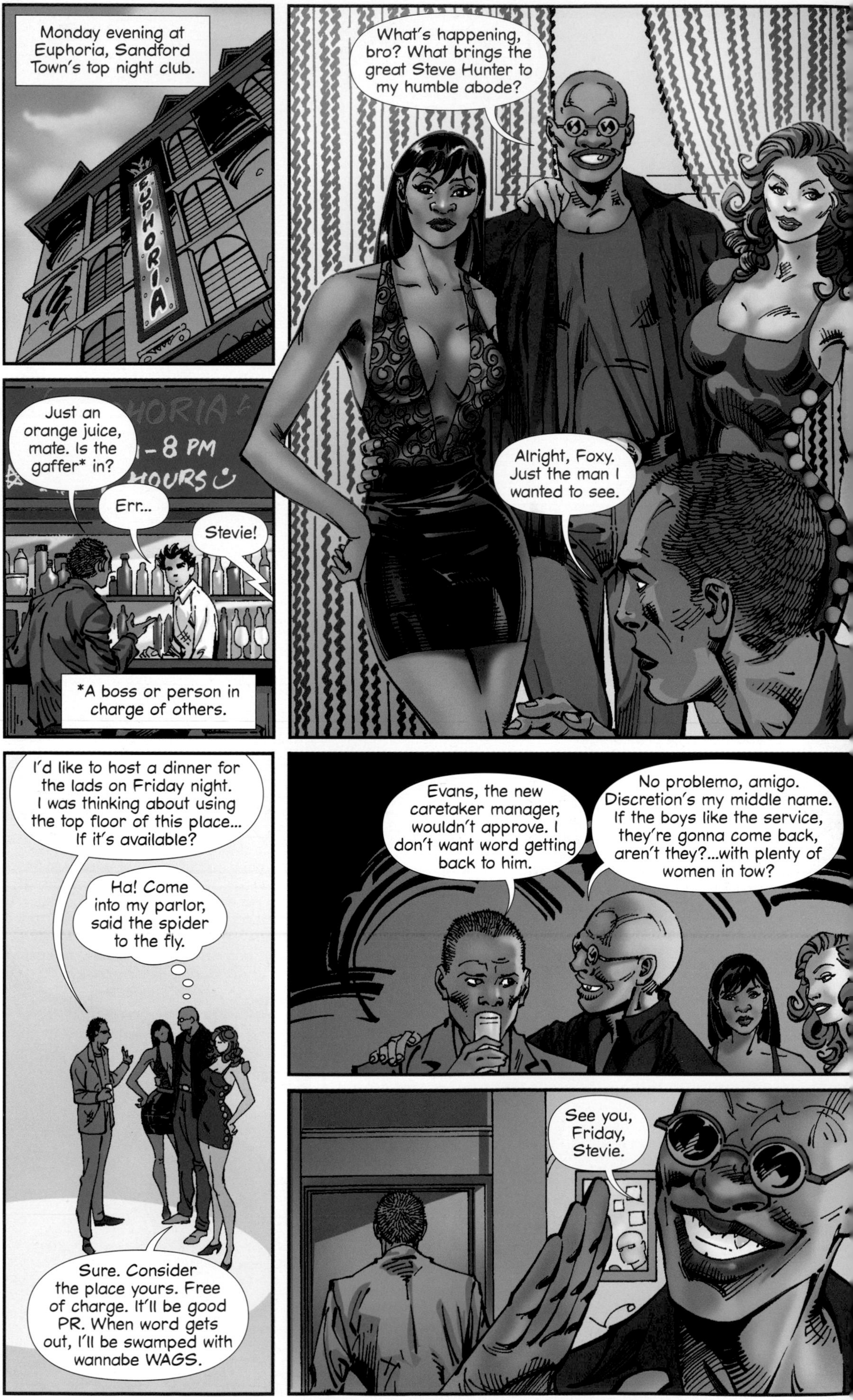
Monday evening at Euphoria, Sandford Town's top night club.
EUPHORIA
What's happening, bro? What brings the great Steve Hunter to my humble abode?
Just an orange juice, mate. Is the gaffer* in?
Err...
Stevie!
*A boss or person in charge of others.
Alright, Foxy. Just the man I wanted to see.
I'd like to host a dinner for the lads on Friday night. I was thinking about using the top floor of this place... If it's available?
Ha! Come into my parlor, said the spider to the fly.
Sure. Consider the place yours. Free of charge. It'll be good PR. When word gets out, I'll be swamped with wannabe WAGS.
Evans, the new caretaker manager, wouldn't approve. I don't want word getting back to him.
No problemo, amigo. Discretion's my middle name. If the boys like the service, they're gonna come back, aren't they?...with plenty of women in tow?
See you, Friday, Stevie.

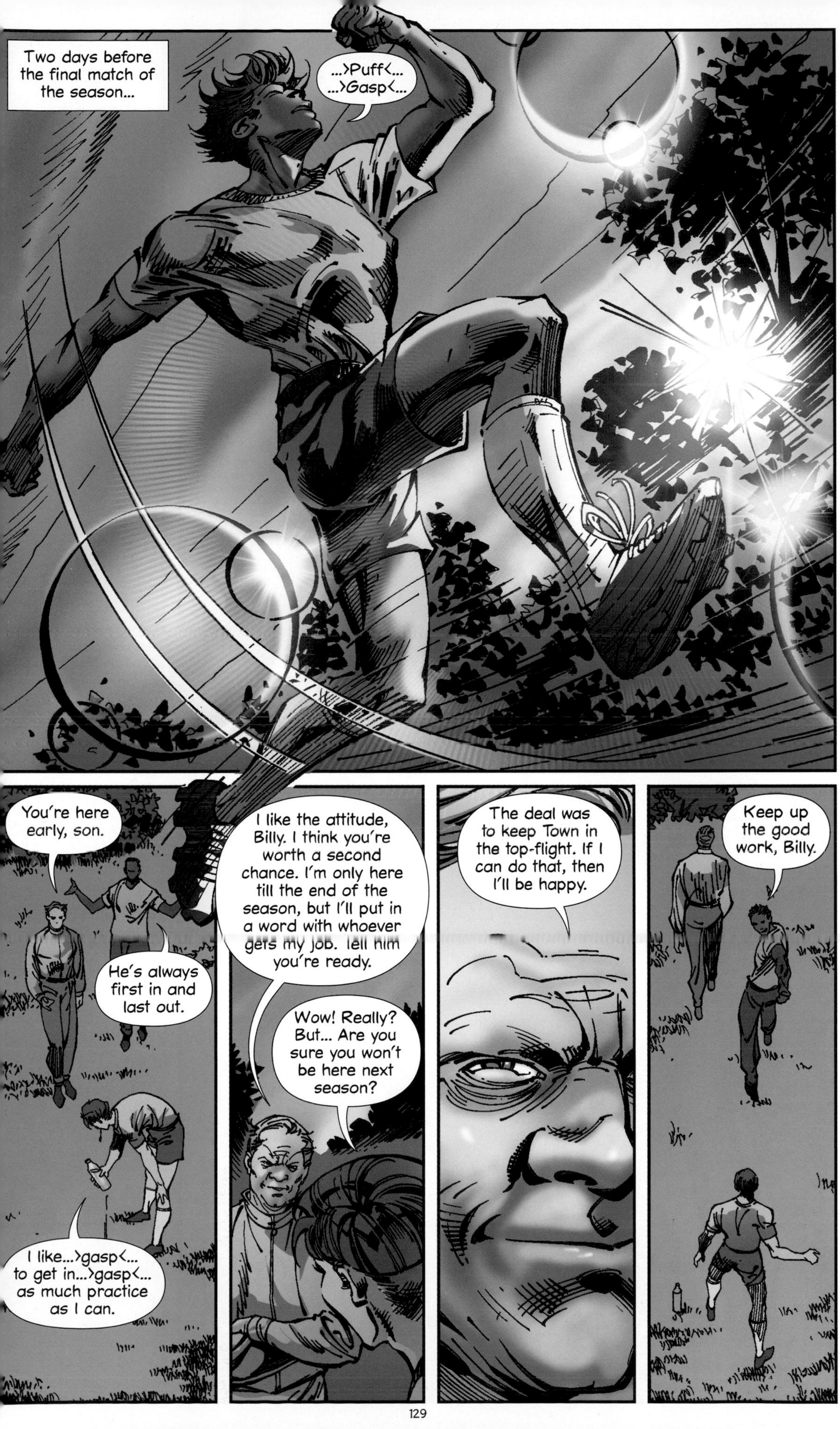
Two days before the final match of the season...
...>Puff<... ...>Gasp<...
You're here early, son.
He's always first in and last out.
I like...>gasp<... to get in...>gasp<... as much practice as I can.
I like the attitude, Billy. I think you're worth a second chance. I'm only here till the end of the season, but I'll put in a word with whoever gets my job. Tell him you're ready.
Wow! Really? But... Are you sure you won't be here next season?
The deal was to keep Town in the top-flight. If I can do that, then I'll be happy.
Keep up the good work, Billy.

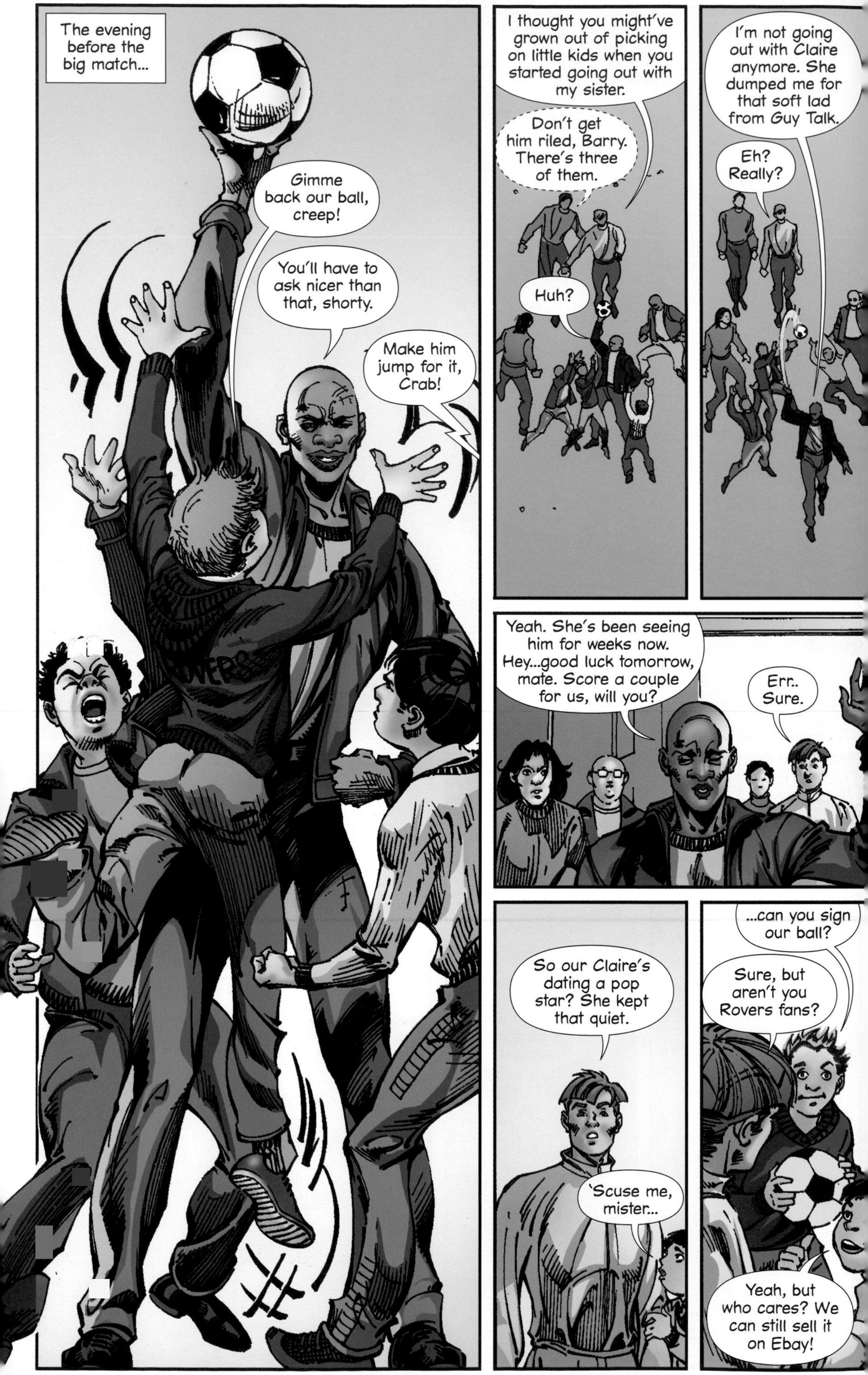

The evening before the big match...
Gimme back our ball, creep!
You'll have to ask nicer than that, shorty.
Make him jump for it, Crab!
I thought you might've grown out of picking on little kids when you started going out with my sister.
Don't get him riled, Barry. There's three of them.
Huh?
I'm not going out with Claire anymore. She dumped me for that soft lad from Guy Talk.
Eh? Really?
Yeah. She's been seeing him for weeks now. Hey...good luck tomorrow, mate. Score a couple for us, will you?
Err.. Sure.
So our Claire's dating a pop star? She kept that quiet.
'Scuse me, mister...
...can you sign our ball?
Sure, but aren't you Rovers fans?
Yeah, but who cares? We can still sell it on Ebay!

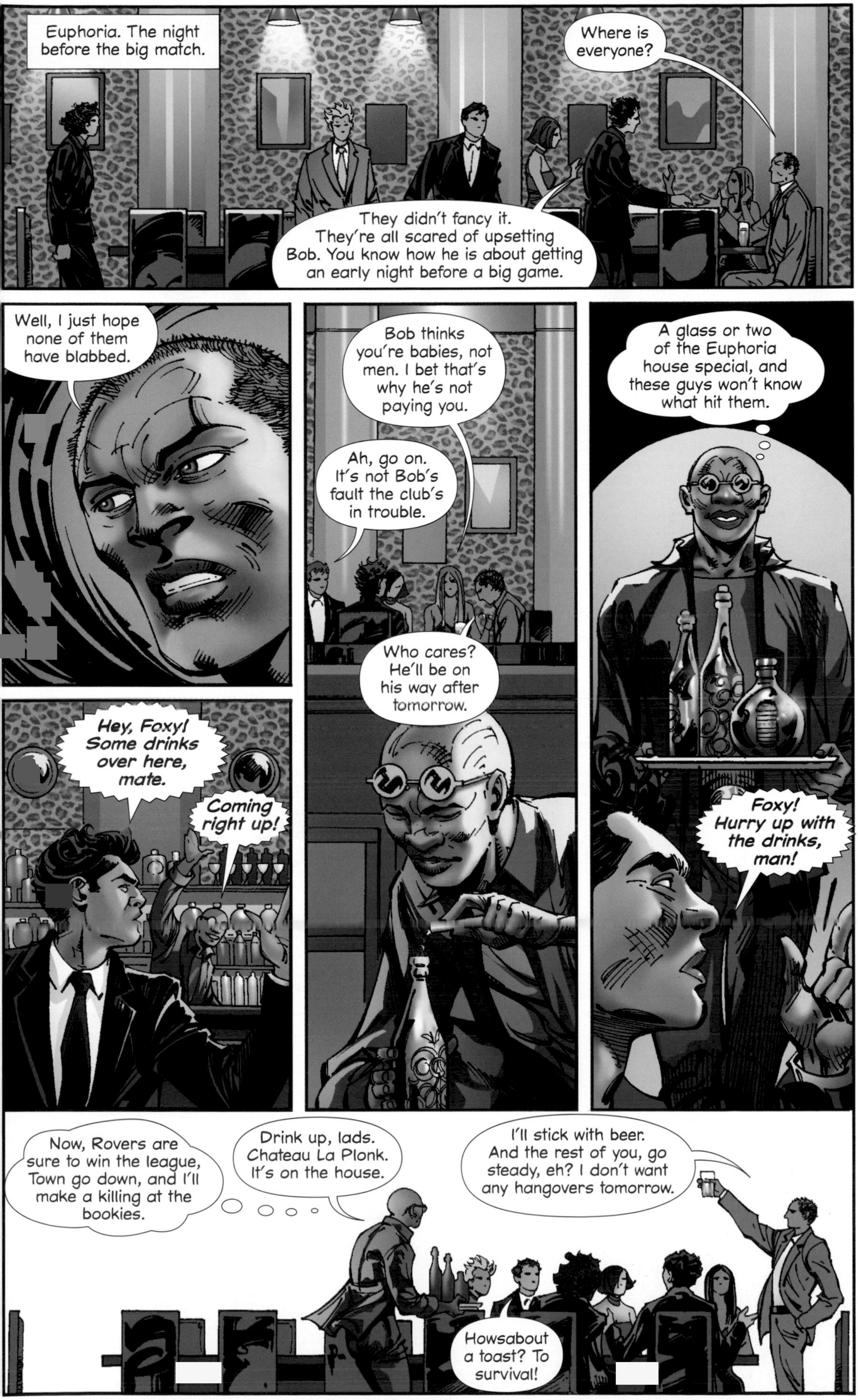
Euphoria. The night before the big match.
Where is everyone?
They didn't fancy it. They're all scared of upsetting Bob. You know how he is about getting an early night before a big game.
Well, I just hope none of them have blabbed.
Bob thinks you're babies, not men. I bet that's why he's not paying you.
Ah, go on. It's not Bob's fault the club's in trouble.
Who cares? He'll be on his way after tomorrow.
A glass or two of the Euphoria house special, and these guys won't know what hit them.
Hey, Foxy! Some drinks over here, mate.
Coming right up!
Foxy! Hurry up with the drinks, man!
Now, Rovers are sure to win the league, Town go down, and I'll make a killing at the bookies.
Drink up, lads. Chateau La Plonk. It's on the house.
I'll stick with beer. And the rest of you, go steady, eh? I don't want any hangovers tomorrow.
Howsabout a toast? To survival!

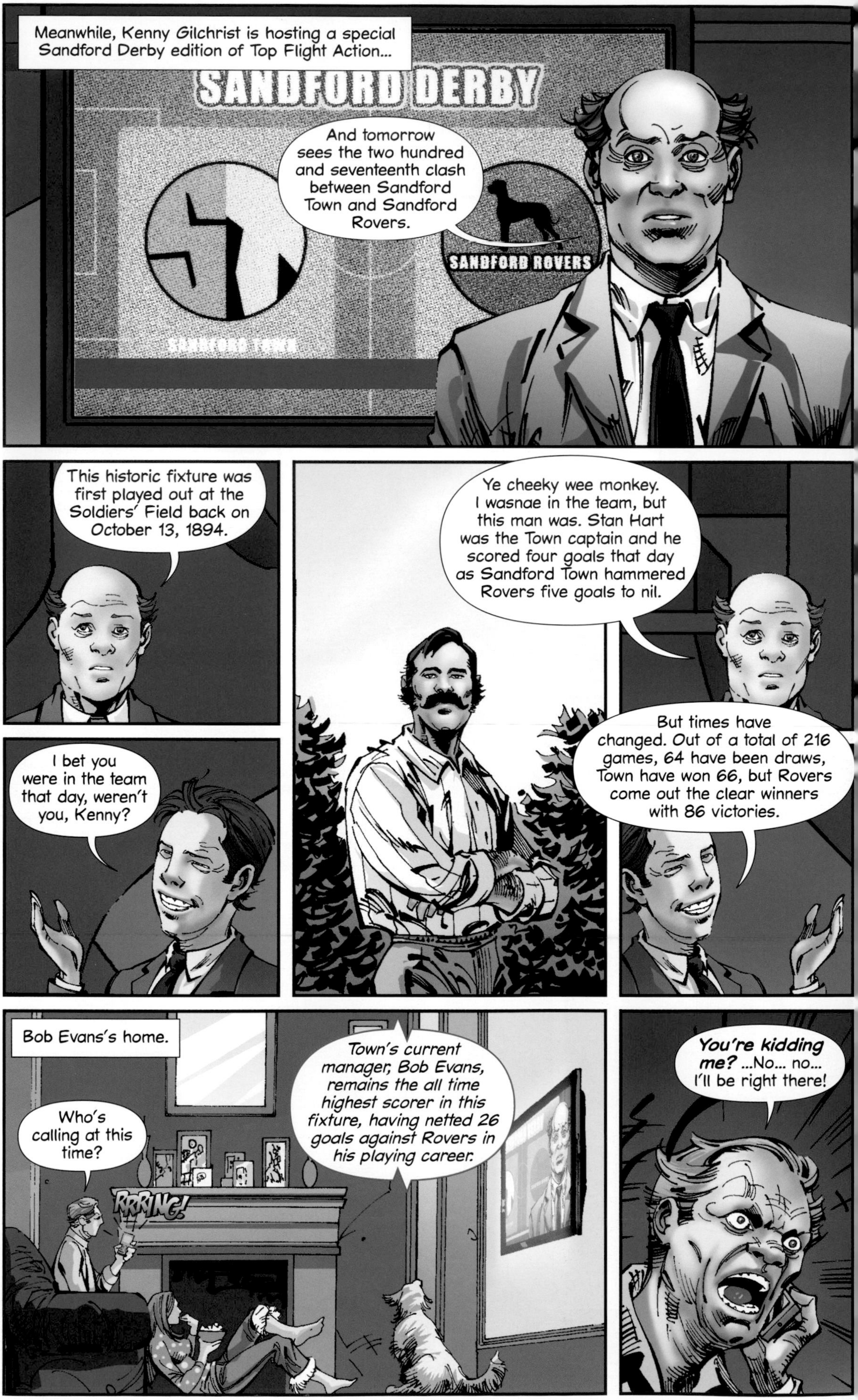
Meanwhile, Kenny Gilchrist is hosting a special Sandford Derby edition of Top Flight Action...
SANDFORD DERBY
SANDFORD ROVERS
SANDFORD TOWN
And tomorrow sees the two hundred and seventeenth clash between Sandford Town and Sandford Rovers.
This historic fixture was first played out at the Soldiers' Field back on October 13, 1894.
I bet you were in the team that day, weren't you, Kenny?
Ye cheeky wee monkey. I wasnae in the team, but this man was. Stan Hart was the Town captain and he scored four goals that day as Sandford Town hammered Rovers five goals to nil.
But times have changed. Out of a total of 216 games, 64 have been draws, Town have won 66, but Rovers come out the clear winners with 86 victories.
Bob Evans's home.
Who's calling at this time?
RRRING!
Town's current manager, Bob Evans, remains the all time highest scorer in this fixture, having netted 26 goals against Rovers in his playing career.
You're kidding me? ...No... no... I'll be right there!

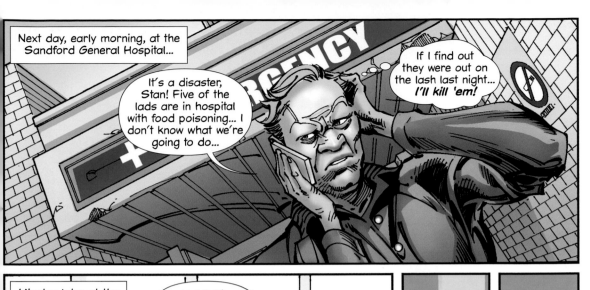

Next day, early morning, at the Sandford General Hospital...

It's a disaster, Stan! Five of the lads are in hospital with food poisoning... I don't know what we're going to do...

If I find out they were out on the lash last night... *I'll kill 'em!*

Minutes later at the Bennett house...

Huh? It's Bob. What does he want?

Pick up the phone and find out, Holmes.

BRRRR

Hello? Boss?

Yeah. Course I'll tell him. He'll be made up.

Where's Billy?! The Boss wants him in the squad!

He's gone to see your mum. Shall I fetch him?

No. I'll get him.

133

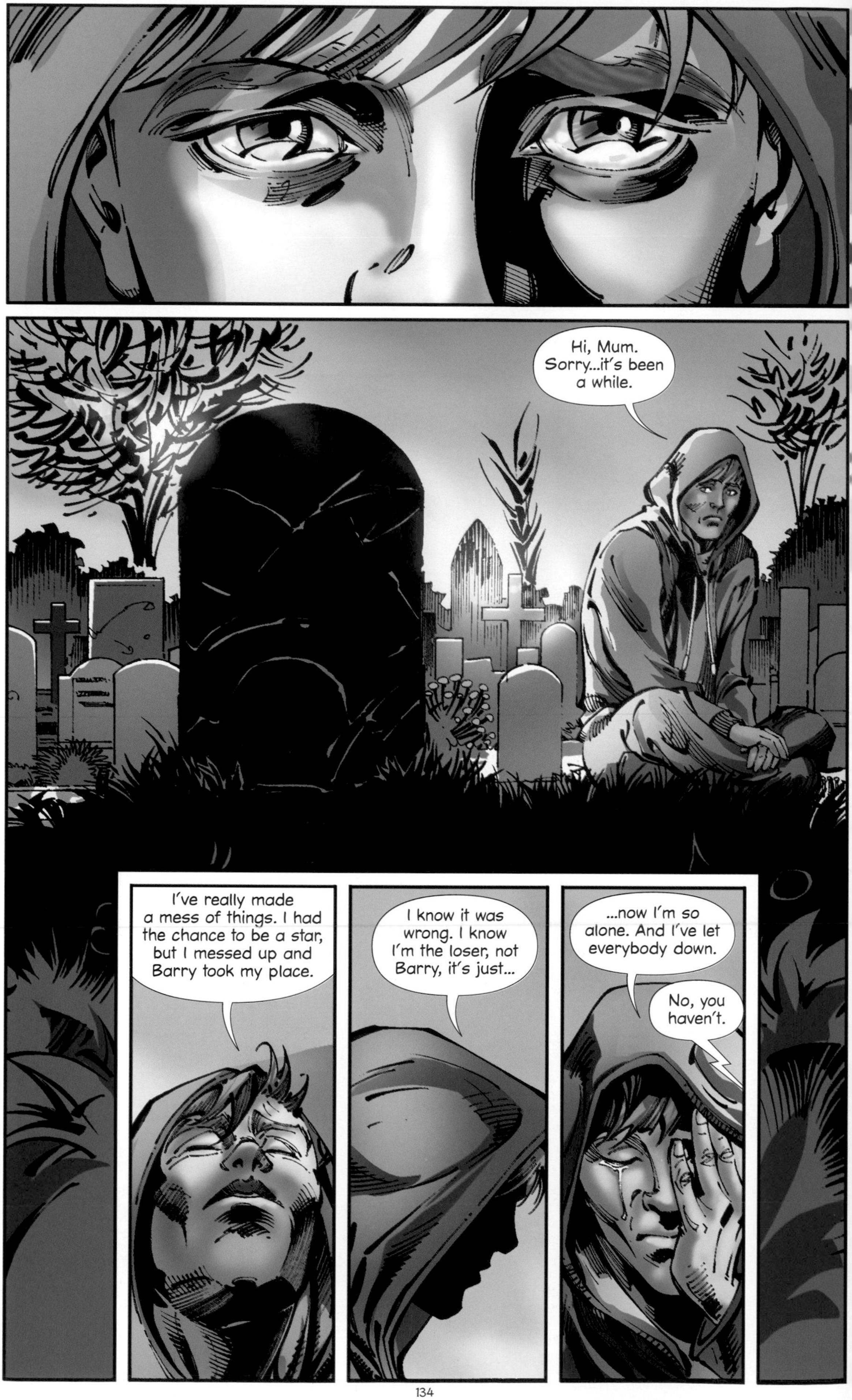
Hi, Mum. Sorry...it's been a while.
I've really made a mess of things. I had the chance to be a star, but I messed up and Barry took my place.
I know it was wrong. I know I'm the loser, not Barry, it's just...
...now I'm so alone. And I've let everybody down.
No, you haven't.

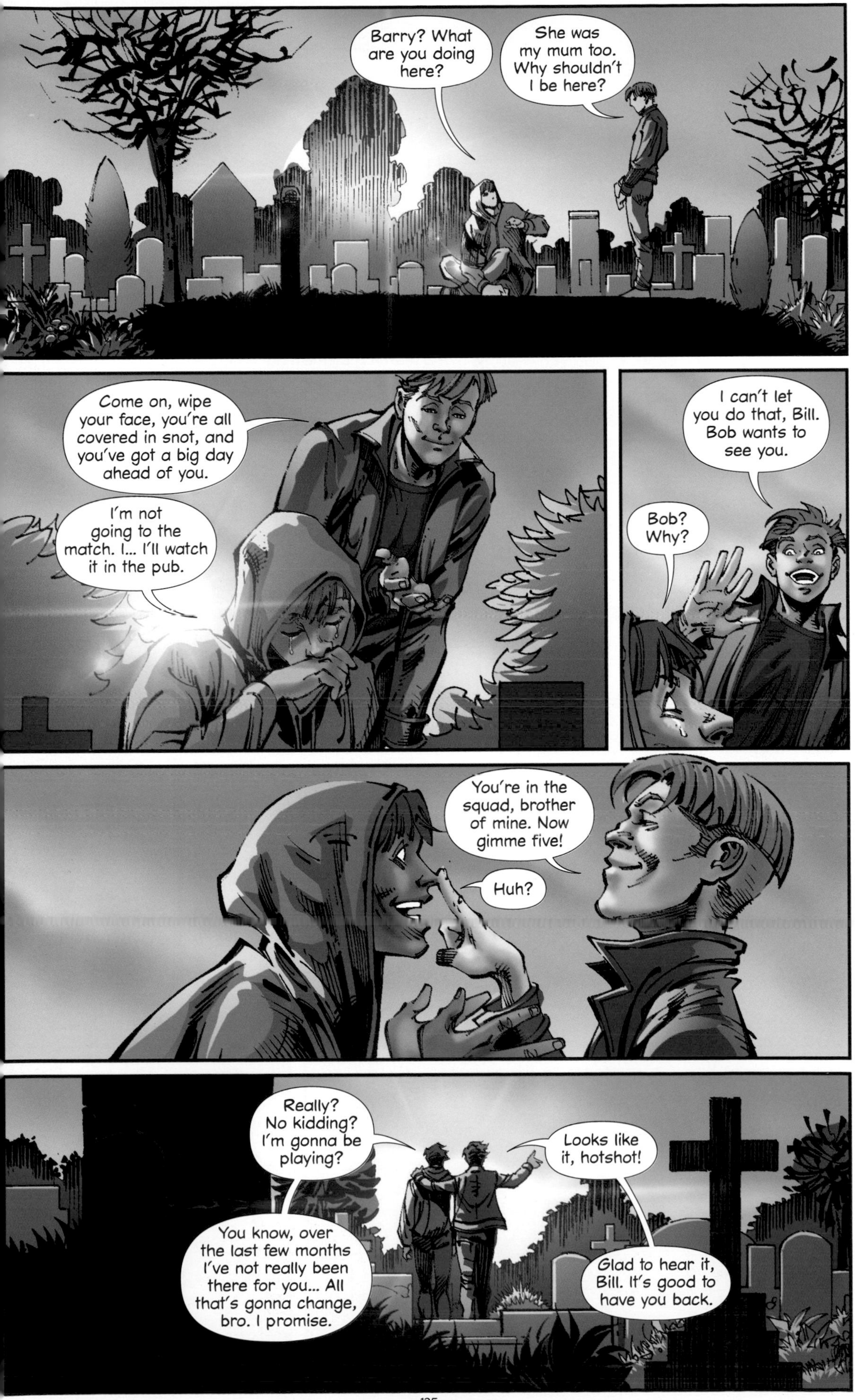
Barry? What are you doing here?
She was my mum too. Why shouldn't I be here?
Come on, wipe your face, you're all covered in snot, and you've got a big day ahead of you.
I'm not going to the match. I... I'll watch it in the pub.
I can't let you do that, Bill. Bob wants to see you.
Bob? Why?
You're in the squad, brother of mine. Now gimme five!
Huh?
Really? No kidding? I'm gonna be playing?
Looks like it, hotshot!
You know, over the last few months I've not really been there for you... All that's gonna change, bro. I promise.
Glad to hear it, Bill. It's good to have you back.

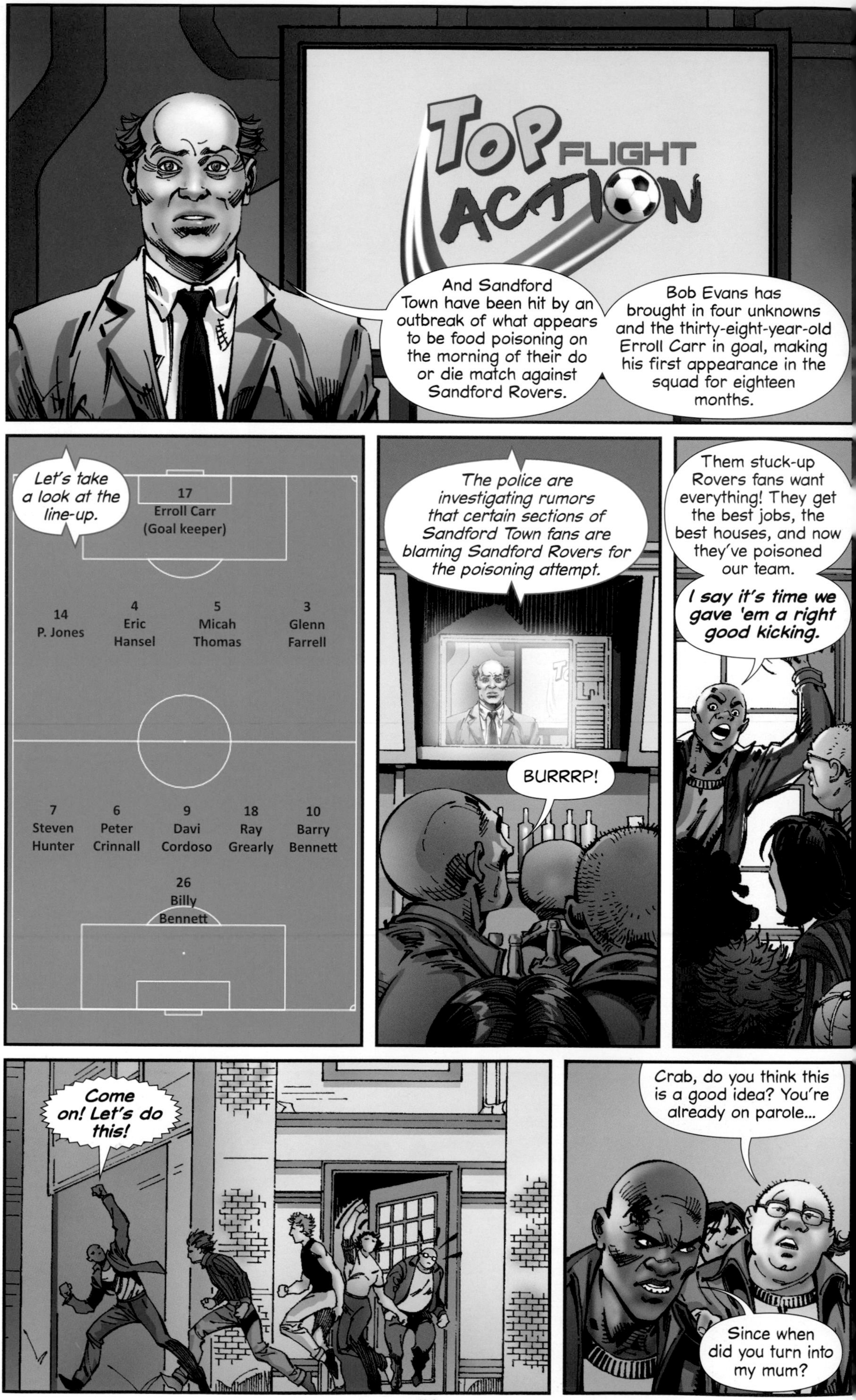
TOP FLIGHT ACTION
And Sandford Town have been hit by an outbreak of what appears to be food poisoning on the morning of their do or die match against Sandford Rovers.
Bob Evans has brought in four unknowns and the thirty-eight-year-old Erroll Carr in goal, making his first appearance in the squad for eighteen months.
Let's take a look at the line-up.
17 Erroll Carr (Goal keeper)
14 P. Jones
4 Eric Hansel
5 Micah Thomas
3 Glenn Farrell
7 Steven Hunter
6 Peter Crinnall
9 Davi Cordoso
18 Ray Grearly
10 Barry Bennett
26 Billy Bennett
The police are investigating rumors that certain sections of Sandford Town fans are blaming Sandford Rovers for the poisoning attempt.
BURRRP!
Them stuck-up Rovers fans want everything! They get the best jobs, the best houses, and now they've poisoned our team.
I say it's time we gave 'em a right good kicking.
Come on! Let's do this!
Crab, do you think this is a good idea? You're already on parole...
Since when did you turn into my mum?

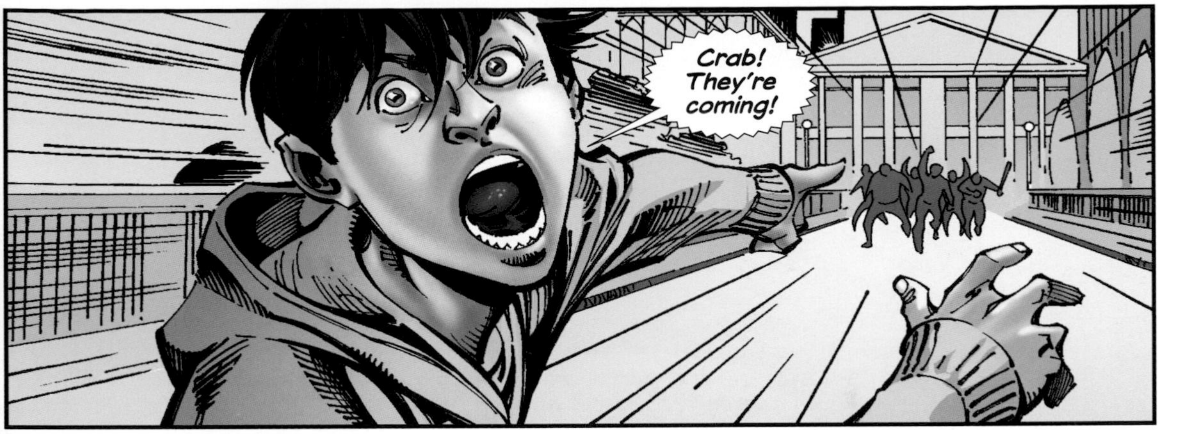
Crab! They're coming!

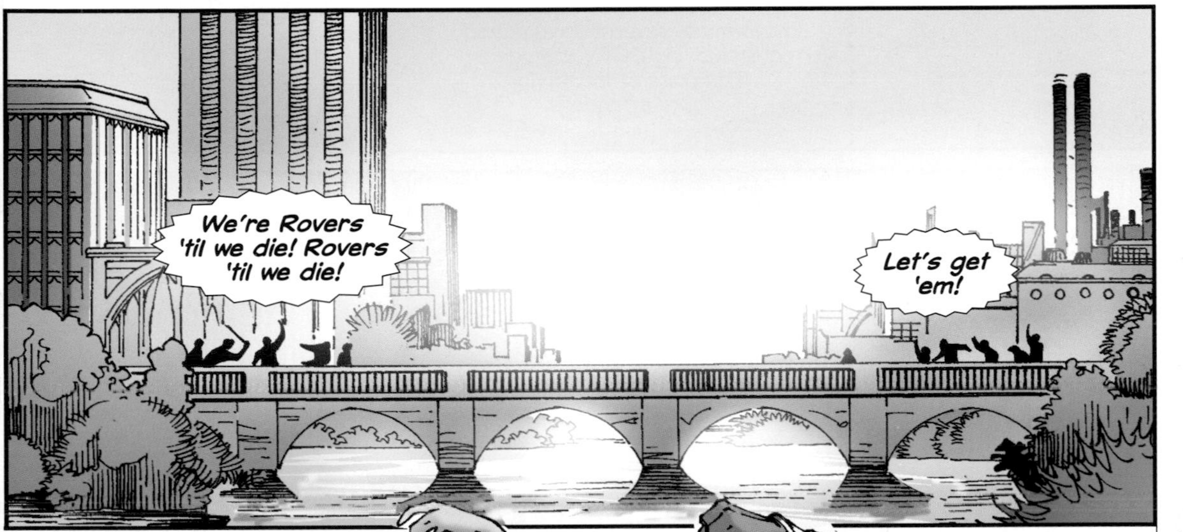
We're Rovers 'til we die! Rovers 'til we die!
Let's get 'em!

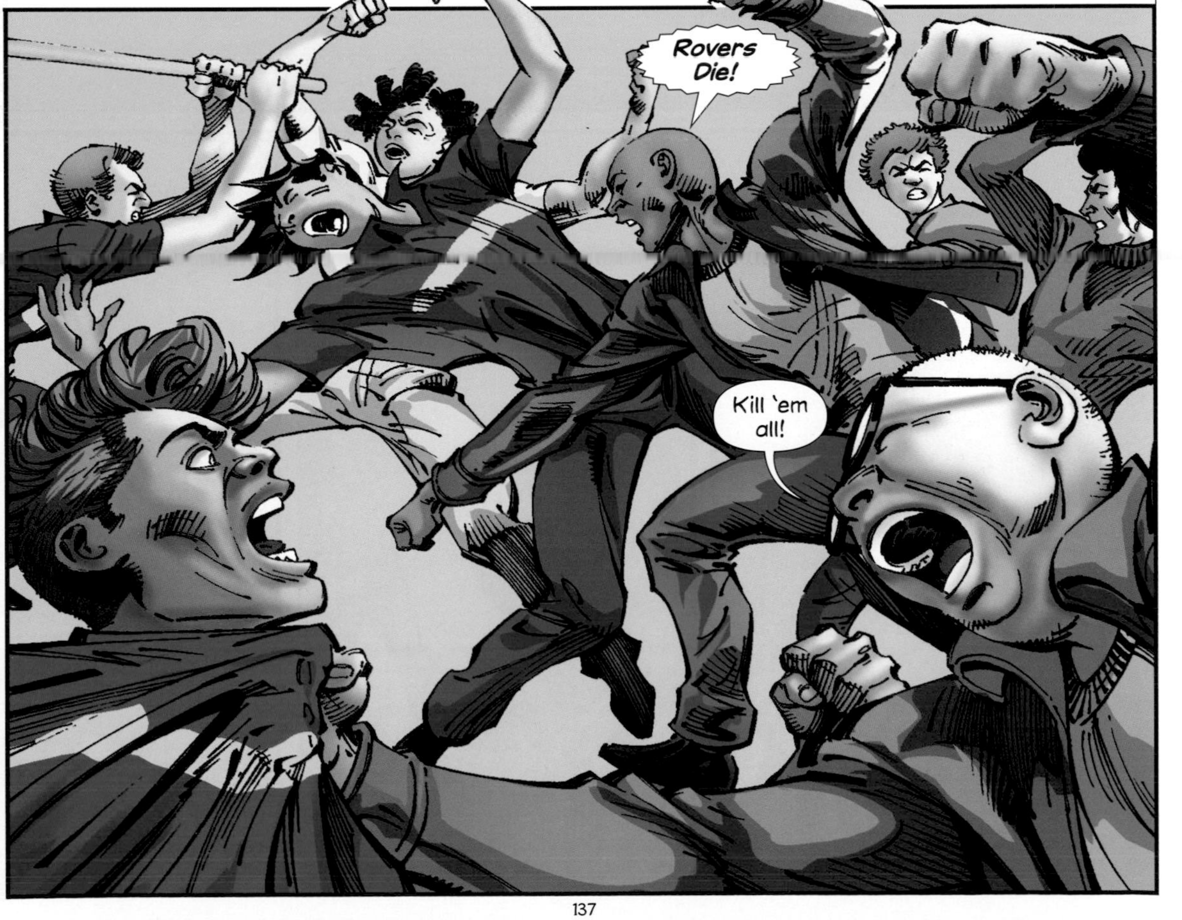
Rovers Die!
Kill 'em all!

And reports are coming in of clashes between rival groups of fans at the Sandford North Bridge. Police have made several arrests and are studying CCTV footage in the hopes of identifying more offenders.

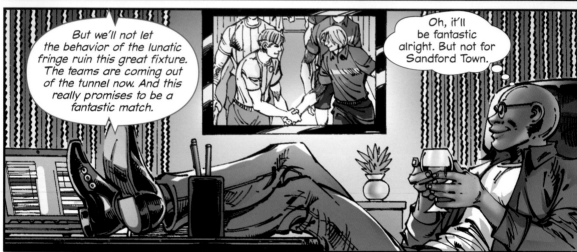

But we'll not let the behavior of the lunatic fringe ruin this great fixture. The teams are coming out of the tunnel now. And this really promises to be a fantastic match.

Oh, it'll be fantastic alright. But not for Sandford Town.

Your first game, eh, kid? Enjoy it.

Cheers!

He's trying to crush my hand. Well, two can play at that game.

Yeeouch!

Hey, Gary, you sound just like a little girl.

Ha! You tell him, Billy.

KRUNCH!

You'll pay for that, kid!

Rovers! Rovers!

Come on Town!

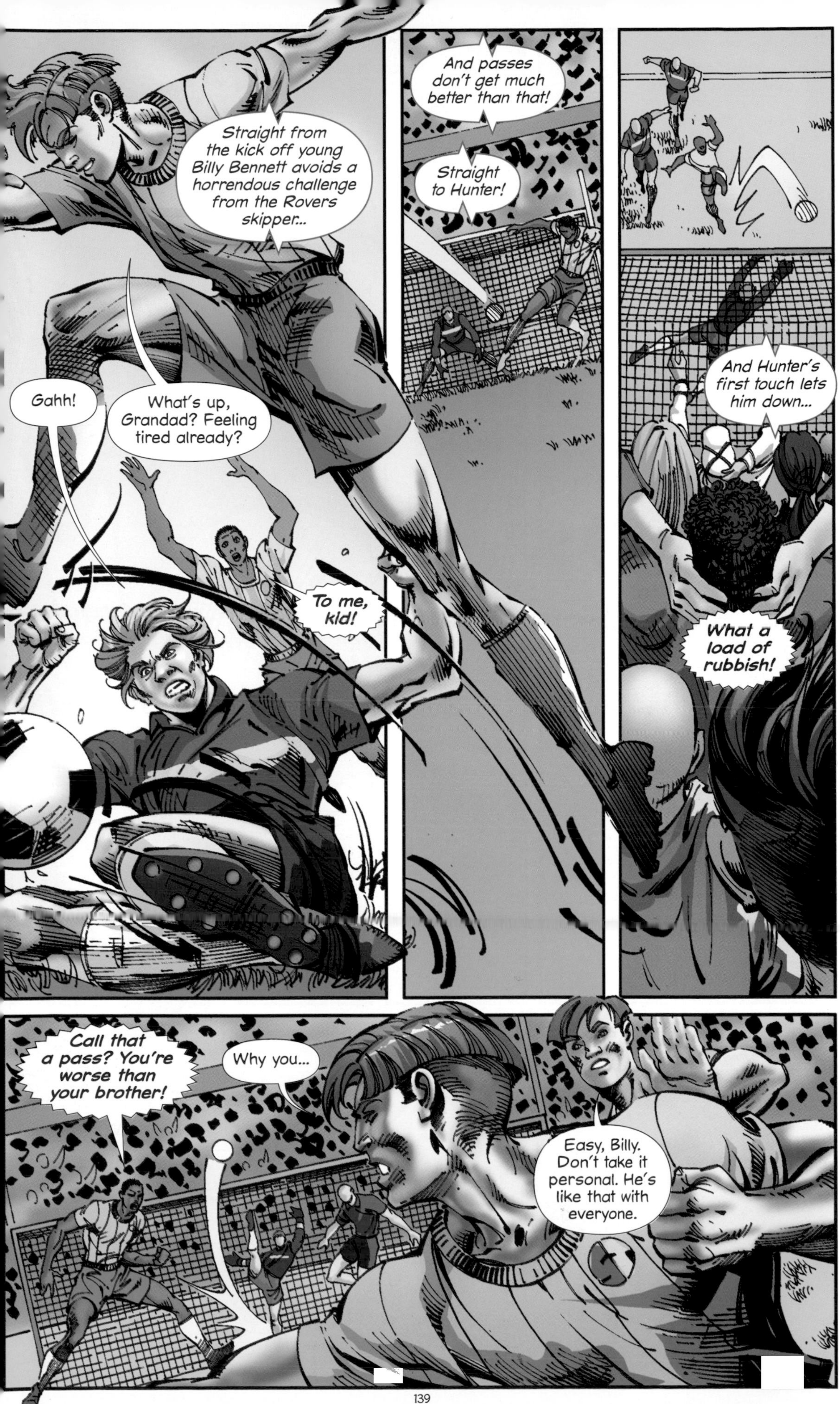
Straight from the kick off young Billy Bennett avoids a horrendous challenge from the Rovers skipper...
What's up, Grandad? Feeling tired already?
Gahh!
To me, kid!
And passes don't get much better than that!
Straight to Hunter!
And Hunter's first touch lets him down...
What a load of rubbish!
Call that a pass? You're worse than your brother!
Why you...
Easy, Billy. Don't take it personal. He's like that with everyone.

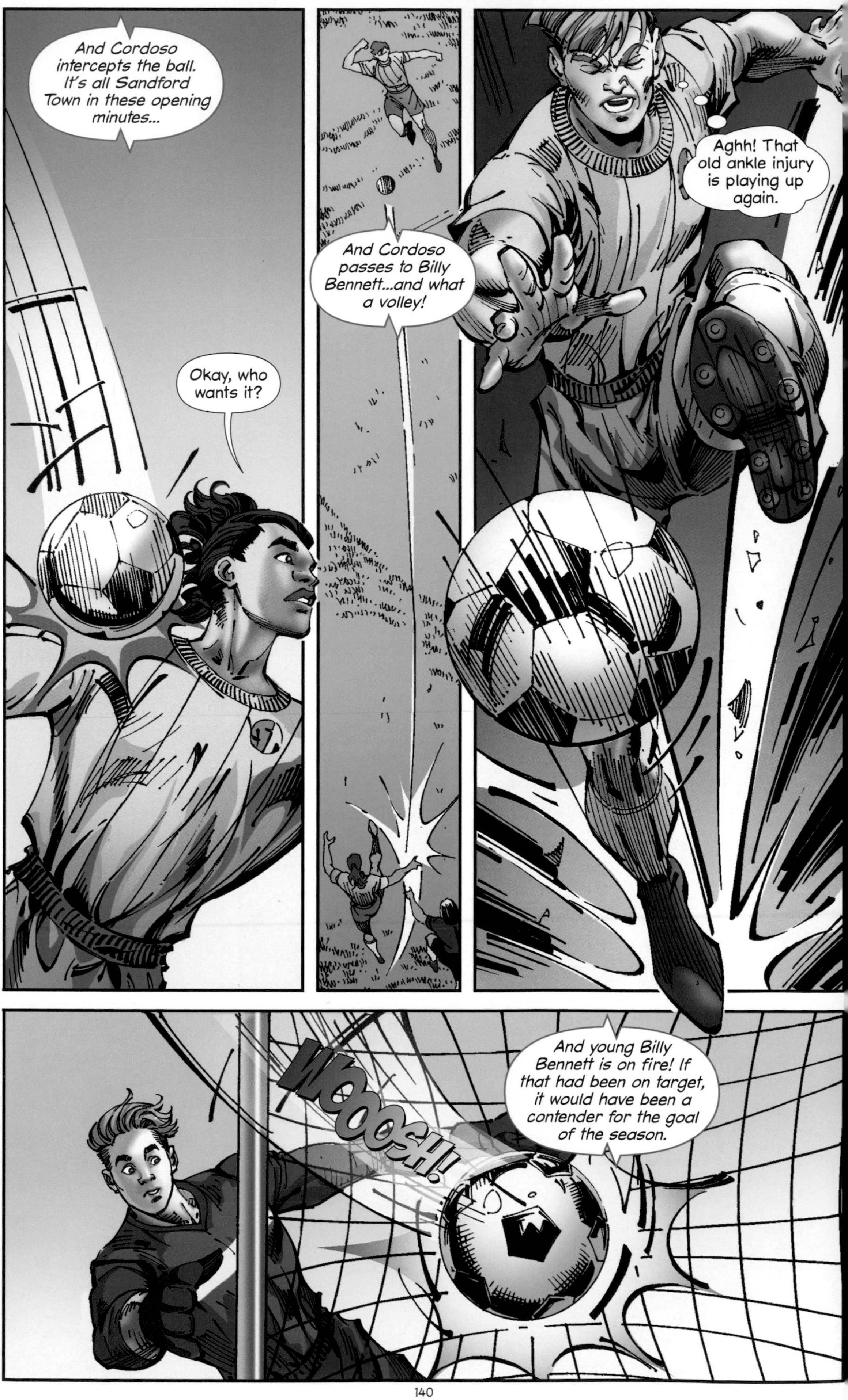
And Cordoso intercepts the ball. It's all Sandford Town in these opening minutes...
Okay, who wants it?
And Cordoso passes to Billy Bennett...and what a volley!
Aghh! That old ankle injury is playing up again.
WOOOSH!
And young Billy Bennett is on fire! If that had been on target, it would have been a contender for the goal of the season.

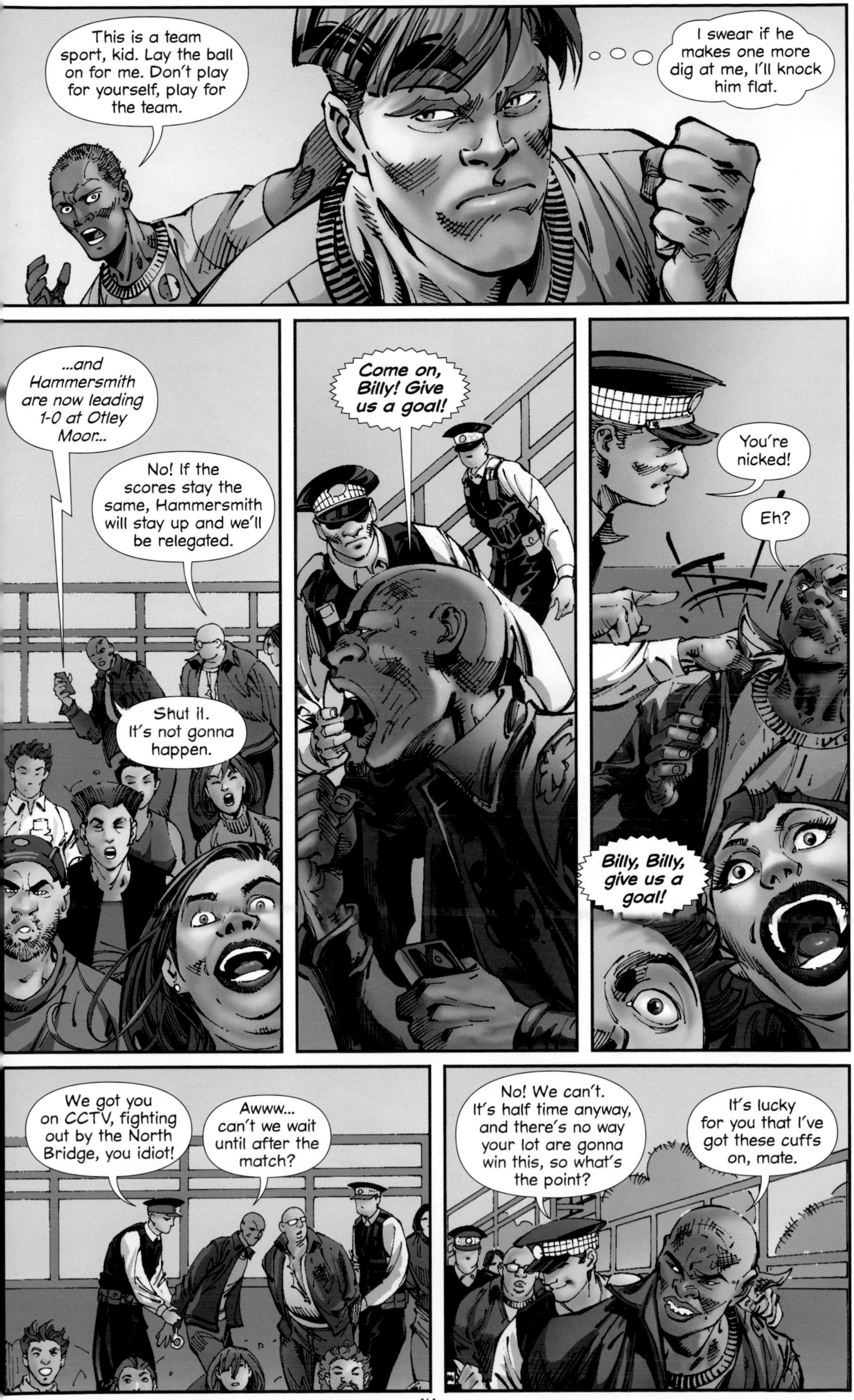
This is a team sport, kid. Lay the ball on for me. Don't play for yourself, play for the team.
I swear if he makes one more dig at me, I'll knock him flat.
...and Hammersmith are now leading 1-0 at Otley Moor...
No! If the scores stay the same, Hammersmith will stay up and we'll be relegated.
Shut it. It's not gonna happen.
Come on, Billy! Give us a goal!
You're nicked!
Eh?
Billy, Billy, give us a goal!
We got you on CCTV, fighting out by the North Bridge, you idiot!
Awww... can't we wait until after the match?
No! We can't. It's half time anyway, and there's no way your lot are gonna win this, so what's the point?
It's lucky for you that I've got these cuffs on, mate.

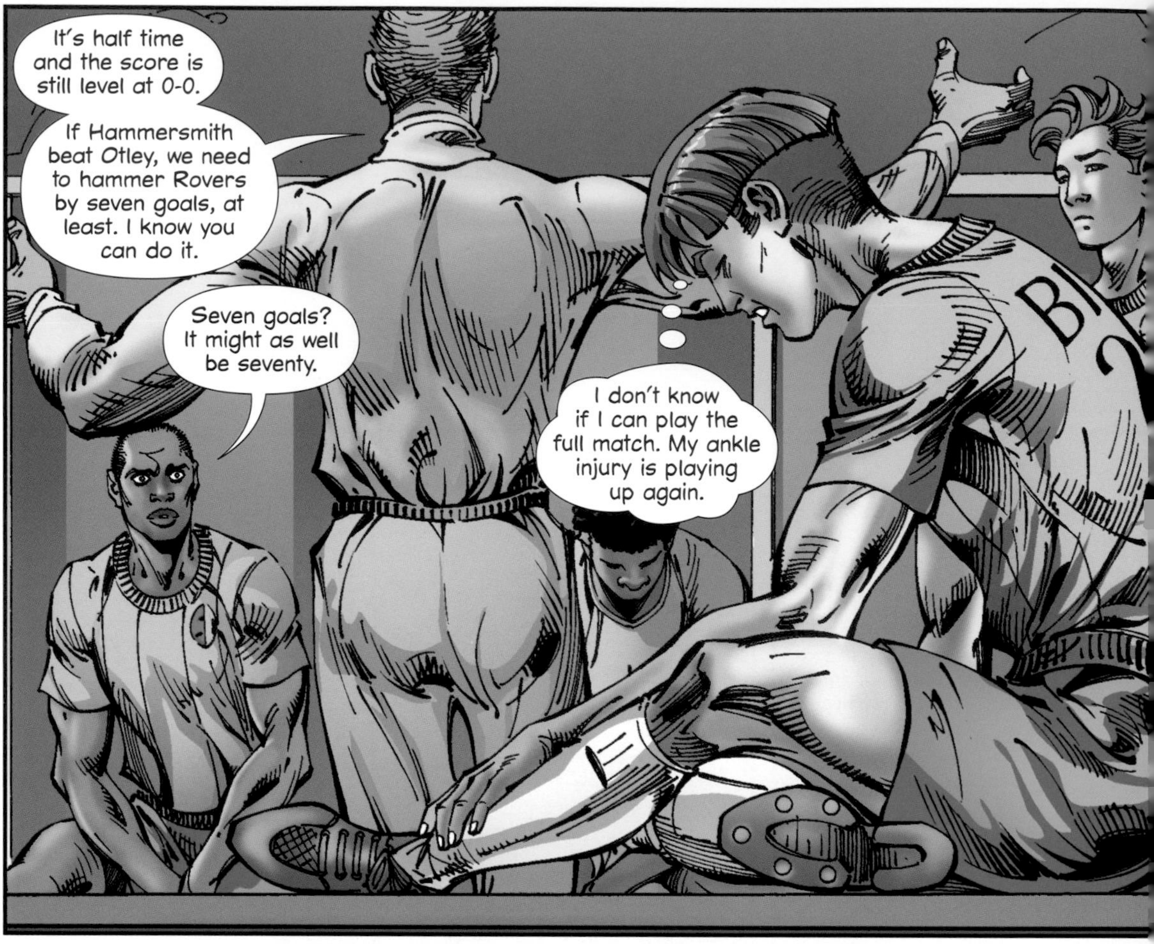
It's half time and the score is still level at 0-0.
If Hammersmith beat Otley, we need to hammer Rovers by seven goals, at least. I know you can do it.
Seven goals? It might as well be seventy.
I don't know if I can play the full match. My ankle injury is playing up again.

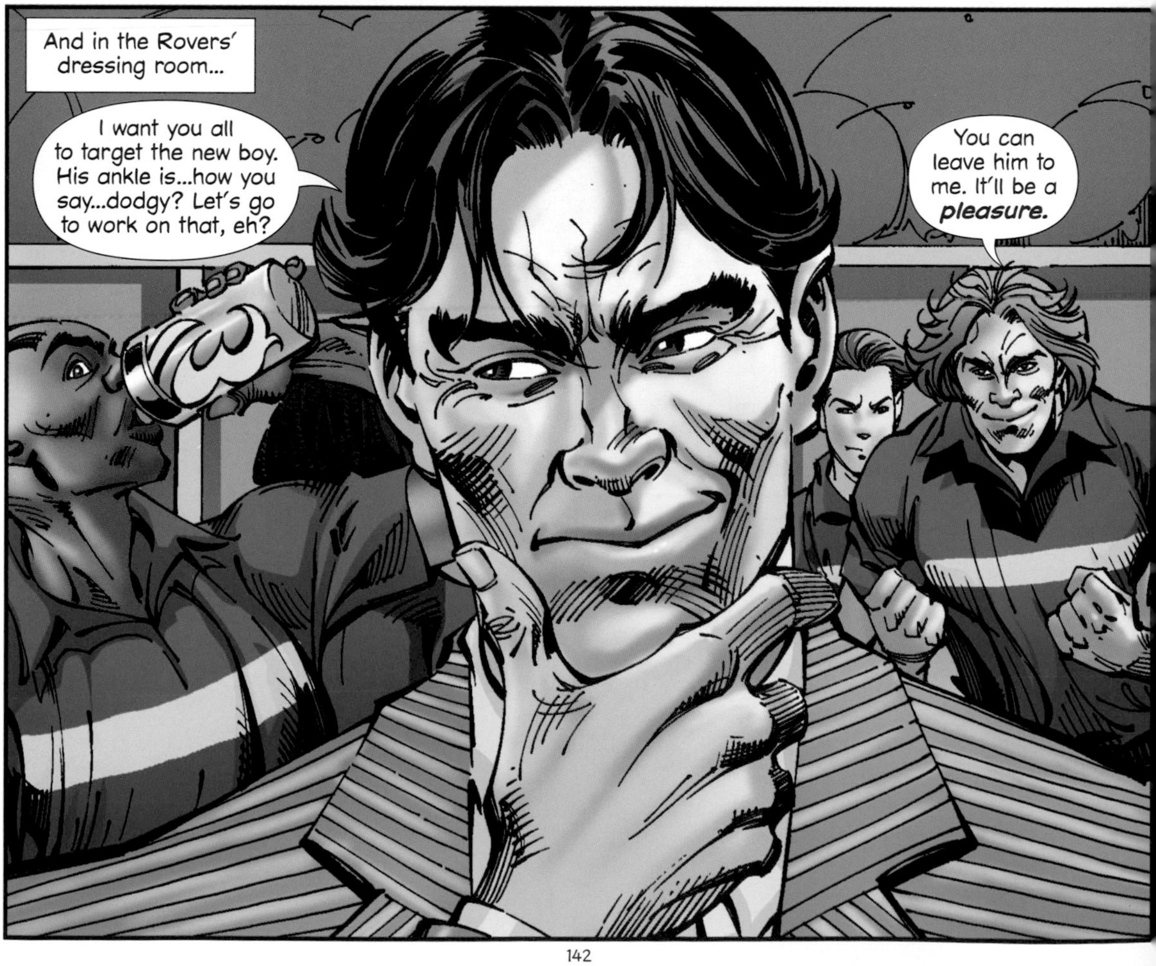
And in the Rovers' dressing room...
I want you all to target the new boy. His ankle is...how you say...dodgy? Let's go to work on that, eh?
You can leave him to me. It'll be a ***pleasure.***

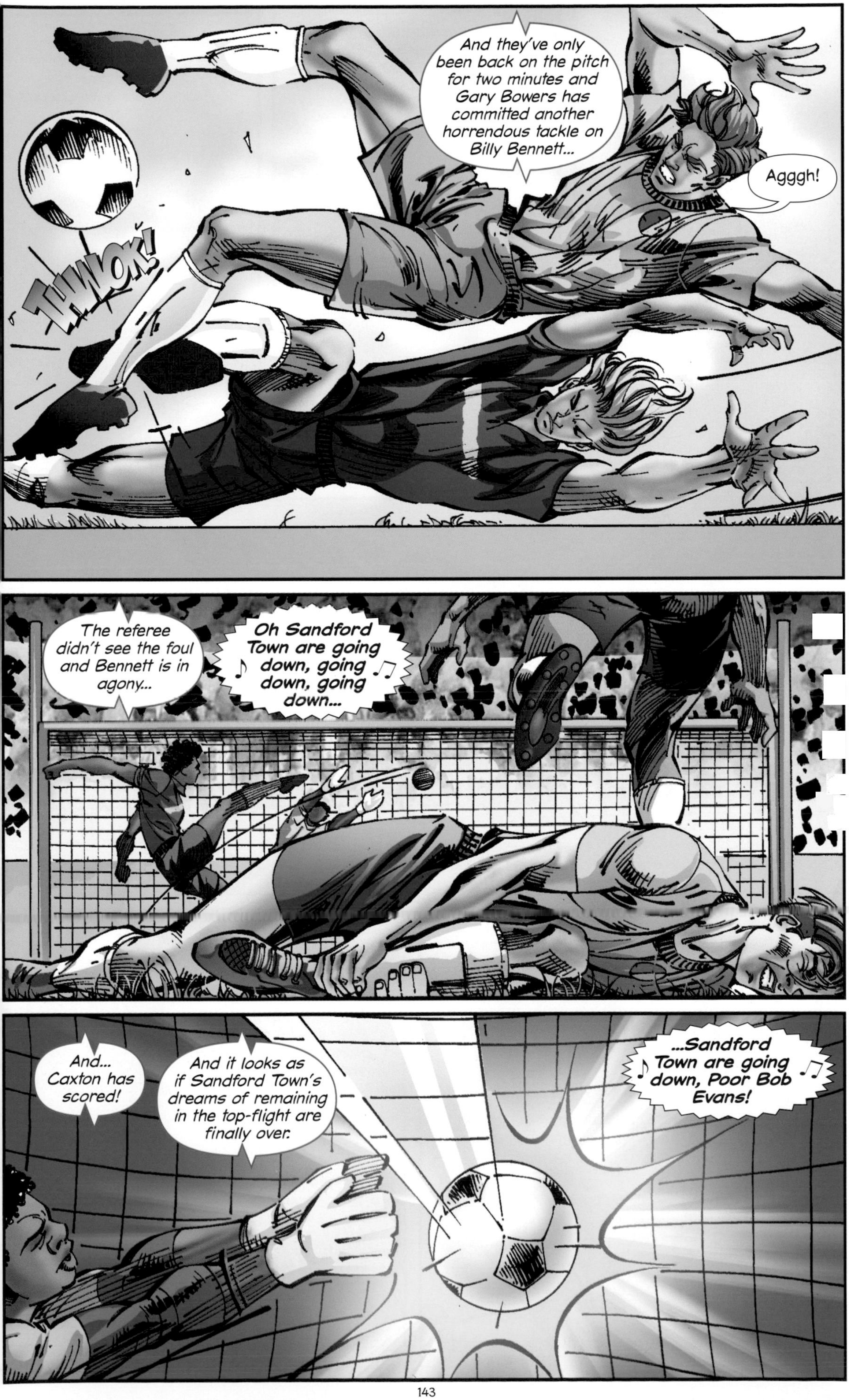
And they've only been back on the pitch for two minutes and Gary Bowers has committed another horrendous tackle on Billy Bennett...
Agggh!
THWOK!
The referee didn't see the foul and Bennett is in agony...
Oh Sandford Town are going down, going down, going down...
And... Caxton has scored!
And it looks as if Sandford Town's dreams of remaining in the top-flight are finally over.
...Sandford Town are going down, Poor Bob Evans!

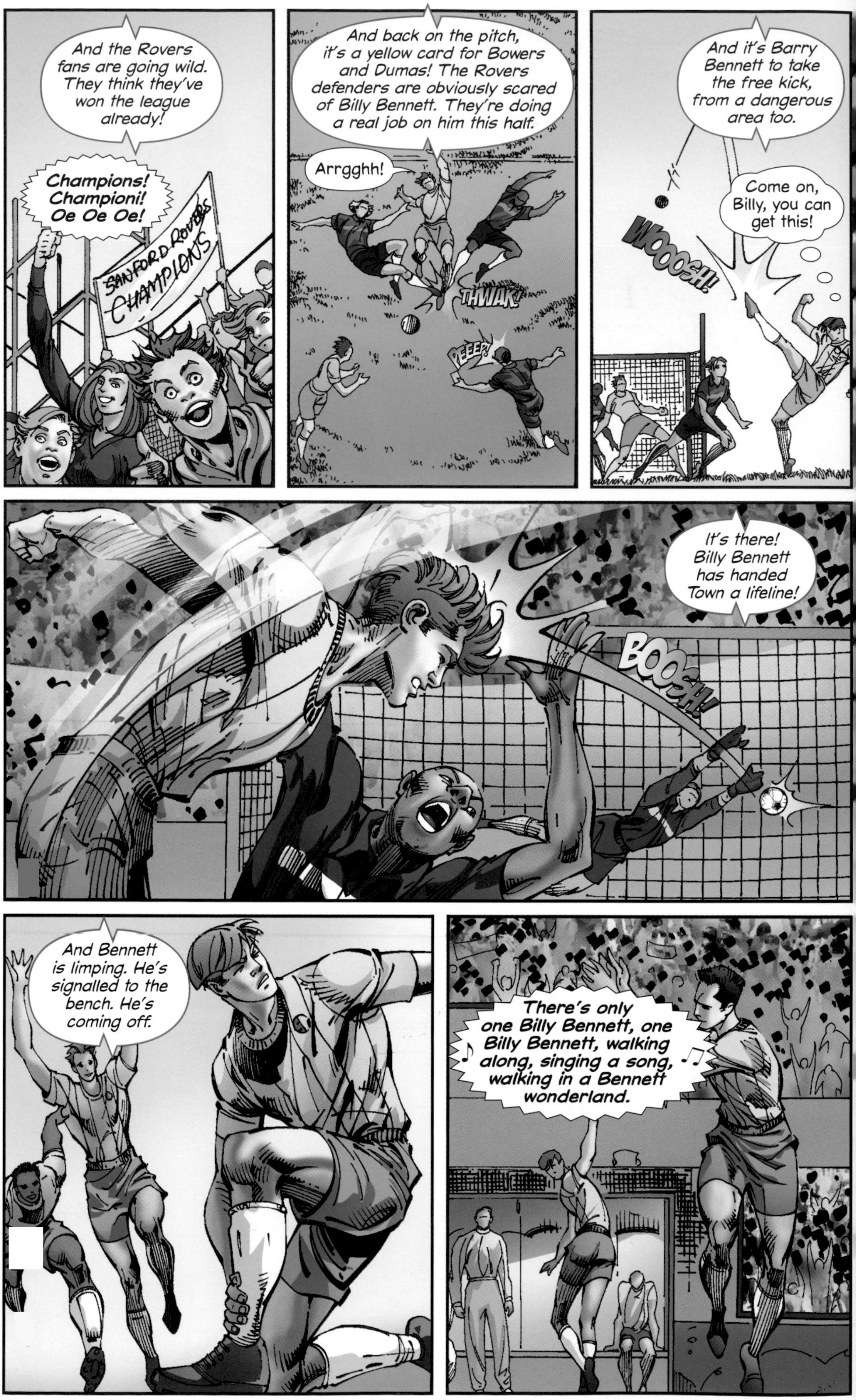
And the Rovers fans are going wild. They think they've won the league already!
Champions! Championi! Oe Oe Oe!
SANFORD ROVERS CHAMPIONS
And back on the pitch, it's a yellow card for Bowers and Dumas! The Rovers defenders are obviously scared of Billy Bennett. They're doing a real job on him this half.
Arrgghh!
THWAK!
PEEEP!
And it's Barry Bennett to take the free kick, from a dangerous area too.
Come on, Billy, you can get this!
WOOOSH!
It's there! Billy Bennett has handed Town a lifeline!
BOOSH!
And Bennett is limping. He's signalled to the bench. He's coming off.
There's only one Billy Bennett, one Billy Bennett, walking along, singing a song, walking in a Bennett wonderland.

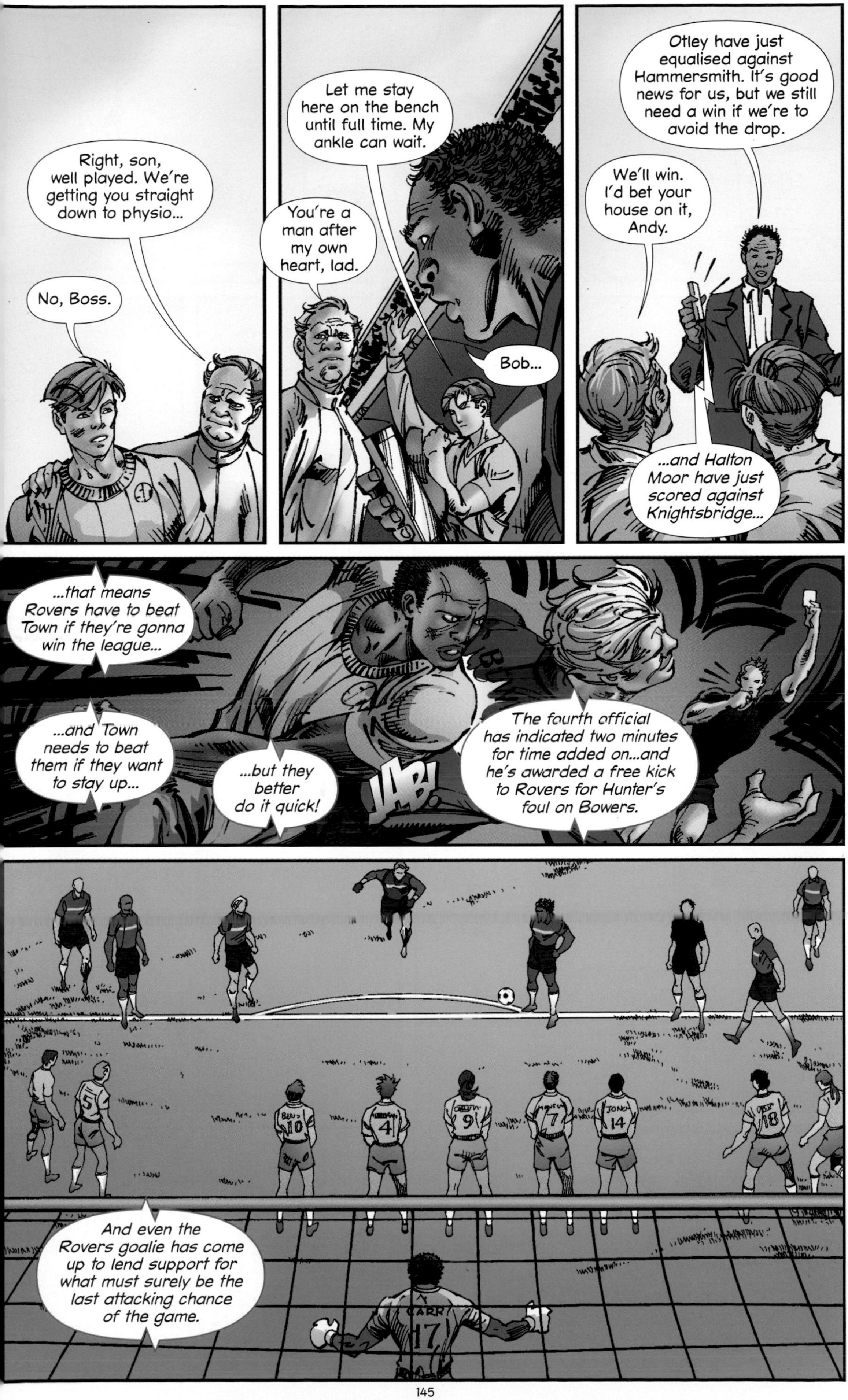

Right, son, well played. We're getting you straight down to physio...
No, Boss.
Let me stay here on the bench until full time. My ankle can wait.
You're a man after my own heart, lad.
Bob...
Otley have just equalised against Hammersmith. It's good news for us, but we still need a win if we're to avoid the drop.
We'll win. I'd bet your house on it, Andy.
...and Halton Moor have just scored against Knightsbridge...
...that means Rovers have to beat Town if they're gonna win the league...
...and Town needs to beat them if they want to stay up...
...but they better do it quick!
JAB!
The fourth official has indicated two minutes for time added on...and he's awarded a free kick to Rovers for Hunter's foul on Bowers.
And even the Rovers goalie has come up to lend support for what must surely be the last attacking chance of the game.

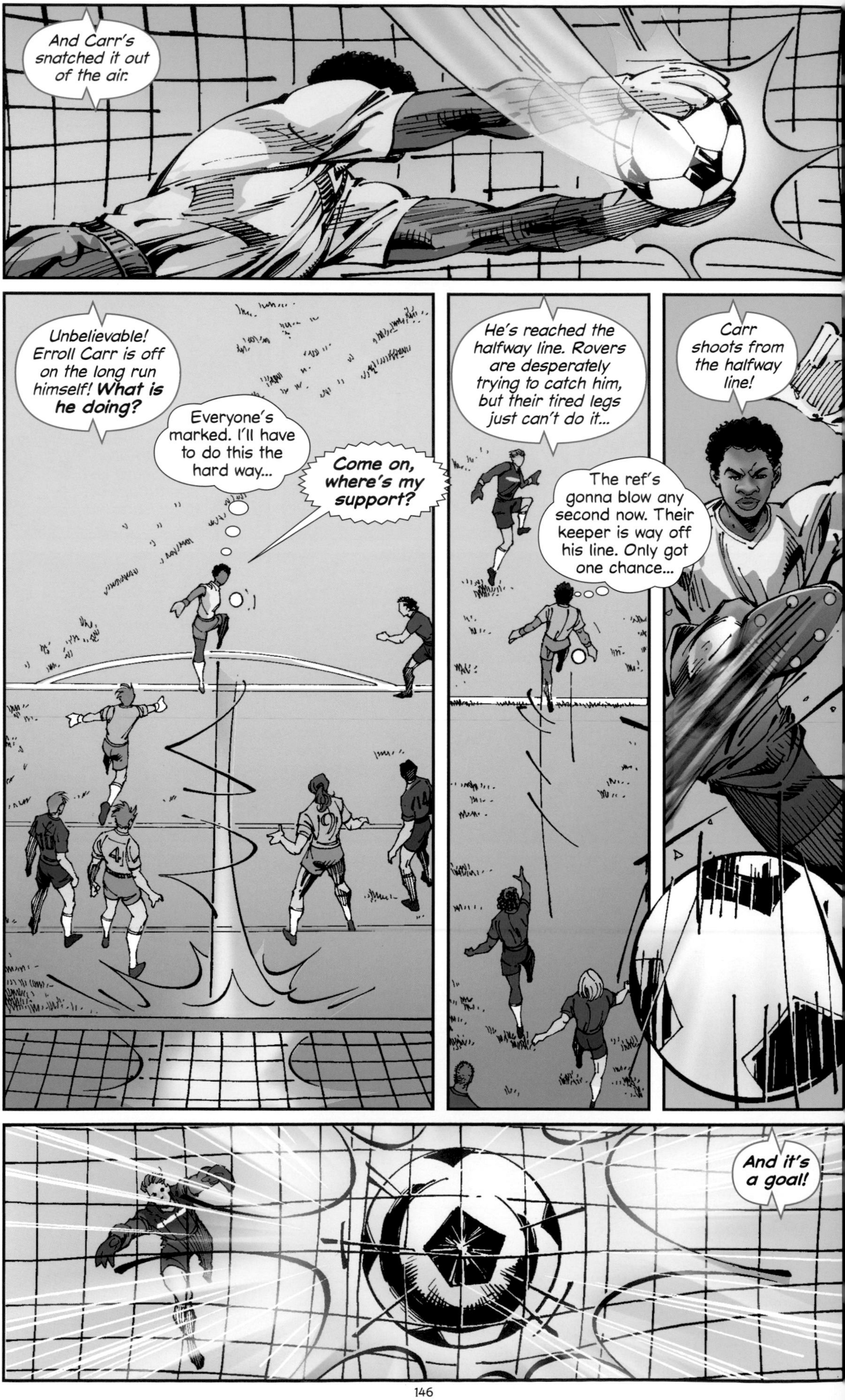
And Carr's snatched it out of the air.
Unbelievable! Erroll Carr is off on the long run himself! **What is he doing?**
Everyone's marked. I'll have to do this the hard way...
Come on, where's my support?
He's reached the halfway line. Rovers are desperately trying to catch him, but their tired legs just can't do it...
The ref's gonna blow any second now. Their keeper is way off his line. Only got one chance...
Carr shoots from the halfway line!
And it's a goal!

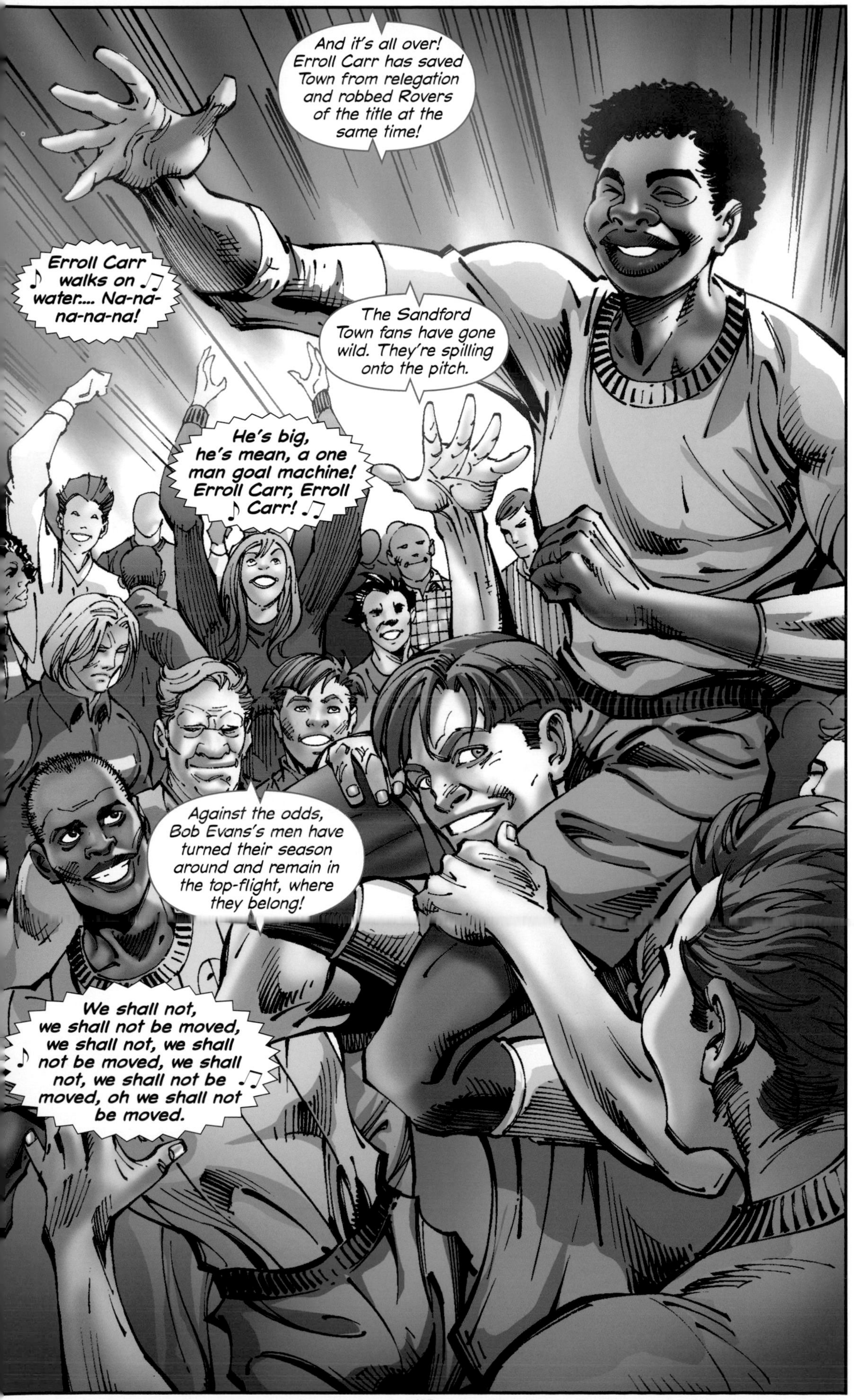
And it's all over! Erroll Carr has saved Town from relegation and robbed Rovers of the title at the same time!
Erroll Carr ♪ walks on ♫ water.... Na-na-na-na-na!
The Sandford Town fans have gone wild. They're spilling onto the pitch.
He's big, he's mean, a one man goal machine! Erroll Carr, Erroll ♪ Carr! ♫
Against the odds, Bob Evans's men have turned their season around and remain in the top-flight, where they belong!
We shall not, we shall not be moved, we shall not, we shall ♪ not be moved, we shall not, we shall not be ♫ moved, oh we shall not be moved.

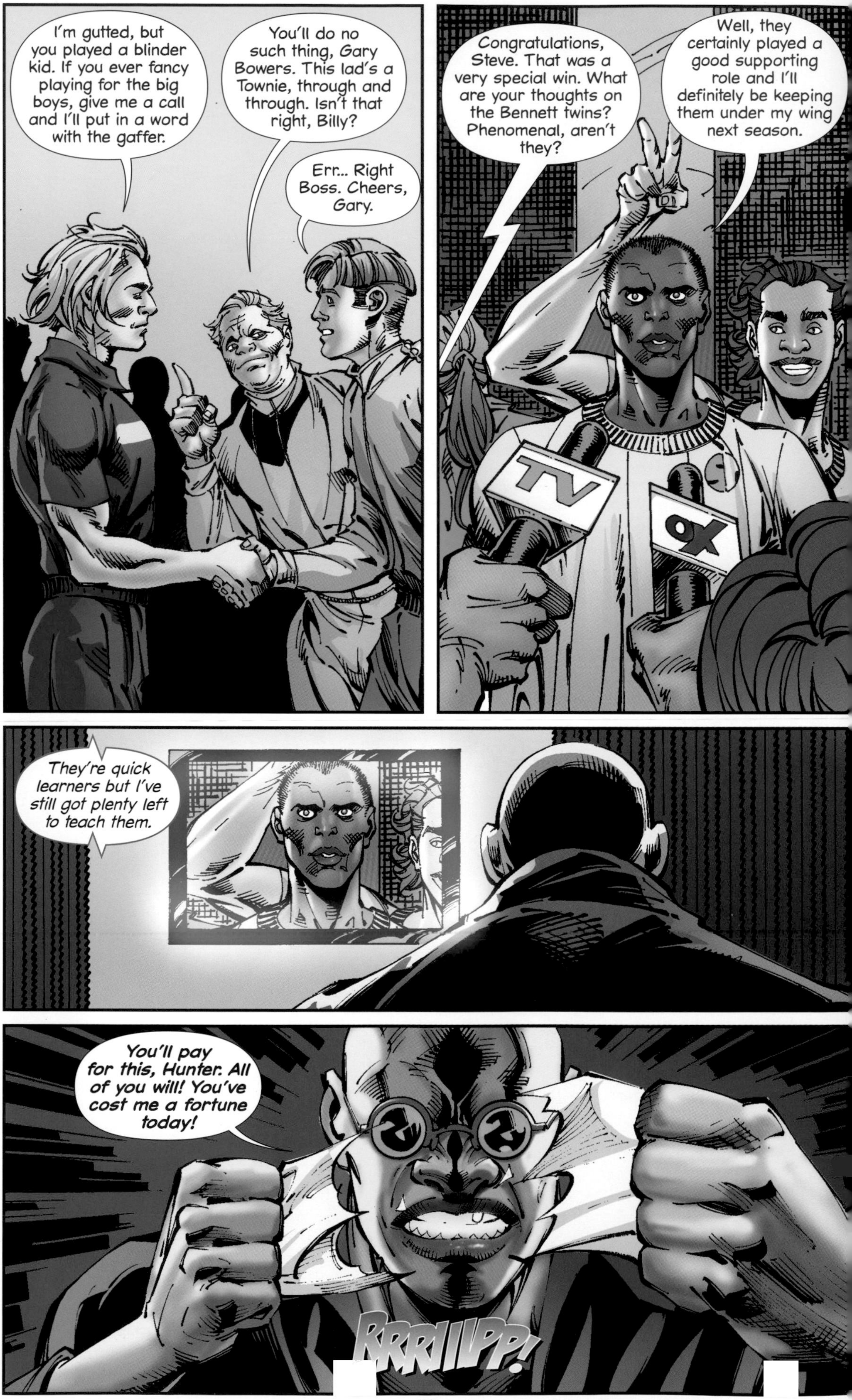
I'm gutted, but you played a blinder kid. If you ever fancy playing for the big boys, give me a call and I'll put in a word with the gaffer.
You'll do no such thing, Gary Bowers. This lad's a Townie, through and through. Isn't that right, Billy?
Err... Right Boss. Cheers, Gary.
Congratulations, Steve. That was a very special win. What are your thoughts on the Bennett twins? Phenomenal, aren't they?
Well, they certainly played a good supporting role and I'll definitely be keeping them under my wing next season.
TV
They're quick learners but I've still got plenty left to teach them.
You'll pay for this, Hunter. All of you will! You've cost me a fortune today!
RRRIIIPP!

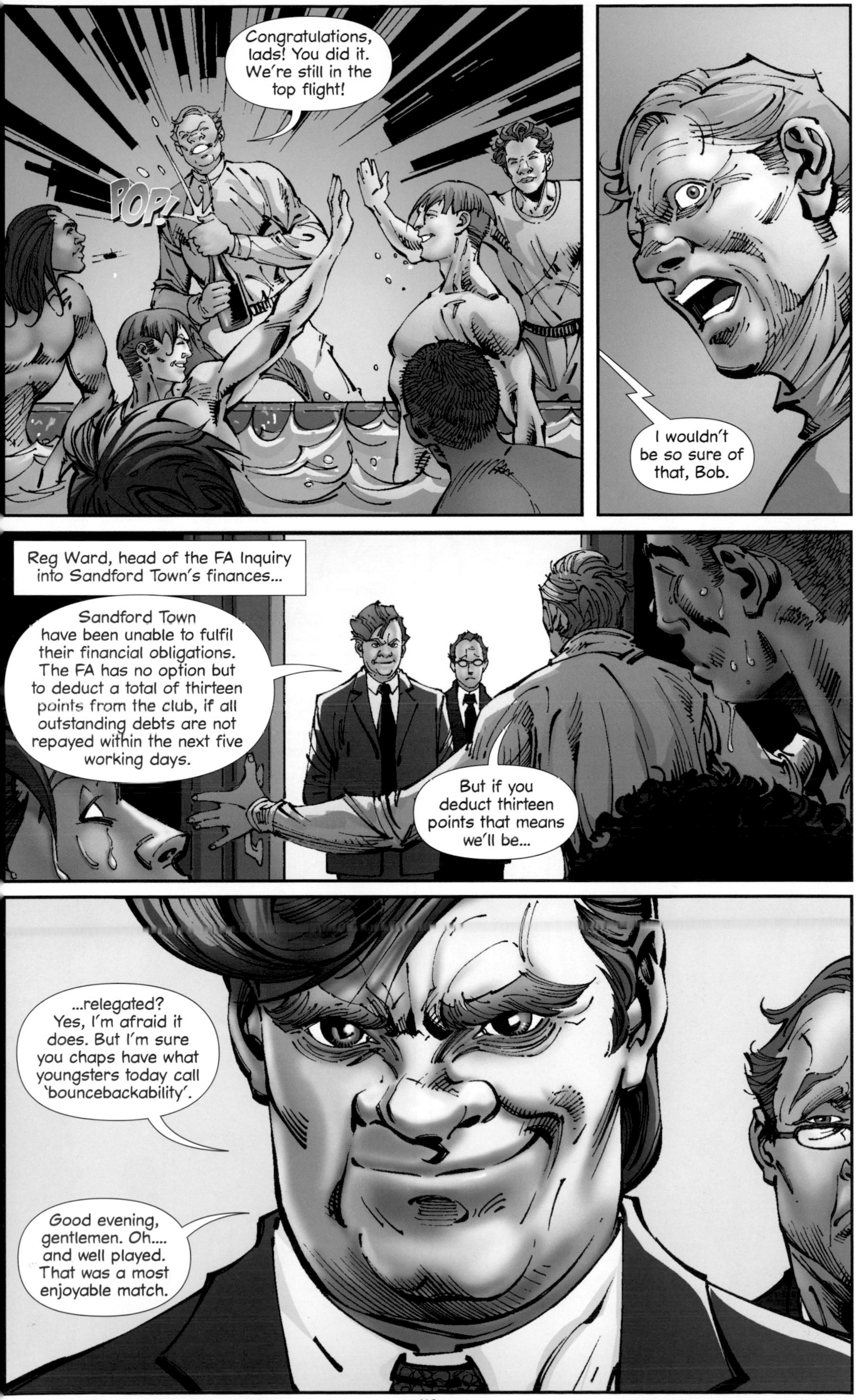
Congratulations, lads! You did it. We're still in the top flight!
POP!
I wouldn't be so sure of that, Bob.
Reg Ward, head of the FA Inquiry into Sandford Town's finances...
Sandford Town have been unable to fulfil their financial obligations. The FA has no option but to deduct a total of thirteen points from the club, if all outstanding debts are not repayed within the next five working days.
But if you deduct thirteen points that means we'll be...
...relegated? Yes, I'm afraid it does. But I'm sure you chaps have what youngsters today call 'bouncebackability'.
Good evening, gentlemen. Oh.... and well played. That was a most enjoyable match.

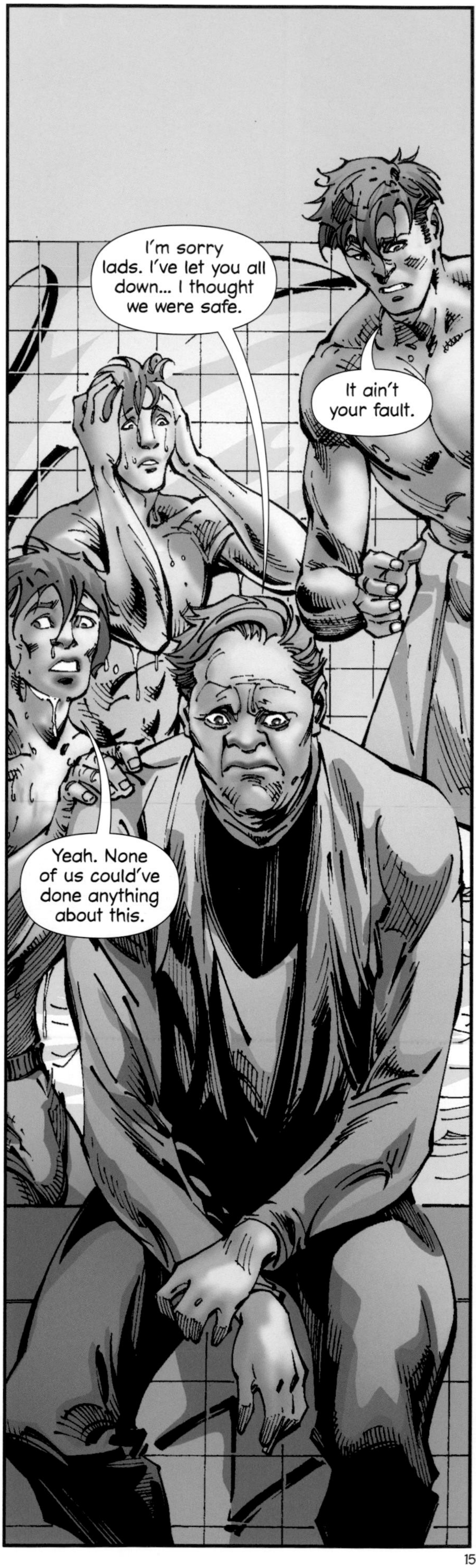
I'm sorry lads. I've let you all down... I thought we were safe.
It ain't your fault.
Yeah. None of us could've done anything about this.

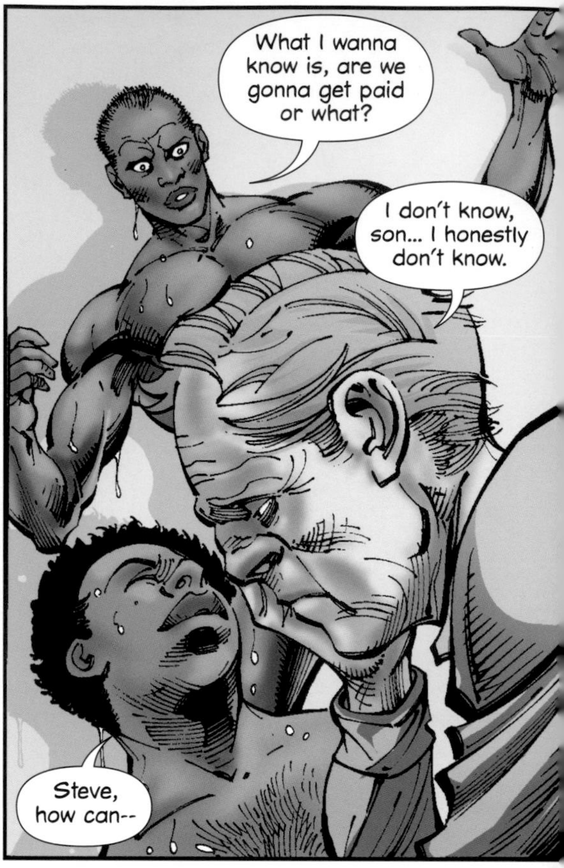
What I wanna know is, are we gonna get paid or what?
I don't know, son... I honestly don't know.
Steve, how can--

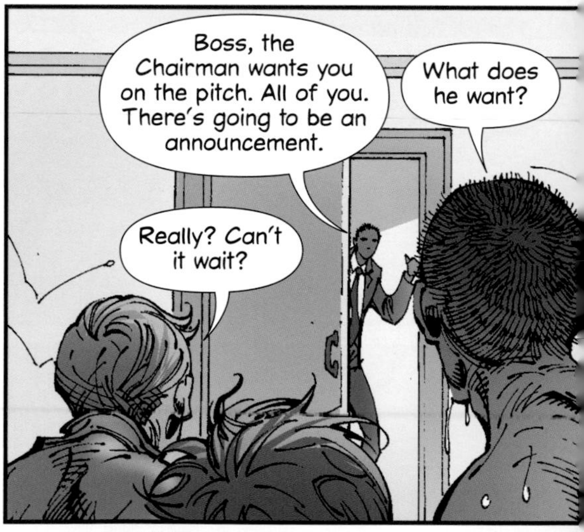
Boss, the Chairman wants you on the pitch. All of you. There's going to be an announcement.
What does he want?
Really? Can't it wait?

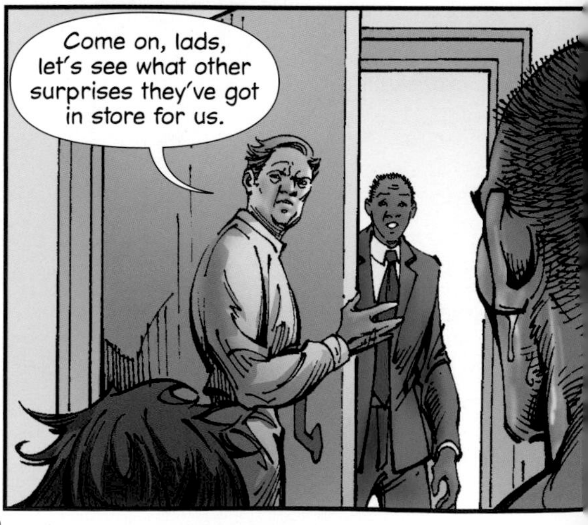
Come on, lads, let's see what other surprises they've got in store for us.

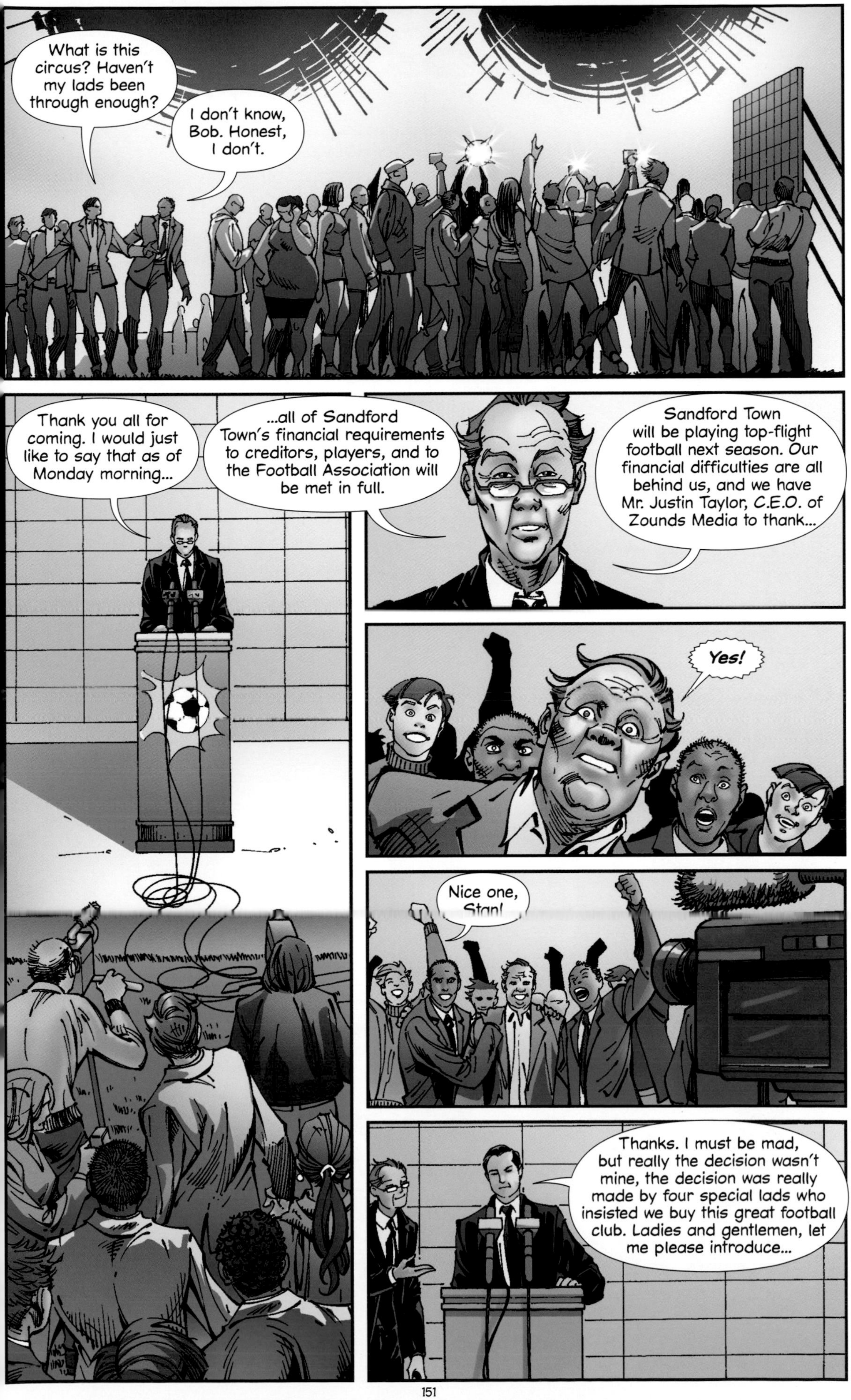
What is this circus? Haven't my lads been through enough?
I don't know, Bob. Honest, I don't.
Thank you all for coming. I would just like to say that as of Monday morning...
...all of Sandford Town's financial requirements to creditors, players, and to the Football Association will be met in full.
Sandford Town will be playing top-flight football next season. Our financial difficulties are all behind us, and we have Mr. Justin Taylor, C.E.O. of Zounds Media to thank...
Yes!
Nice one, Stan!
Thanks. I must be mad, but really the decision wasn't mine, the decision was really made by four special lads who insisted we buy this great football club. Ladies and gentlemen, let me please introduce...

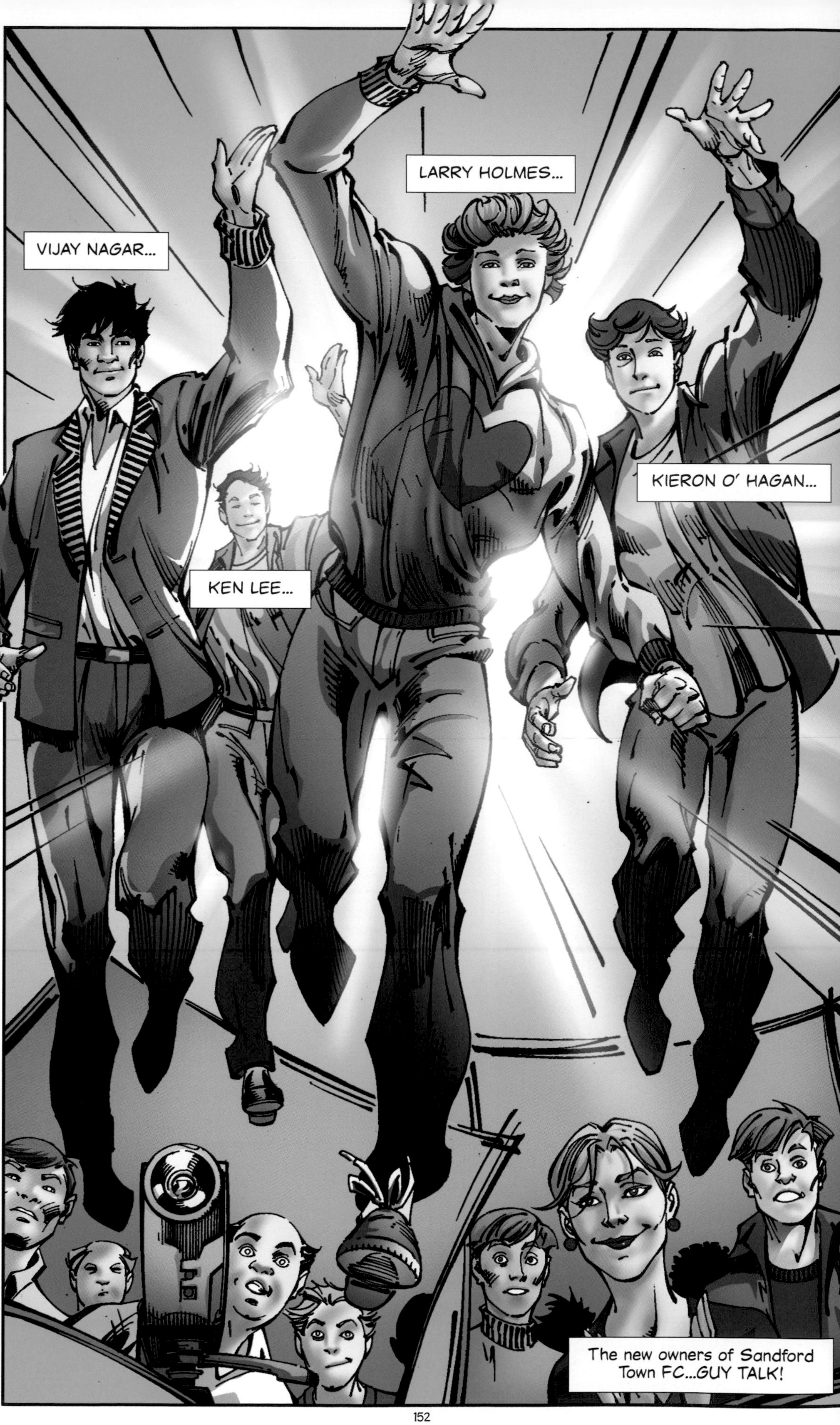
VIJAY NAGAR...
KEN LEE...
LARRY HOLMES...
KIERON O' HAGAN...
The new owners of Sandford Town FC...GUY TALK!

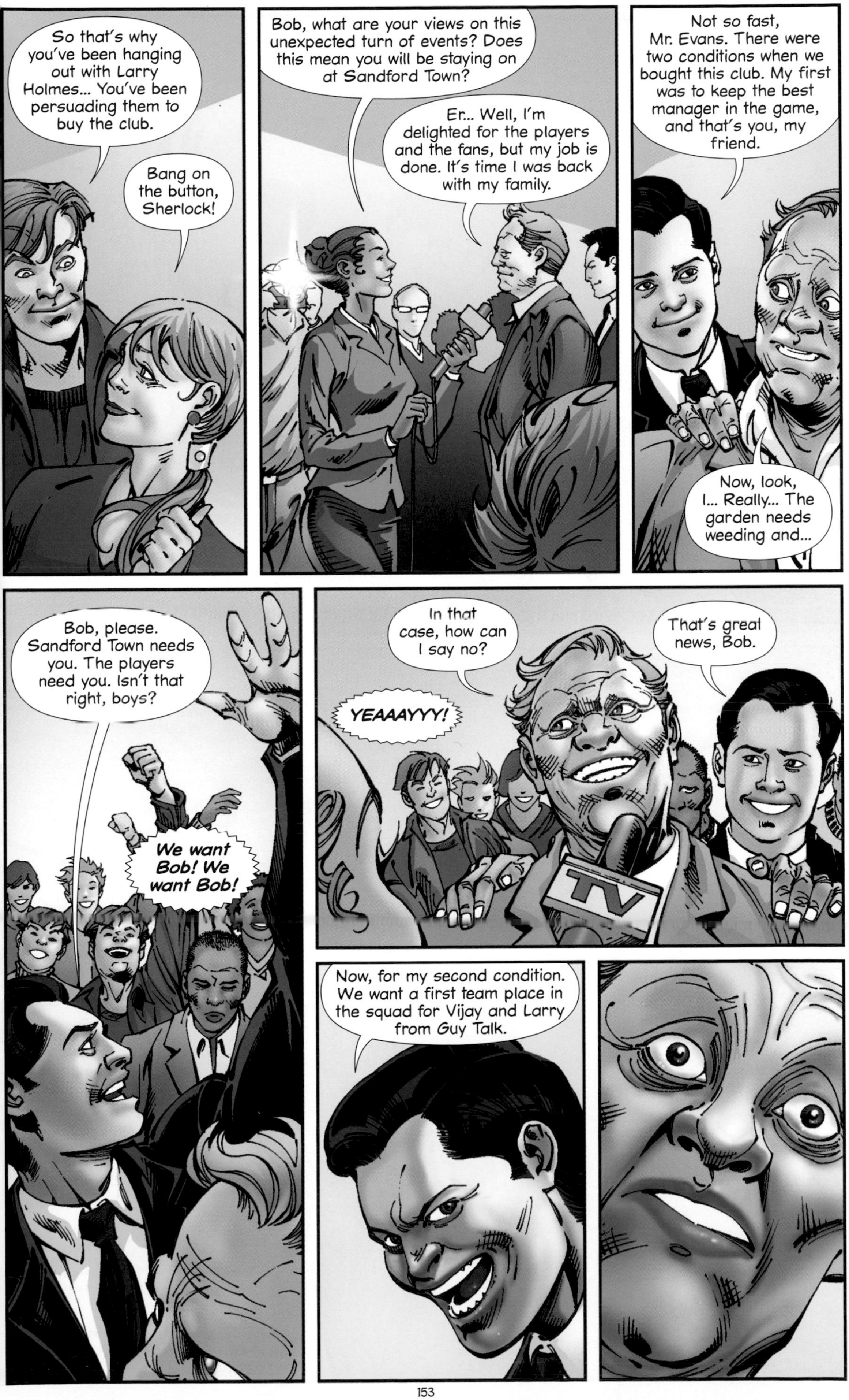

So that's why you've been hanging out with Larry Holmes... You've been persuading them to buy the club.
Bang on the button, Sherlock!
Bob, what are your views on this unexpected turn of events? Does this mean you will be staying on at Sandford Town?
Er... Well, I'm delighted for the players and the fans, but my job is done. It's time I was back with my family.
Not so fast, Mr. Evans. There were two conditions when we bought this club. My first was to keep the best manager in the game, and that's you, my friend.
Now, look, I... Really... The garden needs weeding and...
Bob, please. Sandford Town needs you. The players need you. Isn't that right, boys?
We want Bob! We want Bob!
In that case, how can I say no?
YEAAAYYY!
That's great news, Bob.
TV
Now, for my second condition. We want a first team place in the squad for Vijay and Larry from Guy Talk.

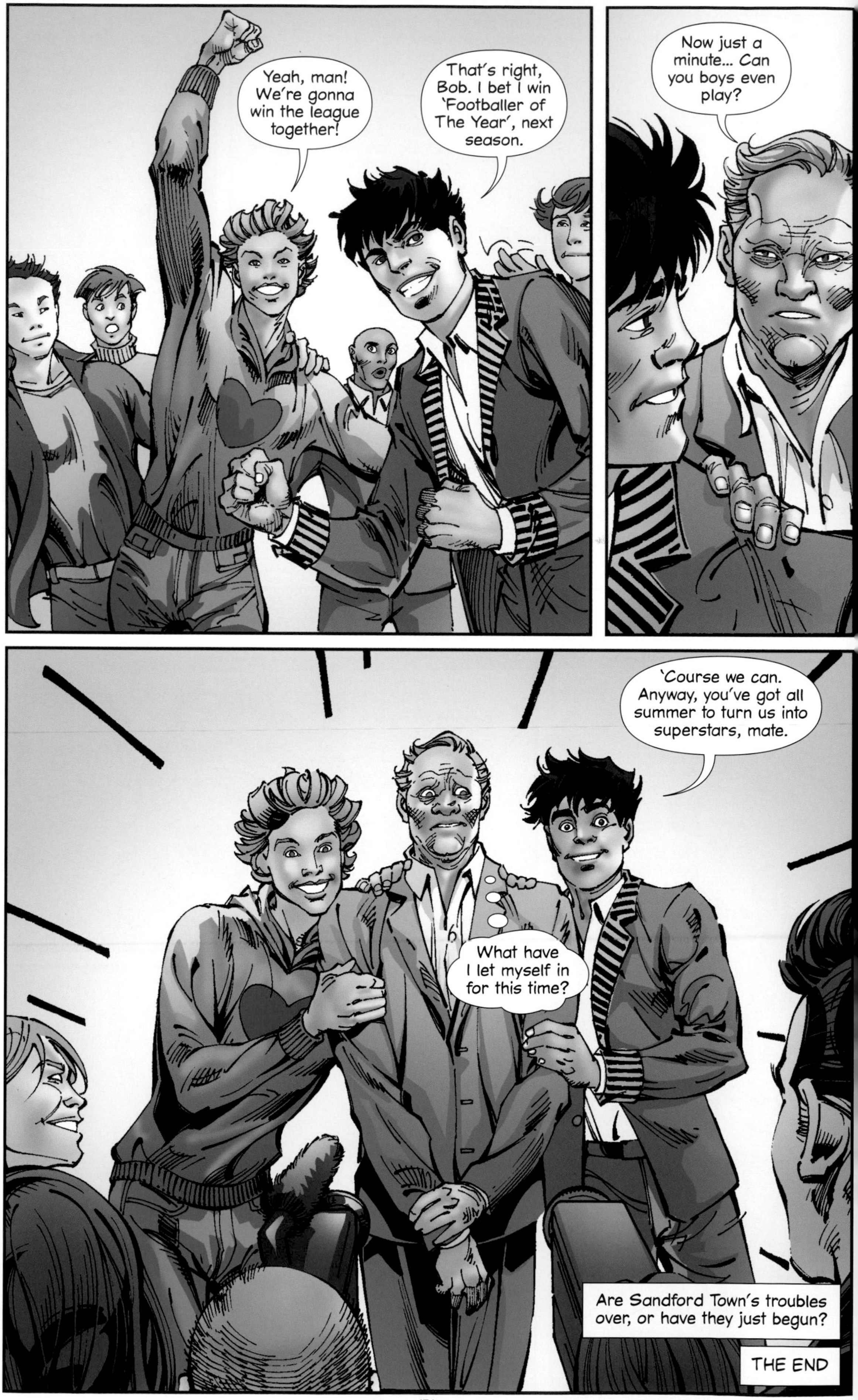
Yeah, man! We're gonna win the league together!
That's right, Bob. I bet I win 'Footballer of The Year', next season.
Now just a minute... Can you boys even play?
'Course we can. Anyway, you've got all summer to turn us into superstars, mate.
What have I let myself in for this time?
Are Sandford Town's troubles over, or have they just begun?
THE END

SANDFORD TOWN FC

A BRIEF HISTORY

Sandford Town FC, formed in 1878, were one of the founding members of the Football League in 1888 and won their first title one year later. This was to be the first of many trophies in their long and glittering history.

Three years later in 1892, Sandford got its second club, Sandford Rovers after Sandford Town moved from Oakwood Park to a new ground, Soldiers' Field, the site of which had been a mustering ground for the British army during the Napoleonic Wars.

The team are nicknamed 'The Townies', and a section of their fanatical fans are known as the Sandford Soldiers. The Rovers team was made up of a breakaway group of players who were against moving away from the docklands where the majority of supporters lived. The ideology behind the move was that there was space for a bigger ground, but Rovers wanted to remain loyal to the original supporters and community. Town supporters dismissively refer to Rovers as the 'Sandford Dogs' on account of Rover being a popular dog name. Sometimes, they are referred to as the 'Mutts'.

Sandford Town won the FA Cup twice in the period running up to World War I, and won the league title three times. In between the wars, they suffered a brief lull in fortune when they were relegated for two seasons, but they bounced back to claim the title once again in 1938. After World War II, Sandford Town entered what is known as their 'Golden Age', claiming the FA Cup on three more occasions and winning the league title twice. Between 1848 and 1960 they never finished lower than t in the league. However, in 1961, after a change in manager they were relegated from the top-flight to the old Division 2. Despite massive loyal support, the side couldn't muster any decent away form and two seasons later they were relegated again to the old Division 3.

By the end of the 1960s the legendary Billy Baines was installed as manager, and he gradually introduced a new generation of young players, including current manager, Bob Evans. The glory years of Billy Baines' reign at Sandford Town were about to begin. Within two seasons they had bounced back to the top-flight, winning the league, FA Cup and League Cup in a sensational 'triple whammy' in 19 . The following year, they made the semi-finals of the European Cup, losing out to Spanish side **Cartagonova** 2-1.

In 1974, they had their revenge against Cartagonova, thrashing them 3-0 in the semi-final before going on to beat West German

giants **Hockenburg**
4–3 in the European Cup
Final in Rome, with Bob
Evans scoring the winning
goal in injury time. They went
on to win the European Cup three
more times in the 1970s.

In spite of the unstoppable success of
Sandford Town throughout the 1970s they
could not carry this forward into the 1980s.
They were last crowned League Champions in
1982 and then, following the death of manager
Billy Baines in a coach crash in Switzerland in
1983, along with three other members of the
squad, the team began to unravel. Bob Evans
was also critically injured in the crash and never
played again. Turning to management, Evans
brought tiny London club Highgate **Wanderers**,
from the Vauxhall Conference, to the top-flight
in just seven seasons. After his success with
Highgate, Evans became National Coach for
the East European nation of **Calaminio**, taking
them to the semi-finals of the World Cup in
1998. He then retired from football, beginning a
successful career as a television pundit.

Sandford Town never managed to recover
completely from the devastating coach crash
of 1983. They have been struggling to maintain
their top-flight status, but the closest they have
come to success was a fourth place finish in the
league in 2004 and the FA Cup semi-finals in
2006. Now, with Bob Evans in charge, the fans'
hopes are high that the glory years are about to
return to Sandford Town.

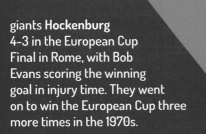

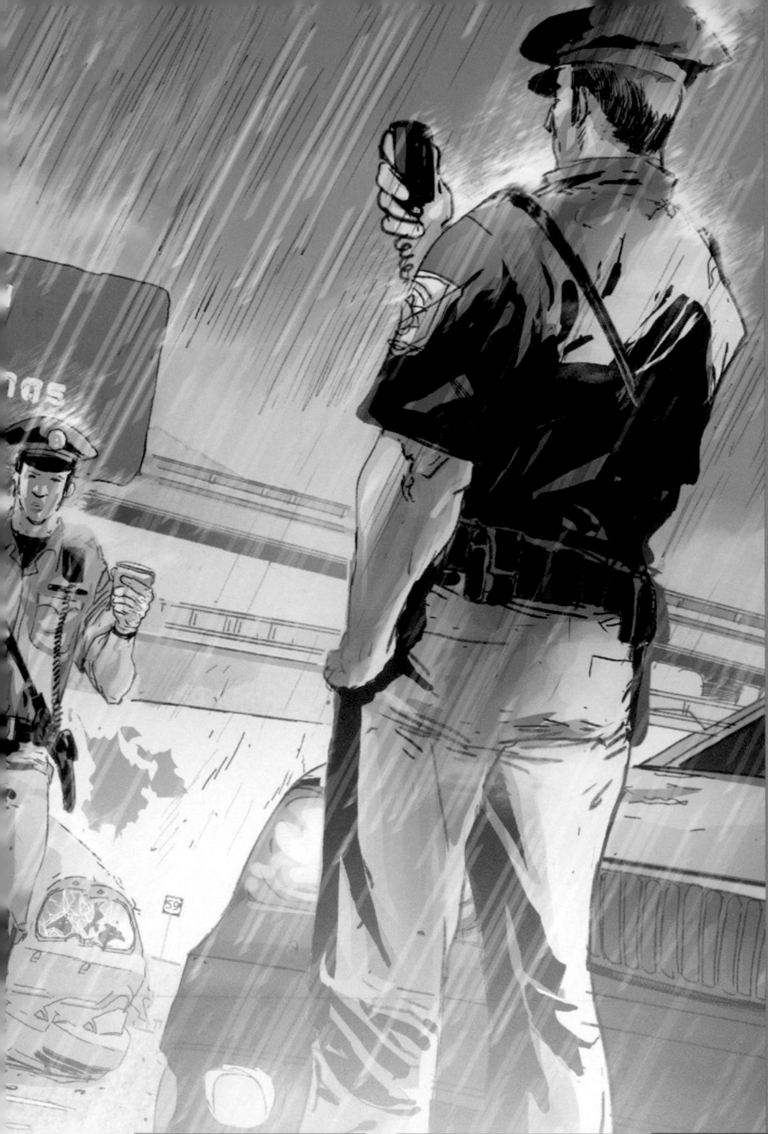

CAMPFIRE®
GRAPHIC NOVELS

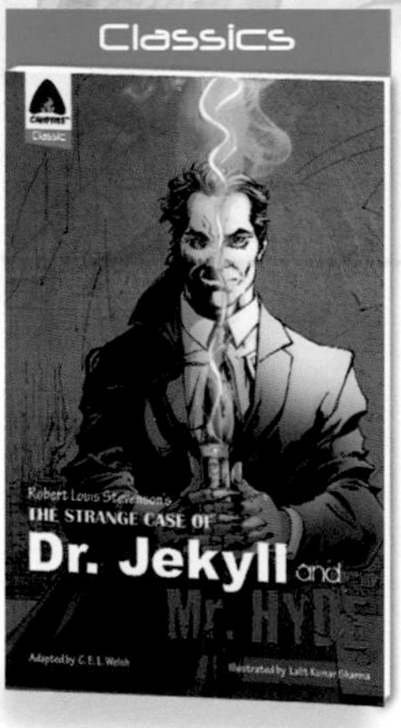
Classics
Robert Louis Stevenson's
THE STRANGE CASE OF
Dr. Jekyll and
Mr. HYDE

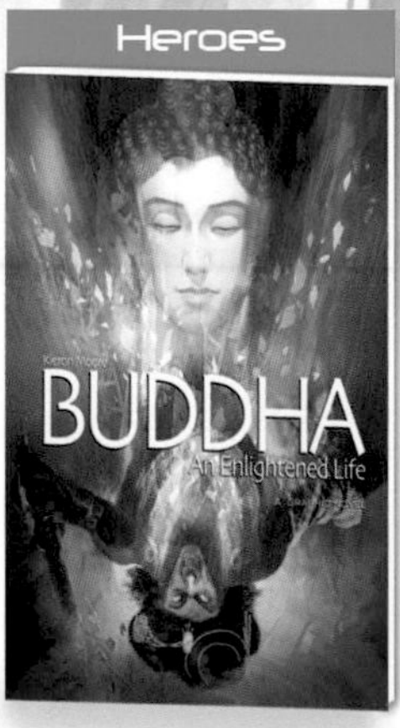
Heroes
BUDDHA
An Enlightened Life

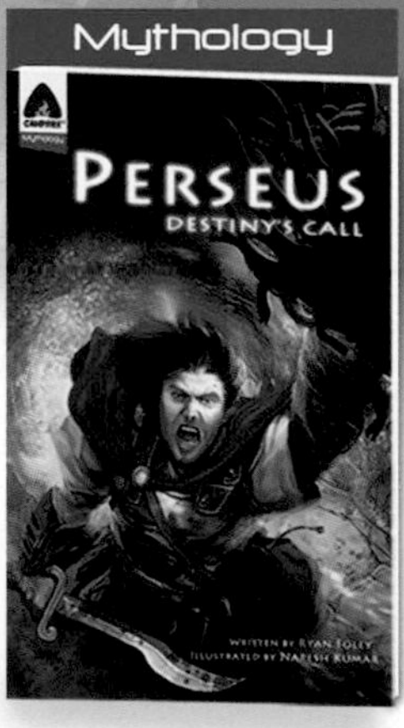
Mythology
PERSEUS
DESTINY'S CALL

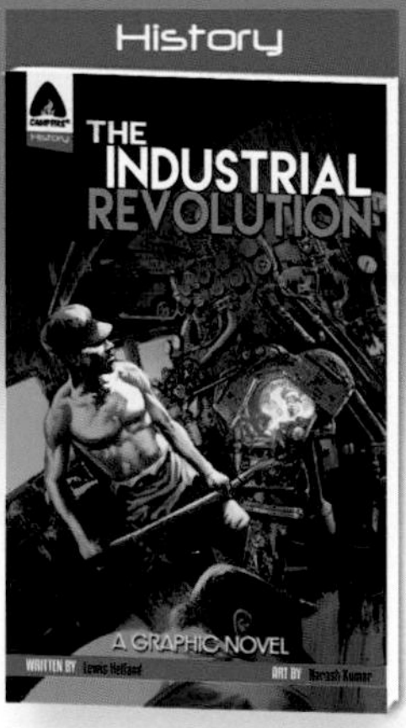
History
THE
INDUSTRIAL
REVOLUTION
A GRAPHIC NOVEL

Find the latest titles from Campfire at:

www.campfire.co.in

GET IT ON Google play

Available on the App Store

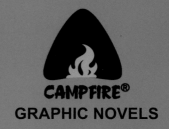

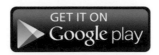

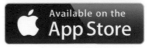